LOVE AND MAGIC IN NEVERLAND

Michael Gary Devloo

Other Books by Michael Gary Devloo:

Casa Construction, Exterior © 2008 ~ An English-Spanish Guide
to home building Construction

The Legend of the Weminuche Ware-pig © 2019 ~ A story of a
hike for Cancer turned wild.

FaceBook and Instagram: michaeldevloo
mikedevloo@gmail.com

A special thanks to all the characters and contributors who helped
intrinsically mold this story of love and magic.

FOR THOMAS AND SEAN

You left this world in an instant, but your essence continues
to breathe in the lives of your children.

Mahalo for this Life

Part I

Part II

Part III

Author's Note

The idea for this book came to me in a dream while camping and sea kayaking on the north shore of the Hawaiian island of Molokai. A dream so real, I had to share it. The intense Ocean-Mother Earth connection found on the Hawaiian Islands provided additional inspiration for this story about love, life, nature, and magic.

Unlike most fiction, this story is written in present tense. It's meant to read raw and unfiltered. If you lose yourself, take a deep breath and let yourself be, then come back.

Lastly, several of the characters in this book are derived from people I've met while traveling the Hawaiian Islands and beyond. I extend my love and gratitude to all who inspired characters in this story! It is my intention that the characters in this story provide depth in demonstrating *human nature*. In this, it is important to realize that both the bright and dark sides of everyone, are in fact both beautiful. In knowing this, we may realize that our own dark sides have love in them too. Love is behind all things after all. This love is the magic of human being.

~ *Part 1* ~

Chapter 1   Wild Speculation

Vaaaaroom! The helicopter buzzes right in front of his camp at 80 miles per hour. He jumps up out of his hammock and scrambles over to the cliff edge to steal a second glimpse. Gone...the sound of the blades is all that's left, it's out of sight already. *Rangers?* Gotta be. His mind analyzes the situation. No heli-tour flies low and fast like that, blazing in just 40 feet off the ocean's surface. *Raid? Is this it? Maybe it's just a maintenance crew, or a reconnaissance mission.*

He scrambles along the rocky bluff trail to gain a view of the beach. *Did it land?* From his lookout spot, he scans the shoreline for some sort of sign. Then he hears the buzzing of the chopper blades rushing back towards him. It zooms right in front of him from the opposite direction. For an instant his eyes focus on two figures inside. They zoom right on by, unfazed by the naked man staring at them from the rocks. *No landing, it's not a raid, it's just a flyby.* His mind decides.

He calms his nerves with a forced exhalation and climbs back into the hammock. He stares up at the tree branches as his mind drifts watching the leaves rustle in the wind. He touches himself slightly, casually. He lets himself fall right back into a sexual daydream taking comfort in his naughty fantasy he shares with no one. In touching himself he releases tension brought on by the chopper, and relaxes back into the daydreams of the morning.

Lustful thoughts, but also dreams of love, spin in his mind and settle in his loins. Normally, his day would not begin without his usual morning masturbation, but the helicopter whizzing by disturbed him. At this point he wants to just go on and get the business over with, but he's unsettled, and thus decides to give it up. *Could there be Rangers ticketing people on the beach right now?* If so, they could be at his camp in an hour. He thinks things over for another second. There were just two of them in the helicopter he saw. If it were a raid, the chopper would have been packed with Rangers. He breathes a sigh of relief and lets it go.

He's not about to base his day off of silly speculation! He might as well get up and light a fire to make breakfast, as usual. Oh, but if he didn't get the business over with he'd be all the more unsettled all morning. But why? Was it a needed fix, or just routine or habit? Or an addiction? Or just part of being human? Why should he even need to justify an act so...natural? Urge or otherwise he continues to touch himself gently. He hears a huff, which stops him suddenly. He instinctively jerks his head around in the hammock to check if anyone is around.

It's Mr. X, with his backpack on. Mr. X darts frantically around the rocks on the bluff-top trail toward him.

He hardly has a chance to pull on his shorts and sit up in the hammock before Mr. X is standing before him.

"Hey, did you see that chopper land? Did it land at the top of the red hill?" X huffs, wiping the sweat off his face.

"Yeah, the chopper zoomed by twice, but it didn't land up here. Did it land on the beach?"

"Not sure. I saw it coming and I just grabbed my bag and bolted. I knew it was a Ranger chopper, that's for sure." Mr. X spits back, his pale blue eyes still stricken with fright.

"I saw two guys in the chopper when it zoomed by. It flew by twice, looked like they were just taking pictures or something."

"Just two guys, huh? Well that doesn't seem like a raid." Mr. X fingers his beard thoughtfully.

"I dunno, I just know they didn't land up here."

"Well shoots, maybe I made the mad dash for nothing!" Mr. X grumbles. Both men smile at each other, acknowledging the silliness of it all.

"Ranger-ready man!" he laughs back at X.

"Well, it's a good day to go up-valley anyway," Mr. X concludes with a sigh, then ambles off humbly.

The day proceeds without further hindrance. He initiates the calming routine of building a fire for breakfast, first making chai tea, then cooking oats. He builds up the fire again to put a medium pot of rice on for later.

"Be present and be free, let go, and live!" he exclaims to the sky, motivating himself for the day.

Still somewhat confused about what to do with himself for the day, he elects to live by his own advice: Go with the flow and see what happens. He wanders up the valley, stopping at familiar pools in the creek and certain spots along the trail that always seem to draw him in.

The day passes seamlessly. He runs into a few other random people along the trail, and up at community gardens, but nothing and no one stirs him. By sunset, he's back at his camp on the bluffs overlooking the great Pacific. He breathes deeply taking in his surroundings. This place is more than just beautiful, special, and free; it's magical, and he knows it. Magic is in the air and all around. He can feel it. He blinks his eyes realizing he is *crazy* for thinking this…For believing in magic.

'*Neverland!*' he exclaims aloud, remembering the name he and others gave this magic land. He shakes his head to arouse some common sense. Magic? Really? He blinks his eyes and looks down at the blue waves thundering at the base of the grassy cliff on which he sits. He watches the wind catch the steep curling waves and blow foamy white spray off their tops. The solid looking foam chunks defy gravity and dance in the wind. He turns and looks up the rugged coastline to the east where a sliver of a rainbow dancing in and out of the clouds holds back an approaching storm. He sees the spectrum of light appear and disappear through the wall of gray. Turning his back to the ocean, he looks up the valley, toward the near vertical cathedral spires of lava rock coated in mossy green. He inhales the vista of the cloud-enshrouded impassable back wall. Turning west he looks to the folding cliffs, the beach, and the setting sun. He sighs heavy. How silly for him to doubt magic in a magical land.

Then he overhears two voices chattering, their volume increasing. He snaps out of his daydream to see a couple of the valley elders approaching his camp. His dreamy thoughts disperse and his rationalizing, analyzing, decision-making brain retakes the helm. He listens as Uncle Dan and Mr. X debate about their first drone encounter, there outside his camp.

"You know this drone sighting isn't just some Babylonian fad, it's a sign of things to come. Yeah man, a precursor." Uncle Dan says.

"Come on! Most of us have heard of these drone-helicopter thingies. It was only a matter of time before some rich tourist got their hands on one and buzzed the beach with it. And that don't mean a damn thing for our little life here!" Mr. X counters.

"Alright man! But then what? More drones! Drones taking pictures! Drones landing. Drone warfare right on our beach, man!" Uncle Dan continues preaching to the heavens.

By now a couple more residents had gathered and a heated, yet frivolous debate is in full swing.

"If I see a drone cruise my camp, I'm gonna throw a rock at it!" an up-valley resident named Kaholo pipes up in a fury.

"Whoa, whoa, whoa! We shouldn't try to stir things up by hurling rocks at the drones, that's not gonna help our outlaw cause! That's asking for drone warfare," Mr. X counters.

"So the first drone hovered over the beach for a few minutes today. Big deal. At least there wasn't a Ranger Raid. Not like the drones are gonna shoot us down." Uncle Dan tries to curb the intensity.

The few that did see the drone agree that it was being flown by a tourist from a boat. It wasn't Rangers or military. Nonetheless, the drone encounter stirs long time residents like Kaholo, Mr. X, and Uncle Dan. Maybe it is a sign of things to come.

"Alright, we know there's nothing we can do to stop the drones, so we might as well just ignore them and go about our lives unbothered. Just like the tourist helicopters, we'll tune them out." Mr. X's partner Ella states attempting to conclude the discussion.

"Yeah, sure, you do that, but I'm gonna give them drones the bird, and then blast 'em out of the sky with whatever I can get my hands on," Kaholo rebukes, causing Mr. X to flare up.

"Bullshit Kaholo! You've been here long enough to know that messing with *the man* is just gonna bring more heat. We're not gonna flick off the drones or fling rocks at them, that's the stupidest thing we can do."

The conversation rolls back and forth. Keith, a carefree bluff resident, seizes the opportunity to spin a song off the ridiculous drone debate.

Feel it when the drone drop,

But we'll still just stay and rock,

They be making one stop,

Checkin' out the hippies, on the bluff top,

'But we'll just take it easy,

Not gonna throw no rock,

Just chillin' on our little island,

Don't want no trou-ble with the man,

And we'll keep on smil-ing,
Until that helicopter land!

The silly song somehow settles the crowd and lightens the mood. The impromptu gathering winds down after a few more songs. It's well past dark now and folks start to reach for their headlamps and bags, to return back to their individual camps for bed. Most are hardly phased by the whole drone debate. The unfettered nature of everyone seems to stir Uncle Dan, and he gets up to speak boldly before the gathering disperses.

"You know we can't always just tune out what the *man* sends at us! I mean, man, one day we might just have to fight for our freedoms, even out here! I don't necessarily propose that we should throw rocks at the drones, or the Rangers, but we should at least think about what to do. Be prepared to defend our freedom, our island, if need be."

"You mean like form and train a hippie militia?" Keith snickers.

"I don't know what I mean, man. We just got to be wary and not complacent, that's all." Uncle Dan concludes.

"Let's build and train the hippie militia!" Kaholo whoops, Enthusiasm builds for a moment, but each outlaw soon starts to gather their things for the walk back to their camps.

With the crowd dispersed, the night is calm once again. He crawls back into his hammock and stares up at the stars. Dreaming.

Chapter 2   The Beach is in Reach

His mind drifts with the wind. The tree branches above sway and creak and the ocean below breathes in and out with each rumble of whitewater. The ocean releases worries from the past, allowing him to travel back in time with Her. He remembers when he first journeyed to Neverland this season, back during the height of the winter swells and before the spring trade winds.

Closing his eyes, he can remember every detail, every feeling from when he hiked in over a month ago. He re-savors the excitement, the exhilaration, and rebirth upon arrival!

The scorching hot sun that day! Panting and sweating carrying two weeks worth of food and a full-size guitar down the 11-mile trail. He feels the sun, the wind, his tired legs, and the red dirt trail beneath his feet.

"I got one word for ya, *Ukulele!*" his good friend Mark spits as he hands the guitar to him sweating in the midday sun.

"Trust me, the guitar is key. Music is really important in there."

"I think you should learn harmonica." Mark grumbles.

They stop short of Neverland and camp about 8 miles in on their first night. They pitch a tent on a grassy bluff-top, footsteps away from a 300 foot drop-off into the roaring sea below. He knows the spot well, certainly worth a night's stay.

The two unpack and get out what they need for dinner. Before cooking, they stop to watch an orange sun dip into the ocean.

"Hey Mark, you see out there, around the corner?" The edge of the cliffs is illuminated in such a way that it's hard to see through the bright rays to the outline of the coast. He takes a break and waits till the sun has dipped below the horizon to finish talking.

"See that little strip of sand around the corner, that's it, that's where we're headed tomorrow. The Beach!"

The twilight fades and the two cook their first meal together over a smoky fire. Not long after, they are sound asleep in their tent.

Morning sun cuts away the clouds and illuminates the head-high surf pounding against the rocks below.

"Just 3 more miles to Neverland," He announces as the duo shoulders their packs. They trot along the trail with fresh legs. After a quick two and a half miles they reach the main valley stream. The duo drops their packs and splashes cool water on their faces and fills their water bottles.

He turns to Mark who is already taking his shoes off to cool is sore feet in the creek. "This valley has powerful vibrations like nowhere I've ever seen. Some say that this water is magical, and others even believe that by drinking it straight you may alter your own DNA."

"Yeah, okay, sure, but I'm still gonna treat it with iodine!" Mark laughs, then stares back at his wide-eyed partner drinking from his hand in the stream.

"Getting transformed already are you? Let's go find a campsite so we can ditch these packs and explore."

They set up a camp by the river mouth underneath a big coconut palm, and then continue along the trail to check out the beach.

"I heard through a couple of resident looking characters that there is gonna be a bonfire on the beach just below the first helipad tonight." Mark announces after he returns from his jog to the end of the beach to check out the waterfall.

They decide to scope out to the informal gathering after dinner. The glow from the bonfire fire welcomes them right in. The two sit down casually in the circle of young backpackers, sand, and stars. Immediately he catches a cute smile from a tall redheaded girl across the fire. His eyes catch hers as his tongue catches on a word, but before any bit of awkward introduction is offered another voice lurches out.

"Que pasa, Mano?" A curly-haired hombre laughs in a mixed Gringo-Spanish meets islander accent. *Mano? Is this guy addressing him? What is he talking about?* His face freezes as his mind struggles to catch up. Mano means *hand* in Spanish. Somehow his mind snaps to with a half-wit response.

"Ok, Mano, just thought we'd say hello, you know, like Mano y Mano and check out your beach fire. It's my first night back on the inside, and my buddy Mark here, it's his first night here ever. We're totally stoked of course."

"That's a good start brotha!" *Spanglish going back to islander slang.* "Warm welcome. Congrats on the escape from Babylonia, they call me Honu."

"And I'm Charlotte," the ginger girl next to him bubbles up before Honu can continue. Other faint faces around the fire offer introduction as well. He can barely keep track of introductions with cross conversation brewing and Charlotte tossing back her fire-lit auburn curls. The discussion from before him and Mark plopped down re-emerges in a fury.

"Candace isn't coming tomorrow. Not with the swell still up like it is." Honu declares before continuing.

"I doubt the boat drop will happen until the surf backs off a good bit. Besides, we heard on the radio from Mr. X that the waves are supposed to be big for three more days."

Eager to engage, he blurts out. "Who's Candace, and What's a boat drop? Uh... Sounds like quite a royal delivery."

"Mano, Mano! You say you've been to The Beach twice before, yet you don't know what a boat drop is! You just wait. The Candace drop is gonna be the bad-dest shit."

"Oh yeah you say that it will be the bad-dest shit. You're gonna flip your shit. It'll be the big Kahuna of boat drops, Yeah that's right, the *Candace Drop!*" Mark busts out a freestyle rap with the confidence and poise of a true showman.

Mark's little rap routine sends Charlotte giggling and rolling back onto the sand. Soon others are rapping right there with him and everyone, misinformed or otherwise is getting amped up about the Candace drop. Everyone just rolls with it and sings and dances under the stars.

The Candace drop doesn't happen the next morning, as predicted, nor the next day, nor the next. The waves are huge; there's no way a boat was getting anywhere near the beach. It's January after all, and 8 to 10-foot swells are the norm and 15 to 20-foot faces aren't out of the ordinary. Honu certainly needed a bit of magic to get a break in the swell for his highly anticipated boat drop.

Although having enough supplies to thrive for an extended stay is always in the back of one's mind in Neverland, he and Mark hardly worry about anything their first week. They had backpacked in ample food and the beauty and pleasures of Neverland were more than enough to sustain them. They had arrived and were set free, living the dream on a tropical remote beach!

Exploring the beach and valley, they meet eccentrics from across the globe. Far out characters that live deep in the valley, tucked away in hidden camps up on ridge tops or along tributaries of the main valley stream. Those that desired socialization stayed close to the beach and those who craved seclusion set up hidden camps miles up the valley.

Most folks stuck to their regular given names, but some did adopt *island* ones. The nickname, *Mano* donned on him by Honu that first night at the bonfire stuck with certitude. In fact, he kind of liked it, so he fully embraced it. He finds out that *Honu* is sea turtle in Hawaiian, and that *Mano* translates to shark, but it also means *Passionate One*.

Chapter 3   Boat Drop

On Mark and Mano's fifth day Candace comes. She arrives on a blue and white boat captained by an Aussie whose name was intentionally kept secret. All the local residents simply referred to him as *The Pro*. The Pro was quick and to the point, and never fashionably late like other local pirate captains. He always picked the perfect day to come in when the swell and winds were down.

Candace's arrival with The Pro is no exception. She arrives first thing in the morning, before any helicopters, under calm seas, during a break in the swell. She swims to the beach off The Pro's boat and bystanders swarm the beach to collect the bags as they float in on the drop. The Pro weaves around sets of waves, motoring toward the beach during the lull then heaving the 50 pound bags overboard into the surf break. He quickly has to zoom back to the outside before big set waves arrive and catch the bags, not his boat, in the impact zone. If the bags get dropped in the sweet spot, the whitewater catches them and pushes them right to the shore. Sometimes wind or current brings some stragglers back out to sea and the captain has to zoom in to retrieve and re-drop them. A perfect boat drop can be smooth and quick like a well-executed magic trick, but sometimes it's a 20 minute iterative circus act.

Locals, who are lucky enough to have arranged a supply bag on the drop, tear into their black trash bags full of food and treats like Christmas presents. The long-awaited arrival of the Candace drop spurs a pizza and wine party which fuel a late night jam session. Guitar, ukulele, hand drums, and joints are passed around a lively crew on the bluffs. Candace herself doesn't join the crew; she stays with her stockpile on the beach not keen on attracting any more attention. Honu, and others had treats and 'pizza essentials' on the drop, so they more or less sponsor the party.

The days begin to blend together and the concept of time starts to fade after a week. Between walking places, making food, music, foraging for food, swimming, and socializing, hours and days just flow. After a week on the *inside*, Mano can't even remember what day it is. The only way to decipher the day of the week was by placing significant events and counting the days between them. Mano could remember his friend Matt hiked in the day after the cruise ship was spotted at dusk on the horizon, which meant it's now Saturday.

The Candace Drop was an excuse to party and the arrival of Matt is yet another. When Matt reveals a handle of whiskey and a 3-pound bag of peanut M&M's out of his backpack, Mark and Mano can't be more thrilled.

"It's the Ma-att drop, he made the whiskey bottle pop, and his bag of M&M's is the panty drop!" Honu and Mano sing out leading a procession of backpackers from the beach to the Heiau for the circus party gathering.

A Heiau is an ancient Hawaiian temple. The Heiau near the beach in Neverland is a wide-open grassy terraced area just up from the river mouth. In Neverland the Heiau is still a sacred place of worship and ritual, but is also used as a community gathering area. The down valley Heiau near the beach has three distinct terraced areas and is a focal point of the whole valley.

Word of a hoedown at the Heiau and the Matt's whiskey bottle pop spreads across the beach and tourist backpackers as well as resident outlaws are drawn out of their camps by the music and hubbub from the sunset gathering. The party is themed to be a gathering of circus acts with glowing poi and wild hula hooping being the highlight.

A Brazilian girl turns more than a few heads during the night's circus show. Daniela, a young traveler, who had couch-surfed her way about the island, found her way to this remote beach with a borrowed crew of dudes and weekend camping gear. Mano notices her right away and is charmed by her sensual attitude and soft lips. Mano's cute boyish grin temps her into asking him to go for a walk in the moonlight. The two wander off toward the end of the party for a passionate night. This turns into two days and nights of pure pleasure! But Mano can't convince her to stay. She leaves with her trail escorts after the typical 3-day stint in paradise. She's just a tourist anyway; she's not an outlaw ready to call Neverland home.

It feels silly for him to chase her down, so he stays in Neverland, swimming and making music, enjoying beach life. Mark hikes out with Matt shortly after Daniela to catch some parties happening on other parts of the island. Just a few days later, Mano caves and manages to justify a trek back to Babylon on a triple purpose mission of pursuing more great sex with Daniela, obtaining a kayak, and a re-supply run.

He could hike to town, buy a sea kayak, and paddle back in with three to four weeks worth of food and treats. His own boat drop! Besides he wants to catch Mark again before he leaves the island, and he lusts for Daniela. These thoughts excite him so much that they carry him along the trail to the outside world light-footed.

The initial blow of Babylon, with its strong odors of tanning oil, perfumes, gasoline, and exhaust fumes, is not too intimidating. The busy people and noise in town can be overwhelming, but this time he's able to push through it and keep his focus. Mano catches up with Mark and Daniela and they shuffle around the island in the rain in borrowed cars. They check out some other beaches, go to the few local bars, and even get put up in a house for two nights by some locals Daniela met couch surfing. It pounds rain for 48 hours, but the lively trio still surf and swim and make fun out of the sunless days. Mano tracks down a used two-person kayak with two paddles on *Craigslist*. He buys the weathered baby blue Zest 2 sit-on-top for two hundred bucks from a grizzled boat mechanic named Steph.

Mano decides to paddle a test voyage from a big protected bay around a rocky reef to a beach park on the northeast side of the island. Simulating his own boat drop, he loads all of his camping gear into a big dry bag and sets off on the open water for a beach-to-beach journey.

A fierce head wind blows hard against the boat, but Mano paddles harder. The said easy hour and a half open ocean test mission turns into a grueling two-hour endurance workout. However, the successful test trip boosts his confidence in his ability to maneuver the loaded kayak in a swell and against the wind. He lands the kayak safely and pulls the boat up on the rocks hurriedly. He rushes to set up his tent at the beach-park campground because he sees a storm about to engulf the whole area. It's pouring down rain by the time he's zipped inside.

Man it sure can rain here! No wonder it's so green! Mano proclaims as if announcing for all to hear. He grows restless, alone in the tent, so he calls Daniela, but only catches her cheerful voicemail greeting. He's already in his sleeping bag eating granola bars when dusk arrives.

There's no way around it. When it's rainy and you are alone in a tent, the sullen fading of day to night from inside that nylon fabric depresses even the brightest spirit. Any luster from Mano's successful test voyage fades. If there was one thing that plagued him it was loneliness. He had always been kind of a loner. He loved people, but he didn't have the patience for friends most of the time. He'd been given the more glorifying moniker of *free spirit*, which he embodied for sure, but he certainly hated the other side of free. Free from sharing. How much better would tent time be if he got to share it with someone? He wishes Mark were here at least!

It's best not to dwell on things, he tells himself sullenly. The next sunny day will come, and there's no shortage of interesting people on the island to meet. He sighs, and then gets up to pee before the grey twilight turns to total dark.

"Maaah-no. Mano, where are you?" The voice is so faint he's sure he's imagining it.

"Hello," he calls out to himself.

"Hello, he-llo! Ma-no." *Wait. That's Daniela's voice, it's not his imagination.*

"Hello, I hear you!" he calls back.

Their voices connect and they find each other. They kiss and embrace in the rainy night. How lucky! How magical is this island! He's so taken aback by Daniela's opportune arrival, that he doesn't even care about the kayak or tent, he just grabs a few essentials and jumps in the Jeep with her. With one headlight, no power steering, and intermittent wipers, they drive the *island car* through a rainstorm back to the couch-surfer place. She commandeers the guest bedroom for them, and they make love to a flickering candle and the rain.

He dreams of what could become of their lives together. Could it be sweet love forever? Somehow, he already knows she is not his soul mate. He just knows; they both know. To be sure, they both intentionally sidestep their way out of any possible transcontinental relationship. Even so, Mano can't help but want her and wonder about more than a short-lived romance.

They wake up simultaneously in the middle of the night and give into temptation again. Making love to such a beautiful, caring woman satisfies more than just a physical desire. This sharing of passion and intimacy creates emotional completion. His heart warms and the feeling, the warmth, is reciprocated in her.

They share orgasms as the candle burns out. Even though he knows she'll soon leave his life, likely forever, he doesn't hold back his passion, his love. The feeling is real. There is care behind each kiss and every caress. They both feel that their touch, their intimacy, has real meaning and purposeful love in that moment. They release all they have and it is beautiful.

It feels like the end of a dream when they part, but parting does feel right, it seems. Mano refocuses his heart and mind to his return trip to Neverland. The surf report shows that the window between winter swells will close soon, so he buys the essentials, filling two big dry bags to carry on board his kayak. Items like huge jars of peanut butter, quinoa, oats, raisins, nuts, wine, and whiskey are packed tight in the bags. Mark drives the jeep with him and the kayak on top to the North Shore for his launch. They unload, embrace, and he watches the taillights of the *island car* disappear down the narrow road.

20

Mano wonders about the fate of his friends in the outside world. Mark and Matt will probably island hop to Maui, and Daniela, she'll continue her world tour and he'll probably never see her again.

Mano is once again alone on his own adventure. *C'est la vie!* It's kind of the way he knew it would be, though. He knew he would have to return to Neverland in the kayak alone. Just like he knew he had to come back to the island this year, just like he knew he had to let Daniela go, he knew he would have to make this journey back to Neverland solo.

But did he have the stomach for the wintertime paddle in? This ocean can be humbling, even life-threatening. Here at the crossroads of the Pacific, *Kai* as the locals called her, is the force that guides and ultimately *decides*. Her currents, winds, and pounding waves have humbled the bravest men for centuries. But the ocean's not misleading. She's not volatile and unstable. The great Pacific has got to be the most stable thing on the planet. Her currents and winds have followed the same seasonal patterns for millions of years, predating this very island he stood upon even.

In some ways her enormity and intricacy can be surprisingly straightforward, though. The Pacific is not unpredictable like a deer in headlights. She's not finicky, she's fluid. You can feel her power, but also you can feel her profound steadiness. He's not sure of how he understands this, or how to explain it, but he can sense Her, like his own intuition.

Staring out at the sea, he sees past the turmoil of crashing waves and into the blue expanse of calmness beyond. The vast ocean humbles him and prompts self-examination. He's paddling back to Neverland, and his friends are staying back. Back in society where they belong. Belong? What went wrong? How did he catch this Neverland bug, and they didn't? He doesn't let this discourage him. Intuition reminds him of the spiritual connection he forged with the place seasons ago. He isn't just going back; Neverland is calling him back. He has to return.

Mano organizes his gear and studies the surf. By early afternoon he's poised for launch with his dry-bags full of provisions, along with a fishing pole, an extra paddle, and a gallon of water, all to be tied onto the sit-on-top kayak with ropes and bungees.

The launch looks rough though. Waves are crashing onto a shallow reef, and there's not a defined channel through the reef to boat out. *There has got to be a better spot to launch,* his mind offers. He decides to catch a ride to a small camping area and beach, farther down the road where there might be an easier, safer place to push off.

He examines the surf at the new location. *Too big, too late a start, not enough cojones. Surely tomorrow will be better... don't push it, tomorrow will be better.* His intuition speaks and he retreats to the grassy field of the beach park camp area to spend the night. He's restless and alone. He wishes he had a car so he could drive twenty miles around the island and crawl into bed with Daniela. Desperate, he tries hitch-hiking, but it's nearly dark and the few cars that pass hardly give notice. Instead, he fights with hot nerves for a sleepless night. Nightmares of the journey alone on the mysterious ocean plague his sleep. Warnings from locals around the island ring through his head.

"Nobody, I mean nobody, kayaks the North Shore in the winter!" Choruses from leather-faced old-timers at the surf shop echo in his brain.

Of course, the guy who sold him the kayak was one who didn't totally agree. Mano relives the awkward dealings in the backyard of broken down boats in one of the island's rougher neighborhoods. Steph's weathered hands and sun-bleached beard were physical proof of a true sea-faring man. His smile was warm, but a slight lazy eye seemed to say, *don't get too close.*

"This boat will get you to the beach, no problem. This boat has gone all the way around the island three times. No problem. This is the boat to do it in!"

Steph went on grumbling pirate-like as he continued his work fixing various decrepit motorboats set-up on blocks in the yard. He said nothing shy of *'this boat is unstoppable.'* But when he helped Mano and Mark strap the boat to the top of the jeep, with the cash in hand, he presented Mano a stern look and a word of caution.

"That's not just any beach you're going to. There's powerful *mana* there! You better be careful and you better paddle in with good intention. Your first time landing on that beach, definitely go when the surf report is below three feet."

The captain's crooked smile fixed on him in the dream just as it did in real life the day he bought the kayak. Mano wakes in a sweat. The dream didn't end in a nightmare, or a revelation, it just ended.

According to the posted surf report, the swell, which had just backed down from a four-day high surf warning, was now slipping to two to four feet, but rising again by tomorrow afternoon. This was the window for his launch.

Honu's advice on beach-landing a kayak, was a mix of terror and comic relief.

'Don't try to surf the boat in. You gotta crash land! Don't worry though, everyone crash-lands! Watch the sets from the outside. When you see a break in the sets, paddle behind the last big wave towards the shore. Don't let a wave catch you, paddle behind it when it's breaking. As soon as the next set of whitewater catches up with you, jump overboard, and swim away from the boat. You don't wanna let the boat crash on top of you of course. Just hang onto your paddle and swim to shore. Don't worry about your boat, the naked hippies on the beach will run out and grab your kayak and all of your shit! Just crash land and you'll be fine. Oh and don't go if the swell picks up, you know that, right.'

'You'll know, and you'll be fine.' Were Honu's final words of wisdom before Mano left Neverland nearly a week ago.

Crash-land! The concept of a crash-landing certainly made Mano feel uneasy. The night's stirrings did not prompt an early launch either.

'I'll know when to go, and I'll be fine,' Mano says to himself. Still, after breakfast he isn't ready. He turns away from the ocean and instead walks to the road to thumb a ride to the other side of the island. He decided he had to see Daniela one last time. He hitches around to the east side of the island and finds the couch surfers house. She's surprised to see him appear at breakfast unannounced. They take a nice walk on the beach and exchange a few more goodbye kisses. It's not as he envisioned though. She's already separated herself from him mentally, preparing to leave the island for the next leg of her world tour. It's a ridiculous re-doing the goodbyes, but the first goodbye just didn't seem real for him.

This one is. One last kiss and he hitches back the other way to launch with the swell rising. From the car he's riding in, Mano sees surfers out on waves in the bay. Waves that weren't there when he rode by earlier that morning. A new swell is coming in. The window for a safe launch is closing! Back at the kayak, he tries to settle his nerves. He re-packs and seals the dry bags before going out to survey the surf conditions once again. This time he doesn't let the voices in his head boss him around.

Dragging the kayak across the sand in preparation to launch, a skinny girl runs toward him in a bikini. She looks at the boat and dry bags full of gear and smiles.

"You're paddling out to that remote beach aren't you?" She asks boldly.

"Well, if I can manage to launch through this split in the waves here, then yeah, I'll be there by sunset."

Mano's gaze moves from the ocean to meet her eyes. In them he finds the confidence boost he is looking for. A sudden smirk of self-confidence charms his face, and she smiles back with the look of a poised diva.

"I know you can do it," she bursts as if reading his dilemma.

The girl's name is Amber and she explains that she'll be hiking the trail back to the Neverland in a of couple days. With another bold look she asks, "Hey can you do a little favor for me?"

"Sure..." He replies curiously. She runs back to her bag and returns with a six-pack of Newcastle beer.

"Here, give this to my friend, Ben, on the beach." He finds just enough room in the large dry bag for the bottles.

Amber helps hold the boat steady in the whitewater for the launch. *Patience,* Mano mumbles to himself. The two wait for a good window in between big sets to push off. Mano jumps onboard and Amber releases the boat. He struggles to steady the kayak after the first wave of whitewater nearly flips him, but he squares up to the next wave then paddles like hell. He pulls fiercely through churns of whitewater, bound for the open ocean! Mano picks his way around boat-breaking waves past the outer reefs where overhead waves crash hard onto rock Along his course he pierces through the crest of a couple of giants. One massive roller almost catches his stern, but luckily it rolls right underneath. Then he's on the outside and he knows he's made it. Still, Mano uses his adrenaline surge to crank way out away from the dangerous reef before even a looking back at the shore. When he finally does, Amber is long gone and he realizes that he's much more than a long swim from land. It's ok though; in the open ocean he's safe, certainly safer away from the crashing waves along the reef.

Now it's just slow and steady paddling, following the rugged coastline. As long as he maintains a safe buffer of a hundred yards off the cliffs, then the swell just flows smoothly underneath. There's no reef or sandbars off the cliffs for miles, just deep water. With little wind or chop, he can almost relax and just cruise. The navigation is simple: just follow the coastline west. It's four hours until sunset, but the current and wind are in his favor, he'll make it to the beach well before. From the smooth, rolling ocean of blue he can see the trail climbing up and down, weaving in and out of the valleys along the coast. The trip by kayak should be less than half the time and half the effort of the trail, with nearly twice the weight in supplies.

———

The swell and the rebound of the swell off the cliffs at times converge, creating weird dips and boils in the deep water he's in. The swell bounces off the cliffs at the same frequency, and nearly the same amplitude, as the swell coming in. At times, two peaks come together to create an even bigger peak right under the boat. Then the bottom falls out when a double valley forms as the waves cross each other. Other times the waves don't meet in sync. Instead they counteract each other, creating a choppy mess of confusing seas. Luckily, he's able to swish through the ups and downs of the competing swells without having to clench his stomach too much. His progress along the coastline feels slow, but the steep valleys to his left unfold with every few paddle strokes.

Two hours into the journey, Mano passes 8-mile valley with its stream plunging in an arcing cascade over hundred-foot cliffs into the sea. He hasn't stopped paddling since the launch. At the sight of the cascading stream dancing over the cliffs and down to the ocean, he rests his paddle and breathes a sigh of relief. He's just two miles from the beach. Tonight he'll be back on the inside. Just as he glances up to eight-mile camp to see if he can see anyone, the hairs on the back of his neck stand on end. A rumbling crash builds from behind.

A rogue wave is breaking right behind him, about to sweep him away! He mouths a scream but his breath is paralyzed. One look back at his impeding doom reveals no crashing wave at all. Instead, a whale's tail smacks down just meters from his kayak. Relieved, but still on edge, he watches humpback whales glide alongside his kayak. At one point, a whale comes so close that he can practically reach it with the paddle. They zoom ahead and leave just as quickly and mysteriously as they came. *Were they just being playful, or did they come to watch over him on his journey?*

The beach ahead is now in clear view and he presses forward squinting with the sun in his eyes. *I'll be landing an hour before sunset,* he thinks to himself. As he rounds the bluffs to the river month and Heiau, he sees people, and people see him! They dance around on the bluff top, waving! Mano lets out a jubilant *Wa-whoee*, as he paddles cautiously towards the breakers with the beach just beyond, trying to decide exactly what to do on the landing.

'*Remember to just crash land.*' Honu's laughing voice echoes in his mind.

So when the whitewater catches me I just jump overboard and let the kayak crash land. He coaches himself as sizable set waves roll underneath him.

He waits behind the break in the deep water just beyond the sandbar, trying to be patient. People start to gather on the shore to receive him as he waits teetering up and down just outside of the crashing waves. The exodus of people from the bluffs reaches the beach, and a small crowd is gathered to welcome him in. Still, he waits outside the break nervously feeling the swells roll under him. Sets of waves come in three or four he decides, monitoring the swell undulating beneath. *One, two, three, okay, wait there's another big one still! Okay, looks calm behind it, now go!*

He paddles frantically just behind the fourth set-wave. He allows himself one nervous look back to see if the next wave is right on his tail. It's not, and after a few hard strokes, he's cleared the impact zone. The next wave comes, but it's not going to break over him. The white water catches up with him though and instantly surfs and spins the kayak. Mano dives off the stern and instinctively goes straight to overhand strokes, towards the shore. After just a few strokes, he realizes he can stand up, he's practically there! Before he can catch his breath, or trudge up to his knees he's knocked over by a blissful naked embrace. Together he and Pulani fall back into the ocean.

"Mano-Banano, you made it. We've been talking about you all day, and then I look up, you know, from where we play music on the bluff, and there you are, paddling in the ocean. I couldn't believe it."

Honu is right behind pulling the upside-down boat to shore.

"Stellar landing! You timed it perfectly, right on the beach!"

"You know, crash-land!" Mano grins.

Chapter 4   Huminals, Hippies, Goddesses and Grizzley

The valley draws Mano in with its beauty and seclusion. He enjoys spending his mornings exploring her many alcoves, side streams, ridge tops, and hidden citrus orchards. The valley garden that he finds himself visiting the most is called Community Garden. Two miles up the valley a man-made diversion of a side stream irrigates several large terraces of fruit trees and flooded lois planted with sugarcane and native Hawaiian taro. A dozen large kukui nut trees were felled to bring light to this food forest oasis in the center of the valley. The felled trees create a portal through the rainforest canopy that allows sun in and bathes hibiscus flowers, bananas and tomatoes in tropical warmth. There's even a cleared grassy terrace beneath a large orange tree where one can soak up the sun and catch a glimpse of the ocean through a window in the canopy.

Mano hikes up to the big mango tree at the center of Community Garden looking for Paul. Paul has been living and caretaking Neverland's most beloved garden for a few seasons. To say Paul is a down-to-earth creature is an understatement. He's a man that feels at home living simply, mostly alone, in the heart of the valley. Mano spots him romping through a muddy taro patch at the edge of the gardens when he arrives.

"Paul, you're such an animal. I think you've been out here so long that now you're more animal than human. You're more like a *huminal!*"

"You know it, Mano-banano, nine years in the valley and I've become a real monkeyman. Wahoo-ohhie!" Paul dances and thrashes about naked in the taro loi muck, completely at home in his jungle world.

"Yeah you, Pulani, and Kaiko have got to be most huminal-like creatures out here. You guys hardly wear clothes even."

"Who needs clothes in a land where you are naked to the core anyway?" Paul replies.

"Ha! You're right! There's no way to hide your personality out here. Why should we even attempt to hide our physical bodies?"

"Well, Mano, your thoughts are like an open book, I'm surprised you're still wearing clothes."

"I guess I haven't been here long enough to lose them all. Plus I'm not quite beyond mosquito molestation, unlike you."

"Yeah alright! I guess you're not a real valley cat, you're more of a beach guy."

"You got it Paul, I'm an ocean guy and I love it. Mama Kai is my maker, and I swim naked with the whales!"

"Yeah we got it all here in Neverland! Monkey men like me, Goddesses, and Grizzlies even." Paul responds as both roll their heads back in a chuckle thinking about a certain character named Grizzley.

The Grizz as he was sometime called, has to be the most famous of all of Neverland's residents. He isn't a huminal of instinct like Paul or Pulani, instead Grizz is his own creature entirely. Grizzley, the oldest of the hippies in Neverland had cool blue eyes and a warm smile that showcased his few, maybe just two, remaining teeth. His beard hadn't been trimmed in decades and its only maintenance was the occasional singe from it blowing over the campfire. Notorious for showing up opportunistically at any food gathering, he'd snatch up any goodies available, and mac em' down. And he'd get away with it, simply because he's the Grizz!

Their thoughts divert from Grizzley as they watch a beautiful butterfly swoop down between them.

"Say, what about the goddesses this season? What do you think about this winter's *women of the valley*?" Mano nudges Paul playfully.

"Well you know how it is, any *wahine* that walks in here is treated like a goddess. But, you know, I'm kinda like you Mano. I go for the ones with that crazy look in their eye. Like that little Brazilian girl you scored with. Ha! You even hiked out for her didn't ya?"

"Yeah, she was special for sure, but she's long gone now. Off-island on her own trip."

"There was no keeping her in Neverland, that's for sure. This place ain't got the pizzazz of Rio. And your pizzazz only goes so far." this time Paul nudges Mano jokingly.

"Yeah, yeah. What about Rainbow, and Honu's little doll, Charlotte?" Paul continues.

"I dunno know much about Miss Giggles, but that Rainbow, she's a firecracker, probably too hot to handle for either of us! I saw her shake everyone down on the bluffs with a terror when someone busted her camp stash a week ago, a real piece of work that one, I tell ya!" Paul laughs out loud before continuing.

"But Charlotte, she's got the sweetness of the most perfectly picked orange from the most famous groves of the back valley. You know, she's the kind that can part a sea of men with a smile. But she don't got the crazy look in her eye, I dunno if she could really do it for me. But your horny ass would do her, I'm sure!" Paul rattles.

"Hey now! I got some control! She's too skinny for my taste anyways."

"Since when do you let any slip by you? Too thin for your taste, whatever!"

"She's Honu's girl, and I'm not one to scam on another dude's lady."

"Yeah sure, Honu's girl. On this island we say it's not your girlfriend, it's just your *turn!*" Paul says with a smirk.

"What is it with Honu? It seems all the ladies are into him." Mano asks.

"He's the classic easygoing hot surfer guy, chicks love that." Paul replies casually.

"I guess I know what you mean. So…what about me?"

"You, Mano, you're charming. You got that thick curly hair, brown eyes and a cheeky smile, sure chicks will melt over you, too. But you're too goofy, your silliness is unrestrained. I think it's kinda funny, beautiful even, but you're not smooth like Honu." Paul teases. Mano feels a bit on the spot and doesn't know how to respond so he diverts the conversation.

"Well what about the up-valley mystiques, Gaia and Keilani, you had a *turn* with either of them yet?" Mano asks.

"Those girls act like they don't need men, meditation is their sex. They're solace is in their singing bowls." Paul announces and they both chuckle, but their minds catch on contemplating these two mysterious goddesses. Gaia, the delicate blue-eyed blond possessed Dali Llama blessings. Keilani, at least a dozen years older, held a dark-eyed Shaman look. Neither were much for conversation or beach parties, however they glowed with something special. They weren't so much hard to talk to, just hard to relate to. How did they end up here anyway? What made them decide to stay? Of course, the reasons for staying were obvious, but here in Neverland no other young girls managed as year-long residents. Mano and Paul and probably every other guy on the beach wanted to know what really juices those two.

Their reflections on the up-valley mystiques leave Paul unsettled. Maybe he did have some sort of 'encounter' with one of them?

"Well, Mano, I think I've had enough valley-girl gossip for the day. I'm gonna head home to my camp." Paul bear hugs Mano then scurries barefoot and bare-skinned farther up valley.

Mano thinks for a moment about Paul's charm as an up-valley naked huminal. He could be quite charming too. What would a woman think if alone on an up-valley walk, she stumbled upon Paul, smiling blued-eyed young and naked with a beard down to his chest. For a tall, strong, hairy, bearded creature man, he has an innocent smile that made him approachable. Mano smiles to himself daydreaming. He ambles along the trail through the java plum trees feeling the coolness of their shadows along the path. Suddenly Kaiko appears, giddy with delight. He jumps up to give Mano a naked embrace.

"I'm in love!" Kaiko exclaims jubilantly.

Kaiko the huminal is in love. In love with his full-power huminal equal Pulani, the beautiful, enchanting, yet completely rugged as the trail, goddess from Uruguay. Both are true-to-themselves animals of instinct, not analyzing, deliberating humans, like Mano. They found each other in this wayward place, and manifested their true love in Neverland.

"This love is so real, but it feels like I'm living in a dream." Kaiko announces.

It's true; the two are living a dream, in love, here in the fantasy realm of Neverland. Mano didn't want to admit it, but he envied their love right then. Their bond feels so solid, so pure and undeniable. They had met in Neverland just weeks ago, but the way their gaze held on each other's eyes, Mano knew they could last. Mano hugs Kaiko again, and feels the true love he is experiencing.

"Let's meditate and pray on your love." Mano offers, truly inspired by Kaiko's feelings.

"Great idea, I should give thanks to the spirits, after all!" Kaiko rejoices.

They sit down on some mossy rocks together and Mano lets his mind drift with thoughts of love. He feels their love and is amazed and inspired, but also jealous. Theirs is the love he yearns for. His heart aches wanting it. They found each other in this incredible place. Would he ever find someone to share true love with? Would he ever overcome his lustful desires that might hinder him to find love?

He tries to release these thoughts and simply meditate. Accept and appreciate their love. But meditation rarely is easy for him and soon he feels restless. Instead of meditating, and releasing all thought, he allows himself to think about love and relationships, his perception of love, and Kaiko and Pulani.

He thinks about love in the outside world. In Babylon love and relationships had to be compatibility tested on multiple levels to make sense. Love had to be mutually beneficial and economically feasible even. But still true love could be so strong, that the power of love itself could overcome any worldly barrier. *Wouldn't that be incredible?* he daydreams.

Kaiko and Pulani's love and togetherness had a unique feeling that Mano could feel. Their love felt powerful, untamed and unrestricted. Though he couldn't even explain it to himself, the very thought of it flusters him and he decides to just abandon it and send simple good intention toward their love. Kaiko and Mano snap out of their meditation simultaneously as a gust of wind rustles the leaves around them.

"Did you feel that!" Kaiko exclaims.

"What? You mean the wind?" Mano stutters.

"No, it's more than just wind, the spirits are bestowing their blessing upon us." Kaiko's eyes widen.

"A blessing of love from the ancients!" Mano declares.

"Yeah Mano-banano, that's it. It's an affirmation that Pulani is the one. She's the product of my manifestation. My wish for true love, realized!"

"That's great, now can you reveal the secret to me, I'm after true love, too, you know!" Mano jokes.

"Power of intention, man! Just like how I got out here. Intention, faith, and luck I guess."

"How did you end up here in Neverland, all the way from Minnesota anyway?" Mano questions.

"Well, it is a pretty damn good story if you really wanna hear it."

"I'm just a lonely guy on an isolated beach, I got time." Mano smiles.

"Alright Mano, here's my story just for you. And it all started with hockey."

"Hockey?" Mano squints, perplexed.

"Yeah, ice hockey…Minnesota, man!" Kaiko folds into a day-dreamy state as he prepares to tell his story.

"Hockey was my whole life growing up. I practiced, and practiced, but didn't make the NHL. I played in the minor leagues for a few years, but I kept getting traded to shittier and shittier places. Hockey was pretty much all I knew, so I just went with it. But it sucked. I was living in Lincoln, Nebraska playing on a shitty team, and then it hit me. Wham! I had my realization. *I don't have to do this anymore.* Then just like that, I quit and went home. My whole life to that point was hockey and I just quit. It was super scary, but totally liberating." Kaiko throws back his shoulder length hair and laughs. Mano's captivated and encourages him to proceed with his story.

"So back in Minnesota, I decide to try to get back with my old girlfriend there. One night we're drinking wine at her dad's house and the conversation moves toward sex. She says we should go get some condoms to be safe, so I jump in her dad's car to go to the store for condoms. I make a wrong turn out of the parking lot and get pulled over and arrested for DUI. Her dad's car gets impounded; he has to bail me out of jail. Everything's destroyed with her, and with the whole DUI charge, I just decided to say *fuck it*, so I skipped bond and fled to California.

Two years in Santa Cruz with no license, no real job, living in the woods and teaching myself guitar, I guess I sort of became a hippie by default. Then I heard of this beach, so I scrounged up some money, and bought a ticket to the island. I must have done something right cause I'm here now!"

"Wow, what a journey," Mano verbalizes wide-eyed. *Must of done something right cause I'm here now.* He lets Kaiko's proclamation fill his own heart.

Huminal, human, outlaw, or otherwise, all of Neverland's residents felt that way. Whatever happened in the past was of little importance. They made it here to paradise now, the past was history!

Whether a true *outlaw* like Kaiko or just a wanderer-in, like Mano, the residents of the valley and beach found their home in Neverland. It was clear for most, normal society was too harsh, too fake, or just too plain hard to keep up with. To Mano, being a *lost boy* on a remote beach was better than being lost in Babylon.

Besides, life in a fantasyland is exciting, and free, and inspiring. Inspiration could grow like a weed in Neverland, and residents did their best to cultivate it. Neverland brings out the best in people, and the best in people bring out the best in everyone else. Because of this, people could positively glow in Neverland. If glow and inspiration reach peak levels, then magic can happen.

32

Chapter 5   Beach Life

Mano, Paul, Kaiko, Pulani and a guy they just nicknamed Hitman hang out in the shade on a hot, cloudless January afternoon. A couple of 2-day tourist backpackers join in a somewhat circular conversation about primitive gardening techniques and various up-valley projects.

"So is this really all you guys do out here-- hang out and talk about the valley?" One tourist asks mid-conversation.

"Well that, hiking, swimming, making food, wandering, dreaming of love, and searching for the meaning of life. You know, typical stuff." Mano rallies back a response casually.

"Well that's great, but haven't you been on all the hikes and seen all the waterfalls? Don't you get bored being so disconnected from society?" The tourist continues to question.

"Disconnected, yes, but bored, hardly!" Mano responds with a laugh before continuing.

"Each day is an opportunity for another adventure. Sometimes I'll do yoga before breakfast. Sometimes I'll start the day with a jump in the ocean, maybe even try to surf or bodysurf if the waves are small. Then there's coffee and food. We call it the morning show. Friends stop by, we jam music, make more food, then who knows? Swimming in the valley stream, beach volleyball, gardening, and guitar. Visiting friends and socializing. There's always fruit and firewood to be gathered and water jugs to fill up. Of course, everything is in the flow and weather and mood dependent. Hobbies and projects like jewelry making, camp building, gardening, and song writing can really eat up your time! If I can find time to read in the hammock or write in my journal, I'm lucky. Just meeting all the new people who come through is enough to fill up an afternoon! Look, it's almost sunset. Time for music and more food and relaxing. Now what do you do out there that you are in such a hurry to get back to?"

Beach life is sweet. There's always something new going on to get excited about. Tonight is another gathering on the bluff and Kaholo is making a homemade pumpkin pie with pumpkins he grew in his garden. Who would want to miss that?

10 or so valley residents as well as a token cute tourist girl or two gathers on the bluffs to serenade the sun to sleep where the ocean meets the sky. After sunset they all duck into Honu's camp at a spot called the lion's den, where Kaiko is making veggies and quinoa. Then Kaholo, the Cheshire Cat, emerges from an unknown trail with his army-green canvas knapsack.

"Check these babies out!" Kaholo opens the bag and pulls out four medium-sized, pale pumpkins.

Charlotte's eyes sparkle examining them.

"Whoa, did those come from the valley?"

"From my garden, up valley," Kaholo answers proudly. He begins work on his pumpkin pie, while regurgitating the highlights from the NPR evening news broadcasts he picks up on his up-valley transistor radio. The fire glows hot with big logs as the crew sits calmly watching Kaholo begin his pie-making process.

Kaholo peels, slices, and boils the pumpkins. Then he mashes them up, and adds sugar to make the filling. Next he reaches into his bag for ingredients to make the crust.

"If you guys wanna see how we do this, look over here." The Cheshire Cat announces pulling out two jars.

"Okay, now, *this* is ganja trim, and *this* is ganja oil. We're just gonna put these right in." He empties both jars straight into a mixing bowl as the eyes around him widen.

"Now we add the flour." He uses an up-valley measuring cup, his bare hand, to scoop up flour into the mix.

"Yeah, maybe a little too much flour, I'll just put some back."

With both hands in the mixing bowl, he kneads together the flour, oil, and trim. Everyone watches as the dough starts to take on the pale green color of his canvas bag.

"Wow, it's really turning the dough green!" Honu nudges Charlotte teasing.

"I know, I know, look at it, looks great, huh!" Kaholo says with a Cheshire grin. Music and storytelling continue while the pie is placed in Dutch oven cast irons on the fire. Glowing hot logs and big coals are placed on top of the cast iron skillet to create the top heat needed for baking. Kaholo keeps the fire stoked and uses a piece of bamboo as a blow stick to send oxygen to the coals. It's nearly midnight by the time the 3 inch thick 17-inch diameter ganja pumpkin pie is finished.

"Ok, we've probably all overdosed on ganja food before, this won't be any different. You can eat your piece now, and in the morning you'll still feel good!" Kaholo announces as he distributes the slices. Few even dare to take a bite till the next day.

The sun rises over the mountains and warms the beach for another fun-filled day. Beach volleyball, Frisbee, pizza, and ganja-pie highs put the crew in a grand mood. The sun gives way to a half-moon that dances in and out of the clouds illuminating the Heiau where everyone comes together for fire and music once more.

The next morning is calm, and Mano decides to take the kayak out for his first fishing outing. He and Paul manage to launch the boat through the shore break. They get tossed by a big set wave on their first attempt, but they flip the boat back upright, right in the sandbar and punch through the break on their second try. They cruise over to a small pocket beach beyond the bluffs, trolling with two fishing poles. They hold the poles in the boat with their bare feet, and paddle with their arms. The lures draw three nibbles, but they can't seem to hook one. Nonetheless, the two bond as brothers, floating on the great Pacific.

Kaiko's day is more impressive. Fueled with love inspiration, he writes a knockout song on guitar in a couple of hours. *Where the River meets the Sea* becomes an instant hit and soars to the Neverland top ten. His lyrics are pure and smooth. Mano and many others draw inspiration from his new song.

Kaiko's song, a love song for his lover Pulani plays in Mano's head and strikes a chord in his heart.

Run, Run, Run Away

Run Away with Me

Where the River Meets the Sea

Our Love will Flow Free

Where the River Meets the Sea...

Hula-hooping, drumming, and dancing highlight the nights leading up to the full moon. Grounding down into the earth and connecting with one's inner child is the theme of the current lunar energy, Mr. X's partner Ella explains. Good vibes build as the group of friends continue to share music, food, and feeling each night and day. Rain doesn't even slow Neverland's increasing positive charge.

On a calm morning, Mano wakes up early, before the first rays of sun touch the beach, and he takes the kayak out in front of the river mouth well before any wind. This time, instead of a lure he uses a prawn from the prawn trap in the stream to bait his fishing hook. He lowers the prawn down to just above the rocks on the bottom.

The small swell rolls underneath him and bobs the kayak and the prawn up and down in the water. He lets himself relax and float with the rhythmic flow of the swell. No more than ten minutes pass and he feels a tug on the line.

It's a fish for sure! He excitedly tries to turn the reel, but he remembers it's so corroded that it can hardly be turned by hand. He sluggishly turns the reel with both hands and pulls the fish in. When the small, floppy, brown fish finally surfaces, it manages to flop off the hook before he can grab it. Somehow, the fish is so tired and disoriented from its slow battle to the surface that it pants defeated at the surface and allows Mano to paddle the kayak over to it and snatch it up with his bare hand. A fluke catch, but still it's his first fish. Excited, he tries again later that evening with a tourist girl, but they only catch an amazing sunset from the water.

Morning kayak cruises and fishing outings become more regular as the winter swell backs down toward the end of February. But the ocean is still the one who grants passage, and timing the sets is not an exact science. He feels the window of calm coming and Mano punches through a couple sets of whitewash, preparing to blast through the impact zone at just the right moment during the lull.

He cranks up the waves quickly passing the point where the small ones are breaking. He's nearly outside the impact zone. Paddling hard for the open ocean, he sees a big wave growing out of the sea. Pumping up the wave with a fury, Mano bursts right through the crest. He lifts off the seat as the thirteen-foot kayak catches air, then drops into the trough of the next wave.

People on the beach stare wide eyed. He cleared it! Then everyone sees the next wave. It's obvious he's not going up and over this monster. Mano takes a couple hard stokes, but he's quickly swept up the face of the wave. At the last second, before the curl catches him for a double overhead body slam, he dives off the boat through the wave to the outside. The boat is taken with the wave, barreling violently towards the beach. Mano's on the outside of the sets, adrenaline pumping. Now, he has to swim back through the break to the shore with his paddle.

Mano can see people on the beach scurrying about as his kayak washes towards them. He waits out the rest of the big set waves still swimming out to sea, not wanting to be caught by them. Eventually there's a lull and he swims hard for the shore, gripping hold of his paddle. Small waves pass under him as he gets closer to the impact zone. He swims with a furry to get through the break, then he looks back and he sees a pretty big one breaking right behind him. It's okay, he's well past the sandbar, he tells himself as the whitewater surge engulfs him. All he can do is hold on and take the pounding.

It's too long before the foamy backwash subsides and he's able to crawl to the surface for air. The next time the whitewater hits, he's more tired and wanting air even more while getting bounced towards the shore in the foam pile. On his next breath he's close enough to shore to touch his feet on the next sandbar. The kayak washes down all the way to the far west end of the beach in the shore rip. Luckily some beach-goers run and grab it in the knee-deep whitewash and drag it up on the sand. Mano nearly collapses on the beach, completely out of energy and breath. He's okay, but he's humbled by the failed launch.

Days of wandering and wondering twist together like a song. Wandering, wishing, and dreaming. Mano contemplates his wishes and dreams for a moment.

He wished for a fish, and he caught one. He lost his only knife, and he wished for one to replace it. A random tourist gave him one without him even asking. He thought about getting drunk on a rainy day, but had no booze, and a tourist offered up a full bottle of rum at the evening jam. His heart yearned wanting to wish for true love, but he decides that he wants it too much, so he waited. What is true love anyway? He lets his mind drift with the wind.

Chapter 6   Khan on the Aina

Kaiko's the first to hear the drone of the motorboat while making morning tea on the bluffs. *A boat is here! It's too early to be a tour boat, this has to be a boat drop. Could it be Honu coming back in on the boat drop as he promised?* Mano rushes over to the edge to scan across the water for a boat. Before he can see anything, he hears a distant shout. "Wah-hoo!" Shouts continue as the boat and a head of bouncing dreadlocks comes into view. Somebody's pumped to be heading back to the inside. Honu is aboard as well as two or three unfamiliar faces. Mano scurries down to the beach to greet them.

"Honu, you made it back! For a moment Charlotte and I thought you'd be forever stuck in Babylon," Mano calls out, embracing him.

"Oh, you knew I'd come back to the valley, I couldn't leave Charlotte stuck here too long with you, Mano-banano."

Mano pulls Honu aside and asks. "Who's the dready dude and the other two with ya?"

"I'm Khan," a voice lurches out before Honu can respond. The tan, blue-eyed, dreadlocked man approaches.

"K-han," Mano annunciates with raised eyebrows.

"Khan!" The man harps back sharply right in Mano's face. "It's spelled K-H-A-N. The 'h' is silent, for you. It is my tribal given name."

"Okay, can do, Khan," Mano smirks, but takes a step back, "Where did you come from, Señor Khan?"

"This whole island is my home, I live here and this beach is my land. Who are you?" Khan's voice is demanding.

Honu jumps in. "Easy there, Khan. This is Mano. He's cool, he's been out here on the beach for a few weeks. He's as pono as Kaholo or anyone else here."

Mano smiles and Khan shrugs. "Where is Kaholo?" Khan asks before marching off.

A softer voice emerges in his wake.

"Hi, I'm Andrew. I'm just happy to be back, safe in paradise." The young bearded redhead offers a polite handshake.

"And I'm Rainbow," the blue-eyed girl with thick brown ringlet hair and an inquisitive gaze chimes in. Mano had heard of Rainbow through Paul but this was their first real meeting.

"Well, great to see some new people arriving, it's been pretty quiet around here. Come up to the bluffs for coffee!" Mano offers.

"Will do, will do. Now where's Charlotte?" Honu chuckles. They carry their bags up to the bluffs and get acquainted. The three new arrivals turn out to be not so new at all. Rainbow had actually just left the beach when Mano arrived and Khan and Andrew are typical seasonal winter characters that all the old timers kinda already knew about.

The stern-faced Khan turns out to be a hardcore surfer, a thundering djembe drummer, and a passionate ukulele player. He's not island-bred like he proclaimed. He's really just a seasonal ganja grower guy from California. Unlike easy-going Honu, Khan felt the need to be the alpha, trying to say Neverland is his beach even! Mano later learns that behind his brash, territorial surfer front is a kind and helping spirit. Still Mano is leery of joining Khan's tribe, as he calls it.

Khan grows to like Mano even. He likes him for the passion and intensity, and generosity he brings to Neverland. He even seems to admire Mano's independence in a funny sort of way. The two become friends and they grow together in Neverland. Khan helps Mano learn to surf the steep beach break and harmonize music in a group. Mano teaches Khan to sea-kayak in winter swells, and coax Rainbow into his arms.

Andrew turns out to be an even more incredible musician than Khan. His flavorful voice is dynamic, crisp, and velvet smooth. Andrew from Austin did his own thing, though. He'd be just as satisfied playing music up in the valley for the birds, as joining in a big group jam session. He doesn't need to be the leader like Khan, and like Mano he didn't care to join Khan's tribe. He was there for the serenity and pleasure of Valley life. He was laid back and suave enough to draw in the ladies, and apparently entertaining enough to keep them coming back to his tent.

Rainbow is shy at first, but her true Alaskan spirit comes out eventually. She'd dance naked in the rain and would speak her mind to any tourist that asked. She wasn't back in Neverland for two weeks before she and Khan became tent-mates. People weren't so surprised by the dozen-plus year age difference, but more by the fact that both Khan and Rainbow are type-A loose cannons. They made it work though. They certainly aren't the lovebirds that Kaiko and Pulani are, but they became a couple, and campmates, nonetheless.

Sometimes a new character would appear out of nowhere in Neverland. Their arrival unannounced, origin and purpose unknown, suddenly showing up in your camp, and like it or not, they instantly became a part of your life. Well, at least momentarily…

Waking with the chirping birds, one morning Mano stumbles out from his tent and walks naked over to the edge of the bluffs to pee and check the surf at the beach. There, a woman is lying on her back, half naked on his front porch, still awaiting the morning sun. He tip toes around her as she lies motionless, but he can sense that her eyes are now open. Her long grey dreadlocks splay out in the grass, her knees butterflied open.

"What are you doing up here?" He questions, as she looks abruptly his way. He swallows, realizing how rude he must have sounded.

She pauses unfazed, before responding. "Reconnecting... and just being."

"Sorry, I didn't mean to sound so abrupt, I guess, I uh just wasn't expecting anyone to be out here in front of my camp this early."

Mano turns to cover his nakedness, and she sits up, still unalarmed.

"It's so great to be back in this powerful place. I've been having incredible visions." the woman announces.

"It surely is powerful, but last night my dreams were more disturbing than incredible." Mano remembers his dream of a shipwreck on the beach.

Mano shuffles around and tells the woman that he will come back to get acquainted after he makes a cup of tea. Really he has an urgent bowel movement and feels uncomfortable being naked. He returns refreshed, and they enjoy a cup of lemongrass tea together as the sun crests the valley's back wall. She gazes off towards the horizon, holding the cup just below her lips. He glances at her then stares out across the ocean as well. Then he glances back to find her staring at him. This time he holds her gaze. They are both intrigued, and they embrace the stare without a word. After some time, she breaks focus and decides to introduce herself.

"My name is Aina, and you must be Mano, the kayaker."

"That's right," he responds, almost skeptical. "How did you know who I am?"

"Oh, I just knew, I heard that surfer guy Khan talking about you, and when I saw you, I just knew you had to be the guy with the kayak."

"Well maybe, but there's *a lot* of guys out here." Mano chuckles.

She smiles to acknowledge him.

"I just guessed. You look like a kayaker, a waterman, I can tell." He turns away, blushing, but then focuses back on her. A thought crosses his mind like he was somehow meant to meet this lady.

"So what does Aina mean?" Mano queries.

"Aina just means island in Hawaiian. I grew up on an island, not here, an island in Alaska. I spent some good times, several seasons of my youth out here living on these same bluffs. You can really live free out here. I did, and I loved it. I guess I still love it, but I'm barely here for a week this time." She sweeps her mop of hair to her other side. Her thick grey dreadlocks and weathered skin are testaments to a hard-earned hippie life. Mano can see the wisdom held in her wrinkled skin and her pale blue eyes. The two of them converse openly as the rising sun warms their skin. The smoothness of her voice makes her easy to listen to, and he listens intently as she tells her story.

"Yeah, we used to stay out here for months at a time, dodging the Rangers, braving the storms, just barely making it on fruit and kick-downs sometimes. Nobody had good flashlights or hi-tech gear back then either. We were tough though."

"What did you do about the storms?" Mano asks, remembering one of Grizzley's tales of the times when it seemed to rain forever.

"Oh, we got wet just like I'm sure you all still do now. When it really got bad, sometimes we'd all make the pilgrimage around to the other side of the island where things are drier. We just banded together and did what we could. That's what you do when you are young, you know." Her voice trails off.

Aina pauses and appears to go back into her original morning reflection. Mano stares down at her hands, watching her as she rubs her fingers together. She keeps her focus forward toward the ocean. Her hands appear as strong as a man's, and surely hold as many stories as her deep eyes.

"What's the hardest thing you've ever done?" he asks randomly. A long silence follows as Aina continues to stare out at the horizon.

"I can only imagine growing up on a remote island in Alaska with a bunch of brothers. It had to be tough." Mano probes a little further.

Aina turns to him and smiles.

"You know, Alaska is an incredible place that makes some hard, hard-headed people, but by far the hardest thing I ever did wasn't here or there. It was in a tree in Northern California."

Mano chuckles. "In a tree in California?"

"Tree sitting in a giant redwood. That was by far the hardest thing I've ever done." Aina smiles wide revealing a couple of silver-crowned back teeth.

"Tree-sitting?" Mano was hoping for a wild story of braving an Alaskan winter melting snow on a woodstove for water and fighting off polar bears. Aina just seemed like that kind of woman.

"Yeah, tree sitting. I was two hundred-fifty feet up a redwood tree north of Arcadia, California for a whole month. It was brutal and crazy and I'll never do it again, but I did it."

Mano looks at her wide-eyed encouraging her to continue with the details of her story.

"The tree I was in was named Anastasia. She was a giant! 280 feet tall. She was nestled in a grove of old growth redwoods called the Freshwater Grove. I stayed up there a whole month on a four-foot by eight-foot sheet of plywood and vowed to protect the tree. It was a trip, being up there in the wind and hail and having people shoot at you and such."

"People shot at you?" Mano stares at her amazed.

"Yeah loggers! The men would come in the evenings and shoot their guns up at us, trying to intimidate us to come down. It was wild. And during the day it was chainsaws all around, all day long."

"Wait, you said 'us.' I thought you were all alone up there?"

"Well, there were other tree-sitters. There was a guy in the tree next to me named Trust, and we were friends. At night sometimes I would come over to his tree."

"So you came down at night."

"Oh no, we never came down, not for a month!"

"Well how'd you get over there?"

She flashes her silver teeth at his unwavering interest.

"Well, Trust had a bow and arrow. He shot over a rope and then I pulled over a cable and attached it to Anastasia. Then I could clip into it with my harness and pull myself across to his tree. You're always clipped in, you know. Even when we slept at night we were in our harnesses."

"So being stuck up there in isolation in the elements all the time was the hardest thing."

"Everything was hard. I was on edge every day. People would try to climb the trees and extract the tree sitters. The hail and wind were brutal at times, and this red dirt from the tree was everywhere."

"So what did you do if someone tried to climb your tree?"

"You bind yourself to the tree. They gave us these metal handcuffs that would attach to the tree so we were locked in. It was nuts, but all of us were really committed so it made it kind of cool, you know? We were tough-ass committed tree sitters. But we were hated. I mean the logging industry up there is way powerful and those trees are the main resource and worth a lot of money. I kind of understood even though my whole island in Alaska was destroyed by logging."

"So, you did it as a tribute for the clear-cutting on your home island?" Mano asks.

"Na, I did it for myself. Whatever you do, you have to do it for yourself first, it's the only way when it really comes down to it."

Silence engulfs them as they both ponder this thought for a moment.

"I can't believe I never even heard of this going on. When was this?" Mano contests.

"Well, I was there the spring after 9/11, so most of the news was caught up on terrorism and such. But reporters and cameras still came to check us out."

"So in the end you came down and your tree was saved?"

"As far as I know yeah. I came down on April 20, 2002 and another tree sitter came up to take my place. I was so covered in that damn red dirt that they had to spray me down head to toe before they would let me in any bar."

"Incredible!"

"No, I was hideous, my friends didn't even wanna take me in their car," she laughs out loud.

"I forgot to ask you what was the best thing about being up there?" Aina sighs deeply before responding.

"Being at the very top right at sunset. I'd climb up to the very last branch and just swing in the wind. You'd swing like crazy, dozens of feet back and forth. It was a trip! But hell, I'm done with that now. To think that was over ten years ago."

They both stare out at the ocean. Mano lets his mind dance around images of Aina the tree sitter. He lies back and lets his thoughts transition into the incredibleness of the place where they sat and his own journey thus far. *Whatever you do, you have to do it for yourself first,* he mutters in his head. It sounded selfish, but somehow it did make sense.

A whale's fin smacks at the water's surface directly in front of them and brings them both back from their trances.

"They're really talking to each other out there, and to us too. The whole ocean and sky have been talking this morning." Aina announces smiling wide.

"You know, magic can reach peak levels here." Mano states humorously.

"You know, a big shift is happening in nature. I can feel it. I've been connected with this place for two decades, but just this year, and last year, I felt it. There's something happening, not just on the earth or from the outside, but from the inside. Deep in the physical core of the planet. I know it sounds silly, but I really felt it this morning just before you walked up. I'm not sure what it means yet, but it sure feels big."

"I hope it's for the good." Mano shrugs.

"Well, things have been getting better here it seems. The gardens are getting better, there's less ranger raids, and the people are better too. Good people like you." She shows him her biggest silver-toothed smile yet.

He looks to the side as if there might be another good person beside him. He thought of himself as a good person, but how did Aina seemingly know? After all, they just met. They break conversation and walk down to the main valley stream together. At the trail crossing she tells him that she must visit a place up valley, so they exchange hugs and part ways. He decides to jump in and cleanse at the river mouth to clear a bit of an unsettled feeling from their conversation. He asks a few people about her later, but he never sees Aina again.

Chapter 7   Sanctuary

An evening storm creeps in from the east and clouds out the sun. There is no sunset, only rain. Mano has dry wood gathered under his tarp, but he opts to crawl into his tent and snack on nuts and raisins for dinner instead. He reads under a headlamp as the rain pelts down. Just a couple-hour storm, he guesses. No need to go crazy adjusting tarps, things will dry up in the morning sun.

But at dawn the rain comes down just the same. It has to be dawn, he decides, opening his eyes to the grey light. There are no birds chirping yet. How is he awake? It's just barely light enough to see.

"Becka!" a voice rings out fierce, but distant and muffled by the pounding rain. It's dawn and that cat named Jason camped nearby is screaming for his girlfriend in the rain. No wonder Mano woke so early. He notices a bowl-sized puddle in the corner of his tent and he delicately pushes an already half-soaked t-shirt towards it to dam off the wetness from the rest of his dry-ish world inside. Why the hell is Jason yelling for Becka at first light in the middle of a storm? His half-asleep mind doesn't want to even think about those two now. So he rolls over and forgets about the shouting and encroaching puddles. Rain is good, but 14 hours of straight rain drains! An hour after dawn, the rain backs off to a drizzle. Mano decides to get up and try and do something, but before he's out of his tent, Jason is calling for him in his camp.

"Have you seen Becka? I don't know where she is. She never came back to camp last night. I'm super worried and it's been raining all night."

"Why isn't she with you?" Mano mutters.

"We got in a fight right as the storm was coming in at dusk. She left and never came back. She didn't even have her headlamp, her jacket or anything."

"Really? I hope she's okay. She's probably freezing and soaked, wherever she is." Mano states grimly as he see's Jason's heart sink.

"I know! I just want to find her and know that she's okay."

Mano walks out to the bluffs with Jason in the cold morning drizzle. The ground is saturated and mud squeezes between his toes. He envisions the valley stream brown and swollen from the all-night rain.

"Where do you think she would have gone?" Mano asks Jason as they push through wet branches on the overgrown bluff-top trail.

"She's not at Khan or Rainbow's camp, I checked. She's not at Keith's, either."

"You don't think she wandered along the edge of the bluffs and slipped and fell, do you?" Mano asks despondently.

"I sss-ure hope not," Jason chatters, his voice weak from the cold. Mano can see his desperation as the rain drips down his pale face.

"Becka, Becka!" Jason howls again like a wounded dog. "Becka, where are you?"

They search all the camps on the bluffs again to no avail, and then proceed down to the river mouth. The valley stream is super high, running like a torrent of chocolate milk toward the ocean. Mano suggests that they walk around the bottom of the bluffs and continue to call for her. Wandering in the dark storm with no light, she could have slipped off the trail that circles the rim of the bluffs. Or into the river to be swept out to sea. He doesn't mention these thoughts to Jason. Instead he offers hope that she could be sheltered under a large boulder at the base of the cliffs. Jason staggers along, sobbing helplessly. The spray from the ocean splashes up against the rocks and rain washes the saltwater back down to the sea. There's not a dry rock anywhere, nor is there a fallen body. Mano is soaked through, and the cold has gotten a hold of him as well. They return to the river mouth camp to regroup, relieved to have found nothing. Still, Jason is becoming unraveled grieving for her.

"She's gone, she's dead. I'll never see her again and it's all my fault."

"Don't say that. It's just a storm, she's probably safe under a tarp somewhere."

Mano looks up to the heavens for an answer as Jason marches around in the mud uselessly.

"Becka, why did you have to leave me!" he bellows over the noise of the raging stream.

Mano turns to Jason.

"Its okay, you're okay, Becka's okay somewhere," he declares, but then pauses to watch a big log tumble down the muddy river.

"Maybe she would have crossed over the stream and gone to the beach camps?" Mano offers.

"No, there's no way she would cross the river flooded like it is now," Jason answers, sharply.

"But...what if she crossed last night before it flooded, and then got stuck on the other side?" Mano theorizes.

"I guess that's possible," Jason replies, sheepishly.

They decide to try to cross the stream and search the beach.

They ford the swollen stream together at a slow spot, but it's still chest-high and pushing hard.

"If you slip, you have to let go of me and swim to the bank right away." Mano tells Jason. They cross without a fumble and slosh along to the beach trail.

Once at the beach, the search ends quickly. Becka is spotted sipping coffee under a tarp at Hitman's camp. Jason approaches her exhausted, soaked and almost in tears.

"We thought you had slipped off the bluffs and were dead!" he cries. She embraces her sobbing, soaked Jason and mumbles out an apology.

The full story unravels over a soothing cup of coffee. She was upset after their fight and crossed the stream at dusk. It kept raining and she didn't want to cross back over at night with no light, so she took refuge at Hitman's camp on the beach.

Mano doesn't stick around for their make-up session. Instead, he leaves to mitigate water damage at his own camp. He collects some clean-ish water off the tarp drip and tries to cut some trenches to drain the puddles around his tent as the drizzle continues. By noon he has all the drips on his tarps dialed and is feeling better about his more weatherproof camp setup. Just when he is about to crawl back into his tent and relax, Khan comes over.

Khan marches right up to him and stares him down with his cold blue eyes.

"Mano! We need to rebuild the Sanctuary. With this storm and what happened with Jason and Becka, it's crucial that we create some community dry space and bring people together."

"But who's gonna stay there to hold it down if we rebuild it?" Mano replies, backpedaling.

"We'll stay there, we'll hold it down." Mano looks at Khan skeptically.

"I don't know, I think the era of the Sanctuary ended when Don the Mayor left." Mano responds half-heartedly.

"That's not true, the concept of *Sanctuary* has been a part of the beach for decades. I've never seen this place without Sanctuary, and frankly, it bothers me. It really does." Khan broadcasts stoically.

"Yeah, but just because it's there doesn't mean people will use it and take care of it," Mano releases, attempting to settle Khan's excitement.

"Mano, you know as well as I do that Sanctuary is a crucial part of this place, and to see it gone..." Khan trails off in thought.

"To see it gone hurts. It hurts my heart even. That whole fiasco of Becka running off, and Jason screaming for hours could have been avoided if the Sanctuary was up and running. It's not just about having a place to party and hangout; it's a place of refuge. A place for tourists to go to when they don't have tarps or good tents and it rains like this. A place where girls can go and feel comfortable when they get into fights with their boyfriends. A place that always has a fire going, and food, and dry space. That's what it's about." Khan pauses, reflecting on what he just said, before continuing.

"With Honu gone, it's up to us to rebuild the Sanctuary. Let's do this today, during the storm!"

It certainly seems a bit ridiculous to take down and set up tarps in the middle of a storm, but Khan's charisma motivates people into action. His brash, tribal, almost anger-driven sensational attitude draws the heat needed to inspire and lead a group effort on the bluffs. Mano doesn't necessarily like him for it, but he admires him and is inspired into action, himself.

The two of them acquire a couple more tarps and move everything from both of their camps to the spot where Sanctuary once was. They set the tarps up over the fire pit and collect and dry out wood for the new community kitchen and gathering area. Sure enough, their motto of, *if we build it, they will come,* holds true. Over a dozen people, including newly arrived tourists, show up for the grand re-opening of the Sanctuary the following night. With Rainbow's help, they serve up food for all, pass around a couple of joints, and celebrate with songs and chants from the season.

"Welcome, my brothers and sisters. It's the grand reopening of the Sanc-tu-ary." Khan sings as he plays the djembe to serenade guests as they walk in. It feels like the beginning of a new era. At one point, Khan stands up and stokes the fire with a couple of nice dry logs. The flames light up his face and he raises a fist in the air.

"It's times like these when we really need to come together and build a community. Let us unite the beach!" All the newbies stare at him wide-eyed, like he is the god of the land. The few long-standing residents shake their heads slightly and sigh. Could this wayward community ever really be united?

Nightly parties at the Sanctuary continue for almost a week and its popularity as a refuge and hang-out zone grows. But after days of extending to whoever came by, Khan and Mano's food supplies are drained. Few people bring items to share. Many more just show up with an empty cup and leave dirty dishes. Khan and Rainbow move their camp back to their original spot on the bluffs, and Mano cooks meals at odd times to avoid having to share with unwanted company. Sanctuary fades as quickly as it was built. The tarps remain and the concept of Sanctuary is still there, perhaps just waiting for the next big storm to draw people back together.

Chapter 8   Tsunami

"Don't camp on the sand, the surf could come up and wash into your tent." Mano overhears Mr. X say to some tourists earlier that day. It's another one of those funky winter days where the swell is down in the morning, but big waves come crashing in before sunset. The beach showed nearly a hundred feet of sand in the morning, but the swell had risen as the day drew on, and at sunset the bigger set waves were washing all the way up to the rocks in places. Nobody had ever been washed away, but there were stories of backpackers who camped on the beach and a winter swell came up and wetted the bottoms of their sleeping bags in the middle of the night.

With so many great spots in the trees, who would want to camp on the sand anyway? Mano contemplates this and imagines what giant waves hitting the beach would be like. How tall could the biggest winter surf be? Twenty-foot, even thirty-foot wave faces had been observed in the recent past. Maybe once a decade, or once a century a fifty-foot wave face could build from a gigantic northwest swell. But a fifty-foot wave would just break farther out offshore and would still just be ankle-deep whitewash once it rolled up to the high, dry sand, right? He's not quite sure; it's hard to even imagine a fifty-foot wave. Eight to ten-foot waves on this steep break could scare away all but the best surfers, even Honu and Khan. Novice swimmers had to be rescued sometimes in as little as two-foot swells. Even the small waves are super powerful on this difficult shore break. Waves, storms, wind, and sun, Mama Kai will protect this land like she always has, Mano reminds himself trying to conclude his own daydream.

What about a tsunami wave? That's different, Mano decides. Not a wind-swell wave like any other, but a seismic wave. A Tsunami wave comes from an underwater earthquake or volcanic eruption. Its source is a seismic event that sends a shockwave of water in all directions. Mano tries to imagine it like a larger version of waves created from a stone dropped into a calm lake. A pulse, a ripple of wave, in all directions, that has to be what a Tsunami is like. He remembers hearing about the tsunamis that struck Thailand and Southeast Asia a few years before. Pictures of upturned boats and destroyed villages several meters up from sea level flash in his mind.

How big were those tsunamis? He looks out across the ocean towards Japan, toward Russia. What really happens out there in the great blue beyond where there are no islands or other landmasses for thousands of miles?

Ancient Hawaiians had lived here for thousands of years without fear of seismic events happening across the ocean. There has to be history or lore of a major tsunami here. Since there is no Internet to cross check for historical facts, Mano decides to consult the next best thing: Mr. X.

"Sure, I've been through a few tsunamis in the 13 years I've been on the beach. All of 'em were small waves, though. None were really even noticeable."

"Really? How did you know about them, then?"

"Oh, they'll announce it on the radio and sometimes they'll send helicopters to warn us. We shouldn't have anything to worry about. Mama Kai protects us here. But if you hear a chopper screaming in at off hours, it usually means something is up. More likely it's the Rangers than some rogue wave. Either way, you know what to do. Run up the valley and hide out.

"Yeah, I know, I shouldn't even be thinking about such nonsense."

"That's right, you shouldn't! You know how things work around here. Good or bad, if you think of something long enough, Mama Kai will just send it!" X sniffs the air with a sly smile.

Less than a week later, an Earthquake unleashes a Tsunami that rocks Japan and sends seismic waves as far as the California coast.

The night the Tsunami occurs, the crew is up well past sunset partying at Edge Camp on the bluffs. Keith tapped a couple of gallons of valley-made lilikoi wine and they are all getting silly, singing to the moon. Keith had a way of changing the rhythm and pitch of popular songs to suit his own style. Sometimes songs could sound even more incredible than their original versions. Other times they were so ridiculous people would just keel over laughing, begging him to stop. But he always persisted unfazed by the group's response. It's one of those classic nights. The Bluffs are lit up by the moon, Keith is buzzed and howling out to the open ocean in song.

Before midnight the booze runs out and the crew drifts off to their individual camps. Mano crawls into his tent at the Sanctuary and falls asleep. He stirs at the odd buzz of a chopper. Is he dreaming? With so many tourist helicopters all day long is he starting to hear them buzzing in his head? The fly over doesn't really stir him. A drunken hippie running and screaming into his tent does.

"Wake the fuck up! Haven't you heard the helicopters? There's a fuckin' tsunami! Run up valley, we gotta move to higher ground!" Keith erupts in frenzy.

Mano emerges from his tent bleary-eyed just as a chopper hovers directly overhead. The helicopter beams down a bright light on him and a voice announces through a loudspeaker. "Tsunami, move to higher ground. Repeat, move to higher ground."

The bright light, careening chopper blades, and loud monotone voice, are a scene from an alien abduction movie. Mano stands paralyzed ready to be sucked away into outer space.

"Come on! We gotta run up valley, the wave is coming!" Keith urges frantically.

Mano snaps back to reality. A giant wave is about to engulf the whole bluff top. He grabs his jacket and headlamp and follows Keith up the hippie highway trail. Up away from the encroaching wave. On their way up they run into Charlotte and Andrew scurrying up to higher ground as well. Mano imagines the wave engulfing the bluffs and narrowly escaping with the surging water right on his heels. He's filled with excitement, allowing himself to believe it. Is this doomsday? They are all nervous yet strangely giddy with the thought of such a crazy catastrophe when they arrive at Kaholo's valley camp at least five hundred feet above sea level.

"We gotta keep going all the way to the back wall. Two, three thousand feet up!" Keith screeches.

"Calm down, lets try to hear the radio!" Kaholo chastises. He carefully turns the dial, fighting the static in the newscast.

"The wave is expected to hit the island at approximately 2 AM," the newscaster drones. "It will be a six…"

"We're all gonna die! The whole world's gonna be washed away! We're all going down! Move to higher ground, they said!" Keith shrieks.

"Pipe down! I can't hear if he said six foot or six hundred foot wave!" Kaholo laments. "Yeah, calm down Keith. Just listen!" Charlotte spits.

The radio crackles out the tsunami warning again. *'The six-foot wave will reach the coast at approximately 2 AM. Evacuation warnings have been issued for all of the island.'*

"A six-foot wave? That's it? What's that gonna do? We've had 12-foot waves crashing on the beach all day!" Mano comments disappointedly.

"We could have just stayed on the bluffs sixty feet up and been fine! I can't believe they beamed down on us with those lights like it was the end of it all!"

"Shhhush," Kaholo fumes.

They continue to listen to the broadcast, now a bit more at ease.

'Okay, we're now taking callers to address anyone's concerns about the wave, which is scheduled to hit land in approximately one hour fifty-five minutes,' the commentator announces. A caller comes on.

"I'm calling to ask if there has been any warning sent to the people out on that remote beach on the north shore. There's no cell phone service out there you know." a woman's voice inquires.

"Hey, they're talking about us out here on the radio! Far out!" Charlotte bursts into a giggle fit, and everyone, even Keith lightens up.

Everyone is asleep at Kaholo's or in various other hideouts by the time the wave actually hits. One beach resident named Cliff had evacuated the whole beach up to the bluffs and had thrown a tsunami party at Sanctuary. Kaiko and a few others slept right through the helicopter warnings and started the next morning just the same as ever. A boat drop is delayed by a day, but other than that the tsunami had no effect on beach life at all. The next day is sunny, with beach volleyball and swimming as usual. A few days later Rainbow comes back in from a town trip and tells people about her experience during the tsunami while in town.

"People were going nuts in Babylon, buying up all the bottled water and food. I just wanted to get my stuff and get back to the beach where people act *normal*. Some lady at the grocery store checkout asked me if I was gonna buy some bottled water before the tsunami hits. I told her, 'Where I'm going we worry about running out of chocolate. There's always plenty of water!'

Mano tries to picture the scene in town. Babylonians everywhere are scrambling to buy up bottled water while Rainbow is searching for chocolate and fun-fetti cake for her friend's birthday on the inside.

Chapter 9   Captain Mano

"Just to let you know, there are two guys camped on the beach willing to pay a lot of money for someone to take them out in a kayak. They are pretty desperate after yesterday's storm. I bet you could get a couple hundred bucks, they seem like the type." Becka tells Mano as they leave the sunset potluck on the Heiau.

It's March 7th, Mr. X's birthday, and all celebrate with an amazing feast of pizza, popcorn, salad, macaroni, lentils, bread, and birthday cake. The crew is jazzed up and ready to continue the party on the Heiau, but Mother Nature has other plans. Another evening of heavy rain follows the sunset. The initial cloudburst sends everyone rushing to their camps to batten down the hatches before an alternative 'under-tarps' party can be arranged. So much for an after-dinner music jam...

Mano shouts to Becka as they scamper down from the Heiau. "Tell those guys that the swell is too high still. Besides, the kayak's not big enough for 2 fat guys, me, and all their gear. They can man up and hike the trail, it's not that wet!"

The next morning is sunny. Sun at last! Even the birds are in a better mood from the warming rays. They sing out with twice the normal enthusiasm at dawn. After his morning routine, Mano scurries down to the beach to dig his toes into the warm sand soaking up divine solar energy.

The gloom of the last couple of days left him feeling cold, internally cold. The cold tickles his ribs and shook through his neck. It unsettled his heart even. The only thing that can warm a body after feeling so cold for so long is a good woman, or tropical sunshine. He has no woman, so he loves the sun, and she warms him like the goddess she is. He sprawls out in the hot sand and lets the rays penetrate his skin. He breathes in the warmth from the thick humid air and just lies there.

By afternoon the clouds lift, and trade winds pick up, blowing out any lingering thought of more rain. The swell backs off too. It appears that the beach and valley are returning to normal pleasant spring weather.

Even the two guys that were desperate for a dangerous kayak ride out yesterday are smiling as they amble down the still muddy beach trail. It's funny how a little time and sunshine can convert a tourist from utterly hopeless and pleading for rescue, to smiling and confident. Babylonians are so pathetically impatient, Mano laughs to himself.

The land is certainly a good teacher of patience, he ponders. He remembers how impatient he was out in Babylon. He could hardly wait at a stoplight for a minute without fidgeting. When he first got to the beach it was such an arduous task to cook rice on an open fire. It felt like hours. Now he's amazed at how fast and easy it is. There's no doubt that time is morphed out here. He can't even remember the last time he saw the weekly cruise ship. He just knows it is spring, early March, and little else matters. The sun has returned, and he feels warm.

With the return of the sun, the beach bounces back to life. By midday people are swimming, Khan is out surfing, and Grizz is recruiting for volleyball.

That evening is another sunset potluck on the Heiau. The crew reunites for Mr. X's birthday and this time there's no rain to deter a late-night music jam. Perhaps it's a celebration for Mr. X, or a celebration of Honu's return from Babylon. Regardless, music flows from the most happily free creatures on earth. Khan's hands careen crisp on his drum as he howls at a rising moon. Honu and Kaiko harmonize guitars, and Kaholo and Andrew duel with their bamboo flutes. Everyone else sings when they know the song as a three-quarter moon rises high to light up the Heiau.

"This is golden, we're really coming together," Andrew comments when they finally break a ten-minute jam.

"Yeah, it's so great to have everyone playing together, that's when the magic happens," Honu chimes in.

"No doubt, it's the Mana, the energy of the valley, speaking through our hearts and being released through our instruments." Khan states poetically, sending Kaiko falling over laughing.

"Come on Khan, we sound good, but you're full of it!"

"No, it's true. When we come together and play with just feeling, not thinking, it's the energy of the valley released. After all, we're here on the Heiau. This is sacred ground. Khan's right!" Honu clarifies and Andrew pauses his picking to add his wit.

"I may just be high, but I feel the energy up from the earth enchanting me like a spell."

"I know, I know, definitely some real *mana* here, real stony *mana!*" Kaholo lurches. This time Mano and Andrew double over laughing.

"The sacred medicine and the mana of the land come together to make the magic and reveal the mystery." Honu serenades.

"Receive the mana and release the Mano to Mama Kai!" Kaholo teases.

"Mano's gone mad! Release him to Mama Kai!" Khan shouts!

Kaiko loses his rhythm to giggling again. "Alright, alright, you guys are tripping me out, lets just keep playing. Enough of this Mano Mana mumbo jumbo."

"Let Mama Kai instill her magic upon Kaiko to lead the next jam." Andrew concludes.

Playing on, releasing the energy of the earth, they let their voices carry to the sky. Each breath, each note, has meaning. For a moment each individual holds their space in the music and they play together as one unified creature channeling mother earth energy on the Heiau. At a slight break in the strumming, an unfamiliar voice disperses the unified energy of the group. A tourist woman appears.

"I'm looking for the kayak rescue guy, the guy with the kayak on the beach. Is he one of you guys?"

"Well, Mano over here is the only outlaw pirate who paddles this coast in the winter," Khan relays to the unknown woman.

"Okay Mr. Mano I need your help, I cut my feet pretty bad on the trail making it out here in the rain, and now they are swollen and I can't hike out. Can you paddle me out in your kayak tomorrow?" The woman squats beside him and shines her headlamp to reveal the minor but painful looking cuts on her feet and ankles.

"Why don't you just stay a few more days and wait for your cuts to heal?" Mano asks. The others nod in agreement.

"I'm almost out of food and I have to make it back. I fly back to Canada in just a few days. I'm a doctor, I can pay you to take me out." Mano stares at her undecidedly.

"And I'll paddle too," she adds with a smirk tossing back her short dark hair.

"Can you swim through the surf break?" Mano asks.

"I can swim. What do you mean?"

"It's usually too hard to launch the boat with two people. You'll have to swim out to the boat and climb aboard on the other side of the breakers."

She gives a suspicious look before replying.

"Yeah, I can do that."

"Okay, two hundred dollars if you want me to paddle you out." Mano throws out without much thought.

"Okay sure, I can get you the money in town." The doctor responds happily.

"We have to leave early, before the trades pick up. Let's meet at the kayak on the beach thirty minutes after sunrise. If all goes well, we'll be in town before lunch."

"I'll be there! Now what time is sunrise?" The doctor responds confidently.

"Time?" Mano's confused for a moment. "Uhh, just meet me thirty minutes after the birds start chirping."

"Okay," She smiles.

"I'll bring a trash bag for your backpack. See you thirty minutes after first bird chirp." She leaves and he returns to music making.

Honu pulls him aside.

"Yo, Mano-banano, are you really gonna leave with that lady in the kayak tomorrow?"

"I guess. She seemed pretty desperate, plus it's a pretty good deal to paddle to town and back for two hundred bucks."

"Look, I wasn't gonna mention it to the group because I wanted it to be a surprise, but I guess I gotta tell you. I'm leaving The Beach to fly back to Cali in two days and I was hoping to record some music up at Kaholo's camp tomorrow at sunset."

"Two days! I had no idea you were leaving that quick, you just got back!"

"I got this little digital recording device. You should stay, it's gonna be a special night."

"Well of course, but I had no idea tomorrow would be your last night. Why don't *you* stay?"

"I know, I know, I wish I could. I gotta go though, I gotta get back for a work gig in California. I fly out in less than a week."

Mano just kind of stands there in awe thinking of Honu's departure. How had nearly 2 months flown by on The Beach? In his mind he kind of thought Honu would never leave.

"Well, I don't want to miss the recording, or possibly your last night here!" Mano exclaims.

"Yeah, you should stay for tomorrow night, just tell the doctor you'll leave the day after, and don't let her fool you with that *doctor line*, she's probably just saying that. You're not obligated to rescue paddle anyone, you know."

"She spoke like she really needed help. Besides I wouldn't want to hoof the trail with cuts on my feet like that, either."

"Well, take her out the next day then, and tomorrow lets record music together."

"Okay, I'll tell her it's too windy or something when I meet her tomorrow morning."

"Never mind that, just tell her the truth. Tell her that your best bro on the island has to have you here. She can wait."

"Alright, alright," Mano sighs. They continue to play music, but the inspiration of the initial session is lost. A cold wind starts to blow and the crew seems to be vying for bed. Honu makes the official announcement of the proposed sunset recording tomorrow, and his subsequent departure from Neverland for the season. Khan, Kaholo and Andrew already knew, but they take in Honu's departure as sullen news nonetheless.

The next morning, Mano wakes and ventures down to the kayak to meet the doctor.

"So, I got some bad news, I can't leave today. I really gotta stay and record music tonight with my good friend Honu, who's leaving soon."

"What are you saying? I thought we had this planned, I gotta get back." Mano just stares at her not knowing what to say.

"Sorry, I can't miss this. If conditions are good I can take you tomorrow."

"Look out at the ocean, it looks calmer than ever, hardly any waves at all," the doctor persists. It's true, the swell had dissipated almost completely overnight. Certainly, the smallest wave day he'd seen all season. Would it still be calm like this tomorrow?

"You could go and take me to town and paddle back in the afternoon. You'll still make it back by sunset for your party." the doctor suggests with puppy dog eyes.

Somehow Mano never really thought of this. It could be a breeze to blow back to the beach with the afternoon trades.

Before he can respond Amber pops up through the bushes with her backpack. He instantly remembers bright-eyed Amber from his first kayak launch.

"I heard you were kayaking to town. I'm sick and can't hike the trail, can you take me in the kayak, too?"

Now he has cute little Amber begging him as well.

"I don't know, it's already getting late, and the winds will pick up soon."

Mano fidgets as the two girls stare at him with puppy dog eyes. He gazes towards the calm ocean and at the kayak and ponders. Three people and two backpacks on a two-man sit-on-top in a headwind. Would it be even possible?

"I'll get you anything you want in town and boat drop it in when I come back!" Amber adds cheerfully.

Little Amber's pleading smile glows. A glowing goddess of the valley is hard to deny. He doesn't want to accept it, but he's being swayed by her heartfelt smile. Then another worry pops into Mano's head. Would the doctor be able to do the trip with her? Would the two women be able to cooperate, keep calm, and friendly while paddling steady, out on the high seas?

He imagines wind pelting their faces and chop crashing over the bow. A disagreement could turn hostile on the small, cramped boat. The chance of such an outbreak should be rare, but in the face of adversity these women may not act themselves. Any sort of social situation on the open ocean could become a disaster and put all their lives in danger. He mentions this concern to them. They look at him and at each other cheerfully and assure him they will cooperate and uphold the Captain's orders in upmost regard.

Mano doesn't know the doctor, but she seems seaworthy enough. He knew Amber as a keep-it-together kind of chick. She helped him on his first kayak launch to the beach weeks ago. Since then she had become a freestanding member of the community, a legitimate up-valley goddess, and in a way, he feels more inclined to help her than the fare-paying doctor. Amber could be the catalyst needed to instill confidence in the team on the open water, and her positive energy could in fact, be crucial to a successful voyage.

Mano's mind tiptoes around all aspects of this tricky ocean passage from beach to Babylon. Could they overcome a stiff headwind, possible storms, and heavy chop? Mano displaces his fears, and instead focuses on the glory of a successful mission. He had to take them both, and do it safely, and make it back by sunset. Mano closes his eyes and asks Mama Kai for her permission. He feels no negative response from her, so he asks her to bless their mission and grant the three of them safe passage over her waters. Then he turns to face his eager crew.

"Well, if you girls are ready to swim and paddle hard, then lets do this!"

They pull the boat down to the water's edge and he bags and ties down the backpacks. He gives the two girls a keen yet grizzled look as he cinches the bags down tight to the deck of the boat.

"You know, going out on the ocean, especially *this Ocean*, isn't something to be taken lightly. There's gonna be wind, swells rolling under the boat, whales! I expect total cooperation out there and commitment to the mission. And if the wind picks up too much we may just have to blow back to the beach." He watches their excited smiles fade to a placid gaze.

Mano goes over the launch plan one more time. The waves are small enough that launching the boat is certainly not his biggest concern. Still, it could be tricky with two girls and their bags.

Instead of the typical game plan of launching the boat himself and having the passengers swim out and climb aboard past the breakers, he decides to launch with the doctor on board and have Amber swim through the waves to climb onto the middle of the boat past the break.

The three of them steady the kayak in the knee-deep whitewash. Holding, watching, waiting for the right launch window. They wait for a lull in between the sets of waves to jump in. He repeats another launch disclaimer.

"There's only a fifty percent chance that we'll make it out past the breakers on the first try." Of course, this proves to be a sour omen. The two launch too early and are swamped by a wall of whitewash from the last big wave of the set. However, they both hold onto their paddles, Mano rights the boat, and they both climb back into the seats. The line looks clear, so they go for it again. This time they slide out past the sand bar during the lull, making it out into the open ocean just as the window between sets closes. They cheer triumphantly in the calm rollers outside the break. When they look back at the beach, Amber is already swimming out to meet them. She dives through the break flawlessly, and backstrokes past the final rollers to reach the boat. She pulls herself on-board and sits her petite body steady on the hatch-cover between the two seats.

Amber sits facing Mano, back to back with the doctor on the tiny spot dubbed the princess perch. Mano fears that the kayak will be tippy and unstable with three of them on board, but they have good balance and it seems to take the rollers without issue. The sun is almost over the back wall of the valley by the time they start paddling east. As they pass the Heiau, the sun fully emerges over the back wall and they get their first blast of headwind. A fierce swirl of wind whips salty spray into their faces and halts their forward progress.

"Here we go!" Mano calls out as they dig in their paddle blades against the wind. The land is heating up from the sun, creating a pressure differential, causing the trade winds to start to blow. He knows the wind will continue to pelt them and become stronger each hour as the sun rises. He encourages the doctor to stay focused and keep a steady rhythm.

She paddles hard and Mano paddles extra-hard, steering against the wind, cutting through the chop.

"One-two, one-two, long and strong!" he calls out to the doctor over the howling wind. The wind whips across from the east, but funnels along the cliffs, often calming for a half-minute then blasting them in unpredictable torrents.

At times the two girls can do little more than just hold on while getting pelted by spray from the trade wind squall. It takes every bit of Mano's strength just to keep the boat straight, perpendicular to the wind. He angles closer to the cliffs in an attempt to gain cover from the pelting gusts. However, the sight of the bone-crushing swell pounding on the cliffs encourages them to keep a safe distance. Their progress is slight, and after only an hour into their journey, both Mano and the doctor are tiring. When the wind picks up, it feels like they are doing little more than just treading water.

Thick clouds blow in from the east, blocking the sun. This sends Amber into a shiver. Her thin, pale body is covered with goose bumps and all she has is her warm spirit inside to keep her from shaking. She clenches the sides of the boat and smiles as chop cresting the bow wets her.

"One-two, one-two, we got this, girls!" Mano exclaims vibrantly trying to keep the crew positive."

"Yeah! You guys got it," Amber screeches, still shivering. Now they are paddling towards an approaching wall of grey, a big squall is blowing in with the wind. Mano tries to remain calm as he stares down a storm front approaching on the horizon. He voices his concern hoping to not lose the faith of his crew.

"How are you girls feeling? Do you think we can make it, or should we turn back? There seems to be a bit of a storm up there."

"Do *you* think we can make it?" the doctor snaps back.

"Well, uh if we keep paddling at this rate we'll make it, in…a couple of hours. But if the front blows in hard, I don't know, we might still get blown back."

He looks at the storm and tries to examine the situation with a keen nautical eye. All he can really defer is that it's coming and they are about to be caught by it no matter what. The wind howls and Amber starts singing to Mama Kai. There are whitecaps well offshore he can see, but close in where they are paddling the wind isn't blowing the tops off the chop just yet. Not only salt spray, but also rain now starts its horizontal pelt at their naked skin. They push on, continuing long deep strokes. He senses the uneasiness of his crew and knows they can feel it in his own voice, too. He combats his own fears by singing a Hawaiian chant he remembers from Khan, belting it out through the pelting rain.

"Come on girls, sing with me. Hold it together, we're gonna make it. *Ohana ono pono, Ohana ohh eh ah. Ohana ono pono…*" Nobody, including Mano, remembers all the words or their meaning, but the rhythmic chanting seems to smooth their paddle strokes and take their minds off the impeding storm.

"How are you doing Amber?" he howls against the wind, even though she's just two feet in front of him. She inhales, shivers, and smiles.

"Just look at how beautiful everything is!" she laughs back, cheeringly.

62

Mano gazes up at the cliffs and the waterfalls shooting down. There are waterfalls everywhere pouring into the ocean from the rain. He stares ahead at the gray wall that is about to engulf the boat. Thousands of pelting raindrops smooth the ocean's surface in front of them. His own confidence rises slightly as he feels the beauty of the storm.

"Keep up those smooth, long strokes!" he encourages the doctor as the front hits them.

"I can hardly see with this rain! I don't know if I can keep this up much longer," she spits into the wind.

"We'll take a break in a bit. We've just got to power through this storm front. Look! We really are making progress. See that big waterfall? It felt like it would be in front of us forever. Now we are nearly alongside it. We're halfway. We'll switch and let Amber paddle to warm up as soon as we get to that next big waterfall."

"I can't wait for hot chocolate and steamy shower," the doctor shouts.

Amber is noticeably freezing, but is still in such high spirits it keeps the two paddlers from whining. The next half-mile to the noted break point takes 10 minutes but it feels like an hour. The rain just keeps coming, and the wind never lets up.

"I don't know about this," Mano huffs under his breath, but they just keep paddling, heads down. Every time he looks up he has to smile at the ridiculousness of the situation, and at Amber. The smiling, shivering, confident mermaid staring back at him.

The storm holds them for what feels like an hour, but it finally lets them go. They pull in close to the cliffs to gain shelter from the wind and Mano mandates a well-deserved break. His hands and arms are cramped and aching after two hours of non-stop paddling. He and the doctor jump in the water and let Amber climb into the front seat. The seventy-degree ocean water gives them a false sense of warmth that soothes them. Underneath the water's surface is a whole new world of calm, separate from the cold and tumultuous air above. They don't want to climb back onto the kayak and allow the wind to scour their newfound warmth from their skin.

He asks the doctor if she wants to sit in the princess perch for a break, but she insists that she keep paddling. Wanting Amber to warm up by paddling, Mano opts to sit in the princess perch while the two girls struggle to maintain the boat in the wind. He soon begins to shiver too, and the girls begin to critique each other's strokes almost to the point of arguing.

"You need to get back in the driver's seat or we're never gonna make it," the doctor shouts.

"Come on! You two girls gotta get us to that next waterfall at least," he laughs as the boat hopelessly teeters against the assaulting wind. They switch back to their original positions and Mano initiates another Khan song to boost morale.

"I like to fly, on the crest of an ocean wave, If I treat her right, she will carry me. See that girls, that's Space Rock, we're getting close." Then, just to spite them, Mama Kai whips up a fierce wind and they pass 2-mile valley at a crawl. The sea is merciless, but the end of the cliff walls is in sight. They have to make it now.

"If we're lucky, the swell will be down enough to land on the reef."

"What do you mean, lucky to land on the reef?" The doctor pipes back.

"Don't worry, I think we're gonna be lucky."

"Ohh cold, ohh," is all Amber can mutter, looking hypothermic now.

"Let us in, storm! Let us in to land, Mama Kai," Mano yells out into the whistling wind like a crazed sea captain. The lifeguard tower that monitors the reef-protected beach at the start of the trail comes into view. Just a few small rogue waves are breaking on the inner reef close to the beach, indicating that landing on the reef could be possible. But with two already worn and weathered maidens, Mano isn't so sure. He doesn't think the doctor with her cut up feet, will be keen on scrambling across the reef in waist high surf, but Amber is shivering so much she may not be able to hold out another two miles to the protected bay landing area.

"Okay girls, we're gonna go for it. I'll do my best to time the sets and not crash-land the boat. But if we do, you know what to do. Just swim away from the kayak so it doesn't crush you against the rocks."

They are all too cold and tired to question him, so he waits, then calls the command to forward paddle and they slide in behind the last big wave of a set. He misjudges the landing spot and misses the keyhole in the reef. Instead they beach the kayak right on the reef in a receding wave.

"Get out, get out, go for it!" He shouts to the girls as the water pools away from the reef. They slip and fall but manage to jump to the calm tidal pool on the other side as Mano wrangles the kayak off the rocks with the next set of waves. Amber is wrapped in an emergency blanket from the lifeguard by the time he pulls the kayak onto the sand.

They run for the doctor's rental car in another downpour. He never thought in the tropics he'd be huddled in a car blasting the heater, but it feels so good. In town they drink hot cocoa and the doctor treats them all to lunch. It isn't until the sun comes out and blasts away the humid air that Mano regains his warmth.

His focus soon shifts to the return trip in. He could still make Honu's sunset recording session, he decides. The doctor pays him the rescue fare plus tip for the incredible voyage, and he gives Amber a wish list for her next boat drop. They all exchange heartfelt hugs and he hitchhikes back to the end of the road, to the kayak. With the swell still down, he launches the kayak through the keyhole with ease. With even greater ease he blows with the wind at his back along the coast towards Neverland. He's using half as much strength to paddle the half-weighted boat with a tailwind, and traveling nearly three times as fast! He's catching the wind swell gliding along the tops of the waves.

He felt at the mercy of Mother Nature on the morning trip out. Now he glides across the waves like he's in charge. He sits tall with the wind at his back, a confident Captain of a tumultuous sea. He envisions the looks from Khan, Honu, Kaiko, and Kaholo when he returns on the almost unheard of out-and-back mission in a single day. He thanks Mama Kai again for allowing him safe passage before picking his way through the surf break to the beach.

He crash-lands the boat on Neverland beach and kneels on the sand, digging his palms into her, thanking her. He kisses the beach with delight. He's safely back in paradise once again.

"Whoa, whoa, whoa. Didn't expect to see you back." Kaholo puts down his flute mid-song as Mano approaches."

"I couldn't miss Honu's big last night jam!"

"Mano banano, you're a quick one. Even I can hardly believe it, delivering the doctor to Babylon and back here before sunset. Quite the show. We watched you come in from the bluffs. You sailed in with the look of a true seaman, a kayak Captain." Honu praises.

"And any good Captain brings back booty for his mates!" Mano reaches into his dry bag and pulls out a twelve-pack of Budweiser beer.

"For my mates!"

"Aye, aye Captain!" Khan praises. "Right on, you really are a Captain. From now on I'm calling you Captain Mano," he announces.

Mano passes the beers around his circle of friends.

"Whoa, they're even still cold! This place is incredible!" Kaiko exclaims, holding the can of beer in awe.

"Fellas, let's toast to Mama Kai for delivering me safely back home."

Khan interjects. "No way, let's toast to Captain Mano for a badass rescue mission and bringing us cold beer in the jungle."

"Aye, aye!" The group roars.

"To Cap-i-tan Mano," Khan initiates.

"To Captain Mano!" They all cheer.

Chapter 10   Journeys to the other side

Honu stays one more day after the recording session, then hikes the trail out solo. He leaves for California, abandoning Charlotte and the rest of the crew on the beach. He doesn't *really* abandon anyone, leaving Charlotte with his guitar and plenty of food and supplies. He had to go back to *'take care of things in the real world,'* but to some it feels like abandonment. He left the beach, the surf, the music, the lifestyle he loved so much as well as his goddess that adored him. Were those magical two months of really *living free* trivial to Honu now? Many felt like Honu was the glue that held everyone together up on the bluffs. He would often be the one to host community meals and initiate music jams. Who would keep unity and keep the good vibes flowing without him?

Naturally, Khan takes it upon himself to pick up where Honu left off.

"Pizza party tonight, right here at the Sanctuary," Khan announces shortly after Honu hits the trail. Mano still can't believe it. It didn't make sense to him, to leave his princess and paradise behind. But most did this…No one could stay in a fantasyland forever right? Besides plane tickets off this remote island weren't easily changed. He wishes his brother well, and lets his own spirit stay present with the island and the crew that remain. The sun sets but rises again.

In an effort to promote Khan's pizza party, Mano walks over to where the faint Sanctuary trail intersects the main trail and writes a simple message in the wet mud hoping to attract some new arrivals. 'Sanctuary Welcome,' he inscribes, with an arrow pointing down the side trail towards the Sanctuary.

Khan attempts to use Honu's parting as a means to summon inspiration.

"Captain, I can feel it this time. You and me. We're gonna bring the Sanctuary back to the heyday of Donnie the Mayor and all those cats that never let the fire die up here. It's up to us, we've gotta make Sanctuary work."

"Well, I made a sign at the trail intersection, we'll see if anyone new shows up." Mano smiles back.

"Yeah, and this time I'm gonna be a little more discerning about people just showing up with a plate wanting to eat. We gotta request that they bring firewood, or water, or something." Khan states with determination.

Mano walks alone up to some pools in the valley for a change of pace then follows the beating of Khan's drum right back to the Sanctuary fire at sunset.

"More firewood for the community kitchen," Mano broadcasts as he sets down a pile he gathered. Already a few new faces have arrived.

"Alright, Captain! See, this is what it's all about, keeping the community going, many hands make life work, right? So who wants to volunteer to fetch water for the tribe?" Khan announces.

A couple of tourists eagerly volunteer to hike down to the stream to fill jugs. Khan is inspired and in a good mood, Mano can tell by the way his dreads shake while he beats his drum. Kaiko and Rainbow start cooking, and a good stew is brewing by dark. The music unfolds between sparks of conversation and the fire burns bright throughout the night.

"Okay, for this great evening, this community gathering, we have a little surprise for ya'll." All eyes fix on Rainbow, who's reaching into her bag.

"For the crew at the Sanctuary tonight, may I present to you this...chocolate cake!"

"Ooooh," the dozen patrons stare at the box cake in excitement.

"And chocolate icing!" Rainbow giggles with delight.

"No way! I'm in heaven already," Kaiko exclaims. The already tired backpackers are coaxed into staying up another full hour while the cake and more music is made.

"This is the most incredible and most welcoming community I've ever experienced," one newcomer announces.

"I have to speak to the leader of this tribe!"

Khan stands up graciously and the two slip away from the fire for a short discussion. *What could it be?* They are back before any ideas can materialize and Khan comes forward proudly with an announcement.

"Brothers and Sisters, My new good brother here, Chris, has invited us all to partake in a special journey tomorrow. He brings with him a vial of sacred medicine and he is offering it up to the tribe for all who are willing. Tomorrow we will journey to the other side!" The fire crackles and lights up Khan's face, and a hint of madness shines in his eyes. Everyone is captivated.

"So tomorrow after breakfast at the Sanctuary, all who are willing can embark on a magical spiritual journey with us!" Khan restates. The group looks at each other with a mix of wonder, excitement, and concern. The fire flares up then smolders. Khan starts beating his drum and chanting in indecipherable tribal fury. The crew bursts with excitement, but then fades with the waning fire to rest for tomorrow's journey.

Heavy morning clouds slowly lift as the dozen or so people meet in the Sanctuary garden to begin the journey. Mano takes a droplet of LSD on the tongue like most, and they all promenade up to outlaw pools halfway up the valley for the day's psychedelic voyage. Jumping off the rock, into the cool pools stimulates the group towards playfulness. Charlotte is overcome with childlike laughter right away.

"I just can't get over how funny everything and everyone is," she exclaims, twirling her toes in one of the smaller side pools. Khan tries to set a tribal tone for the excursion with his drum. Kaiko, Rainbow, and a couple of other tourists are trying to get a dainty little fire going on the terrace beside the pool. They each take turns blowing on it. The wet wood flares up then smolders with each breath. They are *controlling* the little fire with each life-giving breath. Another girl dangles her feet in the pools and blows haphazardly on a harmonica. All the while Chris sits on a sunny rock above the pool in casual observance of everyone. Mano starts to feel the acid coming on, but he feels a little disconnected from the strange sillies all around. He pulls Khan aside.

"I have an idea, how about the two of us sneak up valley and get a bunch of oranges and surprise the group with them. I know of a really good hidden tree. It will be a mission!"

"The vitamin C from the oranges will help extend the trip for the tribe," Khan states agreeing.

"Yeah, we'll get a whole bunch and throw the oranges into the river right above the pools and surprise everybody. There'll be oranges floating everywhere!" Mano teems with excitement.

The two go on their fruit mission. Once they arrive at the said tree, Mano can feel the acid coming on strong. He looks at his hands to confirm. They look foreign to him. Yep, he's definitely tripping.

He climbs the tree and Khan acts as the catcher below. At the first shake of the tree one bright orange falls suddenly. Khan jumps over and reaches out his hand for a miraculous catch. It's as if he paused time for an instant and got right to where the orange would fall. Acid-reflexes. In similar cat-like fashion Khan reaches to catch all but two oranges that Mano shakes loose with a stick.

"Okay, we have at least a dozen of 'em." Khan relays to Mano who is still thirty feet up the tree.

"Let's get a couple more so we're sure to have enough for everyone to get a whole one." Mano says while he scrambles higher up the tree to shake down two more.

"Okay, lets get back to the pools, this is gonna be sweet. Everyone is gonna be so surprised!" Mano prances along the trail with childlike delight.

"Captain, wait!" Khan pauses him on his merry decent.

"How about you and me, Captain? How 'bout we split one of these broken ones first." They stop and tear open one of the split, oozing oranges.

"Brothers in the valley." Khan toasts, staring at him intently while they scrape the sweet fruit from the rind with their teeth. Mano looks into Khan's eyes deeply. He can see right into him. He sees his troublesome youth, his hardship and loss, anger and resentment, but he also sees past it all to the loving man beneath. He sees a hint of madness, too. It's a profound vision. He shakes free from the vision, it almost feels like he's invading Khan's privacy.

"Brothers reborn in the valley," Mano adds.

They hoot and holler and romp down the trail to the pools. Their arrival is no surprise, but when the oranges come rolling down over the falls into the big pool below, everyone is delighted, jumping in to grab the oranges bobbing in the clear water.

"This is awesome!" Kaiko exclaims gleefully.

"Give thanks to Mama Kai and the mana of this valley for providing us these delicious oranges," Khan tells all.

"Hurray for Mama Kai! Hurray for Khan and Mano," the naked hippies splash and cheer.

Mano joins Rainbow by the cheeky little fire to warm up after the swim. He's mesmerized by the way she holds up her curly hair along her neck with one hand and blows on the fire so close.

"He's a good little fire, but you have to blow on him just right to keep him happy," Rainbow says daintily with a smile. Their eyes meeting for a moment.

Her heart seems only slightly open and he cannot read her, but he feels a sudden connection regardless. At least he senses that he feels something. With a few glances around he taps into individual energies of everyone in the group. Somehow he's instantly more aware of the bright and dark sides of everyone. For some, like Khan, the energy is right out there in the open. He hardly has to feel for it. Others keep their essence more hidden, but truth in character can still be detected. Mano wonders what they see in him. His personality is far from hidden. He shudders at the truth of it all. They are all naked to the core.

Mano looks up at Chris on top of the rock. Chris stares back with a smile that fades. Mano brushes his hand against his face almost in shame. He knows the look. He'd seen it several times before, but this time he can *feel* it too. He can feel it in Chris's core and he's touched. He's humbled.

The look or feeling Mano knew instantly, was the look from a man who knew he was less than beautiful into the face of a beautiful man. Not a look of jealousy, but a look of longing. Mano's first reaction in receiving the message through the look makes him feel ashamed. But that's just a reaction. Mano feels into Chris. Feeling deeply, he receives more of a message of appreciation. He wants to send back a message that says, *it's okay you're beautiful, too*. Mano looks back at Chris, straight past the rigid scar on his face, and instead of cowering, Chris smiles with all his heart. Without a word they completely understand each other.

With such strong connections all around it's hard to just space out and enjoy nature, but perhaps they are meant to have this richer, further connected, and more demanding journey.

A burst of sun has Mano feeling instantly overwhelmed. Maybe it's tropical heat or the sharing of energies. He suggests to Rainbow another plunge into the cool pool. They strip down naked, with only slight awkwardness of the group around, then dive into the clear water. Mano opens his eyes to the underwater world around him, it's a whole new world of liquid tranquility. They swim through the bubbles and swirling currents upstream to be engulfed by the white noise of the pounding waterfall. Exploring underwater, Mano finds a hole, a cave behind the waterfall where the surging water passes right over. Inside the underwater cave on the other side of the rushing water it feels eerily calm. The serene quiet past the swirling bubbles from the waterfall mesmerizes him. Inside the cave the current is such that he can remain tucked inside without having to swim up or down, in or out. He feels like an underwater creature in this perfectly protected niche. *If only he could breathe underwater and remain there*. He resurfaces for air elated.

"Just hold your breath and follow me. Take my hand, you can do it." He tries to convince Rainbow to follow him through the turbulent underwater passage to the tranquil cave on the other side.

"I'm too scared, it seems so far," she exclaims after their first failed attempt.

"You can do it, it's just a little bit farther, it's calmer on the other side." Mano tries to reassure her. They try again, but Rainbow comes up again in the turbulent water just in front of the waterfall."

"No way man, it's too intense under there." She gasps.

"But you're almost there. I know you can hold your breath for a lot longer, and once you get there you feel like you could stay forever. The cave of wonders is just on the other side!" Mano coaxes her.

"Alright, I'll try again, but let me go first."

"Just keep swimming along the bottom. Count to fifteen at least before coming up." She swims just barely into the room of calm and then flutters back out of the cave through the waterfall to the surface.

"You did it! You were totally there," Mano encourages.

"Yeah, I see what you mean. It is totally calm under there."

They dive under again. This time they swim like fish side by side. Spending a couple moments in the cave together, a new level of intimacy between them is birthed.

"The cave of wonders really is just on the other side!" She giggles and swims about joyfully.

"I don't think I ever want to leave this perfect water." Rainbow adds.

"I'm a popsicle already, I have to get out," Mano says through chattering teeth.

"How are you so cold? It's great in here, I feel like a mermaid," Rainbow giggles playfully. Mano can stand no more, he's shivering feeling like he may *never* warm up. He gets out of the pool and crouches by the little fire.

"Come on fire, warm me up." He coaxes it with his breath.

It seems to take forever, but he does warm up, and soon he's sweating as Khan and Kaiko jam music together with all sorts of crazies dancing around. Charlotte is giggling at the sight of everyone displaying full on tribal energy. Chris dances like a bear up on his rock.

An elusive up-valley couple Rick and Lisa come down from their camp and join in the group acid trip. Mano envisions a wild animal running through the vibrations of the drum skin, he can *feel* the animal even. Khan's hands fire against the drum with the fury of a wild beast. The group livens with his energy and tribal-like hooting and hollering overtake many of them.

Khan finally tires and slows the group back down with a softer, steadier rhythm. *He really captivates people with his music,* Mano thinks to himself. Mano himself enjoys being captivated by him he decides. Suddenly, Mano senses a chill. They are in the shadow. He notices the sun dipping behind the mountain and instantly he feels a desperate need to get down the valley to feel her solar charge again before dark. He urges Rainbow to come with him down the trail to meet the sun. They should go now and let the group catch up, he thinks to himself. Mano's almost frantic and needy in wanting to be with Rainbow and the setting sun.

"One more swim down to the cave!" Rainbow shouts gleefully. They jump in again. Again they make the underwater passage to the other side. This time Mano is too cold. He cannot stay in the underwater world for long. If only he was cold-blooded like a fish then he could remain in liquid tranquility forever. It's disappointing, but he pays attention to his body and coaxes Rainbow out of the pool. The two dance down the trail in a race to catch the sun.

"Okay, we don't have to run too fast, we'll make it in time," Mano sputters.

"I'm not running, I'm dancing!" she shouts back gleefully.

"Well why don't you stop and have a dance with me." Mano responds coyly.

She turns around and he almost kisses her right then, but something holds him back. Instead, they dance sensually on the trail. He pulls her hips in close and they move, connected to one rhythm. There's no music, but somehow the music in their heads match. He's turned on, but he's still tripping on other, deeper senses. Just when he feels her getting aroused as well, she spins back away, leaving him in a daze.

"Well, we better keep going to catch the sunset." Rainbow laughs as she dances along ahead of him. She's in her own world, he realizes, and they continue down the trail. Just a few more step along and…they're caught! It's the Cheshire Cat, Kaholo. He pops out of nowhere to stop them on the trail.

"Hello there, dancers, where have you two been?"

"Oh, we've been having a fabulous time, day-tripping up at outlaw pools!" Rainbow spouts whimsically. Kaholo smiles coyly, setting down his backpack.

"Alright, alright, I can tell, good to hear. I have the perfect treat for you guys." He reaches into his backpack and pulls out a decorative thermos and a dainty little tea glass on a tiny saucer.

"Alright, alright, now for a little something to keep you up while coming down you know. This here is my special up-valley Ganja Lassie, it will keep you feeling *real* good..." They stare wide-eyed as the Cheshire cat carefully fills the tiny cup on the saucer with his thermos.

"So basically yeah. Just drink the cup and you're good. Yeah one cup of this and you are pretty much good for the rest of the night. Now, you know I like to stay *irie*, so I'll do like...one-and-a-half, okay. But just one... One and you're good, you're *irie*. You may want to stay good for a little longer, you know, I don't know! You know, right, right!" He chuckles, elegantly.

"This is up-valley potion, Rainbow, go easy," Mano warns remembering the pumpkin pie episode. She smiles then downs her little glass daintily.

"Whoa, that is really good. And I can tell it's really strong, too," she giggles.

"I know, I know, it's great." Kaholo smiles as he reaches to pour another for Mano.

"Uh, just a half-glass for me, I'm pretty *irie*, already." Mano stutters.

"Okay, a mini one for Mr. Mano, alright," he charms handing Mano a three-quarter full cup on the saucer.

"Wow, it really is great."

"Yeah, I know, up-valley special!" Kaholo smiles back at Rainbow.

"Can I have a tiny bit more? It's just so good," Rainbow giggles.

"Yeah, I can tell you wanna stay *irie* like your uncle, up-valley. Sure, no problem, a little bonus for the goddess."

"Now don't just drink it because it tastes good, that's potent stuff," Mano continues to urge caution.

"Oh, I'll be fine!" She smirks as she downs an additional cup like a shot of whiskey."

"Alright, great, great, glad I ran into you guys. Let me know how it treats you!" He puts the goodies away in his backpack, preparing to amble on.

"You wanna come down for sunset and food at the Sanctuary?" Mano offers.

"Yeah, I dunno, I'm not really feeling the Khan vibe tonight. But I'll party with you guys some other time, for sure." He hurries off in the opposite direction.

"I can't believe we just got dosed by the Cheshire Cat!" Mano says excitedly.

"I know those little lassies were *sooo good*." Rainbow giggles.

"Yeah, I know, I know, now you're gonna be *really good!*" Mano replies impersonating Kaholo.

It's a rainbow sunset for him and Rainbow down on the bluffs. They sprawl out in the lush grass soaking up the sunset and rainbow energy. The setting sun blasts across the valley and illuminates a spectrum of light shooting from the bluffs up to the back wall. The rest of the group shows up and joins them to watch the final rays of sun fade into the ocean. Kaiko's soft string music brings the group together as twilight sets in.

"You feel the lassie?" Mano asks Rainbow.

"I feel like I'm starting a whole new trip!" Rainbow snickers falling onto her back lazily. Mano's feeling stoned, but coming to his senses otherwise. He laughs to himself thinking of how back at the pools he was imagining a perfectly crafted life for him and Rainbow together. What a fairy tale! Was he just lusting under the dreamy manifesto of the acid trip? He chuckles to himself realizing how silly it would have been to even kiss her. Even if she had kissed him back, there would have been no real heart behind it. Or would there have been? He just wants to give his heart away so badly, it's like he is weighed down by having to hold onto it. He sighs as he watches the first stars twinkle into the evening sky.

Khan senses Mano's surrender and leans in with a smooth ukulele song to charm Rainbow back. They reclaim common ground over a shared rolled cigarette. Still Mano thinks of how his heart pounded as the two of them danced together. How he felt strange wanting to kiss her yet he almost tried anyway. How could he chase down a rainbow? Of course, it would just fade into the mist. He chuckles to himself at the metaphor.

The twilight fades quickly, and soon after it's the great migration back to the Sanctuary for fire and food. Chills rush over Mano as the darkness thickens. Even though the rest of the people near him are rallying along in giggles and chitchat, he feels empty and alone. Suddenly, the cold, lonely feeling is overwhelming. He desires strongly to be held and loved. He's coming down hard off the acid, and he knows it. He knows it's just the drug, but he can't shake the horrible, empty, alone feeling that comes over him. Lisa sits next to him beside the fire and places a calm hand on his shoulder.

"Just relax Mano, you're only coming down. This feeling will pass, you're okay." she tries to comfort him. Still he feels like a lost child.

"Can you just hold my hand?" he pleads to her softly.

She comforts him as he trembles and shakes with cold lonely fear. Just as he felt the childlike day-dreamy joy and fullness of his own love hours ago, he now feels the darkest fear, discomfort and aloneness of his inner child.

The fire and the soft melodies of others thankfully bring him back. He eventually grounds down to the earth and absorbs warmth from the fire. However, melancholy hangs over him. He comes back as half himself after a while. He stays with loving glow of the fire for hours until the flames smolder and the few souls that remain drift off to bed. He's the last one to leave the solemn glow of the dying embers. Eventually, he crawls into his tent and lets the sound of crashing waves wash out his head.

Chapter 11   Fishing

Mano tries to focus and reflect on yesterday's vision quest, but his mind and heart wander. It's hard to decipher what feelings and experiences were real and what incidents and emotions were exaggerated by his drug-influenced imagination. He thinks back to the diffused state of reality where he and others existed with their inner truths revealed. Was that real? At the time it seemed more real than ever, but they were all tripping, his logical brain reminds. The memories that remain are profound, but his rational self wants to write things off. *Live in the now, be present,* he tells himself shaking away the reflection.

He can't let go of his desire for true love, but he's sick of letting himself be so captivated by it. He's an addict for love or sex or both! He laughs to himself. *But how could he be addicted if he wasn't getting either?* To think, he was dreaming of a lifelong workable relationship with Rainbow, yesterday. Oh, how mystical it could be! With the help of just a couple drops of magic potion he thoroughly convinced himself they could be lovers. Sure, anything and everything is possible and free with no consequences in an inebriated state. *A dreamland.*

Live the dream, or try to control it? Or try to create it? He stares at the passing clouds and carefree beauty all around. He better jump in the ocean, maybe he's still tripping. Diving through the whitewash clears his head. *Real life is here, now.* Time to do something real, he decides, confidently. Right now-- in this real world.

"I want to catch a fish," Mano manifests aloud.

He thinks about all the fish that must be lurking amongst the rocks. They are alive and free, in their own mysterious underwater world. They could just sway back and forth with the swell, undeterred by passing waves or storms on the surface. Here, off this remote beach, there is no threat of a hook to spoil their paradise. But are they just living in the present so fully that they would never think to get caught no matter where in the ocean they would swim? That sure seems like a better way to be than to worry and wonder at what you are biting at all the time. These fish don't live in fear of a hook, not in that big ocean out there, Mano concludes. *Ok, enough thinking about being a fish, I wanna think of how to catch a fish.*

He drags his toe through the sand. Patience. To catch a big fish you need big patience, and luck, as well. He knows himself enough to realize that he has only small patience, but maybe he could have luck. Mr. X would fish the shore break with a good pole for hours when the weather was right, and he never seemed to catch anything. He has profound patience! More patience than anyone else on the beach. Not catching a fish after hours trying wouldn't bother him. Yet Mano felt disturbed by just the thought of waiting and waiting for possibly nothing.

On two attempts fishing out of the kayak off the beach he caught only one small fish. It was a pint-sized fish, but its capture was memorable nonetheless, flopping off the hook with its last ounce of strength, only to be scooped up by his bare hand.

It was magic. Mano smiles, re-thanking Mama Kai for her fish. *That little fish barely made a pizza topping*, he sighs. Now he has a working rod and reel, and he wants to catch a big fish.

"Mama Kai, please grant me the patience to catch a big fish," he summons to the horizon.

Kayak, non-corroded fishing rod and reel, weights, lures, blessing from Mama Kai, he has all he needs. He scratches his head and envisions bringing a real catch to the surface. *Help*. He would need help to catch a big fish and bring it to shore on the kayak. He needs a good hand. He needs…Hitman.

Mano seeks out the bearded hermit recluse of few words known locally as Hitman at his beach camp. He finds him lounging in his hammock in the shade with his nose in some hero novel. Hitman nearly jumps out of the hammock at Mano's proposition.

"You want me to go out there with ya! You know my lungs aren't much good for swimming, but I damn well know how to fish!" Hitman heaves at Mano's request.

"And I got a fillet knife. If we catch a big fish, I'll show you how to fillet him up real good. We'll grill 'em up on this here fish cooker grill some tourists gave me. Oh yeah, we're set up to catch a big fish, Mano, but I ain't no waterman. I ain't swimming out through those waves. Ya gotta remember, I'm from Vermont. That ocean scares the piss outta me."

"Hey, I thought you ain't scared of nothing, or nobody. You're Hitman, right?"

"Well, I ain't scared of no-thing or no-body, but that there ocean, she scares the bejesus outta me ever' time I jump in. Pulling me all this way an' that, I can never get enough air out there. But I can ride up on a boat jus' fine. But getting out there, damn! Those waves are tougher than they look, that's for sure."

"The ocean's not a beast, she's more like a woman. She's fluid."

Mano encourages.

"Well that's easy for you to say, you're like a fish out there!"

"*If you treat her right, she will carry you,*" Mano sighs, quoting one of Khan's songs about the ocean.

"Yeah, and if she feels like it, she'll rage on you, beat your ass down, have you gasping for air and begging for mercy. Just like a woman. You got that right!"

"Come on, the waves aren't even that big today. Maybe you can ride on the front of boat when I launch," Mano coaches.

"You got two poles, or jus one?" Hitman asks staring at Mano curiously with his lazy eye.

"Yeah, I got two. I borrowed a good one from Mr. X."

"Oh yeah, he actually lent you one of his. Well that's good luck then, lets do it. You jus' gotta save me if I'm drowning in the waves though!"

"You're not gonna drown. Just let her take you in and swim with her, be patient, go with her flow, and she'll let you slip right through the breakers."

"That's all good talk, but if she starts going senseless on me, thrashing about like a crazy woman, I'll get scared and sink like a stone. Yeah, you ever known a crazy woman like that? That's the kind of woman the ocean is. Passionate as all hell and irrational to the core! '*If you treat her right, she will carry you,*' Shit with oceans and water-based bitches that motto only holds if you're damn lucky. You know, you know the type Mano?"

Mano fumbles, never having seen Hitman so fired up. "Well no, but then, I've never been in love before."

"Well, you better watch out, little ocean-loving Mano-banano. Them crazy women, water-women, they'll love you to death, and make you crazy, too! They'll drown your ass in their craziness. They'll hold you down under so long you'll think you'll never get your head above the foam pile." He pauses to glance out at the breakers.

"See, look out there. She's all cool and beautiful and balanced, but you dive in and the next thing you know she's pounding you over the head and you got to dive deep just to get away. Then you're out there past the sandbar, you can't touch the bottom, and your ass is swimming now!" Hitman's fired up and won't stop. Mano rolls his eyes but lets him continue on his hilarious rant.

"And Mano...I seen you walking the beach with that look of desire in your eye. Boy, you better watch out some woman's gonna suck all that love right outta ya and have you wishing you could just be free. But you can't leave them crazy ones. They're like a rip current, won't let you go, and eventually you just accept and roll with it. Then you look back and realize that land is so far away you'd be better grow gills and become a mermaid, or merman or something."

Hitman loses himself in his own thoughts, while Mano envisions himself as a merman...just for a moment.

"I take it you had a bad experience with one of these *women of the sea*," Mano chuckles.

"Why do you think I'm way the hell out here? I had to get a whole ocean away from the craziness! I tell you, Mano, I just don't trust 'em anymore. I don't trust no woman, or no ocean to just let me float along all easy. No disrespect, but they're both wild, misunderstood creatures. Scary and unpredictable! You don't turn your back on this surf, do ya?"

"Alright Hitman, that's enough. Let's launch this kayak and go fishing before I let your craziness scare me too!"

"Just thought I'd give you my warning. You know, from real experience. I can jus' tell you is hungry for love. And I don't want you to get wrapped up in no crazy woman like I did. A handsome fella like you has gotta be a magnet for them gorgeous water women."

"What do you mean by *'water women'* anyway?"

"Women of the sea, water signs. Their passion comes from the endless ocean. What star sign are you anyway?"

"Cancer," Mano responds.

"Well, it's a damn good thing you're a worthy swimmer, cause it could be quite the voyage!" Hitman chuckles graciously.

"Aye aye, Hitman. I got ya, no need to go any further," Mano says as the two of them drag the kayak across the sand.

Mano coaches Hitman to wait for a good window to duck dive the waves and meet him on the outside of the surf break. Hitman's huffing and puffing by the time he makes it to the boat, but he's quite proud of himself.

"Thank God you were out here with this boat, because I couldn't have made it back. But shit, out here with you, Captain Mano, this is sweet. Totally worth it just to get here, to be on the other side and floating peacefully like this. We don't even need to catch a fish!"

"Hey, don't jinx us. Let's paddle out in front of the Heiau near the river mouth. That's where I think the fish are."

"Yeah, we got to set our lures just a couple feet above the surface."

"You mean just above the rocks on the bottom, right?"

"Yeah, yeah, you know what I mean, I must still be dizzy after diving under all those waves."

They paddle the two-man kayak past the Heiau, staying just a bit outside the break. Mano lowers a lure on a kid's fishing pole with a working reel, and he gives the good rod from Mr. X to Hitman. One hundred yards off the river mouth, they stow their paddles and drop their lures in the clear deep water and wait. The kayak drifts slowly back toward the beach with the wind and current. Mano pictures their little neon worm lures bobbing up and down with the swell just off the rocky bottom. Mano barely puts his pole down to paddle them back up current when Hitman calls out.

"I got a hit!" He quickly reels in a small iridescent reef fish.

"It's a yellow snapper," Hitman claims as he removes the hook with stealth and steady hands in the rocking boat.

"That's great, we haven't even been out here long at all. We know they're biting, we just need *the big one!*" Mano states excited.

"I've got an idea," Hitman declares. He takes his knife and cuts under the head of the snapper and pulls out a piece of flesh.

"What did you do that for? That little guy could have at least made a pizza topping."

"Fish eat fish." Hitman answers back, unassumingly. Mano stares blankly, still confused to Hitman's idea.

"Big fish eat little fish, right? We can take this snapper belly and bait our hooks with it. That's how you get the big fish."

Without hesitation Mano puts faith in Hitman's idea and they both re-set their hooks with a smooth piece of snapper belly. Drifting along, Mano lifts and lowers his rod, trying to initiate some sort of action.

"Oh, yep, got another hit," Hitman casually reels in another small yellow snapper.

"I wanna catch a fish *too*, maybe we should switch poles," Mano mumbles. Just then, he feels a tug and he grips his pole tightly as he watches the reel spin wildly.

"I got a fish! What do I do? It's taking all the line out, What now?" Mano fidgets as the reel spins wildly and line feeds out into the deep blue.

"Just hold on," Hitman tells him patiently.

"But it's taking all the line out so fast. How do I reel it in?"

"Just be patient. Let him take the line out."

"Man, this thing sure seems big. I hope I can hold onto him. Look at this pole!" He gasps as he grips the pole tighter. The tiny rod is completely bent over like a candy cane!

"That's small test line. We just gotta wait and wear him out a bit." Hitman instructs.

Eventually, Mano is able to pull a little line back, reeling him in bit by bit. Unlike the first two little snappers, when this fish wants to run, there's nothing Mano can do to stop him. The fish just goes. But little by little Mano reels him closer.

"Oh, I can see him now. Yeah, he is big! You gotta pull him in close to the boat." Hitman instructs.

Mano keeps tugging and reeling and pulls him in close, but the fish is all twist and tail at the surface.

"Now what do we do?" Mano yelps.

"What, you don't have a gaff?" Hitman laughs as the fish flutters about and Mano struggles to gain any additional line. Then, like a poised hunter, Hitman leans over the boat and lunges for the fish with his hand. He pulls up his arm and slaps the fish onto the deck of the kayak. He gaffed the giant fish by the gills with his bare hand. Mano is frantic, but Hitman remains poised, his body leaning on the wiggling fish, pinning it down like a wrestler.

"Get me that rope," Hitman commands. Mano hands him a piece of rope and he strings it through the gills and out the fish's mouth and ties it off. He then slides the dying bloody fish overboard. Hitman must have given it quite the beating in pinning it down, cause there's blood all over the deck of the kayak and it's oozing into the water.

"Man, that's some fish, I can't believe you just reached out and grabbed that thing." Mano is in awe.

"Yeah, this fish will make a meal for half the beach."

"Well, now what do we do?" Mano questions the mighty fish grabber.

"We keep fishing." Hitman responds dryly.

"This fish bleeding into the water will help attract more fish," he adds.

"Alright, let's re-bait the hooks and keep at it!" Mano hardly skips a breath to consider any negative repercussions from stringing the fish overboard. They simply lower another chunk of snapper flesh and wait excitedly.

No more than ten minutes lapse before Mano peers down into the water at his fish. His heart soars to his throat.

"Shark, shark, pull the fish in!" Mano erupts as he sees the shark through the deep water, accelerating upward towards the kayak. Hitman quickly pulls the fish up onto the deck and the shark comes within a foot of the kayak then darts straight back into the deep blue like a billiard ball bouncing off a rail at a right angle.

Mano's heart is still in his throat. "D-did you see that thing?" He manages to stutter.

"Yeah, amazing, black-tipped reef shark nearly seven foot long." Hitman announces.

"Yeah...seven foot shark. Let's get out of here!"

The two decide they've caught their limit, and quickly reel in the lines and prepare to paddle back. Hitman seems only slightly phased by the shark encounter, but Mano is looking back over his shoulder constantly as they paddle the boat back toward the beach. The face of the shark zooming up to the boat clear through the water makes him shudder. Each paddle stroke is more cautious, more delicate. He can hardly let his hands touch the water, thinking the shark might be right under them lurking. Their fish is still dripping blood on the deck of the kayak as they pull in fast to the beach break.

"So what's the protocol for landing this thing?" Hitman spits with a tinge of uncertainty.

"We crash-land with glory and true water-man style," Mano calls back.

"Crash-land? Does that mean we jump off and crash, or hold on 'til we crash?" Hitman gulps as a bigger swell rolls underneath. Mano teases Hitman for a moment this time. The boat bobs outside the break and Mano sings.

"If you treat her right…"

"Oh shut up and sail us in proper! We've had enough adventure already."

The swell is even smaller than when they launched, and the beach is just thirty yards from the break. Still, Hitman needs encouragement and direction.

"We gotta time the sets just right, and paddle in behind the last big one," Mano instructs. Hitman scrambles, and while looking back he almost flies right out of his seat when a big wave rolls underneath.

"Okay, when I say go, paddle like hell for the shore, and if a wave catches us, jump overboard and swim hard. Ok…now! Paddle forward!" Mano shouts.

They blast toward the inside and are just boat lengths away from the sand when the first set wave of whitewash rushes against the stern of the kayak.

"Jump off, bail! Bail!" Mano calls frantically as the whitewash surfs the boat. Hitman jumps out into waist-deep water and Mano stays in the boat until it glides easily onto the sand.

"Very funny!" Hitman smiles as he trudges up to meet him.

"Yeah, about as smooth as your idea to chum the water with that fish, just so you could scare the piss out of me by luring that shark right to the boat!"

"Hey, I said it would attract more fish, right?"

"Yeah, big fish eat little fish. Shark eats big fish, bigger shark eats two dudes in a kayak!"

"Sharks don't like to eat people," Hitman huffs as the two drag the kayak up onto the rocks.

"Catch anything out there, guys?" Q calls out from the beach trail.

"I got a couple of small snapper and Captain Merman here managed to land this one." Hitman lifts the two-foot fish on the stringer.

"Whoa, nice catch, that's gotta be 20 pounds!"

"Yep, we're feasting tonight. Tell the boys on the bluffs to come on down to the beach for seafood night."

"Alright, fish feast on the beach!" Q rattles back as he disappears in the milo forest.

Back at Hitman's camp in the milo grove there's another catch: a bird in the bird trap.

"I can't believe this homemade, third-grade box trap actually worked. I got me an Urkel!" Hitman does a mini Irish jig he's so elated. The still alive island chicken in the trap coos and dances with him.

"Now we can have surf and turf," Mano chuckles!

Hitman cleans and dresses the bird then he shows Mano how to push the fillet knife flat against the skin of the fish to separate the flesh into nice fillets. Word spreads via coconut wireless of the big catch and hippies come out of the jungle for the feast. Several help prepare a big pot of pasta salad filled with fresh tomatoes and basil from the land as well. A couple of homemade wine jugs are brought down from up-valley stashes to add to the beautiful meal at Hitman's beach camp. There's practically as much fish as people care to eat.

"So when are you gonna take me fishing?" Rainbow asks Mano mid-meal.

"Well, Hitman's the one to go with. He's the one who you need on board to land the big one." Mano attempts to bait the hook for his female-fearing comrade.

"Oh, I don't wanna go with Hitman, he's scary, he'll try to use me as shark bait!"

Mano falls back laughing and Hitman offers his big fish handling hand to her with a sort of backwoods charm. His lazy eye twinkles as he smiles.

"Chum with me, my dear."

"Eww, eww, eww!" Rainbow jumps and shakes her arms like a scared school girl.

Chapter 12   Rainbow's Goat

Hitman, in all his eloquence, must have made an impression on Rainbow, for she does in fact *chum with him.* She lets him bestow upon her his knowledge of various backwoods survival skills and they go on excursions in the valley together. She bounces between his and Khan's camp as she pleases and somehow it doesn't evoke any jealousy between the two egocentric men. The night before Mano is set to embark on a kayak trip to the west side of the island, Rainbow makes a declaration around the campfire.

"Tomorrow, with Hitman's help, I'm going to kill and butcher a goat, and therefore justify my carnivorous nature." Rainbow proclaims. Silence settles around the fire, the declaration caught everyone off-guard.

"I've never killed anything, and I figured since I'm eating meat, I should learn how to take the life of an animal." She explains.

"Alright! This should be a show! Mano, I think you are gonna have to stay an extra day for this," Khan declares wide-eyed.

"So do you have the goat already?" Mano asks."

"Q has a goat he captured on a tether and has been fattening him up with basil and other greens for nearly a week now. He's agreed to donate it to the cause," Hitman asserts.

"So, this is a *cause* now?" someone snickers.

"Yes, it's a cause for celebration— Rainbow's first kill!" Hitman exclaims.

Eyes roll and a buzz of different voices fill the air. A few comment on how cute the goat appeared, walking the beach trail with Q on a leash even. Khan breaks up the snickering with a bold proposition.

"Hitman, I'd like to put this here bag of weed down to buy the filming rights to the goat slaying tomorrow," Khan announces, holding up a small bag of shake for all to see.

"We'll start the ceremony tomorrow afternoon," Hitman rallies, winking at Khan in agreement."

"So this is a *ceremony* now?" Grizz grumbles. The rest of the crews roll their eyes as if to say, *here we go again.*

The next day Rainbow kills, skins and quarters the goat. Well, Rainbow kills it with Hitman's help, and Khan films. It hardly flinches when Rainbow slits its throat with a single pull of a sharp knife. Mano turns away at the slit of the knife but his eyes catch with awe how the goat's blood flows generously from the fatal wound in its neck. He sees its body tense only slightly at the glint of the knife. In another fleeting glance he notices the careful holding of the animal by Hitman as if it were his own precious kin. He holds the goat as it bleeds till its last heartbeat. Most are standoffish during the whole *ceremony*. Few watch Khan's video, but all enjoy the delicious goat stew Hitman prepares.

There's something discerning and almost unnatural about watching the life fade out of a living creature. Mano felt it even when he sliced into his first fish. You are taking away a life that's literally held in your hands. But it feels natural, death to sustain life. Still gutting a live fish, or spearing a prawn is one thing. Slicing the throat of a wide-eyed, fuzzy bleating goat is a whole new level of killing a helpless creature for its meat. Mano doesn't think he could do what tiny Rainbow did, slice a goat and watch the life fade from the eyes of the living mammal.

Sustainable or righteous or not, the full-grown goat quartered and boiled down in a big pot, hardly yields enough cooked meat to fill an overturned Frisbee to the top. It seems unfair, the effort and size of an animal involved for such little meat, but the *ceremony* and sharing aspect makes it worthwhile perhaps? Maybe the goat's skin will get properly tanned and will live on as a drumhead and its spirit will fill the valley with music.

The crew sits on the grassy helipad and enjoys goat stew in the sun. They contemplate life and death and the death of the goat to sustain their life. One valley resident brings a pet baby goat on a leash to the meal. The cute little bleating goat wags its tail and sniffs the stew of its brethren curiously. They ponder the beautiful mystery of it all.

Chapter 13   Full Moon Mission

The morning ocean is calm and he feels mentally ready. Mano launches the kayak smoothly through the surf break and paddles westward. He was nervous about the launch and the solo journey to the west side of the island, but once he is alone out on the open water he feels comfortable in his element. He'll float with the current and the trade winds west to where the jagged spires of the north shore eventually fade to rolling hills and a long, sandy beach where a road re-joins the coastline. With the wind at his back, he paddles with ease, leaving Neverland like a soul set free.

Looking west from Neverland beach one can see the folding verdant cliffs extending down like curtains for thousands of feet to the ocean. 5 miles west there is a point that marks the furthest one can see along the coast from Neverland. Here the landscape changes drastically. A jagged wall undercut by the ocean is a landmark on the island that divides the north shore from the drier leeward west side of the island. Once around this farthest visible point, the cliffs that tower above the sea change from verdant green to a barren, deep red color. Mano paddles around this pivotal point to where he can no longer see Neverland beach where he started. After a few more miles he can see the take-out beach where he would re-enter society. He's in no hurry, so he paddles into a quiet alcove up along the cliff-lined shore. A small barrier reef blocks the encroaching surf from the great Pacific, creating a calm lagoon on the inside, perfect for swimming. Mano slides off the kayak and into the cool blue. The underwater world below is serene. Even without goggles he can see an assortment of reef fish scattering about as he swims through the lagoon. The jagged, black lava-rock reef and white sand create a stunning contrast along the ocean floor. He comes back to the surface for air and just floats peacefully next to the kayak. He's as free as a fish in the infinite Pacific.

After another mile of paddling, he's at the landing beach. The expanse of white sand stretches westward for as far as he can see. Even though he's never been there before, he knows there's a road at the end of the beach, and it's beach-break the whole way. There's no reef with waves crashing over it to worry about. He approaches the surf-break and prepares to land. There are people on the beach. There are cars and trucks on the beach! *Babylon here I come!* He holds his breath and pushes to shore.

At the rural beach park, Captain Mano is well received. He meets some cool travelers his age and is invited to party with them. They are eager to hear tales from Neverland, the remote, beautiful world within a world they've heard about on the other side of the cliffs.

"Thomas, you've got to make the hike in and check it out. You'll love it there! Just think of the gardens you could plant and the music..." Mano glows with inspiration and he encourages these new men and women to backpack the trail to the inside. He stays that night and the next before hitching a ride all the way around the island with his kayak.

Riding in a car, he feels out of his element and sick to his stomach. The travel time is warp speed compared to his bare feet or kayak that he's used to. Stepping onto the pavement and into a store is even more disorienting. The traffic, noise, and smells of exhaust fumes overwhelm his senses. *Babylon.* Somehow this time he just isn't prepared for the intensity.

Town felt intense on his first re-supply trip, but he could still relate with people there, and the typical annoyances like cars and gardeners running loud weed eaters were not so disturbing. This time, he feels more bothered and more distant from society. People are colder than he remembers, buildings feel more uncomfortable, and traffic is way louder than he imagined.

He can hardly consider stopping at the tourist spots to encourage cute girls to make the trek to his fantasyland. He just wants to blast back to the inside as soon as possible. So that becomes his mission. He hitches back to the north shore with daylight fading and an onset of rain. He'll have to wait until dawn to launch, he groans. With his tent still pitched back at Sanctuary, he's forced to take shelter in a cave at the road's end to keep out of the rain. It's a miserable night full of mosquitos in the cold damp cave.

Although worn out from no sleep, he's ready to launch at first light. The rising sun and calm ocean liven him for the return voyage, and he launches the kayak with ease.

With the assistance of an encouraging tailwind, he zips along the coast, landing back home in Neverland before the sun has even crested the back wall. He'll surprise Khan on the bluffs before he's even finished his coffee!

"Captain!" Khan receives him in a euphoric embrace. "Great to see you back, brother!" Mano sits down to enjoy a coffee with him and Rainbow.

"So, what was it like paddling out to the remote west side?" Rainbow asks curiously. Mano elatedly tells them about his journey beyond the verdant cliffs to the barren red-rock walls and the incredible reef-bound lagoon, but Khan stops his excitement.

"Did you hear about the raid?" Khan halts Mano mid-sentence.

"Raid? What raid?" Mano queries.

"The morning after the full moon." Khan's voice slows. A spoon clinks against a steel bowl and all falls silent.

"Have you been back to your spot at the Sanctuary yet?" Khan asks.

"No. I just landed and came straight here," Mano sputters.

"Well, there was a Ranger Raid, and most of us got off pretty light. Rainbow and I got tickets, but you Captain…You got hit hard. The Rangers hacked Sanctuary to bits.

"You're kidding me, brotha!" Mano spouts back jokingly. Khan's gaze is stone cold.

"Maybe you should go see for yourself," Khan sort of smiles. Mano's taken aback by Khan's serious face. He swallows then shuffles over to his camp at the Sanctuary.

He finds his camp a smashed up pile of rubbish. His tarps and hammock are slashed, and his tent is hacked to bits. Even the tent poles are purposely broken. The rangers found a sealed bucket full of his food too. They just dumped it out on the ground. If that weren't enough, they took his cooking oil and poured it all over the food to encourage ants to come. And come they did. Ants are everywhere! He can hardly believe it. His camp that was left neatly buttoned up three days before is now a pile of rubble. Even the giant bag of peanut M&M's Amber had brought him are scattered everywhere. He unravels his destroyed tent and finds his sleeping bag and a few articles of clothing intact inside. His guitar is undamaged, still in its case. He sighs in relief. The theory that the rangers have a superstition about destroying musical instruments must be true.

Discouraged, he doesn't even know where to begin as far as cleanup. He can't bear to look at the ant-infested food pile anymore. Thus, he packs up what is salvageable and moves to the beach, taking his sleeping bag, guitar, and a few dishes without looking back.

Other locals have sympathy for his plight. Khan gives him a tarp for shelter, and Grizz kicks him down some food and lends him a couple of pots and pans. It isn't the end of the world, and thankfully, to the Rangers, Mano still remained an outlaw unknown.

He runs into Hitman down on the beach. He's quick to fill Mano in on the full moon show he missed.

"So Rick and Lisa brought down this giant wine bottle filled with homemade up-valley wine. Rick unveiled it and called out to the crowd on the Heiau, *Bring out your cups!* He started pouring from this massive glass bottle and people began to get silly as the moon rose. Then Cliff started blabbering and chanting to Khan's drumming and the dancing began." Mano listens bright-eyed as Hitman continues.

"The moon was dancing in and out of the clouds and it was sort of misting. I guess Cliff knew conditions were prime so he rallied a chant to the gods. '*Moonbow, moonbow, moonbow!*' He's yelling all crisp and fast, then everyone around joins in. Quick and rhythmic, and together we chanted as the drums beat in sync. I tell you Mano, we all just kept chanting '*moonbow*' for like ten minutes! Chanting like madmen as the full moon danced in and out of the mist. Then, wham! The spectrum of light arced down into the ocean right in front of the Heiau, bright as can be. This night rainbow beamed down just for us. It had to be the most incredible thing I've ever seen here, or anywhere. We all screamed with delight. It was incredible. The moonbow lasted for almost an hour before it started to rain. Then everyone scattered. And the next morning was the raid..."

A long silence engulfs them as they both just stare out at the horizon. Mano breaks the stillness.

"Wow, what a trip, and the Rangers came the next day. What was that like?"

"They came first thing in the morning, of course. They must have landed on the bluffs at dawn. Might have been two helicopter crews. I know they dropped off a couple guys up-valley at least. Of course, everyone was still asleep after the big moonbow wine party. Q was up taking a duce and he got awarded the first ticket. But like a true outlaw, after he got his ticket he ran down to the beach to warn everyone. Besides Q, Khan, Rainbow, and Grizz, we all got away. The rest of us ran and hid up valley, and I guess they hung out on the beach to write tourist tickets for a bit, then flew out early afternoon."

"Man, I knew I shouldn't have missed the full moon!" Mano exclaims.

"Yeah, you missed a good one, but spring break's just started, we'll be partying down all week for sure!" Hitman whoops.

"I've always wanted to see a night rainbow," Mano says looking up to the sky."

"Yeah, I tell you Captain, it was magic!"

Chapter 14   Spring Break

Finally, spring break is here! The last week of March brings an influx of college students from Oahu. The curious, adventurous ones fly over to this remote island in order to check a backpack trip to the beach off their bucket lists. There is by no means a horde of spring breakers, but the 2-dozen or so new arrivals that trickle in over the course of a week are young, fun, and ready to throw down. It's enough even to draw up-valley recluses like Kaholo and Keilani out of their hideouts and down to the beach.

Neverland's spring break began with the big moonbow event. Then things kicked into high gear with the arrival of some cute college girls and Mano's return with fifteen liters of wine on the kayak. Khan and Mano host a big wine party down at Hitman's beach camp after a sunset jam. They planned to tap just one five-liter bag of wine, but once the crew gets started, holding back the two remaining wine boobs just isn't an option. They dance and sing as a big java plum log burns in half and the bag of wine gets passed around. Once finished, it's ceremoniously popped in a beach party ritual known as 'The Naked Popping of the Boob.'

Once finished, the empty plastic bladder is inflated tight then set on the ground for drunken folk to earn the glory of being the one to implode the air-filled pillow by springing onto it with their naked ass. It's quite a challenge, but the boom it makes upon successful implosion is louder than a firecracker. It's not just the tourists who are blown away by this ridiculous party stunt; it gets Khan and Hitman rolling in the sand too. The first boob goes all the way around the circle, bouncing naked butts right off of it. The suspense heightens as liquid courage prompts a few to really crash down on the boob. But this first boob just won't pop. It just flops naked butts right off. Then, going against everyone's advice, a scrawny newcomer, well lubricated, insists that he'll pop the boob by jumping onto it from up in a tree.

"Don't do it, man!" Kaholo yells as everyone watches him careen off a tree branch six feet up. He hits the boob dead on and it bursts so loudly, that it echoes across the valley. It breaks his fall flawlessly and he's deemed a hero. The next boob is quickly tapped and finished for round two. This time, after one round of failed attempts, Rick stomps on it with his big army boot and it implodes. The crowd boos him for his unfair technique, but this means the final boob must be tapped, finished and popped for a redo.

By now everyone smells of cheap wine and the party proceeds in a haze. Smoke in the eyes is no longer bothersome and clothes become less necessary. The last boob bounces a couple people off, but liquid courage prompts forceful body slams, and it soon bursts.

Then the party's over. There are no more boobs of wine, or booze of any kind. Somehow the couple of cute college girls scurry away before Hitman, Khan, or Mano can put any moves on them. Still they all sink into the sand satisfied. Another epic party they will never forget.

Mano, with his camp on the beach in the mix of the spring break scene, can hardly contain himself with the daily influx of hot college girls. *Just relax and have fun*, he tells himself. *Your spring break is nearly over, too.* Mano sighs, feeling confused in his purpose and dumbfounded with sexual desire. Even with the beach buzzing with life, he can't help but feel lonely. He yearns for the comfort and companionship of a partner beside him. The discomfort of loneliness is even stronger when he realizes that he must soon forge ahead in Babylon alone once more. A good woman, or even just a youthful lover who cared and wanted to stay, could be enough for him to forget about the real world and just stay. He wanted to live his fantasy in Neverland and forget about Babylon, but without a partner it just didn't seem feasible for him. *Never ever*, he huffs to himself pessimistically.

Mama Kai calls him and he washes away his pessimism in her cool blue. *Live in the now* he reminds himself. He wanders back to his beach camp vowing to not burden himself with thoughts of the future...at least for the rest of the day, anyway.

"Hey, Captain Mano, can you take us up to community garden?" two tourist girls ask him in passing.

"Right now?" he hesitates, taken aback. He just stopped thinking about girls and now two appear. Mano recognizes the girls from the big boob blowout party a couple of days ago. They backpacked in with their boyfriends and a bunch of other physics students from Oahu, but of course he can't remember their names. They continue to talk as he stares at them dumbly.

"Oh whenever, maybe this afternoon? We just figured we'd ask. We heard about the gardens and we'd love to see them, but we have no idea how to find our way around up there."

"Yeah, they're kind of hidden, purposefully hidden from tourists. If I take you there you have to promise not to tell any other tourists about the way there." Mano tells them coyly.

"We can keep it a secret," one girl giggles and whispers something to the other. Mano's heart livens, are these two *'girlfriends'* interested in him?

The three amble up the Hippie Highway together after lunch. He makes a good bit of suggestive conversation the whole way up the trail, but neither seems to really be interested. He actually relaxes more, knowing that this may purely be just a nature walk in good company.

Physics students, with boyfriends, leaving to go back to Oahu in a couple of days. No need to get excited. He tells them the names of all sorts of plants he knows and pulls mint for them to taste out of outlaw pools. They wade across a small side stream and walk through a thick muddy taro patch.

"Where are we going now?" the more talkative girl asks doubtingly as they push through the mud.

"Yeah, I think we are off of the Hippie Highway now," the other one comments. Without a word he lets the girls line up behind him in the muddy taro patch. He reaches in front of him to pull back a big taro stalk, revealing a trail of mud out of the taro patch and up to a grassy clearing beyond.

"This way," he instructs, holding back the taro stalk to let them proceed. From the grassy platform the view opens up to a giant terrace covered with banana, papaya, and edible hibiscus.

"Welcome to Neverland's community gardens!" Mano exclaims.

"Whoa! People weren't kidding—this place is unreal!" The talkative one gasps as they all stare wide-eyed at the garden.

Mano's about to continue the tour of the cultivated terrace of edible fruits and vegetables, but he pauses when he notices a brown tarp pitched under the big guava tree near the center of the garden.

"Someone's camped here," he mutters to himself.

Then an unfamiliar voice springs up singing from behind them.

"Well, hello there. Hello, hello. Welcome, hide-dee-ho. Three for tea, I see."

They all turn around and find themselves face to face with a short Asian man with a shaved head.

"Well, well! It's Mr. Kayak and his two scientist friends. Good afternoon, and welcome. Welcome to my garden."

Two thoughts rush into Mano's head. How did this guy know who he was? He'd never seen him before. And why was he calling the community gardens *his* garden. Before he can respond, the little man grasps the thin brunette's hand daintily and introduces himself.

"I am Coco Lele and this is my garden of Eden. Welcome! Come, sit! Have a tea with me, oh you must sit and have tea, tea for three. Well, four if we include Mr. Kayak here, he he!"

Coco Lele escorts them to his simple camp under the big guava tree near the center of the garden. Mano can hardly get a word in with Coco Lele's quick-witted singsong discourse bouncing from one rhyme to the next. But, like the girls, he lets himself be swept into this little man's whimsical tour without questioning. Curious, or helpless, they follow along without much thought. Coco Lele captivates his audience with historical up-valley lore as he stokes a small fire for tea. With the tea steeping he calms to a meditative silence, and asks the girls if they'd like to see his handmade shell leis. They both nod agreeably so he carefully reaches for a decorative box tucked just out of sight. He opens the little treasure chest, allowing just himself to take in the wonder of what's inside. He looks lovingly at his box of treasures before showing the group. He pulls out a few handcrafted Kahelelani shell necklaces and bracelets and shows them to the trio. The leis are made of rare shells endemic to just a few Hawaiian islands, and they shine with vibrant cream, pink, and burgundy colors.

"Where did you get those? They're so brilliant!" one girl exclaims.

"Girls, girls, I did not get these…I made them. Most of these are rare Ni'ihau shells from the forbidden island," he explains smugly. The beauty of the man in the garden with his precious leis and his fairy-tale style of speech captivates them all.

"And this one here, this is my personal power piece. This one you cannot touch, but I will show you." He proudly displays a thick, multi-strand lei whose shells are aligned to create an interlacing rainbow of colors. It's an intricate piece worthy of Hawaiian royalty. He delicately puts the lei back in the box and tucks it into its hidden place. He closes his eyes for a breath and a moment of silence.

"Now the tea!" His eyes pop open with a big smile.

They sip tea and let themselves become immersed in the quiet natural world of the garden. Mano allows any lingering intentions to vanish and he and the girls slip into a daydream with this Asian garden muse. Maybe it's the tea, or the garden, or just Coco Lele's light, witty voice. Who knows, but they're all captivated and mesmerized.

"I'd like to read your energy," Coco Lele states abruptly, focusing on the one brunette girl. She brushes her hair back, looking away shyly.

"What do you mean, read my energy?" she asks.

"I have a gift, and I would like to read you. I sense something interesting. Just give me your hand." She extends her hand. She's practically hypnotized, she has no other option, Coco Lele's speech is so captivating.

He sits directly across from her, his knees nearly touching hers, and places one hand above and one below her hand, lightly clasping it between his. Mano and the other blonde girl look on inquisitively as Coco Lele and his subject close their eyes. Coco Lele's eyelashes flutter and his head lifts with a growing smile.

"I see...interesting," he chuckles to himself, quite pleased with his findings.

"Well, that wasn't so hard," she exhales in release. Mano and the other girl stare at them curiously.

"So, what did you receive?" she asks Coco Lele, intently.

"Oh, I do not receive, I was just reading." he smirks.

"Well," she says fumbling, overcome with anticipation.

"If you are comfortable, I'll share what I found with you and your friends."

"Well, uh, I'm not sure, but if you are...reasonable?" She hesitates. Coco Lele leaves little time for a change of heart, and quickly continues.

"Well, the way I like to do this is...a little different. It's quite unique...I'll describe you, or my impression of you as something. There is...so much, of course, but I prefer to just use a few simple words, it's how I do it."

"Okay..." She draws out her response with more than a hint of skepticism, but curiosity overcomes her.

"Okay, just tell it!" she releases.

Coco Lele glances at Mano and the other girl, then sitting in lotus, he closes his eyes and smiles to himself. Like before, his eyelids flutter as if to aid in his concentration.

"You are..." he hesitates, then opens his eyes and stares at her intently.

"You are a force pushing..." Silence falls over the group as the two stare into each other for a long moment. "You are like a hand pushing on a chest. Pressing, pushing." A Russian accent is suddenly apparent when he enunciates *pushing*.

"That's it?" Her response is questioning and accepting at the same time.

"Pushing," Coco Lele reiterates.

She seems to take in and accept the reading then she looks cautiously toward her friend whose face is overcome with curiosity.

"Okay, try me," the blonde girl giggles. Mano feels a tinge of nervousness, knowing that his turn will likely follow. Coco Lele takes the girl's soft hand, then allows himself to sit back and focus in on her energy. He chuckles to himself as her *aura* is read. He sits back and meditates like before, prior to responding.

"You are...Ice-Cream-Land!" He proclaims enthusiastically.

"Yes, ice-cream-land. Not ice cream, not candy-land, but ice-cream-land. You understand the difference?"

"Yes I do," she giggles.

"Ice-cream-land. People want to be in your fun land because it is full of ice cream! You are soft and sweet and people want to lick you, taste your goodness."

Mano didn't quite get the first reading, but he agrees the second girl really is certainly ice-cream-land. Once Coco Lele actually said it, it fit perfectly. Coco Lele goes on about ice-cream-land for a bit in a fantastical tone. Then all eyes turn to Mano. He can't even imagine what one word would describe him. He gulps, knowing that his energy is strong and right out in the open.

Mano bravely extends his hand forward. During the reading he tries to let his energy be open and be true, he thinks of love and his daydreams of it as usual.

Coco Lele's eyes flutter just the same and he sits back. This time his smile broadens to the point of showing all of his teeth.

"Now Mano, I didn't even have to look deep to read you. Your energy is right out in the open." He pauses for a moment, then speaks again looking straight into his eyes.

"You are...a very passionate man." He takes another breath for reflection.

"You are a man's man. You like to provide and are good at it. You are a good forager." He smiles and emits a little laugh.

"A very passionate man…" He reiterates then sits back and trails off speaking softly to himself. Mano and him share a wide smile then Coco Lele speaks again.

"Now that we have that out of the way, tell me what's going on down at the beach. You know, spring break and all." Coco Lele's tone lightens, but Mano remains transfixed, still trying to derive meaning out of what he already knew about himself. The girls start to tell of their trip in on the trail and how they witnessed a boat drop.

"Ahh a boat drop! Is Captain Bligh here? I know he's a big spring-breaker." Coco Lele chuckles.

"No, it was probably The Pro, I haven't seen Captain Bligh all winter. He must be hanging out in town." Mano answers.

"You know, I don't make it down to the beach much, but I do like to hear of the happenings. I find it amusing. I did hear about you, Mr. Kayak and some of your missions even way up here. Say, is Grizzley still out rounding up chicks for volleyball?"

"As always, nothing new there," Mano laughs.

"These girls you brought up here, they have got to be the best girls on the beach right now, is that right, Mr. Kayak?" Mano nods in agreement, as the two ladies look away shyly.

"Well, I figured that much with you, Mr. Mano." Coco Lele laughs, while smiling dreamily into the girls' blue eyes.

"Keep trying, you'll get to use your passion, don't worry." Coco Lele insists. He tries to keep them all up at his camp in the garden as long as possible with stories of spearing wild pigs in snares, as well as his journey as an up-valley celibate soloist. The girls eventually express their need to return to their boyfriends on the beach because the sun is sinking low and their counterparts may be worried that they are up-valley getting more than just their energy read.

The trio heads down after gathering a few handfuls of greens from the garden. Mano daydreams of trying to get *Pushing* to kiss *Ice-cream-land,* but any slight suggestiveness he hints at just seems to make him look silly.

The weeklong festival of young, fun newcomers ends as quickly as it began. After the weekend, the beach is practically deserted, aside from the familiar few. Andrew, Hitman, Q, Mano, and four or five random *touri* are the only ones left at the beachfront campsites. The rest of the outlaws scattered along the creek, bluff, and way up valley, manage to fall back to their usual soloist routines.

Grizz is quick to stop by Mano's camp as soon as the action dies down.

"Hey, I can't find anyone to play volleyball with, what's with people just leaving so quick all the time? I mean, I just woke up from a nap and it's like wham, spring break's over." Grizz chuckles as he bounces the ball in front of him.

"Those college kids, they don't know where it's at. They could be here at *Neverland University*, learning all they need to know from guys like us, right Grizz?"

"Yeah, Neverland U, that's where I go to school. I got an A in Grizz-olgy and a B-plus on my graduate level Grizzertation." Grizz laughs at his own *Grizz-ism*.

"Come on Captain Mano, I got to think that you, with your Hollywood moves, could manage to keep just one of those hotties here with ya!"

"They're not into bearded kayak guys like me, they're all about Babylonian boyfriends and Grizzertations and such."

"What, they think you're like, too *grizzly* for them?" Grizz teases.

"No, but *you're* too grizzly for them." Mano bounces the volleyball delicately off of Grizz's head and catches it, leaving Grizz unphased.

"Come on, there's no way I'm too *grizzly*, I'm the Grizz! Nowooooh!" he yells out, caveman-like. Mano chuckles and Grizz just keeps at it.

"Now what about that one girl you were kinda hanging with, Christina? Kristi? You know, that little yoga hottie that showed up with the physics team."

"You mean, Kristen," Mano clarifies.

"Yeah, her! She seemed ready to take your class, right? Whatever happened to her?"

"She went back to Oahu with the physics team. She's no outlaw."

"Well she could have been. You just couldn't convince her," Grizz jokes.

"Grizz, do you know what intimacy is?"

"Let's see, uhh, *Grizzlentamacy*—snuggling up to the Grizz! Just kidding, I know what intimacy is," he releases with a sigh.

"Well, Kristen and I shared some beautiful intimacy for a few days, but there wasn't much outside of that. The love just wasn't there."

"Oh, whatever. You could have still convinced her to stay! That's no fun, at least you could have sent her to me!"

"I don't know if I can even convince myself to stay." Mano exhales deeply.

"What, so you're gonna go and get all Babaloney, too?"

"If I stay here with no woman, I'll just get grizzlier and more out of touch with the world. I need to find a good girl on the mainland and bring her back next season."

"Yeah, a real stayer-girl, Neverland material!" Grizz snarls.

"Yeah, something like that." Mano replies.

Mano ponders the idea of a stayer-girl a bit more and the possibility of meeting his true love on remote Neverland beach and there seems no real solution in staying. He could try to be a celibate soloist up valley like Coco Lele, but that certainly wasn't him. He would have to forge ahead in Babylon. The Neverland forever dream must wait. Mano bites his tongue at his humble acceptance of his dream unrealized. He'll leave the island and give Babylon another whirl he decides. He must continue his quest for true love as a passionate man on the outside.

He promises Mama Kai he will return to her sacred beach, and in the meantime he will share her beauty, joy, and love with the world. He vows that he does believe in magic, and pledges to keep it alive in his heart.

~ Part II ~

Chapter 15   Eleanor

He slips in and out of her turbulent waters with ease. A few smooth strokes at the right time are all he needs. The ocean had shown her calming touch and he glides back to the sand, relaxed. He's still breathing to her pulse, the rhythm of the swell, after he surfaces and walks onto the dry sand. He exhales fully to change his breath.

Back to doing the daily chores and wanderings in Neverland, fetching water and preparing food. It's almost evening and there's a potluck gathering on the Heiau at sunset. He makes a wonderful dessert, a mango pie with browned coconut and sesame seed crust that is a highlight of the party. Soft string music serenades the setting sun. This is the life. For a moment he wonders why he ever left.

Mano left, but he found his way back. It's a new beginning, a new winter. He still has most of his old friends in the valley, but the excitement of a new season with new characters stirs him. He has high hopes that this season will be the next great adventure, another great escape from the pressures of the real world that had been weighing him down for months and months...

He landed on the island in mid January and Khan picked him up at the airport along with his friend, Sierra. Khan had already been on the island for nearly a month and is super stoked, more than ready to blast back to Neverland beach for the winter season.

"They're waiting for us," Khan exclaims as he throws Mano's bags in the back of the truck.

"Oh yeah, great! I've been waiting 9 months to get back here," Mano jokes.

"No, really! It's been high surf for weeks and we haven't been able to do a drop. We're overdue, man. We gotta get in there, brother!"

"What about The Pro?" Mano asks.

"He's not doing the boat drop anymore. He kind of got ousted by the local Hawaiians. The Pro was just too good, he charged too little, and he was just too on point, you know." Mano shrugs, not knowing what to say. Khan continues.

"You know, Honu and I kind of suspected this was bound to happen with The Pro being Australian and not a real local. The Hawaiians probably probed the authorities to find something to stick him with. Honu and I planted a coconut tree in his honor last spring. We kinda thought it might be his last season.

"What about Captain Bligh?" Mano queries.

"You know Captain Bligh and I don't really see eye to eye. Besides, I think the Rangers seized his boat and he doesn't even have one anymore."

"Okay, so who's gonna do the drop, and when?"

Khan pulls him in close. "There's another guy, local, and the swell is down now. We're leaving tomorrow."

"Whoa, this is all happening in a whirlwind! I'm fresh off the plane and now we are boat dropping in tomorrow." Mano digs in his heels at Khan's ambitious proposal.

"That's right, Captain. The window is tomorrow. We have to take the chances we got. We can't wait on waves." Khan's getting so hyped up Mano can see his pupils constricting.

"Alright, so Sierra will hike in, and I'll paddle there in my kayak. Then we'll all meet up at the beach tomorrow evening."

"No, you don't get it Captain, I need you with me on that boat!"

"I never take the boat in, I'll kayak, you just take the food bags for me and Sierra."

"Captain, we've got forty-two bags on the drop and hungry people in there. I need your help on the boat with the bags. I'll even pay for your drop." Mano finally grasps the situation, and agrees to the motorized ride in.

"And he's a good Captain, a solid guy. The boat, I'm not so sure about, but I'm sure it's fine."

"What do you mean not so sure, but sure it's fine?" Mano's tone changes from excited to concerned.

"Don't worry, Captain. Forget what I said. *Eleanor*, the boat, she'll be fine, she'll get us there no problem." Khan pledges. Mano shouldn't be nervous, but just being at the mercy of another Captain on a motorboat left things out of his control. He had learned about surrendering to the flow, but he still couldn't help but feel nervous that the mission in, Khan's mission in, his first boat ride in, would be without any of his own direction.

But the scenario couldn't be more perfect, Mano realizes. Khan and Mano, spearheading the long-awaited big winter boat drop to Neverland on their first trip back of the new year.

The next morning, they board the boat piled high with plastic boat drop bags. They push off into a calm Pacific dawn. A young girl unexpectedly shows up at the boat with her bag ready to join the crew. She's from the island and knows the drill, so the four of them launch from the North Shore and head west.

The new Captain is chipper as can be out on the water. He goes into full detail of his life as a *true-local* fisherman and boat captain of this glorious Pacific coast.

Pods of dolphins and even humpback whales guide them as they cruise along the coast. Mano and the new girl are giddy with excitement, but Khan simmers them with a prayer reminding them that any mission into Neverland should not be taken for granted. The excited trio, as wells as the Captain, hold hands in the boat and pray for their safe arrival. They pray for the safe delivery of all the bags, and the safety of the Captain, and the crew too. They humbly ask for Mama Kai's blessing to allow them safe passage over her waters. Khan wants to stop the boat so they can all have a moment of silence together, but the Captain is in a zone and doesn't want to stop. Their eyes shimmer with the cool morning light. They are fortunate for sure, going back to the land of magic, and even luckier to be on a boat fast-tracking around the cliffs.

"Twenty minutes and we'll be at the beach," the Captain shouts into the wind. They come about the bluffs just as the sun is cresting the back wall of the valley, and they get their first glance of Neverland. People are on the beach; they heard the boat coming.

"There's already a bunch of hippies ready on the beach. This boat drop should be a snap," the Captain shouts.

"Yeah, but they're not swimmers." Khan reminds him.

"Okay, I'll bring us about, and we'll toss the bags off this side," the Captain instructs as he barrels towards the set break. Khan and Mano scramble over the pile of bags as the captain circles *Eleanor* about, turning with the wind and paralleling the beach. He waits for a window between sets, and then zooms ahead.

"Okay, go!" The Captain shouts. Mano and Khan throw 20 bags overboard like bombs out of an airplane as the Captain slides between waves at trolling speed.

"Get going, let her rip...Okay, okay, stop, that's it." The Captain directs as he turns the boat back out to sea as big sets of waves roll under them. They wait out the set then back around they go as the plastic lined flotsam spreads wide in the surf.

"Coming around again, same drill!" They shuffle 10 more bags overboard once more in another twenty-second fury.

"That's over half of them," Mano shouts as they head back out to sea to avoid the big sets closing in. The crew looks back at the disbursing bags.

"See that. The ones we threw on the far side are catching the surf and the first ones we tossed are drifting out of the impact zone and aren't making it in."

They circle back around, pick up the stragglers, and re-toss them in the sweet spot. By this time, dozens of hippies and bystanders on the beach are at the water's edge as the first lucky bags wash in.

"Ready! Up! Go, go, go!" The rest of the bags are tossed overboard right in the sweet spot. Now there are bags everywhere. Forty-two bags are spread through the surf and are starting to get washed up onto the beach.

"Okay, now the surfboards," the Captain continues. Khan paddles in one of the short boards and swims back out to help paddle in a local girl on a long board. Mano jumps off on another board with a box of five-dozen eggs, a special delivery for Mr. X, and paddles for the shore. It's quite the scene on the beach with bags starting to form into piles and hippies running around trying to find their order. Mano tries to direct traffic and keep everything together on the beach so no one's bag disappears. It looks like everybody and everything made it in fine. Mano pauses to glance back out to the ocean while carrying two heavy bags across the sand.

He's back in Neverland once again! Mano smiles as he scans the vibrant scene on the beach in the morning light. But his eye catches on the boat. What's the Captain doing? Mano sees the boat paused in the shore break and the Captain is scrambling around the back of the boat seemingly adjusting the motors.

"Why is the boat stopped!" he shouts out loud to no one. Then he sees the big waves coming in. The boat surges up on the first big wave. The Captain scrambles to hold on as the boat is lifted nearly vertical in the wave.

"Oh my God it's going to dump-truck right over!" Mano's mouth gapes open in horror. The wave passes just under and lets the boat slam back down into the trough. Then *Eleanor* is turned sideways and Mano can tell it's all over. The next, even bigger wave approaches and the Captain bails overboard just as a wall of water completely barrels the boat. Is this really happening? Mano's mind flashes. The Captain swims for shore and the boat gets pushed upside down against the rocks on the east end of the beach. *Eleanor* is shipwrecked.

Suddenly, it's a panic-induced boat rescue on the beach.

"Let's try to swim over to her and get her flipped back over before it's too late," Khan commands, ushering Mano and several locals on the beach to swim out to the overturned boat that is teetering against the rocks on the Heiau side of the beach. They try to salvage the boat but it's just too dangerous. With the help of seven or eight guys they actually manage to right her. On their second attempt they heave her upright while she's being pounded against the rocks, but she's full of water and the motors are already trashed. They salvage what they can from inside the boat, managing to retrieve the sealed gas cans with minimal fuel spilling into the ocean. Everyone is in awe.

The boat crash leaves a sour taste in Mano's and Khan's mouths on what should have been a jubilant arrival. Khan blames himself for not mentioning the safety of the boat in the prayer, and not taking the time to properly bless the voyage with the boat stopped. The Captain claims the engines failed because he hit a sea turtle in the surf. That can't be a good sign. They are all saddened by the environmental impact the crashed boat will have on the beach. *'At least no one got hurt,'* are the echoing, consoling words of everyone around. The sour taste of their shipwrecked arrival lingers amongst Mano and the crew. Mr. X sends solace in an assertion of a few simple words.

"Mama Kai giveth, and Mama Kai taketh away." This of all things seems to calm any wonderings about whether the voyage was mysteriously cursed or not. Ultimately, it is the Ocean, Mother Nature, Mama Kai, who decides. She is the one who grants passage to the beach. The boat Captain is probably the least upset. *Eleanor* was heavily insured! Still, the thought of Khan's prayer lingers in Mano's head. Khan mentioned everything in his prayer for safe passage. The Captain, the crew, the bags, but he failed to ask for the safety of the boat. It affirmed what Mano had refused to believe. That Khan truly is connected with the spirits of the island. He shakes it off. It could be just plain bad luck that the boat crashed. Right? *Mama giveth and Mama taketh away.*

Khan and Mano go to find a campsite and settle in. No sooner than ten steps down the trail they run into a messenger.

"I'm relaying a message from Cliff. Your camp has already been set up. Come this way to Surf Camp." They look at each other and smile. The two follow their guide to a fully stoked-out campsite just off the beach. They can hardly believe it. Laid out for them in a tucked away spot is a two-man tent with tarps, a fire pit complete with a grill, pots and pans, plates, bowls, cups, spoons, and a stack of firewood. Cut pieces, arms length, of all sizes, stacked and ready to go for them. They are set up like royalty. They glance at each other and smile. They are the kings of the beach!

Chapter 16   Return to Rock and Roll

Sierra arrives off the trail early that same afternoon. With her comes a message that they have an exclusive invite to a pizza party on the bluffs with a guy named Krazy Red. Another messenger stops by Surf Camp that evening. It's the weather report relayed from Mr. X.

"The outer edge of a small hurricane is going to brush the island tonight, so be sure to batten down the hatches, there'll be some significant rain and heavy winds!"

"Great, we just got here and now we have to deal with a storm," Mano grumbles. Thankfully, their camp is already set up, and dialed for weather. They fare just fine in the heavy winds and rains that pelt their tarps for twenty-four hours. Khan grows restless the next day during the storm, and decides to motivate the crew to re-create Sanctuary during the rainstorm. Mano remembers how the two of them re-built and held down Sanctuary on the bluffs last winter, only to have his tent hacked up and destroyed by a Ranger raid.

But Khan and Mano still believe in the concept of Sanctuary and community space in Neverland. Bringing people together and protecting those who may not be well prepared is important, especially during trying times. Who knows how long the storm could last? A group shelter close to the beach could be critical to keep people safe and dry and in good spirits for the days to come. They were the leaders, the kings of the beach, so they should take it upon themselves to help out and protect everyone else who happened to be there. With the help of six or seven newly acquired *tribe members*, Khan and Mano construct the Happy Buddha Sanctuary just off the trail in between the beach and the Heiau. A Sanctuary for all to use and share and take shelter from any storm, is Khan's declared foresight. Their second night back, they sponsor a huge pizza party in the drizzle underneath tarps at the new Happy Buddha Sanctuary spot.

Word spreads and those without adequate shelter come to share food under the spacious, dry tarp set-up. Music, food, and good vibes flow. They rock and roll as a beach community again!

The next day the storm clears, and the good vibes continue. The buzz of Khan and Mano's arrival even carries to the way back, and up-valley folk like Gaia, Keilani, and Kaholo come down and join for food and music and ganja at the Buddha. Khan and Mano are pumped to be back in their fantasy beach paradise again.

Khan's even more stoked to have *sponsored* three or four guys who would otherwise have to hike out for food—his newest tribe forming. They are employed to cook, clean, and gather firewood for the group in exchange for food and weed. They are happy to be part of a team and be able to stay in paradise. Mano's not bothered by Khan's indentured servants. He's happy to have new faces to jam with and good food to share. Sierra is thriving as the newest member of this wayward wilderness fantasyland, joyously soaking up all the attention a cute girl can get on a remote beach.

"Every guy out here is a healer and they all want to do body work on me!" she tells Khan and Mano, who are not the least bit surprised! Sierra's a strong-willed, well-grounded mountain girl and they both have no doubt she'll find her place in Neverland.

With the storm cleared, and the weather pattern back to typical dry trade winds, Mano and Khan fear word of the boat crash will bring the heat. A wrecked boat pushed up on the rocks is clearly a red flag for tourist helicopters to see and report. They almost expect a raid, but they try not to be on edge anticipating one. The first tourist copters that fly by every morning certainly perk up Mano's ears though.

Mr. X provides a little insight to help Mano differentiate between the tourist copters and the Ranger copter, because Mano had only seen the Rangers once and they didn't even land.

'You can tell a Ranger copter just by the way it sounds. The tourist copters are slow and sputtery, but a Ranger copter buzzes in fast and loud like a bee right in your face. They always zoom in low, right off the deck, hot-roddin' you know. If it don't sound like anger, then it ain't a Ranger.'

With the boat wreck, Mano is sure the Rangers will come and investigate. Of course, boats wrecking on this beach is nothing new. Apparently, Mama Kai took three boats since Mano's departure last spring. Over the last year, the ocean had been a bit unpredictable. Even in the middle of summer when the north swell is completely down, a rogue swell came up for a day and wrecked a sailboat somebody had anchored off the beach. It was crushed against the rocks and washed onto shore. Some had brought parts from the mast and hull to the beach cave and built a tiki bar of sorts. But it was all gone now. The winter swells had washed the cave clean. *Eleanor* would meet the same fate. Soon she would get crushed and weathered to bits by the great Pacific.

Music, swimming, hiking, sun, and surf prevail as thoughts of a raid stemming from the boat crash dissipate with each passing day. They have red wine or rum cocktails in the evenings and there is plenty of ganja to go around. Life is good back on the beach.

The calm mornings allow deeper thoughts to surface. Mano still thinks about love. He meditates about his quest for true love one morning by himself on the Heiau as he watches the rising sun shoot golden rays up from a cloud before fully emerging from behind the back wall. He ventures up-valley all day to wander and wonder but returns to the Heiau for sunset. He watches the piercing orange globe descend under the horizon with a sigh of loneliness.

The Sun is not lonely, Mano ponders as the first stars twinkle in to take its place. But it sits in the universe alone. Out there, no other stars come close enough to shine on its equal light. The planets revolve around it, but it has no partner in shining its light. Could the sun shine its light upon another equal star far far away? It seems too distant and too different than all the rest to have a partner. He asks the heavens, but receives no response. He resolves to walk back to camp before the twilight fades because he doesn't have his headlamp with him.

In Neverland, darkness can bring loneliness and he can feel it sinking in. Luckily there is a solution for that. With his ukulele over his shoulder he simply walks toward the drumming. Toward friends, food, music, and fun. When he sees the fire he sighs, knowing that fire, like the sun is also a good companion. He sits down in the circle and lets the warmth and music soak in.

"Hey Andrew, play Vitamin D!" Mano shouts his request during a break in the strumming. Andrew's smooth voice and unique style are unmatched by anybody in the group. He lets his lyrics melt sweetly like raindrops from an afternoon sprinkle. Teasing. Mano's favorite song of his is an ode to the sun.

'Ev-ery day, I can't stop, lovin you-ooo. A kiss from your sunrise oh you tease me yes you do...Everybody loves you because you help with photosynthesis and shower us with vitamin D.'

Dozens of songs are played and four or five pizzas are consumed at the Buddha that night. Heart energy is pumping big like the north swell and everyone lets their souls shine through their music. The handmade food slow-cooked on a fire, words sung with such feeling and meaning, the centeredness of the group, and the primitive pureness of the setting create a beautiful scene that is beyond this world. The tourists that come to witness and become entranced in it are blown away; they can feel the magic in the open air. Magic is alive, open and abundant at the Buddha Sanctuary!

Khan's intensity soars with the group's causing some, like Mano, to tremble. Khan's feelings are so intense they disrupt Mano's own heart frequency somehow. Maybe he's not as comfortable with himself as he thought. Powerful heart rhythms do reach a climax, and many are almost overwhelmed. Drained somehow. Mano decides to leave before the show is over and walks back to his camp.

Back in his own zone, Mano is comfortable and fulfilled alone with his thoughts and the cool night air. His feelings of loneliness are gone. He feels the warmth from the community around him in his stomach. He breathes in the love from his friends and it makes his chest full and his heart steady. He breathes with the steady rhythm of the swell, the pulse of mother earth.

When he wakes at dawn with the birds, he feels refreshed. He starts the day with a hot chai, then morning yoga on the Heiau. On the Heiau, facing the ocean, he prays. He prays to Mama Kai, prays in thanks for his safe return to the inside. He asks humbly for her to send him true love. It feels like a silly fairytale wish, but he wishes it anyway and sends his prayer off to the Pacific. A distant whale spouts and dives when he opens his eyes after his final prayerful Ohm. Another day of mystery and magic has begun.

He opts for a morning swim and then a walk to bathe in the valley stream. Back along the trail outside the Buddha Sanctuary, he spots Gaia skipping down towards the beach. She's just as bright-eyed as ever, but her pace seems unduly quick for such a calm morning.

Oh, how he yearns to captivate her attention. It certainly wasn't love or even lust at first sight, but she has an attractive mystique about her. Her aura could be Coco Lele simplified to *'child of the light.'* To him at least, she possessed a noticeable glow of enlightenment; enlightenment from a young age, possibly even from birth.

When he sees her, he's not so much attracted, but intrigued. She excites him differently than any other cute girl, but she's a feminist soloist creature from the way back, an up-valley goddess mystic. To him her heart seemed buried deep in the valley, on lockdown for some reason. He wanted to snap her out of it and show her a wild time. He could show her what a passionate, caring, sensual man he is....

"Just to let you know, I think a helicopter landed on the bluffs just now," Gaia comments casually in passing, unfettered by his dizzying fatuous day-dreamy state. Mano snaps back to real-time.

"Are you are kidding me, did you see it land?"

"No, I didn't see it, but I swear it is the Rangers. I could feel it, I was sure enough that I stopped my yoga practice."

"So, do you think this is it? Do you think this is a Raid?"

"I don't know, but I'm getting out of here." Gaia replies.

"Well, you're fine, all you have to worry about is your blanket," Mano jokes to her as she wisps away.

Sierra is still having her morning coffee and relaxing in the sunshine, when Mano climbs back up the hill to her camp to warn her.

"So, I ran into Gaia and she thinks…she thinks she heard a helicopter land on the bluffs. So, I guess there's a raid!" Mano huffs, out of breath from the steep climb.

"Are you serious?"

"Well, not a hundred percent, but when Gaia senses a raid, I think we should listen. You know she's lived here on her own for like four years. If anybody can sense a raid, she can!"

Mano goes to a rock perch where he has a clear view of the beach, and scans for anything unusual. Nada. It's the classic dilemma, to stash the stuff and prepare for a full-on raid, or just wait and see.

"How about this, I'll go back to the Heiau and see if I can see anything happening on the bluffs. I'll signal back to you if there's really a raid." Mano offers.

"What kind of signal?" Sierra asks.

"Okay, if I wave two hands in the air that means it's a raid and you should totally get your stuff and ninja up valley, but if I wave with one hand then it's okay. One hand wave means no raid."

"Okay I got it, one hand is hello and two hands is run like hell."

At the Heiau, Mano looks towards the bluffs for any sign of the Rangers. Nothing. Maybe Gaia's intuition was incorrect.

"We're all okay, false alarm," he yells jubilantly to Sierra, waving a one-hand hello. She's already coming down the trail with her backpack fully loaded, tent and everything ready to hide up-valley in fear of a raid. "False alarm," he shouts again and waves the walks to meet her.

"I'm already inspired into action. I'm going to camp up-valley anyway on my own!"

Chapter 17   Pau-hana

"I just got this sudden strange feeling that Len may be at the end of his life," Khan speaks abruptly during Sierra and Mano's debate over cooking techniques.

"He's probably hiked out already, he's out of food and he's hiked out," Mano replies, attempting to snub out any negative energy and any further thought on the Lennie situation.

Lennie, or Len-dog, as Khan often called him, is some weirdo living on the island that went a bit off his rocker and decided that he'd just go to the end of the road. And when the road ended, he just kept on to the end of the trail, to Neverland. But his weird energy estranged him from any group. At first glance he seemed harmless, but just looking into his eyes, you could see into his disturbed side. Schizophrenia, split personalities, and paranoia are right there on the surface. He came to Neverland and thoroughly crept out Sierra and the other girls for a few days, then simply vanished up in the way back valley.

"I don't know. I've just been having some bad visions that Len is going to get smoked on these rocks out here," Khan continues.

"No, I'm sure he'll be fine, he'll hike out. Everyone hikes out. He'll go back to his family on the outside and get better. He's probably drinking an iced coffee in town right now! He's Len-dog, Screwy Lennie, he's just finding himself— he's hiked out," Mano persists.

"You know some people don't just come out here to have fun and to get away. Some people don't come to Neverland to 'find themselves' either. Some people come out here to end it all!" Khan reaches his left hand above his head and then smacks it down upon his right, making a dramatic slap.

"Pau, he's done. Pau-hana, There's no more work for him. He's off his rocker and soon to be smoked by the valley," Khan declares.

"Hey! Don't say that. It's not like that with Lennie," Mano snaps. Khan's energy seems poisonous.

"Yeah, knock it off, Khan! Quit thinking negative thoughts like that. Why don't you grab some more wood for the fire if you are gonna eat with us. These potatoes are taking forever." Mano slips out of frustration.

"Well if Mama Kai smokes Len-dog on these cliffs, then so be it." Sierra's tone rings so cold it makes both men wince.

"Lennie will make it. He's not pau hana!" Mano spits back, but with a tone of uncertainty.

Please make it. Take care of yourself Lennie, hike out, get better. Mano prays alone later that evening. The thought of Lennie weighs on him heavy and he can hardly sleep. Did Lennie come out to Neverland and walk the 11 miles beyond the end of the road to end it all? Will the valley bring him back? The valley can cure and heal and save, but it can also teach hard lessons, and spit people out. Or as Khan said, smoke them on her jagged cliffs.

The next day a report comes through the coconut wireless that the infamous Lennie had been spotted still here in the valley. It's been five or six days since he was last seen, destroying beautiful flowers in the sanctuary garden. Now he was supposedly spotted by Kaholo raging around deep in the back valley and his body was said to be deteriorating already. He had almost nothing with him Kaholo said. His feet and legs had some rough cuts on them too, and he had surely been getting eaten alive by mosquitoes.

"He's certainly out of food by now." Mano proclaims grimly as they mull over the Lennie situation.

"Captain, if he comes back down to the beach we can't let him stay. We gotta get him outta here. He could endanger the community. You're gonna have to paddle him out!" Khan demands.

"What! I'm not going to paddle out Screwy Lennie—he's too unstable. What if he just jumps off the kayak halfway down the coast? Then what?"

"Chill out Captain, I see your point, it's just that I'm worried about Len-dog, and if he comes down here and starts running amok and freakin' people out, that's not good. We'll have to extract him somehow, that's all."

"Well, that's if he comes back and doesn't get spat out by Mama Kai," Sierra laments.

"He's pau-hana," Mano mumbles to himself.

'Wait! I take it back, I don't mean to say that. He's not pau-hana, he's fine. Mama Kai, please let Len-dog be fine and make it safe out of the valley. Help him fix his body and his spirit and deliver him safe back to Babylon.' Mano prays, then releases, trying to clear his head of it all.

The next day Mano wakes with the birds just the same and serenades the dawn with them. He takes the usual morning bowel movement and glances out to the ocean to survey the waves before yoga practice. He notices *Eleanor* is still in the same spot wedged up on the rocks, but it seems like the splash around her has grown. The waves must be bigger today. Maybe a new swell is coming in? Mano trots down to the creek to fill up water jugs. It's cold enough for a sweater on this January morning. The sun is slow to rise. Maybe it's earlier than he thinks.

Halfway through his yoga routine he glances over toward the beach and he notices *Eleanor* being carried out by the swell. The surf rises beneath her and takes her out to sea. He doubts she'll go far, but he secretly hopes that she'll get carried away into blue the abyss where they will never have her as an eyesore again.

He continues his solo practice allowing his energy and gaze to focus on the back wall of the valley with the sun illuminating the clouds behind it. The sun breaks free as he moves through his final poses, filling the Heiau with warmth and light. The ocean breathes with him, and he releases three Ohms before opening his eyes to her.

He looks over to the beach and Eleanor is gone. She's not wedged up on the rocks or taken out to sea. The boat is now in four or five big pieces and spread along the rocks. The swell came up, took her out to the break, and then slammed her back onto the rocks harder than ever. Overhead waves work what's left of her for the rest of the day. She's now just mangled steel and fiberglass. After a full week of high surf, she's hardly recognizable.

A few scavenger parties come down to pull out any sizable pieces of fiberglass that could be made into tables or other camp furniture. But the boat, the eyesore, the stain on Mano and Khan's arrival, is gone. Mama Kai giveth and Mama taketh away. There are no more superstitions floating about anymore. The boat is gone, pau-hana, just like the two others before it this same year. Now, the only question is if Lennie would meet the same fate? Mano grimaces, imagining a limp body washing up on the shore just like the mangled boat.

Chapter 18   Island Girl

'Don't let your emotions rule you!' Mano scolds himself. He hated being emotionally driven, and he would chastise himself for it.

'Let go! Be comfortable wherever you are.' He would tell himself. But he can't discount his dreams or feelings. Is he just living in a dreamer's world full of wishful thinking? He sighs trying to release his dreams, his feeling. He smiles to himself in acceptance. What's a fantasyland without dreams and feelings, anyway? He sighs once more, letting his being be.

Mano allows himself to be entranced by any new cute tourist girl that hikes in. Sure enough, on a walk down to Cliff's garden on the beach to collect basil, he runs into a pair of dark-eyed smiling sisters. New arrivals, from rural eastern Canada. Right away he can tell these two aren't the typical overnight backpackers. They seem less rushed, more in touch, and connected to the earth. He's quick to invite them to the evening pizza party jam at the Buddha. He's drawn to the older sister, Summer, so he sits next to her around the evening campfire circle.

Summer is the big sister that acts more like a little sister. She is loud and fun and enthusiastic, yet sensitive and sincere. Mano moves behind her and massages her by the fire. She lets herself melt under his touch and that ignites a spark inside him. Receptive and sensual, she receives his love through the massage. If there is one thing Mano knew he could do well, it's how to touch a woman just right. His touch is strong yet delicate and meaningful. Through his hands and body he can feel a real connection with her. Maybe it's just the essence of the evening, or maybe it's something more. A goodnight kiss seems to prove the latter. Mano holds her in his arms and kisses her slowly before letting her walk back down the trail to fall asleep alongside her sister Natalie. He dances back to his camp dreamily.

The next morning Summer joins him on the Heiau for yoga. After a great sunlit practice, she accepts his invite back for morning tea in his little garden spot on the perch. He pulls her close and presses her body against his. They give in to full body kissing, falling over each other in the garden.

He yearns so desperately to love. He lets his heart out in his touch and kiss and words. Later she tells her sister how he captivated her in the garden. They giggle wondering what may happen next. After another community dinner and music show at the Buddha that evening, neither can hold back. She stays with him in his tent. He pulls her close. Being with a woman makes him feel whole, complete, even more a part of this world.

For the next couple of days they explore the valley together. They swim and cook together and spend nights in each other's arms.

Mano envisions a long-term relationship with her right away. Somehow, though, his heart tells him that he can't let Summer get too close. Something holds back the full love he wants to extend. He wants her comfort, her love, but something in his heart is holding him back. He doesn't understand.

"Just be with this girl so you can be stable and satisfied out here," he tries to encourage himself.

Summer is the hottest girl on the beach now. She's nice too, and she wants to stay and be with him. Why does he feel this way? He knows he wants so desperately to fall in love, why can't he just love her, and be with her?

After a full day of wandering and pondering, he decides he could extend his love pure and free to her. He would be with her. It makes sense. He wouldn't resist the opportunity to share his love.

It never occurs to Mano that perhaps Summer isn't so concerned with love. Maybe she just wants a male companion or an island fling. But that's not how Mano's mind turns. He'd always ponder love with nearly every girl he is intimate with.

Of course, Summer's encounter with Mano, sprouts a change in the sister's planned island tour. They are supposed to catch a plane off the island in a couple days. Like most, their travel plans allowed for less than a week in Neverland. They decide to hike out, re-supply with food, change their plane tickets, and hike back in after three or four days to stay a whole month or more. Summer kisses Mano and promises to be back in less than a week.

"Maybe in just two or three days," she giggles as they part. So that's it. He will wait patiently, here in the protection of Neverland for the return of the Canadian sisters.

Mano is protected from the outside world, but not from temptation. Of course, right after they leave, a new girl arrives that catches his eye. Two girls, another pair of sisters even. He resists temptation at first, but he can't help but catch smiles from the tall curly-haired blonde.

She's way too young, he thinks to himself instantly. Nonetheless, he finds a moment to introduce himself. Mano rejects any lustful thoughts he has for Melanie immediately, but he can't discount his natural attraction to her. She has the sweet smile of Charlotte, and the body of a bikini model. In fact, she said she had even done some bikini modeling! But, she's an island girl. Surely, she would be more into her many friends on the outside than some mainlander hanging out in Neverland.

He had a taste of pleasure with Summer, so now his hunger for love and sex is less easily subdued. He can't resist. At least he can't resist *trying* to get to know her. It doesn't make sense, and he is sure it will never work out, but somehow it seems stupid not to try. Would the Canadian sisters *really* be back like they said? For a second, he tries to believe that they won't be back, just like the countless tourists that left their tents pitched with plans to return after a quick supply run, yet were never heard from again. The Canadian sisters would be back though; of course, Summer would be back. She was practically in love with him when they parted yesterday, right? He shakes his head. He isn't sure about her anyway. His mind twists and his stomach tries to digest the situation. Ego or arrogance takes over. He has to at least try something with this island girl! Just thinking about her arouses him. She's so steamy hot.

"So Melanie, you say you do yoga, would you like to join me for a yoga practice on the Heiau tomorrow morning?"

"Yeah, if you see me up at my camp, come get me," she answers effortlessly.

She's up and roaming about when he walks over to the Heiau early the next morning. She waves at him and he motions for her to walk down to join. From the middle of the three verdant Heiau terraces, there is a clear panoramic view of the ocean. Looking out towards the sea, the beach is on the far left and the valley stream tumbles down to meet the ocean on the right. It's the physical and spiritual center of Neverland. He knows this and is almost shy about leading her in a yoga practice there.

It's clearly not Melanie's first-time doing a yoga routine and her strong, limber body forms perfect poses. He tries not to get turned on, but watching her blond curls dangle over her tanned skin makes this a real challenge. Afterwards, he offers her breakfast and morning tea at his camp. The routine is déjà vu from what he practiced with Summer less than a week before. Tea turns into talking, then touching, and then kissing and lying down together. The midmorning sun keeps the warmth on their skin and she's not shy about letting her top slip off.

Her skin is simply amazing. The smoothness and tightness of it makes him want to lick her all over. He teases her nipples with his teeth as he holds her close with a hand around the back of her neck. He kisses her again, flipping her over on top of him. He squeezes her tight butt and pulls her towards him. Touch and kisses are still fluid, but heat is building and movements are becoming powerful and instinctive. He thrusts her upright so she's sitting on top of him. For a moment they just stare at each other in the blazing sun. He places her hand on his erection. A big black bee buzzes over head.

"You know, I shouldn't really be…" He silences her by bending her down slowly onto her back. Moving more slowly now, he kisses her down her side, to her belly button. Then he pulls her shorts and panties down just enough to skim his mouth over her peach fuzz. With just the slightest taste she squirms and releases a quick but audible chirp. She pushes him back slightly. He looks up and smiles.

"You really are a wild man, aren't you!" She says with a broad smile.

She pulls her shorts up and continues, "I really got to get back. My mom and sister are probably wondering where I am!…Not to say I don't want…" she swallows her words and he hugs her calmly without a word and watches her scurry away down the trail.

Mano falls back on his yoga mat and sighs. *She tasted so good.*

He avoids contact with her for the rest of the day, but he can't help but think of their racy encounter that morning in the garden. Then he thinks of Summer and his heart sinks. What is he doing? He doesn't know what to think or feel— pleasure or remorse? He decides pleasure suits him better and under the moonlight he makes a quick pass by Melanie's camp.

She's already in her sleeping bag out on the grassy terrace, lying awake staring up at the moon and stars. He forgets about Summer completely, and just lets passion flow freely. At first she's cautious, but as soon as she's wet and aroused, neither can hold back. They make love and hold each other tight all through the clear night. At dawn they decide to continue up in the valley.

"I know of a secret spot next to a pool where we could be just ourselves," Mano tells her. He packs his backpack complete with blankets and lunch and they escape up valley. The spot he takes her to is neither secret nor hidden, but it's a good spot next to a wonderful, natural swimming pool in the creek. Soon they're on top of each other again. This time, she's as loud as she wants to be with no one around. After they're both finished, she lies naked on top of him in the open air. Again the feeling of wholeness and comfort from sharing his love with a beautiful woman engulfs him. They giggle as they cuddle in their own little world. Their laughing stops abruptly when they both hear the crunch of a stick.

"Shush," Mano whispers.

"Did you hear that? Somebody's coming," Melanie mutters.

"Yeah, I hear voices on the trail. There's definitely somebody walking right up here," Mano confirms.

Then Melanie begins to recognize one of the voices. "That's my sister!" she squeals in a whisper. "And that guy that's with her, he's practically my uncle."

"What?" Mano swallows.

"Yeah, he must have just gotten here."

"Just be quiet. If we're quiet and don't move, no one can see us over this little rock wall." Mano assures her.

"What should we do, we're totally naked and they're headed right over here!"

"Just be quiet, they won't see us, they'll just walk right past."

"And if they do see us?" Melanie twitches.

"There's nothing we can do now. Just hold still and be quiet or they *will* see us!" The group of four walks past, including Melanie's sister and her family friend. They pause at the pools just above them, putting the two even more on edge.

"Look up over the wall and see what they're doing," Melanie whispers.

"It looks like they're taking their clothes off to jump in this big pool right here."

"What?" she gasps.

"If they swim over to this side, they'll surely see us." Not wanting to get caught in the act, Mano and Melanie's minds scramble for what to do.

"We are already naked, I guess we could just jump in the pool with them," Mano suggests. So in an awkward burst, they jump out from behind the wall and into the pool joining the four other naked tourists.

"Where did you come from?" they all ask.

"We were just hiding over there waiting for you guys to jump in, so we could surprise you," Mano explains casually. The *uncle* smirks and they all just giggle and swim in the water. The whole group then proceeds to have a giant fern costume party. It's an anything-but-clothes party, and everyone romps around wildly in costumes made of ferns, banana leaves, vines, and ti leaves. The lively crew adopts the fern fantasy for the rest of the afternoon. Now Mano is completely second-guessing the feelings he had for Summer and is somehow wondering if something could work out with this new barely 19-year-old fern fairy princess. He lets himself daydream as they walk hand in hand back down to the Heiau to catch the sunset.

They approach the Heiau still giggling. As they crest onto the top grassy terrace, Mano takes in a sight that makes his stomach churn. It's Summer and Natalie sitting on the middle level of the Heiau, partaking in an evening meditation with Ella.

He quickly retracts his hand and he and Melanie quiet their conversation. The group is still in meditation with their eyes closed. How are *the sisters* back already? It's barely even been three days, he thinks to himself. Now, he's in quite the situation. Summer has no idea about Melanie, nor does Melanie know that he was with Summer just a few days prior. He takes a deep breath and allows himself to smile at the irony of it all. The meditation ends and he approaches Summer, casually.

She tells him that she's super tired from hiking back in with a fully loaded pack, and she'll just have to wait to hang out with him till the morning. So the secret is safe for the rest the evening. Still, the situation Mano brought upon himself is on the brink of biting him in the ass.

He expressed love for both girls, but assumed it would never work out with either. Summer may cling to him and provide good love and company for a while, but she'll eventually want to go back to Canada and he'll likely be unwilling to chase her. Although Melanie is so hot and fun, he can hardly trick himself into thinking that their encounter could be anything more than a flash in the pan. After all, she's an island girl, and nineteen.

He hopes to somehow maintain relationships and not just screw it up with both of them. It would be hard to go back to Summer after being with Melanie. He is certainly more attracted to her. But to break Summer's heart after she hiked back in to be with him would be awful. It would crush him, too, because she is such a sweet girl.

All the sisters, all four of them would eventually find out everything, and he'd be regarded a scoundrel by all of them. He sighs. If only Mark were here, he'd figure out a way to make it work with both girls. But that's not him; he's a one-woman man. He needs to show his love to just one girl, the right girl, which neither of them is! Still, he should try to make it work with one of them, right? He doesn't want to be lonely on the beach all winter.

Talking to the heavens, he yells out, *'Oh Mama Kai, how you tease me! Not even two weeks here, and I'm praying on the Heiau for you to send me true love, to send me a woman. You send me two. Two goddesses! And how am I to have true love if I can't be true to either of them?'* His own impatience and promiscuity soured his wish. Will he now be punished for such disgrace?

He cannot go backwards, so he must rally forward. With Summer gone to bed with her sister, he continues the night with Melanie. Their passion deepens and he begins to dream of what it might be like to travel with her on the mainland. He's really just getting to know her. Maybe they could be together. He knows she is special. An incredible kisser. She tasted as sweet as a mango too. He lets himself be mesmerized just thinking of her in her banana-leaf outfit again.

The next morning the situation becomes more precarious. Both pairs of sisters show up to join him for his morning yoga routine on the sacred Heiau. Somehow he manages to keep it together and he leads a sound practice for all five of them. But when it's over, he doesn't even know whom he should invite up to his camp for tea. He scrambles and tells them all that he is going on a solo mission way up valley to look for papayas and other fruits to bring to the evening potluck. So he runs off, avoiding the dilemma altogether.

He stops at Grizzley's on his way up valley.

"Grizzley, you gotta help me. I think I just screwed it up with two amazing goddesses."

"Two goddesses? I thought you were with Summer!"

"Well, just the other day I met this girl Melanie and…"

"Melanie! I saw her! Man, super cute, She's a real hottie. You really got with her too?"

"Well…"

"Oh, I see how is, take all the ladies and don't leave any for the Grizz!"

"You know I'm on the lookout for a girlfriend for you too, Grizzley Bear!"

"Yeah I see how it is. I'm pretty much off the market, I guess."

"Oh, come on Grizz, just listen to me for a second. So far right now I still don't think Melanie or Summer knows that I've been with the other."

"So you really hooked up with Melanie?"

"Yes, just over the last two days, but Summer and I had such a connection that…I don't know, I feel so horrible."

"Well you've probably already screwed it up with her now." Grizz bursts.

"Just listen! So tonight's the potluck and I don't even know who to sit next to. I don't know how to tell Summer about Melanie. Or should I just try to forget about Melanie and go back to Summer?"

"Well Melanie is an *island girl*. I don't know if you really want to get involved with that kind of thing. She's young, too. You'd have the local boys all over you on the outside. But she's hot, and Summer is too." Grizz pauses, puzzled, then continues.

"I kinda thought Summer could be a real valley girl, like she'd really want to be here, you know." Grizz pauses again in contemplation. "I don't know what to tell you. I guess just don't stop having sex. That's where I screwed up. Once you stop you totally lose it you know. Look at me, I never get laid! Once I stopped, that was like…it. I totally lost my mojo or something."

"I don't care so much about getting laid, I just want to find true love," Mano replies disgruntled.

"Well if that's the case, then I guess try not to jump on every hot thing that walks in here!"

"Good advice, Grizz. I will definitely remember that the next time I'm cruising the beach. However, that's not going to resolve this twisted sister situation."

"We'll you're just going to have to blow one of them off and go with the other one, I guess. I dunno, unless you think they'd go for the whole threesome thing… pretty unlikely though."

"No, I don't think they're gonna go for that. That'd be a stretch, even out here in fantasyland."

"I guess you'll figure out who still likes you at the potluck," Grizz chuckles.

"Grizz, this is going nowhere. I'm going up valley, see you at the beach at sunset."

Grizz certainly twisted things up in Mano's head even more. Mano spends the rest of the day gathering fruit, trying to gather himself. He rallies his conscience and decides to cruise by Natalie and Summer's camp just prior to the potluck.

"Hey there, Captain Mano, check out these cool cards I got in town." Summer charms him.

"Are they the animal instinct ones or the inspirational spirit ones?" Mano jokes.

"Actually, this deck is called Ancient Deities. You wanna draw a card?" Summer smiles.

Mano sighs. What would his fate be? He takes the deck and shuffles it several times to clear the energy. He tries to set an intention, as both sisters look on. He truly wants his passion and love to be for good. He takes a deep breath and silently asks the ancient deities, *'Where should I focus my energy and love?'*

He draws the Jesus card. It reads, "Open your heart to love." It goes on to say that Jesus was a prophet that loved unconditionally. He loved all creatures great and small. He even loved those who hated and killed him. Mano's unsure if this answers his question. He ponders deeply about what the card means. He should accept love and in return love unselfishly without greed or desire, like Jesus did. He's no prophet, though, he muses. He's plagued by excessive desire for love.

Still, Mano doesn't really know what to do about the two girls, but the card certainly means something. Everything that happens here has meaning. He clears the deck and hands it back to the sisters.

Summer draws a card. Hers reads: *Let it go.* Mano gulps, and she looks confused. Natalie then shuffles the deck and draws. Hers reads: *Come out of the closet.* They all laugh at that one. He leaves them on this airy note to prepare his dish for the potluck, still carrying his dilemma.

Summer is such a sweet girl, but he cannot not shake his thoughts from his recent encounter with Melanie. She'd be less of a sure thing, and Summer would probably make a better girlfriend, but he knew he couldn't hold her in his heart. Why should he deceive her with his love? He didn't want to lead her on. Would either want anything to do with him once they found out?

One way or another it would all go down at sunset. Who would he be with and who would he be forced to burn? It sounded like some heartless TV drama. So shallow. So horrible, so without love at all!

How could he be a loving man and be like this? He shudders at the circumstances, the strange irony of it. A week ago, he was desperate for any woman and he readied himself to be a loyal lover. He certainly doesn't feel like the caring, compassionate man he previously considered himself to be. There was nothing left to mull over, he sighs. He might as well just be positive and try not to lose them both.

Mano shows up late to the potluck. Everyone is already circled around ready to bless the food. Melanie notices him first so he just goes over and sits next to her. Fate? That pretty much settles it. He hardly speaks to Summer, almost pretending like she isn't there.

That was dumb, he later decides. He tries to bounce back to her after dinner when everyone is jamming around the fire, but she senses what's going on and gives him the cold shoulder. From then on, every time he sees her he feels ashamed.

He spends that night with Melanie under the stars on the Heiau. That's the peak of their relationship right there. She eventually finds out about his prior experience with Summer, but she doesn't hold it against him. However, what little thread was spun of their blissful bond they formed in those first four days unravels in her remaining two weeks in Neverland. Their love withers even as he attempts to grow it. Of course, it isn't supposed to work anyway. She's a nineteen year-old island girl! She doesn't want to be made a princess in Neverland. She is just cruising.

When he tries to approach Summer alone the day after the potluck to apologize and explain himself, she shoots him down immediately, refusing to hear him, whatsoever. Even though they had known each other for less than a week, he feels like he crushed her open heart. The fact that she would likely close her heart more based on this experience is what bothers him the most. He really feels that love is meant to be open and shared. He remembers the Jesus card he drew and tries to spread love to his self and others unconditionally. Still it pains him that he cheated on Summer when he knew she really would have treated him well.

Chapter 19   It Is Written

Mano roams the valley alone, soul searching. The valley provides him with no more direction than Grizzley's conflicting words of advice. Desperate for direction, he decides to take up Melanie's mom's offer to do a spiritual card reading for him. He thinks of the whole thing as silly, but others who visited her had positive reviews. It could be worth a shot.

"I think you should totally do a reading with her," Sierra encourages him.

"She may act all hairy fairy when you talk to her, but as far as interpreting the cards and the signs, I think she knows her shit. Her reading for me was pretty spot on." she continues.

"But if she reads me, then she'll know everything about me and Melanie, and who I am."

"It's not like you hold back much anyways, Captain silly. Besides, she probably already knows everything about you and Melanie. She's psychic!"

"Yeah, she probably knows everything already. I just find it a bit weird, spilling out my issues and having my mind opened up and read by some lady who knows I had sex with her teenage daughter."

"Mano, this isn't Babylon, there's no conflict of interest here. This kind of stuff is totally fine." With that thought and his heart open to receive, he goes to the mom for a reading.

Patricia is a soft-spoken scatterbrained British woman just a touch older than Mano's own mother. She shares Melanie's curly long blonde hair, but her skin is pale and freckled and her eyes are a much lighter shade of blue.

The reading is just as magical and ambiguous as Mano expects. He asks about his typical dilemmas regarding love and the direction he should take with his life. He questions her about going back to living full-time in the outside world, or remaining in Neverland. He draws an assortment of animal cards including Buffalo, Tiger, Deer and Raven for his basic questions about love and life and direction. She interprets the meanings of the cards for him and suggests new things to ask to then clarify the questions with new cards.

After 10 or so cards are drawn that yield quite a mixed array of signals, Mano decides to change his approach. He decides to ask just one simple question.

"Where should I go this summer after the winter season here in Neverland?"

Patricia sits back and summons the spirits to give her an answer. She waits for a long time for a response from the heavens before finally speaking.

"You will find your answer in Peru. Before you can proceed to the next big step in your life you must first go to Peru. There you will find the answers you're looking for."

"Peru?" Mano repeats, confused.

"Yes, Peru." Patricia confirms authoritatively.

"Peru! Really?" Mano can't help but chuckle at the seriousness of her response.

"So, I have to go to Peru to find out what to do with my life. I have nothing to do with Peru, I have no real interest in going to Peru. Why do I need to go to Peru?"

"I don't know why exactly, that's just what the spirits told me."

"So, what am I supposed to do once I get to Peru?"

"You will find a shaman, a medicine man, and he'll teach you what you need to know."

"What? What type of shaman, and where will I find him? This all seems really far-fetched. Fly to Peru and find a shaman and do whatever he says."

"No, no, Mano. It's not like that. You have to pay attention to the signs and they will lead you to the right medicine man." Mano is still perplexed.

"Is there any way you can ask the spirits if there's anywhere else I can meet this medicine man? Maybe somewhere a little closer to home? Can I meet a shaman and learn *my lesson* on the mainland somewhere?"

Patricia sighs. "Well, let's see. We can try and ask if you can meet your medicine man some other place. Why don't you ask that question and draw another card and we'll see?"

He's surprised by her response, but without hesitation he reaches for the deck. He asks intently if he really has to go to Peru to find direction as he slips out a card. When he turns the card over the image surprises them both. It's the whale card!

"It is written, you must go to Peru!" Patricia exclaims as she looks up and stares into his eyes.

Mano swallows. Strangely he sort of expected the whale to come up somewhere in his reading. He was thinking about whales before he even touched the card even.

"You know about the whale song, right?" Patricia questions.

"Well, sort of. I know that male humpback whales sing underwater. I hear them here all the time when I'm swimming in the Ocean."

"Yes! Whales carry a unique song with them during mating season, and they return to the same spot across thousands of miles of ocean each year. It is said that their distinct song holds true and transmits great distances underwater. Through the constant medium of the seawater whales can communicate with each other. Their singing here can be heard as far as Alaska even. They are considered the most important animal in the ocean by the native Hawaiians and their song speaks the message of eternal truth." She looks directly into Mano's eyes to be sure she has his full attention before continuing.

"Since the whale holds the truth, the whale card means what is said to happen must certainly happen. Even more powerful than that, the whale writes the song and yours has already been written. You must go to Peru."

"Okay, I got it, I guess I really gotta go to Peru."

"Yes, and the sooner you can make the journey, the sooner you may find the answers and direction you are looking for."

"Got it. Cancel all other plans and go to Peru. Find Shaman, go on vision quest, and find the truth which will lead to happiness and fulfillment."

"Yes Mano," Patricia replies, ignoring his sarcasm.

"Then can I ride a whale back to the land of magic, back here to Neverland!"

"If that's what the shaman reveals, then sure!"

"So, what do you mean by 'follow the signs to get there,' exactly?" he asks, already disenchanted.

"Don't follow, but pay attention to the signs. You know. If you see something at random pointing towards Peru, don't take it for granted. Listen. Listen to the people too." He asks a few more questions and draws a few more cards, but none sing to him like the whale card. He receives a blessing from Patricia and continues back to his camp.

Sierra is there, lounging in her hammock reading a book when he arrives.

"So, how was your reading with Patricia?" Sierra draws out the sentence with a smirk.

"It went pretty well, I drew a lot of great animals and she communicated with the spirits for me. I drew the whale card so apparently I'm destined to go to Peru and have some vision quest with a shaman there in order to find my true direction in life."

"Peru vision quest? Sounds pretty intense."

"You know the whole whale thing! You can't really argue with what the whales sing, especially here! I guess I'm out there swimming with them so much that now they wanna take over and write my song." Mano laughs.

"The whales here are really special, maybe you shouldn't take it for granted." Sierra voices.

"I know, I know. I just still feel a bit lost— lost and craving love, still."

"So, Melanie isn't falling for your charm anymore?"

"Charm's not the problem, I'm just too intense for her. She's not ready for love, she's just cruising."

"Yeah, I know what you mean, I think most people here are just cruising." Sierra states nonchalantly. She and Mano just stare blankly at a pair of doves as they peck around their kitchen for scraps. Eventually, Mano breaks the silence.

"I'm going up to the bluffs to jam some guitar and talk to my whale friends about the upcoming Peru trip."

"I'll just be cruising in this here hammock." Sierra smiles.

On the bluffs, Mano looks out to the ocean and sees humpback whales breaching. They slap their tails and fins on the surface of the water with such carefree bliss. How lucky are they, not only are they the greatest creatures of the ocean, but they are also beholders of the truth of the earth. He wonders about the songs they write and sing for him and other souls beyond.

He chuckles to himself, thinking about the excitement Patricia released when trying to convince him to go to Peru to seek out his destiny. Maybe if he just listens to the whales here long enough he could understand the song that is written for him. He sighs at the next whale breach. Maybe he just needs to relax and cruise here on the beach and not get caught up worrying about purpose, love, and direction.

"Hey Mano, what are you doing all alone on this side of the stream? Let me see that guitar there, I recognize that ol' piece of work!"

"Yeah, it's the *Guava Infusion,* still rocking the guava infused sound from the bridge I fixed with a stick of guava wood last year."

Krazy Red takes the guitar and bangs out a lead from *The Dark side of the Moon* like it's nothing. Unlike most of the male permanent residents of the valley, Krazy Red managed to secure a nice goddess for a camping partner. Red notices Mano's state of contemplation and confusion and attempts to instill upon him some of his own outlaw wisdom.

"All I ever think about is pizza and sex. Pizza, sex. Sex, pizza, that's about it. Well, and the end of the world, of course. Throw in booze and some of the random drama that occurs around here, and there really isn't much more to think about. I can tell you're always thinking, Mano I could tell you were thinking hard when I saw you up here. That's why I came over and bugged ya. Just quit it! This is a simple place. Just think sex and pizza, that's it. Have good sex, make good pizza, and you'll be fine." They both laugh.

"Easy enough for you to say, you've got the best pie cooker in the valley and Bella's teenage titties to come home to every night." They both laugh again. But Red is right. Once you can just get a nice girl and hold on to her here, all you'd need to worry about would be pleasing her sexually and making a damn good pizza. Everything else requires minimal thought.

Chapter 20   Boat Launch

"I should have tried to paddle out with Q this morning. He must have left his spot on the perch real early," Mano mentions, amid the supply run discussion between him, Khan, and Sierra.

"I never saw him launch his boat," Khan comments.

"When I went to do yoga I noticed his stuff was gone. I talked to Mr. X and he confirmed it. Said he had a clean launch outta here, blasted out on calm seas," Mano confirms.

"Captain Mano, I thought you were the only North Shore winter kayak Captain," Khan chuckles.

"Apparently not anymore. I got to go out and get my boat just so I can prove myself and keep the Captain Mano namesake."

"Well, we've all got to go out, We should just all hike together," Sierra chimes in. Two weeks had flown by since the boat crash, and Mano, Sierra, and Khan were nearly out of food.

"Actually, I'm gonna paddle out with this guy, Kawika tomorrow morning if the swell is still down," Khan announces.

"What? Where is there another kayak, and who's Kawika?" Mano asks perturbed. He certainly believed he knew of all that's going on down on the beach!

"Yeah, there's another two-man kayak stashed down by surf camp. This guy Kawika has been holding it all winter for another guy, but apparently we can use it." Khan continues.

"Well, I wanna go out on the boat!" Mano whines.

"Well, I kind of already made a trade with this Kawika guy to get to paddle out with him, so I guess you're hiking."

"Oh, I see how it is, sneaky pirate. I better get my kayak back in here!"

"Oh, come on! The trail is beautiful. You can hike with me," Sierra suggests.

"Alright, alright, I guess I don't really mind hiking."

Khan's smile broadens. "So, we go tomorrow. We'll all meet up in town, get food and come back the next day."

"Deal." Mano and Sierra nod in agreement.

The next morning Sierra and Mano pack their backpacks and get ready to make the long trek out. Kawika is in the shore break launching the kayak when Mano looks up from his cup of tea.

"You gotta check this out Sierra! Come right now, this guy Kawika is about to get totally humbled!" Mano sees big sets coming and he can already tell that the novice Kawika is too far out to make any kind of retreat. He doesn't even bail off the boat before a wave catches him. The wave scoops up the kayak, then careens it down. Bam!

"You see that!" Mano shouts.

"Yeah he's getting totally worked!" Sierra acknowledges, as they watch Kawika get body slammed in the surf.

"I don't think he's gonna be ready for another attempt after that one," Mano commentates.

"You probably should go down there and try and help them," Sierra says, somewhat concerned. No sooner than Mano steps foot onto the sand does Khan run over to him.

"Captain, we need your help to launch the boat. Kawika nearly drowned trying to swim back in after he got hammered by that big set."

"Yep, trying to launch a da kayak wif-out Captain Mano in wintertime surf, brotha I could a told ya, dat's a bad idea." Mano spouts back to Khan impersonating pigeon talk. Khan smiles widely.

"We just need you to launch the boat, then we can swim out and paddle it fine from outside the break."

"Well, if I go out and launch, I'm on the mission. I'm paddling to town. I'm not just gonna launch and swim back in!"

"Well," Khan stutters.

"My backpack is already packed. Kawika can just take it and hike to town and I'll take his stuff which is already on the boat."

"I don't mind hiking at all, that sounds fine," Kawika responds humbly.

"Alright, Captain. See if you can get us out of here!" Khan bursts.

Khan and Mano hold the kayak in the whitewash and wait for a window to launch, then Mano jumps in and pumps the paddle through the water and shoots right out through the break to the outside at the perfect moment in the lull. Khan swims out to meet him and off they go.

"Captain, I'll tell you that was style there! You ripped right through those waves, made it look easy. You the man, Captain!"

Khan and Mano paddle steadily together like two true watermen and they land on the protected bay beach in Babylon like pros, surfing the boat to shore right in front of the lifeguard tower. Even the local surfers size them up, impressed. Nobody paddles the North Shore in the winter!

In town everything happens seamlessly. Khan calls and finds out a boat drop is happening the next morning, so he and Mano hustle to go buy food and drop off bags. Of course, Sierra and Kawika aren't off the trail yet with Mano's backpack, so Mano has to borrow cash from Khan to buy two hundred dollars of food. Somehow they don't all connect back until the next morning. But the two groups reunite and Mano and Kawika switch back backpacks. Khan reunites with his daughter and convinces her mom to let him take her back in on the boat drop with The Pro. The tried and true sea captain is now back in action after the boat crash. Mano paddles the kayak back in solo, weighed down with a hundred pounds of food. Sierra and Kawika will likely be back in off the trail in a few more days.

It's a smooth solo kayak landing back on the beach. Mano is back home after less than forty-eight hours in Babylon.

Chapter 21   From Russia with Love

Who is this guy? He looks like a real character. Mano thinks to himself instantly when he catches a glimpse of a blond buff man up at the Sanctuary. Mano could just tell at first glance this newcomer is more than the typical mainland tourist; he's a real *character* worth getting to know. Some people just have a look that screams, *I didn't just come here just for the photos.* He notices the muscular man sitting around Sanctuary fire making friends with Kaholo and Thomas. He still can't get past the obvious. This guy is ripped! He's built like a bodybuilder, yet lean like a boxer.

"Hello, I am Dmitri. I come from Siberia," he announces in a heavy Russian accent, as Mano walks over to him. Fascinated, Mano, Kaholo, and Thomas probe into his background. It turns out that Dmitri really was a Siberian bodybuilder. In his twenties he even trained to be on the Russian Olympic powerlifting team. Although he said he once dead lifted eight-hundred pounds, he didn't make the cut. His story continues as the trio stare at his rippling muscles in amazement. After he gave up his bodybuilding dream, Dmitri got into acting in Russian action films, but he was always cast to play the part of the guy who rarely spoke and always got killed early on, so he gave that up too. He went to California, married a Mexican girl, something didn't work out with her, and now he's here. In a sense, it didn't really matter where he was, Dmitri the yogi is just living in the moment. He is living in the present and this is where he was supposed to be right now, here at the Sanctuary kitchen in Neverland. Mano still had to ask how a Siberian bodybuilder found his way to this remote beach on this most remote Pacific island.

'In California I heard of this place, and I just had to come here.'

Typical answer. Mano can't help but think of what it must take to feed this guy. Like most, he hiked in with just a small backpack of supplies, probably only two days worth of food.

"Can you believe this trail you guys take to get here? When I saw those cliff parts I almost turned back." Dmitri describes his frightening and humbling journey to the inside.

"Dude, I've seen little old ladies carry twice as much as you down that trail. I mean, you look like freakin' *Thor*. If people saw you turning back, nobody would come!" Kaholo erupts, sending both Thomas and Mano doubling over laughing.

Dmitri is welcomed into the group. His simple childlike silly charm makes him more than likable. He manages to fit in just fine with the eclectic bunch. He enjoys beach life and *loves* living simply and freely in the present moment. He's helpful too— almost too helpful. However, Dmitri is not an initiator like Khan. He sorely needs someone to instruct him. Otherwise, he'd still just *'be in his moment'*. Everyone is puzzled trying to figure this out. After all, most came to this place to seek freedom from the oppressive rules and order of the outside world. Dmitri doesn't think to plan or prepare— he doesn't feel the need to. Dmitri isn't inclined to set up a camp of his own, he'd rather serve those who could care for and direct him. Many might see Dmitri as a burden or even a hindrance, but Khan, on the other hand, sees him as an opportunity. In Dmitri Khan found his ultimate tribe member. A friendly six-foot four Russian bodybuilder who actually wanted to be told what to do.

Overnight Dmitri becomes Khan's right-hand man and indentured servant, so to speak. He's enlisted as a *warrior* in Khan's tribe. Dmitri totally loves it, and Khan is delighted. Dmitri could haul water and firewood, cook, set-up camp— he'd do whatever Khan asked, and he never complained. Dmitri was completely elated to serve Khan and his tribe for the simple exchange of food, shelter, and companionship. Even Grizz couldn't quite figure him out.

"I don't get it. He just follows Khan around and does whatever he says. Is Dmitri just stupid or something?" The same thought was kind of in the back of everyone's head, but Grizz is the only one brash enough to just announce it, straight up.

But maybe instead of being big and dumb and gullible, he so advanced in his own present state of being that he *could* just *'be'* in Khan's tribe. No one could really figure him out for sure. The Russian's *'in the moment'* essence is baffling, yet also so strangely appealing, that he becomes the highlight of many conversations. Could it really be possible for an intellect be so free of ego? Is Dmitri an example of present bliss attained? Or is he an example of ignorance is bliss?

Even tourists take notice. Random People would stop by Sanctuary and ask what the Russian was up to. Usually the answer was simple. Find Khan and you'd find Dmitri, usually carrying something for him.

When he wasn't assigned to cooking or load carrying duties, he'd take part in Khan's warrior training regiment. They'd build elaborate hideout camps and drum and chant Khan's warrior anthems. To most, it only seemed like they were just acting tribal, being boys in the fantasy realm of Neverland. However, when Dmitri charms a sleepy monk seal into a head bobbing dance with his off-beat drumming, some start to begin to believe that he too is connected to the magic of the island. Maybe he is even more *in tune* than he realizes himself. The way he sat on the beach and played for the seal, and the seal just crawled right up to him and smiled into his eyes. It wasn't just coincidence; it was much more. *A genuine understanding?*

One day, Dmitri's carefree, living in the moment attitude, gets himself into a fair bit of trouble. He clambers through thorny lantana bushes on some Khan mission and ends up covered in tiny abrasions. He then decides to climb a large mango tree up in the valley to reach some premature fruits. The noxious mango sap from the tree limbs rubs into his open cuts and causes an allergic reaction. For some, mango sap can be only mildly irritating, but Dmitri develops a mango rash that worsened to full body hives.

And Dmitri being Dmitri, itches them. He itches his hives wildly and the welts spread and blister. The blistering hives cover his armpits and inner thighs — and even his face.

'Don't itch it, just put the pulp of the noni fruit on it,' Some insist.

'Jump in the ocean, and rub aloe all over,' others recommend.

'Just put aloe and ti leaves all over, and bathe in the cold stream.'

Dmitri tries every hippie remedy suggested and only gets worse. Even the aloe has an adverse effect. Maybe he is allergic to aloe too!

No antihistamine is strong enough to clear Dmitri's horrible reaction, either. He's incapacitated for days while the sores blister grotesquely. His face becomes horrific. The once handsome bodybuilder is now a hideous gargoyle. But despite the horribleness of it all, Dmitri keeps a great attitude. Not once does he even consider leaving Neverland to seek real medical attention. He plays the Djembe drum and sings his heart song to distract himself.

Just to be in the moment, like a child pure and free.

Just to be in the moment like a child let it all go.

Dmitri really is like a child. Even covered in sores, others can see the beauty in his childlike present state of peace.

"I just want to make peace with the mango tree," he announces, humbly. So Dmitri ventures up into the valley to *talk* to the very mango tree that poisoned him.

Although he had been warned not to eat mangos because that was likely what caused his allergic reaction, he eats them anyway. He just wanted to *'make peace with the plant.'* Not good. The festering sores around his mouth become more inflamed and he can't help but touch his face. Then he touches his genitalia. The inflammation that spreads there has him scratching himself all night. Even the most disciplined yogi cannot remain unfettered. The next morning he pleads to Khan for help, showing him his swollen genitalia.

"My balls are like baseballs." Dmitri announces, indiscreetly.

Khan comes straight to Mano with news of Dmitri's plight.

"Captain, I need you to paddle Dmitri out of here. There's no way he can walk the trail. I've seen his balls and they're even worse than his face. He needs to get out of here and get medical help quick!"

So Khan and Mano ready Q's kayak for launch. Dmitri needs help and it's up to Mano to get him out of there. Luckily, the swell is down and the launch is smooth. But sore-covered Dmitri refuses to wear clothes in the boat. He won't even put on his sarong, claiming his balls are too chafed to have anything touch them. He simply ties the sarong around his neck for the whole journey to the outside world.

Halfway to Babylon the trades pick up, but the Siberian paddles strong. Strong, but not steady. His paddling rhythm mimics his offbeat drumming and his broad shoulders and bulky upper body make the kayak extra tippy. The boat shifts drastically with each heavy paddle stroke.

"Keep a steady rhythm and try not to lean so much every time you paddle," Mano shouts, nervously. Mano starts to chant a Khan song and encourages Dmitri to focus.

"Be like a warrior," Mano declares. This seems to help as they teeter-totter forward in the headwind. Then a gust catches them and Dmitri wobbles and leans. There's no counterbalance from Mano and the two-person kayak overturns. Splash! They are both in the water hanging on to the flipped boat in the choppy waves.

"You never said we could flip!" Dmitri gasps, flailing in the sea.

The boat is upside down in the middle of the ocean! This had never happened to Mano or Dmitri before. But the kayak is a self-bailing sit-on-top, so they simply flip it back over and climb back aboard. Somehow the ill-fated duo manages to reach the take-out beach in Babylon without a second capsize. Captain Mano prepares for another crash-landing.

"Okay Dmitri, when we land in Babylon the first thing you need to do is put your sarong on! You hear me? As soon as we jump out of the boat and pull it to shore, untie your sarong from your neck and put it on. Better yet, have the sarong in your hand ready when we land. You can't be running around naked in Babylon, especially all rashed-out like you are!"

Mano times the sets coming in like an expert boatman and they land the boat right up onto the sand.

"Put your sarong on, Dmitri. There are tourists on the beach!"

Mano watches in dismay as Dmitri struggles to untie the sarong from his neck, fearing that the lifeguards may be watching the whole scene.

Miraculously, nobody notices a naked, flailing, hive-covered Russian bodybuilder, right in front of the lifeguard tower. They aren't even questioned. The duo hitches a ride to town and Mano tells Dmitri that he must get medical help. Somehow Dmitri still believes he can get better on his own and he refuses to go straight to the clinic. Instead Mano drops Dmitri off with some Russian friends of his and they take him to the doctor.

"Get better Dmitri! See you back in Neverland." Mano yells as they drive away.

Chapter 22   Classic

Mano looks across the bluffs, taking in the panorama of the setting sun. His gaze catches on *her* in the afterglow. Just a glimpse of her silhouette sends a tingling feeling down his spine that prompts him to look away. He's enchanted, so he glances at her again. The beautiful topless blond had just sat down on the edge of the bluffs to take in the sunset as well. Alone she sits paying no mind to the thirteen people laughing and playing music nearby. Mano can't shake the tingly feeling; he's more than intrigued. Her aura enchants him, and the fading light makes the encounter feel like a dream. Should he go and talk to her? He teeters on edge. He's not intimidated, she just seems so *in the moment,* in her own moment, so he turns to join the rest of the group. A half moon is up and beaming down bright as the sun's afterglow withers to darkness.

They had started an LSD trip, and already his senses are heightened. Time and space begin to morph with the fading light, as he tries to tune into his surroundings, into Mother Earth.

Some new guy off the trail dosed 13 or 15 of them on the bluffs at sunset. Mano almost didn't take his, but he decided that if Dmitri took his, then he might as well be *'in the moment'* too. The situation certainly caught him by surprise. He didn't at all prepare for a journey, but maybe it wasn't for him to decide anyway. The moment felt right and the energy of the group seemed pure and clean. So down the rabbit hole they go. Together, and on their own, they transcend into a world within a world.

Mano tunes into the sound of the ocean. He hears and feels the waves pounding against the rocky coast. The beating of the ocean swell becomes the pulse of his heart. To him, the rhythmic churning of the swell symbolizes the power of life and death. His thoughts, his feelings surrounding life, love, and death echo in his brain for the rest of the night. He curls his toes into the earth to feel her depth. He feels the grass beneath his feet. He hones into her, connecting to the center of the Earth herself as he feels her pulse and breath with each thundering wave. The heartbeat of Mother Earth rises and falls with his chest. The connection he feels is so deep, it's intimidating. He pulls away from Mother Earth and tunes into the group. He can feel the energy like heat waves radiating from everyone around him.

She's not looking for company or dinner— Mano can feel without asking when he sees *her* walk toward him from the other side of the fire. He can sense *her*. Not clearly, but he senses that she's intrigued. She offers a smirk and asks him who he is.

Taken aback by her approach, he contests, "Well, a better question would be, who are *yooou?*" Mano exhales, mocking the caterpillar from *Alice and Wonderland*.

"Well okay, mister," she teases with the same smirk, perhaps attuned to his strangeness. "I'm Heidi, but you can call me Classic!"

She extends her hand forward and he kisses it with utmost delicateness.

"Classic, huh? Like classic cars, classical music, classic what now?" Mano puffs.

"Just Classic." She smiles.

"We'll then, Classic it is! They call me Captain Mano," he proclaims with a grin.

"Captain Silly Mano," another voice speaks up from across the fire.

"Well, Captain Silly," Classic announces cheerfully, "I've got to get back to my camp on the beach, but I hope to see you again sometime."

"I'm sure we'll be seeing each other soon, Miss Classic." he stutters, but manages a casual wink.

She tramps off. Mano's working on trying to lighten his approach, so he's happy to let her go, besides he and the whole Sanctuary crew are tripping.

"Ooooh, Classic!" Gaia snickers, sensing Mano's interest.

"She's probably hiking out tomorrow," Mano exclaims, attempting to throw out any lingering thoughts of her so he can continue connecting with Mother Earth.

Mano decides to volunteer for a water run and fill up some jugs for the group. It's no surprise, he's already super thirsty! By the time he gets down to the creek he can feel the acid take hold, but he can tell the small dose isn't going to last all night. Mano's a touch relieved at that. He feels he can handle tripping for 4 or 5 hours, but an all night psychedelic excursion seems beyond his current energy level.

"What's going on up there at Sanctuary?" A couple asks him from the riverside camp.

"It's Leia's fifth birthday party, and we are all dosed!" Mano exclaims, still in caterpillar voice. They chuckle and wish him well on his excursion.

Back at the Sanctuary it seems like the rest of the group is catching up to him. Khan is hammering on the drum and Keith is wailing on his guitar and singing. Thomas has five pots of five different dishes and coffee going at once on the Sanctuary fire pit, and is calling out orders for more wood. Another couple is off on the *Prawn Team*, trying to spear freshwater prawns in the stream while tripping face. Others are dancing around and hula-hooping in the firelight. Still feeling the pulse of the waves and the rhythm of the earth inside him, Mano seizes a Djembe drum and starts yelping and hammering away. His hands spatter rapidly as he releases the energy of an animal running, through the tightened skin.

He's in his own world for a moment, but he lets his rhythm slow and allows himself to rejoin the energy of the group. He hears and feels the energies around him as his deeper sense of feeling picks up on the vibrations from the bodies beside the fire. Personalities are unmasked and feelings are out in the open. Khan's fire is felt through his drumming. A good energy builds within the group as chanting and singing and drumming start to come together.

Soulful rhythms and words erupt in freestyle fashion. Mano's mind is so warped that he can't hold a conversation, but somehow he can sing and rap from the heart. The music controls the pace and the mood. Heart energy is released with each sacred note. A girl named Sofia takes the guitar and instantly all divert their focus to her. A new song. Her smooth, seductive voice carries the group into a daydream. They all feel and even for a moment live her daydream of being singer in a band as a young girl. The loud, soulful music livens the atmosphere and allows each to release. Two hours in the group is more alive than ever.

Everyone takes his or her turn singing or rapping and releasing soul feeling through music. Keith takes everyone to the *Dark side of the Moon* and back. Khan drums to draw out tribal energy and has people stomping their feet, dancing wildly like monkeys. But Sofia simmers the team to a hush with her calm, bold voice and smooth strumming.

Mano turns to Keith. "I wanna try to play guitar, but I don't know if I can right now. I don't know if I can even hold it or hold a rhythm."

"Just don't look at your hands. Don't try to look at where the strings are. Don't even try to sing a song. Just play, and sing to what you are playing," Keith coaches him.

His warped mind catches on the neck of the guitar and how it feels bent and twisted in his grasp. The guitar looks and feels like a foreign object, he can hardly hold it. He tricks his mind by closing his eyes to start. Mano tries not to think and just lets the words and chords flow. He finds the groove and plays. He smears the cords at first unsure of himself, but he fights through and finds his space in the music, releasing an impromptu psychedelic jam. Each chord, each note, vibrates through the instrument and into his own heart to resonate with a feeling. The sensation is in part jarring, but some notes feel so spot on, that he's inspired into singing. He lets his heart sing and releases unpredictable words. It's not the words that matter to him, it's just the sounds, the feeling coming from his body and soul. He can 'feel' the music even before he can hear it. Experimenting with music in this altered state of consciousness is incredible.

Eventually, his fingers tire and he loses his grip, loses the groove. He hands the guitar back to Sofia, and she and Keith bring the group and the groove back. The fire flickers and Mano reads into every soul through their faces surrounding him. Just slight inferences of truth, but powerful revelations of character. He feels Sofia's childhood pain of a father who didn't care, but also her joy from being a self-made woman. He feels Khan's desire for family from him being estranged by his actual one. He feels his hunger for control, too. Again, Mano wonders what they see in him. He can feel his own truths weighing upon him. The beauty and ugliness he carries inside. He quivers at the thought of his own ingrained culpabilities.

"We got boilage, put em' in!" Thomas instructs. They all watch as the living creatures recoil and their bodies quake in the billowing bubbles. Mano swears that he can hear the prawns scream as they touch the boiling surface. He knows it's just in his head, but he can hardly watch because he can *feel* them so strongly. Their death for the group's sustenance does not seem unjust though, and he feels humility, not disgrace in taking the life energy from the prawn. The mana of the valley fills his body and he tastes not just the flesh of the prawn, but the energy of the valley through it. Life, death, love!

Thoughts dissipate and his fire sinks into his chest where his heart still pounds with the pulse of the Pacific. The feeling of the pulse of Mother Earth is so intense that Mano must leave the group by the fire. He walks in the moonlight to the Sanctuary garden and sits to tune in by a small rock-bordered garden within it shaped like a heart with peace-sign divisions through it. The peace-heart garden. He sits in lotus and allows himself to feel the pure energy of the garden around him. Away from the noise of the group, the beating of the Pacific on the cliffs pulses louder and fuller than ever. He closes his eyes once again and connects with the earth.

He can feels a feeling of love through the peace-heart garden. He connects with the vibrant affection of Kaiko and Pulani that bloomed there last winter. Some of the seeds Kaiko sowed in this little garden patch a year ago managed to grow and reseed themselves this winter. The tiny verdant sprouts represent their love to Mano now. They forged their bond in love here in this valley and carried it with them. Mano feels a powerful connection to their love and to the land where they first grew it. He asks the valley again to send him true love, which would be the peace within his heart. Mother Earth wants him to have true love— he can feel that, too.

All night he is restless coming down from the trip. But he embraces his loud heartbeat in cadence with the crashing waves. Love, like the ocean waves, pulses in his heart and it feels good.

'It's a new day, a new dawn, it's a new life, for me,' Mano sings with the birds the next morning. He feels whole and inspired, but still lonely. His morning routine is slower than usual. He makes his way down to the Heiau for yoga by himself. He tries to practice without being deterred by his lingering thoughts from the night before. It's hard to deduce if what he thought and felt last night was real or just drug-induced fiction. He shakes himself from the trance. Of course everything he feels is real. After all, this island does not permit fakeness.

Back at his camp his mind catches on his encounter with Classic at the start of last night's journey. How she captivated him at first glance at sunset. He sighs. Could she be the one? His soul mate. He lets his impression of her tickle and excite him. *But she could be leaving today, down the trail already.* Even if she were still here, she could be lackluster or mean, or not interested in him altogether. She could be amazing, too. But how could he ever know if he simply lingered in camp? He stops touching himself and sits up to try to think about her honestly. He reconsiders the glow she possessed when she sat alone on the bluffs. She is a special girl— he knows that much. He must at least try. Go down to the beach and find her. He pauses to calm his excitement. First, a song to calm this pent-up passion. He decides to sing a song he wrote about loneliness, just for the birds and whales to hear of course.

Hello, Hello

I guess I'm all alone

When you're alone

You breathe alone

When you're alone

You grieve alone

No one to walk beside you but your own shadow

Shout and all you hear is your own echo

Hello, Hello

Is there anybody home?

Won't somebody just hold my hand

As I cross this distant land?

I'm too far gone

To still…be alone

Be on my own

Hello…hello!

"Hello," A voice giggles out of the bushes. It's certainly not his own echo.

"Hello?" he questions the mysterious someone.

"Well, hello there, Captain Silly!" Classic erupts, emerging from a side trail bright-eyed.

"Well, what a surprise, Classic. What have you been up to on this beautiful day?"

"Oh, just swimming, watching the rainbows and dolphins, the magic all around!" She twirls around like a fairy.

She dances about so lightheartedly, so dreamily, that Mano nearly falls over in a daze. She sits down next to him and they lounge in his camp in the shade. Soon their conversation steers towards deep topics. Religion and spirituality, love and societal expectations, even magic and earth's mysteries.

"So you said you came to this place because you saw it in a dream. Why do think your dream led you here?" He digs into her story, fascinated. She clasps his hand, as if wanting to transmit her energy to him as well as her words.

"Well, I'm a surfer and I was daydreaming of beaches. I envisioned this beautiful beach surrounded by verdant cliffs. I could picture it in my mind. Then I had a real dream about the beach, the exact one I was daydreaming about. I was swimming to the beach in the dream. I was swimming with the whales. They were like, escorting me." Classic stops and reflects as if trying to remember a feeling or something from the dream.

"Really, swimming alongside the whales?" Mano interjects.

"Well, not right next to me, but when I'd look up, I could see the splash from their tails and fins and I could hear them. I remember I could hear them guiding me. I could hear the whale's song, and I knew I must swim with them here, to the beach. You know about the whale's song, right?"

Mano chokes, remembering his meeting with Patricia just over a week ago. "Uhh, yeah, I hear them singing almost every time I go underwater past the break."

"No, do you know, *the meaning?*" She pulls his hand in close to her chest and looks out over the water.

"Uhh, you mean, '*it is written.*'" Mano stutters with a tinge of cynicism.

"Yes, exactly!" They both pause, embracing a moment of deeper understanding looking into each-other's eyes. Classic breaks the silence and gets up. Mano blinks to pull himself together.

"Let's continue this story about following the whales down at the beach." Mano suggests.

"That's a great idea, Mano." She offers her hand and the two walk together. There's something noticeably special about just holding her hand, he decides. Once settled on the sand, he prompts her to continue the story of her dream.

"So there was something in the water. I could feel movement underneath, like something swimming by me. It startled me and I stopped swimming and looked around at the surface and the beach was gone, it was just open ocean all around me. I started really panicking, really freaking out, and then I woke up." Classic exhales in release.

"Wow, so you think you were right out there with them?" He points out to the ocean where the whales are swimming and singing just beyond.

"Yeah, right out there." she animates before diving back into her own thoughts, then looks straight into Mano and continues.

"Well, I still knew just what the beach looked like from my dream, so I went and tried to find a picture of it on the Internet. I was Googling tropical beaches with whales and a bunch of different photos came up. Then I saw the photo of this beach, here, and it was it, the one from my dream, exactly."

"So you had to come here!" He pulls her hand to his heart this time.

"Yeah, at the end of the holiday season in Wisconsin, I bought my ticket to the island and hiked out to the beach. You must think I'm crazy."

"That's pretty par for the course as far as stories of how people get here. I've heard of more than a few people having a vision of this beach in a dream."

"Isn't it all so amazing! Synchronistic, intentional, even!"

"Magic!" Mano smiles, squeezing her hand.

"Do you believe in magic, Mano?"

"Absolutely. Once I didn't believe, but now I do. Now I am certain that this is the most magical beach in the world." He goes on to tell her his theroy that magic perpetuates in this place. He explains how when people's guards are down, and intentions are pure and clear, inspiration soars and magic is allowed to happen. She lightheartedly agrees and continues to tell of her journey to the island, and her trek to the beach.

"But why? Why do you think the whales led you here, and why did *you* come?" He hopes he already knows her response for this one.

"Well, I had to get out of Wisconsin, for several reasons. I had to get away and find myself on my own."

"You know why the whales come here?" He looks into her eyes and pauses. She smiles and swishes her sun-kissed hair over one shoulder.

"I guess you better tell me, Captain Silly!" she giggles.

He tells her how he asked the same question to some old-timers up at the Sanctuary on his very first trip in. He swallows and repeats verbatim what he heard.

"This is where they come to make love." he releases in the same calm, low voice he heard years ago.

"If you believe in magic, do you believe in love?" Mano continues.

"Sure I believe in love, but love can't be forced. It just happens."

"What about love at first sight?" he continues curiously.

"I don't know about that. Love is a tricky thing, you know."

Mano changes the subject back to magic. They talk about each of their experiences with coincidences, fate, and the mystic here on the island. How they each came to accept and follow the signs that led them to Neverland.

Even after much discussion, neither can really enumerate this idea of magic, although they each *feel* more than just some understanding of it. Maybe one of the valley's elders can provide some more insight to explaining this mystery Mano ponders. Immediately, Ella comes to his mind. He thinks about her claims that she could communicate with the ancients of the land. Could she explain this magic? He voices this thought to Classic.

"Have you met Ella, the older Australian lady here at the beach?"

"Isn't that her over there walking towards us right now?" Classic points out.

"That's classic, Classic! See what I mean about synchronicity!"

They both look over towards Ella as she approaches, casually walking along the shell-line.

"We were just talking about you!" Mano tells Ella when she reaches them.

"Well, here I am," she replies in her sunny Aussie accent.

Mano tells her about their discussion of love and magic, hoping for some sort of a lead-in for him. Ella can tell that he's interested in this new tourist girl and she does make an effort to encourage her to stay longer than she's planned at the beach. Of course, she'd encourage any good soul to stay.

"You know the formula for magic, right?" Ella probes Classic, then turns to Mano. "I know you know it, Captain Mano." He stares at her mesmerized in the midday sun.

"Well, it's a simple formula anyway. Beauty, plus love plus joy make magic. Beauty like in these beautiful surroundings, or the beauty of her." She says staring right at Classic then continues.

"Love in the purest of form, and joy. Happiness and jubilation for what you see, allow you to believe, and then comes magic. It's really that simple. We can all see it. You got to have these three things for magic to happen. Then it's easy!" Mano and Classic nod in agreement.

"With people opening up to beauty, creating joy, and extending love, magic happens. I see it all the time. And now with the world changing, I believe that there will be even more magic all around!"

"Do you think that it makes sense that I saw this place in a dream...Like I was meant to come here?" Classic asks Ella.

"Absolutely! Of course, even if you didn't dream it at all you were still meant to be here now."

They all start to smile at the serendipity of it all. 'You should be here now.' What a great idea! Ella waves goodbye and continues along the shell-line without another word.

"Let's jump in! It's already getting hot, and all these thoughts of love and magic and living in a fantasyland are making me even hotter." Mano proclaims, feeling the need to release his own excitement.

They swim together in the cool Pacific. They do not hear the whales because they stay in the channel and just let the whitewater wash against their naked bodies. They feel Mama Kai's power and rhythm letting themselves get tossed by her waves. They are water creatures destined by forces of magic to be here. They are dreamers living in a dream world. They both followed their dreams to this place and are now not just experiencing the magic there— they are a part of it. What could become if they let their beauty, love, and joy flow freely? What could manifest if they combined their love and joy together? They embrace under water and let themselves wash to shore together in a wave.

Out of the water, they feel more naked. But still they walk along the shell line together as clouds dance overhead. Mano's drawn to a small patch of sand illuminated by a burst of sun through the clouds. He kneels down in the tiny patch of warmth no bigger than him. He fingers the sand and feels a shell. He feels it in his fingers and without even looking at it, he hands it to Classic.

"A gift from your whale friends," he smiles. It's a rare bumpy cowry shell with a beautiful peach colored hue. Did the light lead him to it? She holds the shell against her nipple and smiles.

"Thank you. You naked sun-god," she giggles.

"Miss Classic, would you care to join me for lunch?" Mano offers politely. She agrees and follows him up to his camp at a lookout just above the beach. Mano continues their conversation of what it may be like to escape society and live completely removed in Neverland.

"Here you can do almost anything you want and you don't have to worry about time or money." Mano advocates. Classic contemplates the thought of escaping it all. *Could this fantasy be real? She's thinking it.* Mano can sense it.

"But, I could only manage to stay here forever if I had a partner, a lover." Mano adds smoothly, trying not to startle her. She tosses her hair back and chuckles.

"Love shouldn't be what limits you. You should just stay here because *you* love it. That's what I think," Classic declares.

"Do *you* love it here enough to stay?"

"Well I do love it here, but I love the outside world, too. I've only been here a few days, so I guess it's too early to tell." she responds, playfully.

"No fantasy is complete without love," Mano states plainly as he reaches to put some water on the fire for lemongrass tea.

They continue to talk and relax in the shade. He's trying his hardest to be patient, but he's anxious to make something happen, knowing well that Classic may stay just a night or two more. He pulls her in close for a kiss. Their lips touch softly and hold for a brief moment, but she backs away, not allowing either the full enjoyment of a first kiss. Feeling a bit awkward, he settles back and they just look at each other and smile. What does she really desire? He thinks to himself, unsettled. He feels excited but still awkward so he gets up and walks over to glance toward the beach.

He can see half of the beach through a view window Dmitri cut out through the trees for part of Khan's master development plan. Immediately, his eyes catch on a blue kayak paused just outside the surf break. It's Q and Kawika on the SS salvation!

"I can't believe it! They're here." Mano speaks aloud.

"Classic, it's a kayak! My boat, the SS Salvation American Spirit, it's here! Those guys are finally bringing it back in from town. They are trying to land on the beach right now! I've got to get down there, they must be nervous about the landing in the swell or they wouldn't be just waiting behind the waves like they are." he lurches, a bit overexcited.

"What about the tea?" Classic asks.

"Just leave the tea," he hollers preparing to scramble down to the beach to receive Kawika and Q landing with his boat.

"Wait." Classic pauses him as they shuffle down through the oleander.

She pulls him in for a real kiss this time. It's certainly more sensual, but her mouth isn't fully open. She's still holding back some.

"Well, that was better," Mano jokes as they hurry down to the beach.

Khan is already in the water by the time Mano and Classic get to the sand.

"It looks like Khan's going to help them land the boat," Mano comments. So he runs into the ocean naked in celebration to receive them. He swims through the breakers to the kayak to say hello and congratulate the team for bringing his boat in. He's elated, but Q is scared and seems more than ready for dry land. Q doesn't want to crash-land the boat on-board with Khan and Kawika so he decides he will just swim in through the break. Somehow Mano doesn't catch this passenger switch, and he swims back to shore as well.

Khan and Kawika time the landing perfectly and the boat doesn't even flip. By the time Mano gets ashore himself, Khan is already swimming back out to help Q, who seems to be having more than a bit of trouble swimming in through the surf break. Mano pays little attention. After all, Khan's there to help and probably Q just needs a swim coach anyways. It's not *that* big out there. Naked beach goers start to gather around, asking about the boat and the journey in. Mano inspects the kayak that he hasn't seen in almost a year.

All of a sudden, someone yells out that Khan needs help. Really? Khan? Mano turns back to the ocean to see both him and Q getting pounded in the whitewash from a huge set that just came in. Mano immediately swims out to them where they are still treading water in surges of heavy whitewash. Q is so panicky he is clawing at Khan, nearly drowning him as well.

By the time Mano gets out there the two of them are completely exhausted and Khan has moved away from Q. Not a good swimmer, Q is more or less doggy paddling, barely keeping his head above water in the whitewash. The rush of the next wave comes and pulls him under. He comes up gasping for air as he struggles to get his head above the foam pile. Mano tries to calm Q down and just get him to paddle toward him a bit. But Q's freaking out, calling for help, making minimal effort to swim to the beach at all.

After being pummeled by a half dozen waves Q's now coming up with less and less strength each time. Mano can see the fear in his eyes. Q's disoriented and his little confidence is drowned, knowing he's failing to make forward progress in the whitewash. Mano yells to remind him to duck as the next wave barrels over him. He comes up in even more of a panic. Without a rescue buoy, Mano decides he will try to push Q up into the coming surf so as to let the whitewater catch his body and push him towards the shore. Khan is spent and spitting up water, so Mano just motions for him to swim in. Mano and Q take a few waves together and let themselves be pushed towards the shore. By now Q is too tired to even keep his head above water in between waves.

"Grab onto my legs, I'm going to try to paddle you in," Mano instructs alternatively. Q cooperates and it works. After some of Mano's hard strokes through the whitewash with Q just holding on, they're both able to stand with their heads above water. Mano can see it in Q's eyes, he's thanking him with the look of a man who's been given a rare second chance. He helps pull Q, who can barely stand, onto the sand. Khan's collapsed on the beach, spitting up seawater and panting when they arrive.

"Dmitri's out there, you've got to go back out there for Dmitri." Khan spits.

"What?" Mano turns and sees the Russian getting hammered in the whitewash. Apparently, Dmitri saw Khan struggling and went out to save him, only to get caught in the rip along the channel and dragged into deep water himself. He's not as far out or as far gone as Q was, and Mano is able to swim out there and coach him in.

———

152

Both Khan and Q lie collapsed on the sand for ten minutes before getting up. The naked hippies who wouldn't dare swim out for a rescue thank Mano for his valiant effort.

"You're a hero," some claim.

"Q was done for, you totally saved his life!" Mano didn't think it was that big of a deal. Was Q really that close to drowning?

Khan, eventually comes around too. "Thank God you went out there, Captain!

"Props to Captain Mano for saving the day again," Andrew adds. "Oh, and you really looked good in front of the girl," he whispers to him with a smirk.

They all hang out on the beach for a good while. But instead of whisking away up valley hand in hand with her lifeguard hero, Classic just says she'll see him later. Apparently, she had already signed up with some other guys to get *spiritual healing* and *bodywork* done. Mano doesn't really understand her vibe, but he remains intrigued nonetheless. She went from all that serious deep conversation of love and life that morning, to a feather in the wind. Caught in limbo, he doesn't know whether to like her or not.

Who knows what she's after, if anything? Is she just a feather in the wind like most young girls that cruise here? He can't tell. His feelings are already out in the open as usual, she knew he wanted her, now he just has to wait. Ahh, how he hated waiting! And he can't help but remember how good she looked naked. A perfect surfer-girl body. Even if she isn't his soul mate, at least she could be his mermaid. He grabs his ukulele and tromps off to write a silly love song for Classic.

The song, *Water Signs,* comes together in an hour and a half spurt alone on the Heiau. Simple and cheesy as can be, but he still likes the way it sounds. He decides he could sing it to Classic. Why not? He'd sing it for her later that evening. She'll either like it, or it will be way too over-the-top, but that doesn't matter. Why should it? He wants to express himself and release. Open his heart to love!

He rushes down to the river mouth to get a fellow goddess's opinion. He runs into Keilani and tells her about the *classic* beach day he is having. Maybe she can offer some advice on the whole Classic situation. He tells her about how he is trying to be careful with his words, actions, thoughts, and love, but also the excitement and enchantment he feels. He explains to her how he felt when he first saw Classic during that sunset on the bluffs, and of the lustful desire he had for her that he could not shake.

He admires Keilani's loving spirit, but also her independence. She is not one to be held down by any man. She's a delicate woman that surely desires a man, but somehow she is just fine on her own. Out here, she seems at peace, alone in her hidden up-valley camp. She certainly doesn't seem to be needy for love like him. He plays his ukulele for her and she smiles an endearing, sweet smile that shows an understanding for his passion. He smiles back, and they share a special moment of appreciation of passion by two passionate people.

"Well, what do you think of the chords? What do you think of the chorus? I mean, *'Not just a wet dream'* is kind of cheesy, but I kind of like it."

"I like it, I really like it, and the chords totally work. It's great."

"Well, do you think I should play it for her?" Mano finally asks.

"Sure, play it for her, why not? The song is totally you, it's authentic Captain Silly Mano, of course you should play it for her."

"I don't know why, but I'm so excited about her. Maybe even in love with her."

"Don't get ahead of yourself now. Have you had sex with this girl already?"

Taken aback, he answers, "No, not even close. We barely even kissed today."

"Well here's my one bit of advice for you: if you really like her, take it slow."

"Yeah, I know, that's the way to go, take it slow."

"I know it's not really your style, but that's my advice."

"You have my word Keilani. With Classic, I'm taking it slow and smooth." He walks off back towards the Heiau.

"Good luck," she shouts behind him.

Ella is about to lead an afternoon meditation when he passes over the top Heiau terrace. He decides to join in so as to ground back into the earth before running into Classic again. As luck would have it, just as they are starting the meditation, Classic shows up, topless and radiant to join them. They all sink their roots deep, deep, deep into Mother Earth and find their own relaxed states of being. He works to purge all lingering thoughts from his mind and actually gets quite close to really reaching that pure meditative state. After less than an hour, they open their eyes to rejoin the fantasy they are living all around them. Each blade of grass, each breath, has life and meaning. They all watch the sunset on the Heiau together and he plays his new song, *Water Signs* for Classic. The sun glows pink and shoots golden rays from behind clouds before breaking free in its final plunge into the sea.

Mano takes it slow. Instead of an intimate candlelight dinner at his camp, they bring food up to the bluff top Sanctuary to cook with Khan, Thomas, Dmitri, Q, Sofia and the rest of the gang. He offers to walk her back to her camp near the beach, but she says she'd rather spend a night with him. They hardly kiss and just spoon a bit in their sleeping bags. After all, it had been an exhausting day.

The next morning they are both up early. Before he can cook her breakfast, she runs off to retrieve some stuff from her camp. She comes back with her backpack fully packed.

"I've been completely out of food for a day. I'm gonna hike out, re-supply, and probably hike right back in." she declares suddenly.

"What? You're hiking out now? We're just getting to know each other. I was just starting to like you," Mano jokes.

"Well, I'm out of food, I really should hike out."

"Don't be silly. You can stay here with me and eat my food — I've got plenty. Then in a week or so we can both hike out together and get more."

"No, no I can't do that, I can't just be eating your food."

"Well if you really feel that way, I'll sell you some food. I've got lots of extra quinoa and pancake mix right here. Whatever you need. You don't even have to hike out to go to the store."

"I have to go to town for other stuff too, you know. But I'll come back. I'll come back in like two or three days."

"Sure, that's what they all say. But hardly anybody comes back. Once you're out there you get so caught up in the mix it's really hard to get back. Believe me, I know. You should just stay. Stay a week," Mano pesters.

"I'm all packed up. I got to go, but I'll come back. I promise."

What else can he say? She's ready with her backpack on.

"Don't promise me anything. Just come back and have an amazing time here with me. Here, take some granola bars for your hike out."

She takes a couple of bars and tramps off. Maybe she is just a wet dream after all. He certainly isn't going to let any hopes of her coming back weigh him down. He sighs, then bites his tongue, feeling like he should've put the moves on her sooner. Taking it slow certainly didn't keep her interested. He tries to let it go completely, just another tourist girl in the valley of wandering souls...

'Valley of wandering dudes,' He huffs to himself in disgust. Still, he has no other woman to think about, so he thinks about her. He dreams about Classic and he counts the days. Two days, three days, four. After four days he decides he should begin to forget. Then on the fifth day Kona winds prompt him to make a town mission. He decided he was over her, but the placid ocean temps him to town anyway.

He has Classic's number so why not try to give her a call while he's out there. At least see where she ended up, just for curiosity's sake...

He runs into Dmitri when going to launch the boat, and he prompts him to reconnect with Classic.

"You should, Mano. Go and find this girl, this Classic, she is a good girl for you, I can tell. Yes, yes you will make good with this girl, this Classic."

So Mano dials her up while in town.

"You're in town by the bay, me too, I just paddled out, we should meet up for a drink." He asks eagerly.

Over cocktails, he asks her why she never made the trip back in. She claims that the classic difficulties of dealing with missed phone calls and e-mails and not wanting to hike back in the rain.

"Don't you want to go back and be with the whales like your dream called you to do?" he offers. She doesn't give a definitive answer.

It's almost sunset so Mano suggests that they continue their conversation over sunset beers on the bay.

So Mano and Classic watch the sunset together and hold each other close and kiss. She kisses him back fully and he tastes the essence of love. The light fades and they decide to walk back to town.

———

156

"You know, if you want to come back to Neverland with me you won't have to hike in," Mano suggests coyly.

"I just happen to have one seat available on the *SS Salvation* for one lovely lady. We could just pick up some more supplies and set sail by midday tomorrow. We'll be back in Neverland fully stocked for weeks by sunset." He's already daydreaming.

Classic cuts in.

"Well, all my stuff is at this guy's house on the east side of the island. And I don't know if I could really go back with you."

"Whoa, timeout. Who's *this guy*?"

"Oh, his name's Bucky."

"Bucky?" Mano says with obvious predisposition as her phone interrupts.

"Oh, that's him calling me right now." she laughs.

"So you're right here in town to pick me up? Yeah I'm here...Okay...I think I can hear your truck right now. I'm right here on the main road."

Mano can hardly believe what he's hearing.

He mumbles to himself, 'Bucky better not be some backwards-hat-wearing surfer driving a beat up truck with squeaky brakes.'

He sees the truck and doesn't even care to look at whoever's in it.

"Bye, Captain Silly." Classic hugs him half-heartedly and gets in. The truck rolls off, squeaking down the lane.

Ouch! He's totally crushed. Left on the side of the road for a 2-bit surfer named Bucky. He can hardly believe it. Then it starts to pour rain. It's dark, he has no tent, and it's pouring rain. With nowhere to go, he steps into the grocery store and just stares at the brightly colored vegetables. Classic!

Chapter 23   Ocean Outings

He should have just stayed in Neverland and ate granola bars. Mano huffs to himself. But he didn't. He had to go and chase down Classic. The whole Classic ordeal leaves a sour taste in his mouth. His lust for love left him sour. He's more than groggy after a wet sleepless night without a tent in Babylon. He is so sour and perturbed he can hardly handle a trip to the grocery store.

The whole Babylonian scene just annoys him. Incessant noise from cars and lawn equipment makes his ears ring. Everywhere he looks someone's either talking or texting on their phones. Somehow born out of months of purity in nature in Neverland, he feels easily into the life frequencies of those on the street. Just like he felt more exposed than ever, with his heart rhythm felt by those around him on LSD back in Neverland, he feels into people's thoughts and actions there in Babylon. In his hypersensitive state, he can feel inside the people there. The trip through town feels like an acid trip almost.

He can grasp it and try to tune in like a guitar riff to a vocal melody or a drumbeat, but he can tune things out, too. However he can't help but notice the difference in the flow between these people and the residents in Neverland. What he perceives just makes him sour and despise the Babylonian world. These hurried people seem all too careful with what they do or say. Guards are up as they go about day-to-day tasks, some fearful of displaying their true character. *It's all image*, he mouths to himself. Everyone is so caught up in themselves. Where's the love?

Even the smells he perceives are phony. Chemical fragrances bought on plastic cards from islands far away. One out of a dozen, or one in two dozen people he feels into seem to express their true self, emitting an aura that's not just a cover up. He feels like an alien amongst society. In the community where he just kayaked from, water flowed clean from the stream, and words and music came from the heart. Here, words could be deceiving and the music on the loudspeaker at the grocery store is simply tuned out.

He buys his vegetables, cheese, and chocolate and doesn't look back. It's a smooth ride back home with the wind switched to westbound trades. With wind at his back both ways, he feels that Mama Kai and the land, her Neverland, are still on his side. With every paddle stroke he feels closer to home. The whales sing their song of truth, waving him home with splashing fins as the beach comes into view.

The next day it's sun, surf, yoga, music, and home-cooked food as usual. Life is simple. Things aren't necessarily easy or predictable, but they are pure. Grizzley's left on a kayak mission west to search for shells at an even more remote pocket beach around the point. Khan and his tribe of minions are still holding down Sanctuary on the bluffs. Thomas is clearing trees and building terraces for a new garden up valley. Sierra is concocting a scheme to boat drop in a beehive to potentially double the honeybee population way up valley and improve natural pollination in the gardens. The valley winemakers, Rick and Lisa, just arrived back for the season and are eager to pop the top on a batch of banana wine they had been fermenting in their up-valley stash for nearly a year.

Cliff, who said he planned to leave the day the boat crashed, is still here. His latest kick is promoting large-scale bonfire parties on the beach. But where are Honu, Hitman, Charlotte, Rainbow, Kaiko, and Pulani? These crucial characters from the winter before would have to come back, right? It's almost March already. Maybe they wouldn't come back. Well, Charlotte wouldn't be back. She couldn't get a visa extension. Hitman is said to be hard at work in California. Kaiko and Pulani, now married are probably still in Mexico. No one had a clue what happened to Rainbow and Honu must still be caught up in some mainland business venture. If he's not here by mid-March, he won't make it, Mano decides. Regardless of friends here and away Mano settles back into beach life. He cleans and re-organizes his camp and relaxes in his hammock with a good book.

The next afternoon the most notorious and loved outlaw pirate, Captain Bligh, drops in for a surprise pizza party and jam session. He slips his Jet Ski right in between big sets of waves and lands on the beach in full helicopter view. He drops off gear, gets drunk, makes a pizza, plays a few songs on ukulele, then leaves. However, his exit isn't quite as smooth as his entry. It takes a good thirty tries to get the Jet Ski started, then he's dodging head high sets in a left-right weave to slip out of the shore break. He gets out of the break and down the beach before he spins back around to get a bag he left sitting on the sand. It certainly seems age has not slowed this wild pirate's reckless lifestyle. Some of his stories have become lore and legend in Neverland.

'Did you hear about the time he wrecked his Zodiac on the beach last year?'

'Yeah, he's crashed like three boats out here!'

'Once, his kayak was sinking so badly on the way in that he had to give up and swim in from eight-mile, and the boat just magically floated in to the beach.'

'I heard that he rode in on the fin of a tiger shark!'

Another morning, a Ranger scare keeps everyone on their toes. Louder and faster than normal, a copter swoops in from the west. That's a Ranger copter Mano instantly thinks. It zooms past for a reconnaissance mission then leaves only to return an hour later. He sees it coming again, and it's carrying something, it's got a sling. Raid?

The helicopter lands with the sling attached. The uniformed men from the helicopter carry only shovels and weed whackers, not pistols and ticket ledgers. So the hippies on the beach welcome the maintenance men and make their job extremely easy. They gather up any trash on the beach camps and the bluffs and take it to the helicopter to carry it out for easy disposal. They clear out any camps in places where less responsible tourists and outlaws left a wake of debris. The crew of hippies even makes the workers a chocolate cake with dark chocolate and coconut icing. It's sort of a peace offering. Of course, they don't accept, as some of the maintenance crew fear the food is dosed with either ganja or LSD.

The lightweight helicopter speeds off with the cabin full of park maintenance workers then returns to carry out the load of trash in the sling. All the naked hippies on the beach cheer as the pilot spins up off the beach in an amazing double helix twist. With their departure, it seems that any stress of a potential raid is now over. But who knows when the real raid is coming?

Two days later, another chopper lands just before sunset. Alarm spreads across the beach via coconut wireless.

A bunch of up-valley cats are sitting around an evening potluck at the other end of the beach at Mr. X's camp and they see it come in. It's not the red one, someone confirms, so it's not a tourist medical evacuation.

"It looks like it's dropping people off," X shouts.

"But for a raid, surely they'd come at dawn and get the jump on everyone here. That's how they always do it." Andrew counters.

"Okay, okay, no need for alarm, people. Let's not assume anything," Kaholo chimes in.

"Well if it is a raid, I'm sure someone will run down and tell us," Mano says. The group continues with the potluck party in the fading light. Darkness approaches and people get a little bit anxious and start talking more.

"Do you think they might do something like drop a couple of guys off tonight and then come with ten more tomorrow morning, and it will be a full on raid?" Andrew questions.

"You know, I've seen them do it like that before," Mr. X. answers him. "Two years ago, spring break, they came in with two guys, spent the night and the next morning they brought in eight or ten more early and it was a full three-day raid. I don't know, maybe we should prepare for that. There hasn't been a raid since September. We all know we are due."

"Surely somebody's already gone over to talk to them. We should just wait and relax. We'll get the news here and then we'll decide what to do. They're not going to do anything tonight— it's practically dark." Kaholo says, trying to calm the vibe. Sure enough, a messenger comes a few minutes later.

"So, did you talk to the people in the helicopter? Is it the Rangers? What's going on down there?" The whole crew demands answers.

"Yeah, it's the Rangers. I talked to them. There's gonna be a raid tomorrow." The crowd shudders. Music stops and all eyes focus on the tourist as he relays the news. "Yeah, I saw two of them in the helicopter, a guy and a girl, and they were wearing police jackets.

"So, you talked to them and they said tomorrow would be a Ranger Raid." Kaholo questions him.

"Yeah, the guy asked if I had a permit, and I said no. Then he was like, *'Well you better pack up and leave right now because the heat is coming and it's gonna be a thousand dollar fine tomorrow morning.'*"

"But if there's gonna be a raid why would he tell you? That doesn't make sense." Mano interjects.

"I don't know, but they did it like this before. Two guys first, then the next day it was the raid. We should consider ourselves fortunate for the tip-off and take the time to stash our stuff now," Mr. X warns.

"I don't know. I don't think it's a raid. I bet it's a bluff. Maybe they're just coming to check on the work the maintenance guys did just a few days ago." Kaholo says.

Mr. X and Ella leave to stash their buckets of supplies to prepare for a raid. Mr. X doesn't move his camp for a hurricane, and will hardly even put his book down when a maintenance guy walks by, so seeing him spark into defense mode puts the fear of God into any seasoned outlaw. When the crew at the potluck sees him and Ella pack up at night and hike up valley to hide out, everyone trembles with true concern.

Andrew's next to start stashing his buckets. A few others follow suit.

"I'm gonna get my essentials in a dry bag and launch the *SS Salvation* first thing in the morning. If I see that it's a raid from the ocean, I'll just head to town," Mano proclaims.

"Then you can sound the alarm from the ocean to everyone on the bluffs." Gaia suggests.

"Let's not get too excited, people. I think it's a bit too early in the season for *the big raid*. The tourist report still sounds a bit fishy. It might be just some sort of hype," Kaholo declares, still confident.

"I'll go talk to them. I'll get the real story from the Rangers." Q finally says getting up to go down the trail with his headlamp.

"Alright, go shake 'em down and give us the real news! The good news," Mano teases.

Thirty minutes later, Q comes back.

"Alright, I got the real report. I talked to the woman and she says that she's just here with her husband on their honeymoon and they are friends with the head lady at the DLNR and somehow they arranged to be dropped off in the helicopter to stay on the beach for a few days. They didn't have guns and I don't think they're the Rangers. It's just some guy and his wife and they have some sort of connection with the DLNR lady."

"Well, I like the sound of that story a lot better," Kaholo chuckles.

"What if they realized they spilled the beans by tipping the one tourist guy off, and now they are coming up with this whole honeymoon story to recover?" Andrew asks twisting things around again.

"Do you really think they'd go through all that? It's obvious that the first tourist guy went over there and the man just wanted to scare him. These tourists got a special ride in. I'm gonna go with the second story," Kaholo tells them.

"Well we know the head of the DLNR is a lady-what if it is her, the head lady, that arrived in the helicopter. Maybe she's here to supervise the whole raid and see how they do it. What if that's the case?"

"Enough! We already know it's not going to be a raid now, so let's just forget about it. I'm sick of hearing about it, already." Kaholo speaks up loudly to break up the negative chatter.

It turns out that Kaholo and Q are right. The pair is a couple on their honeymoon with some epic hook-up. Everyone remains safe in paradise.

Chapter 24   The Great Goat Getaway

"So tell me about this Avocado Box." Mano pesters Thomas after breakfast at the Sanctuary.

Thomas turns to Mano to explain with bright eyes.

"You know about the few avocado trees that produce this time of year growing up in two-mile valley, near the start of the trail?"

"Yeah, up two-mile stream, I know."

"So anyone can hike up that side trail and harvest avocados to bring in, but you can only really carry in a couple because everyone has the usual backpack full of supplies, and two or three is really all the extra weight anyone can handle. Plus, there's rarely more than a couple of ripe ones at one time anyway."

"Yeah, I get it, but what's this box for?" Mano questions.

"So, I built this box out of stones right off the main trail at two-mile valley and I gathered about ten unripe avocados and put them in it. And I hiked in with a couple of ripe ones. Now every time someone we know is going out for re-supply, we can tell them to gather more avocados, put them in the box, and take just the ripest ones to the Sanctuary. So you see, it could be like this continuous flow of avocados into the valley. Brilliant huh!"

"Whoa! That is a pretty kickass idea. Do you think it will really work?"

"Well, I don't know. People have to actually hike out of their way to get new avocados to fill the box."

"Yeah, you know how people are." Mano shrugs.

"But it *could* totally work—that's the whole point. It makes sense, right?" Thomas pipes back.

"Yeah, totally. I think it's a great idea. Fresh avocados arriving daily to Neverland, it's incredible." Mano responds with a smile, but his tone is a bit halfhearted.

Thomas breaks a piece of firewood over his knee. "I know, its kind of wishful thinking."

"We'll see, I still think it's pretty clever." Mano adds with a smile that warms.

They both catch themselves daydreaming over the creamy taste of a perfectly ripe Hawaiian avocado.

The two stop daydreaming at the sound of a Shaman bird's call and get up to hike down to the beach to enjoy an afternoon of sun. The day is so sunny and warm that even some of the up-valley recluses are on the beach sprawling out naked in the sunbaked sand. Mano and Thomas join Grizz and Kaholo for a round of Frisbee with a new naked goddess from Maui who calls herself Lilikoi. They dive into the water and jump in the hot sand catching the disc and a full-body tan. Then they gather atop a big dune to snack and pass around a couple of joints. Lilikoi's friends stop by with a tiny baby goat and a bottle of store-bought powdered goat milk to feed it.

"Hey guys, this is my pet goat, Luna. I found her stranded on the trail on my hike in and rescued her." Lilikoi explains.

The resident outlaws look on cheekily, watching the blue-eyed naked goddess coax the spunky black baby goat into taking a bottle. The little goat guzzles the milk then bleats gleefully. Kaholo and Mano practically fall over off the dune in laughter.

"You know we had another hippie chick just like you with a pet goat last year, and she made some real grizzly-good goat stew." Grizz cackles, in a poor attempt to crack a joke.

Lilikoi, and Luna the goat found their home in Neverland. Lilikoi's soft, calm demeanor made her likable by all and unlike many women she was totally comfortable in her own tan naked skin. She had short almost boyish hair, but the way she carried herself was purely feminine. Rubbing herself with coconut oil and sweet fragrances, preparing fancy cacao drinks, and wearing beautiful self-crafted jewelry, gave her an aura of elegance in a community of rough and tattered critter-people.

She'd practice naked headstands on the sand with her legs splayed out, and all the dudes would pretend not to watch.

"Mano, I think Lilikoi has got you beat for the tannest cat on the beach." Kaholo declares, while watching her smoothly exit out of an inversion into a sandy sprawl towards the sun.

With the welcoming of Lilikoi and Luna into the resident circle, the crew gets an idea to throw a big beach bash, as the weather and ocean conditions are prime for fun in the sun. The surf is down enough that even a novice swimmer could swim through the beach break. Tomorrow could be calmer and warmer even! Discussion continues around planning potluck dishes, beach games, and the like as the sun fades. Gaia and Keilani even come down from the valley to set up temporary beach camps for tomorrow morning's big beach blowout.

"Mano, you can help us launch an air mattress out beyond the break and we'll have a swim-to floating island to lounge on— it will be so sweet!" Gaia and Lilikoi giggle excitedly.

The next morning is the most glorious beach day of the year so far. The sun beams in hot first thing in the morning and the waves are small enough to longboard. Khan pulls out the 10-0 long board from his stashed quiver and puts on quite a show while the rest of the crew sips coffee from the same sandy dune they hung out on yesterday. The cute little goat Luna prances around wagging her tail gleefully. Mano catches a few waves on the long board as well and floats merrily in the channel with Gaia and Kaholo. Grizzley goes looking for some bamboo at his camp to setup the volleyball net and Lilikoi is nearly finished blowing up the queen-sized air mattress to launch for their floating island lounge when Thomas comes running down the beach trail.

"Boots on the ground! Boots on the ground!" He yells to sound the alarm to the crew.

Immediately, the casual sunbathers spring into action. Several Rangers shuffle toward the main beach camp by the big date palm and everyone who sees them scatters. Khan and Q who happened to be standing next to the *SS Salvation* quickly pull her into the water and launch the kayak through the beach break for an ocean getaway. Kaholo and a few others sprint down the beach toward the valley hoping to escape to jungle beyond. Mano rushes to the trail to grab his ukulele and water bottle, but he's instantly caught by Titus the lead Ranger coming from the other direction.

"Sit down!" Titus commands aggressively. Not wanting additional trouble, Mano promptly abides and takes a seat on a rock wall that divides the trail from the main camp at the center of the beach. Four then Five other tourists are corralled by other Rangers and seated with him. Titus stands over them all with his clipboard and calls for their camping permits. Even if Mano had a permit it would be long expired, for the Beach, which existed in a Hawaii state park, allowed a maximum stay of 5 days. A couple of the other tourists claim to have the permit and Titus fingers through his list of named allowed campers. Mano's mind races trying conjure up some sort of *reasonable* story. Then he looks out to the ocean and see's Lilikoi, Luna the goat, and another backpacker launching the air mattress into the ocean in an ill-fated getaway. Mano seizes the opportunity and blurts out:

"Hey Titus, is that a goat...on a boat?"

The Ranger spins around and glances at the trio floundering their craft through the whitewash.

"Oh no way!" Titus exclaims, sounding purely Hawaiian. Then he marches down to the beach in a fury. Mano's equally dumbstruck as he watches the air mattress team paddle like hell and miraculously escape to the outside of the surf break scrambling goat and all.

"Mano!" He hears Gaia's voice call out in a sharp whisper from the bushes on the other side of the trail. Suddenly he realizes that this is his chance at escape. He jumps up and the two run down the trail toward the Heiau. Three Rangers are down at the water's edge waving angrily to Lilikoi, the other guy, and the goat, now floating calmly outside the surf break. Mano and Gaia don't look back, and in moments they are at the side trail to the perch to cut over to the Heiau. They avoid the main trail trying to make their escape up and over where Mano and Sierra's overlook camps are. Halfway up the side trail they spin around at the sight of a big Hawaiian Ranger known by all the outlaws as *The Rock* due to obvious resemblance to the Hollywood star.

"Oh my god, it's *The Rock*— go back the other way!" Gaia yelps.

The Rangers can't keep up with the fleeing hippies on their well-known foot trails and make little effort to pursue them. Near the Heiau they run into Sierra and they all hide out for a half hour to try to let things settle down. Afterward, Mano elects to do a quick reconnaissance mission on the Heiau. From there he gets a glimpse of the beach and tries to figure out what's going on. The crew on the air mattress is still out there in the ocean and Khan and Q are still floating in the kayak, too. Mano scans the beach; the Rangers are certainly still there. Maybe they are staying the night. He sees Khan and Q on the kayak and he motions for them to paddle in close to the rocks so they can communicate.

"I think they are staying the night!" Q manages to shout over the churn of the ocean. This is what Mano guessed too.

"Try to land at the pocket beach on the other side of the bluffs and let's meet up at Three Mangos, up-valley."

Khan nods and holds his paddle vertically in agreement. Mano and the two girls hike clandestinely up-valley and wait at a small camp tucked below Three Mangos. Khan and Q signal to them with a wahooie and they chime back to motion them in to their convert spot.

They play the waiting game for the rest of the afternoon, hanging out passing joints and the ukulele back and forth, getting hungrier and more restless each hour. Everyone else who got away is likely in the same situation, hunkering down somewhere. It's a cat and mouse game all the residents know too well. Rangers vs. Outlaws. Mano still can't believe he escaped with the '*goat on a boat*' diversion.

The free five trickle back to the bluffs to watch the sunset with plans to sneak back to their camps near the beach under the cover of darkness. They all crave sustenance, as there is nothing at Sanctuary. Mano doesn't have a headlamp or a shirt so he's the first to cave and hike down in the twilight. He feels any remaining Rangers must be preparing for bed. He descends the steep trail down to the river, casually. Turning down the steepest, narrowest corner he runs right into Titus sneaking up to the bluffs with his crossbow. Mano gulps as *the moment of truth* is upon him. Instead of sprinting away in fear or floundering a half-wit response, he looks the man who captured him in the eye. A man-to-man look of mutual respect is exchanged, and Mano steps to the side a bit to let Titus pass him going up the trail. The seasoned head Ranger continues uphill and lets Mano slip down to the stream without a word. Mano's heart sinks to his stomach; he can't believe what just happened, Titus simply let him go without question.

He makes it back to his camp undeterred and avoids any further Ranger contact the next morning. The whole Ranger crew departs via helicopter by noon. Mano tracks down Grizz to get the scoop on the rest of the raid on the beach yesterday morning.

"Yeah, I just crawled in my tent and took a nap. A Ranger passed right over me and I was all cool. Kaholo escaped up-valley, I think most of the locals got away."

"What about Lilikoi and the other dude on the air mattress and the goat?" Mano asks.

"Goat-girl and SPF-man!" Grizz chuckles. "Yeah, they hung out there on the ocean for hours, but they eventually got too thirsty and had to come in. They bailed and got their tickets."

"SPF-man?" Mano askes perplexed.

"Yeah that's what everyone's calling him now. He got so sunburnt out on that raft that now he thinks he's some kind of superhero or something. I dunno man, pretty wild though. At least that goat helped you get away. I would have loved to see the look on Titus's face when he watched that goat launch through the waves!"

"There's a goat on a boat...no way!" Mano impersonates Titus in his best pidgin accent. They both roll in laughter.

Chapter 25   Stayer Girl

On an impulse, Mano turns off the valley trail and crosses over to the hippie highway to cruise by Community Garden to look for Paul. He had heard Paul was back in the valley and he thought to find him at his usual spot below the garden. Paul has a way of captivating women that intrigued Mano and he thought that maybe he could offer him some good advice. With nearly nine years living in the valley, he must have some worthy guidance on finding a real *stayer girl*. Mano remembers his conversation with him over a year ago when he came upon him in the garden taro patch. He and Paul are a lot alike, he decides. They are both more than just monkey men like Paul once joked. They are loving, caring, genuine, passionate men. Paul is all alone relaxing at his primitive camp he set up in the guava forest when Mano approaches.

"Hey Mano-banano, what are you doing way up here? I thought you'd be chasing girls down on the beach on a sunny day like today."

"I figured for once I'd try your strategy. Just wait for them to come to me."

"Well, sometimes that works, sometimes it don't, but most of the time it takes a little of both." Paul laughs back to him.

"Well, easy enough for you to say! You're more of a charmer than me! And you don't fall on your face mad in love with them like I do. You let *them* do that."

Paul laughs. "I do what I do, just like you— we can't really change who we are."

Well, I want to learn more about you, and what you do. I'm curious how you attract girls way up in the valley yet you're not discouraged when they head back to Babylon and leave you up here all alone."

"Well, I won't say I don't get discouraged, but I try not to let girls get to me, I don't let them mess with my head. But don't get me wrong, I'm still hoping to find a *stayer girl* who won't go running back to Babylon. Life is certainly better here with a woman. We both know that much. There's no better place to be with a woman than in the simple serenity of the valley. But if you care too much, that just spoils it somehow. Chicks are weird like that." Paul finishes with a raised eyebrow stare.

"I know you are a caring man, so I'm not sure I understand your philosophy. You'll have to put things into monkey terms for me. " Mano replies with a smile.

"Well I can tell you that half your problem is you care too damn much about what will happen! You are so bending to please a lady to make it work and maybe that's not *really* you anyway. As soon as you stop caring all the time, stop giving everything you have, then you'll have girls crawling all over you, wanting to make you care more. But if you do too much, and you pour your focus onto them, they don't have to win you over and there's like nothing left for them to do. They'll either get bored and just go for some asshole and try to convert them, to make them care...Or they'll just manipulate you to death because they can. Yeah, don't care too much. You gotta kinda stand your ground and be an asshole, but not all the time. Women need their freedom and support from their men too. But too much support and care will make them feel trapped. At least for the young ones, it's like they don't respect you if you care too much."

"That doesn't really make sense. Chicks hate asshole guys."

"Is that so? Look at Andrew and Khan, do they seem to have a problem getting girls to like them?"

Mano pulls his own hair, frustrated. "I just don't get the logic, Paul. I know that a woman wants to be loved and cared for, I know how good it makes them feel." Paul laughs hard seeing Mano release his feelings.

"Of course you do Mano, I know you. You'll make a woman feel so cared for she'll freak out and run away!" Mano is still confused. Paul looks directly at him and speaks to him slowly like he's talking to a toddler.

"If you give them exactly what they want, you're screwed! That's the logic." Mano shakes his head frustrated. Paul just continues on.

"Take Honu for example. Super nice guy, right? Every girl wants to get close to him because he's so nice."

"Right, it's hard to out-nice Honu. He's the most generous guy in Neverland for sure."

"Okay, remember last year when he had that beautiful girl everybody called Princess? Charlotte, yeah that was her name."

"Yeah, of course. How could I forget?"

"Well, he took good care of her but he never made her his sole focus. He would go to the outside to meet friends and surf, and in the end he just left Neverland and went back to California, leaving her here on the bluffs guessing. And what did she do? She wrote that beautiful song about him and adored him even more. I think she even tracked him down last summer in California, to try and make him care. But you see, even if Honu does really care about her, he's smart enough to not let on that he does. That's why he does so well. And you, you're Captain Mano— with your charisma, you should be able to pull in chicks twice as hot as Charlotte, once you stop being so *concerned*. You've got to not want them— to make them really want you. Ya hear what I'm saying?"

Mano smiles at the thought, then sighs. "I just don't really know if that's me."

"I don't know, Mano. I'm just trying to help you out, tell you what I know. You've gotta remember, women are not like us. Us men, we want good things, right? We want good things to happen to us, and when they do, we take them, and we are happy. Pretty much the more good things and the easier they come, the better, right? Now women on the other hand, especially the beautiful ones who already get a bunch of attention, they don't really know what they want. And what's more difficult is that good things don't necessarily make them happy. It's harder and more complicated for them, unfortunately."

They both stop to scratch their heads in wonder of what Paul just said. Then Paul tries again to shed some light.

"You know, man was made from the dust of the earth, and woman came from the womb of Mother Earth. Almost more like they're from liquid, from the sea…" Paul trails off and they both just stare at the forest perplexed. Their eyes catch on the shaman birds that sing high up in the guava trees above them. Mano slaps at a few mosquitos in frustration, and turns back to Paul.

"What about just getting a woman to want to stay here. Really stay here in the valley."

"A *stayer girl*. Yep that's what you want. I wanna take it beyond that even. I want to create a whole Neverland lineage, men and women with children. Families here on the inside."

"But first you need a woman to stay here," Mano says.

"Well of course. As soon as I find a woman who wants to stay, who really wants to be here and live in the valley with me, then I'm gonna try my best to get her pregnant. That's one way, at least, as I see it."

"Whoa, Whoa, Whoa. How do you think knocking a girl up is gonna make her want to stay in the valley?"

"Well, I don't mean it like that. I mean, have a baby, consensually. But, if a girl really wants to be out here, having a baby and raising the child here is just the next step toward togetherness and lasting existence here. Women want to be nurtured and to have a nurturing environment to raise a baby. Can you think of a more nurturing, purer environment than these gardens?" Paul motions grandiosely toward the lush terraces of community gardens behind his camp.

"True, but I think you'll have a hell of a time trying to convince a modern woman of that."

"Sure, but once they see past all that material crap and understand the nurturing love of Mother Nature here, they'll realize that there really is no better place."

"Maybe you are on to something, Paul. The Neverland Huminal lineage!"

"Hey, like I said, she's got to really want to stay here first."

"Yeah, a *stayer girl* — that's what you want in a woman."

"That's my dream, at least," Paul smiles to himself.

"It's a good dream, and yeah without all the burdens of the outside world, maybe it could actually be easy. Why shouldn't it be?

"A pure life in nature should be simple."

"Paul, you're right. So how about we just manifest it? Right here, right now. Let's manifest great stayer girls in Neverland for the both of us!"

Chapter 26　Moonlight Madness

"How many moons has it been since we got here?" Mano asks Khan, smiling.

"Let's see. There have been two full moons already but it was kind of cloudy and rainy for both of them. With this half moon on the rise, the full moon is just another week or so away. Maybe this time it'll be full and bright and not cloudy at all!" Khan declares, manifesting.

"Wow, two months since our boat ride in together. Doesn't it seem like just a few weeks ago?"

"Two weeks, two months, it don't matter Captain. Time stops at the end of the road, right?" Mano watches as Khan's spliff burns slowly between his fingers.

"Sierra and I were thinking of paddling out in a couple days for resupply." Mano continues.

"Yeah, me and the boys on the bluffs will be out of food soon, too."

"It's been a good while. We've been out of rum for a week!" Mano resonates.

"Yeah, it would be nice to go out and come back in fully stoked for spring break and full moon parties." Khan states, staring into the moonlight, spliff still burning in hand. He holds the end of the spliff up to Mano. Mano takes a puff and passes it back.

"Remember the triple nipple boob blowout last March?"

"Yeah, that was pretty epic!" Mano laughs. Khan stares back at him, brotherly with a cheeky grin.

"You and Sierra paddling out for resupply…Captain, it should be us! Me and you makin' the mission."

"I told Sierra she can come out on the *SS Salvation*. She said her knees are bothering her and she doesn't feel like hiking the trail."

"You sure treat that girl well, especially for some chick you're not even sleeping with." Khan chums up to him, nudging his shoulder.

"Whatever! She's my friend and she's never done the ocean journey. I should give her the kayak experience."

"What's the swell looking like?" Khan probes.

"Mr. X says nada for swell, at least for the next couple of days." They stare out to the ocean. No one speaks for a good minute or so.

"I still think it should be a warrior mission— me and you Captain."

"Well, how about all three of us go then? Me, you, and Sierra, who can ride in the princess perch." Mano offers.

"Alright Captain! Let's launch, the three of us, tomorrow right at sunset!" Khan glows with excitement.

"Maybe a couple of hours before sunset so we arrive in time to still hitch a ride into town." Mano attempts to keep Khan's veering mind corralled.

"Whatever. Me, you, and the woman tomorrow right before sunset."

"We can put supply bags on the boat drop and come back the next day," Mano suggests.

"Sounds good to me. I'm turning in. See you tomorrow." Khan hugs Mano goodnight. He pulls back still holding Mano on each shoulder looking at him face to face.

"You know, Captain, you're like a brother I never had." The compliment catches Mano off guard.

"You're my best friend on the beach." Mano replies.

"Right on! So tomorrow we sail to Babylon as brothers."

"Alright, brother, see ya tomorrow."

The half moon is high in the sky and shines bright. Its reflection glimmers smoothly on the ocean and illuminates the cliffs to the west. There's almost no wind. Mano walks back up to his camp on the perch without a headlamp. An enchanting calm settles over the beach and valley.

The next day the typical afternoon trades are steady but the swell is almost nonexistent. Another fifty feet of beach is exposed because the north swell has backed down so much. Mano's excited about a smooth journey back to Babylon as a team of three. Sierra, himself, and Khan will cruise back for resupply in the evening light. The journey should be perfect.

"Are you ready to pack the dry-bag and prepare for launch?" Mano beckons to Khan as he approaches on the trail.

"Mano catches a crafty look in Khan's eye when he draws near."

"We should wait until the middle of the night and launch under the light of the half moon," Khan conspires.

"No, let's pack the stuff and get ready to go right now. Sierra and I are almost ready."

"Captain, I've got an even better idea. Let's all take acid right now and leave at four in the morning." Mano rolls his eyes as Khan continues grandiosely.

"We'll be coming down by then. We'll paddle in the calm of night and arrive in town at dawn. We'll go to the store all strung out, do the boat drop, and kayak right back in, no sleep!"

"No way, man. That's completely ridiculous. We're not gonna do that! Whatever happened to the original plan? We leave right now, arrive at sunset, and hitch a ride to town for beers. We'll get some good sleep and come back the next day."

"Look at this moon and this calm ocean, Captain! We should make this a mission, a *vision quest*!" Khan waves wildly toward the moon. Mano stares confused yet captivated.

"No. Let's stick to the original plan. Stay straight, paddle into town, get some good rest, and paddle back the next day. I'm not tripping on acid in the middle of the Pacific with you and Sierra. Not on my boat!" Mano concludes defiantly.

Still, Mano smiles to himself when he lets Khan's wild idea settle his mind. Talk about a journey!

He shakes his head at the craziness of it. *Khan just thrives on moonlit intensity.* Certainly Sierra would not go for it, so why is he even the least bit captivated? It would be his first moonlit voyage, and her first ocean kayak experience ever. A journey enough! They didn't need any crazy Khan variables. Sierra comes down from camp and hears Khan's new proposal.

"This doesn't need to be a warrior mission! Let's just have a fun, calm, sunset paddle out together. We don't need or do any drugs!" Sierra states, like a schoolteacher matter-of-factly.

Mano can tell that Sierra's strict feminine voice only riles Khan up more.

"I'm sick and tired of saving drugs!" Khan shouts out. Sierra and Mano both laugh out loud at the complete ridiculousness of his statement. But all of a sudden their well-thought-out plan is in limbo and the mission out is becoming quite the ordeal, with sunset approaching.

Mano thinks to tell Khan to just bugger off and just paddle with Sierra right now. Of course, he realizes that Khan is not the kind of guy that you can just tell off. He's a hothead, and a blowup from him would put a major damper on what should be a beautiful, peaceful paddle out. Plus, he takes things so personally. He'd be a cantankerous pain in the ass for everyone for a whole week or worse if they left him. Mano decides to shoot for what he believes to be a fair compromise.

"Okay, Khan. How about we leave at 11 PM, when the moon's just overhead? We're not going to take acid, but you do whatever you want, you've tripped enough to where you'll probably paddle the same either way. We'll sleep on the beach when we arrive in Babylon and the next day we'll do the town run, get groceries and come back."

"Okay fine! But I still think it should be just me and you Captain. Let's make this a vision quest." Khan grits his teeth, digesting the decision being not of his control.

"That's not happening Khan. Sierra is coming."

"Instead, let's leave at 1 AM." Khan tests.

"We'll leave when the moon is just overhead. Be ready." Mano points up to the sky and whisks his arm down rapidly, turning away.

"Aye, aye, Captain. Sounds decent." Khan nods.

"All right! Now let's just enjoy this sunset," Sierra consoles.

The sunset is a beautiful combination of layered clouds that settle into calm waters. Still there is a strange staleness in the air, like a fog is rolling in.

Khan doesn't save his drugs, as expected. He doses with his new girlfriend Amy and Dmitri. Amy and Khan drift into their altered states around the campfire. For the second time, LSD has no effect on Dmitri, but he's in the zone with them anyway. Mano tries to just kick back and play music. Sierra's not even interested in hanging out at all, and just heads back to her camp.

"I'll be reading up in my hammock. Just come and get me when you guys are ready," she says with a yawn.

A couple hours into their *journey*, Khan has a *vision*.

"The woman can't go. This has to be a warrior mission. It should be me, you, and Dmitri." he declares.

"Not a chance. Sierra's going. That's been decided. We are not changing plans now." Mano shoots him down immediately.

"Captain, this is meant to be a warrior mission. I had a vision. Look at this moon! It should be me, you and Dmitri— you know it should be."

"Don't push my buttons, Khan! Besides, me, you and Dmitri's giant body in the boat just wouldn't work. He's way too big and tippy. We'd never make it. Three in the kayak at night with you tripping is pushing our luck as it is."

"Just look at this night! We could totally make it. Look at how calm it is out there. No waves or wind at all! We could practically push the boat through the waves." Dmitri giggles in agreement.

"Khan!" Now Mano is starting to boil.

Dmitri tries to put in his own convincing words.

"Captain, please. Would you just let me make this mission? I could be like your servant for one whole day when we get back. I just want to make this mission." Dmitri truly is so endearing looking bright-eyed and dumb in the moonlight wearing just his airline blanket poncho Khan made for him. Mano nearly falls for his *moment-man* charm.

"I'm not talking about this to you guys anymore. I'll see you in an hour, Khan. You better be ready!" Mano shouts as he storms off toward the beach.

"I know that you know that you're making the wrong decision, Captain!" *He just has to have the last word*, Mano thinks to himself.

The moon drifts overhead and Mano goes to get Sierra for the journey. He's angry and nervous. Khan pressuring him has him aggravated and unsettled. The four do meet back in Goddess Gardens as planned. Khan and Dmitri are still trying to pressure for a substitution.

"You know what? You guys just go, I don't even want to paddle with you guys anymore. Besides with theses clouds moving in and covering up the moon, it's freaking me out. I'm too scared to kayak, you guys just go," Sierra says again, in haste.

Mano knows that she knows rocking the boat with Khan will just be a recipe for a bad time. She doesn't want to be out at sea with a bossy, tripping Khan for 2 hours any more than he does. Perhaps she sees the whole journey as more of a pain in the ass than it's worth. She's right about the clouds, too. They're really coming in and dimming the half moon. The half moon seems only half as bright as it was an hour ago. Mano grits his teeth thinking of how Khan will get his way anyway.

"Sierra, you have to go, because with me, Khan, and Dmitri there's just too much weight in the boat."

"Now it's cloudy, it's late, and I'm tired of dealing with all of this stupidity. I'm not going. I'll hike out tomorrow and see you guys in town." Mano can tell she's upset but there's little more he can propose.

Again, he imagines himself, Khan, and the Russian paddling in the moonlit glassy ocean, tripping on LSD. He chuckles out loud at his own mental image of the three of them.

He'd be in the back in the captain's seat, Dmitri would be in front paddling, and Khan would sit in the princess perch playing ukulele the whole way. Mano and Dmitri hike down to the beach to prepare the boat while Khan goes to say a quick goodbye to Amy. Khan had said something earlier to her by the campfire that made her leave in a huff, and now they needed to patch things up before he leaves her for a few days in town. Patching things up from an argument that occurred on acid while still on acid doesn't really work though.

The minutes tick by as Mano and Dmitri wait on the moonlit beach. After half an hour Mano says, "You know, I don't think Khan can make this mission."

"But Khan, you know...he is coming. Khan will come, he must come, we must wait for him," Dmitri wagers.

"No, Dmitri, you've got to understand. Khan and Amy are arguing while tripping on acid. He wants Amy to go back to California with him and she's considering it, but now she is doubting the whole situation. Things are being revealed under the influence of the acid. This is a key turning point. You may not know it, but I can sense it. Amy is seeing Khan's true character unveiled through the drug, and she doesn't like it. Khan's supposed to go buy plane tickets for them to go back to California on this trip out, and now she's having second thoughts. It's going to take more than a thirty-minute conversation for them to hash things out. Besides, they're both still tripping hard. There's no chance for them to figure this out until tomorrow morning over coffee, if then. Khan's not coming. He's out. Maybe our only chance to make this mission is just you and I."

"But please, Captain. We must wait for Khan. Khan will come. Khan will be here."

"Dmitri, you don't understand. Khan and Amy are not going to have this thing resolved in the next hour, maybe not even by tomorrow. Khan cannot make this mission."

Still, the Russian insists on waiting. He's more loyal to Khan than a Labrador retriever. Eventually, Khan comes with just the news Mano expected. Over the course of a few hours, Khan and Amy's future together had become indeterminate.

"Amy's freaking out about the whole idea of coming to the ranch in California, I don't know if I can leave just yet. We just spent the last hour crying in each other's arms."

"Well by the sound of it, I don't think you guys can have this thing resolved until tomorrow morning."

"I don't know, Captain. Do you think I should just go right now with you and Dmitri?" Khan questions.

"No, I think you should stay here with Amy and figure out whatever you guys need to figure out. I'll tell you for certain, if you really want her to go back with you to California then the two of you should hike the trail out together and go buy the plane tickets together. If you really want to be with her, you should be with her right now when she needs you the most. Show her that you care, and mean it. Dmitri and I will just meet you in town somehow."

"No! I don't like that plan. Maybe we should just postpone this whole thing till the morning." Khan whines.

"Maybe I'll just leave in the morning by myself! Frankly, I don't feel like waiting around, planning this whole mission around your latest whim," Mano barks.

"This is a team mission, a warrior mission."

"I don't care about a warrior mission! The *SS* is gonna set sail when I feel like it. This whole deal doesn't revolve around you, Khan!"

Mano expects an out-lash of childishness, but instead he gets some forceful, manipulative B.S. Khan certainly has a way of manipulating things to suit him, but this had gone altogether too far. Now, Mano is at ends enough to leave him pissed off right there on the beach. But that isn't a good idea.

"Khan, why don't you just go and be with Amy, be with her when she needs you, and tomorrow morning we'll consider our options. Maybe we can leave tomorrow."

"Okay, I'll go back over and talk to Amy for just ten more minutes and I'll see if I can go. I'll shout back two woo-hooie's if I'm coming or just one yelp if I'm not. And if not, we'll leave first thing in the morning."

Mano pretends like he's listening, but really he's just blocking out whatever Khan says to keep himself from getting more pissed. He's too annoyed to really listen, yet too cautious and careful to really say what he wants to say. He knows Khan will pull any manipulative move he can just to keep from having to hike the 11-mile trail. Khan feels like he is above the trail. He almost never hikes the trail. *This time he'd be hiking, all 11 knee-grinding miles of it.* Mano clenches.

Khan goes back to Amy. Mano and Dmitri hear just one yelp, and Mano's satisfied at that.

Mano then turns to the Russian and asks, "Dmitri, do you still want to make this mission?" The Russian looks up at the half moon, now near the horizon with the clouds dashing across it. He looks out at the glassy, calm Pacific and back at Mano.

"Yes, I want to make this mission."

"Okay, let's go wake up Sierra. She probably wont want to go, but we should just see. At least tell her what's up."

They hike up to the perch and gently rouse her in the hammock. She's asleep but she snaps right up.

"Sierra, Khan's out of the picture. Do you still want to go on this midnight sea kayak mission?" He isn't expecting her to be anything but perturbed for waking her, but he still needs to at least convey what happened with Khan and plan a meet-up on the outside. To their surprise, she's entirely enthusiastic.

"I'm ready, let's just make some tea first," she responds with a yawn.

"Let's make tea and oatmeal and then go." Mano agrees. Sierra stokes the fire from her hammock. They send Dmitri down to fetch some more water for tea.

"So, I guess now it's you, me, and Dmitri," Mano grumbles.

"Are you sure about this? I mean, taking Dmitri with us in the boat," she asks.

"It's not ideal, but it's possible. He's a good paddler but he's tippy as all hell, I will say that. The only time I ever flipped in the open ocean was when I paddled him out when he had that horrible rash."

"Well, even if the three of us do make it, what do we do with Dmitri in town? I mean, all he has is an airline blanket and a sarong."

"Good point, Sierra. He will definitely slow us down for town duties, and we'll have to feed him and watch over him out there, it will be ridiculous." Mano's heart sinks thinking about leaving the humble carefree warrior Dmitri who *'just wanted to make this mission.'*

"Well, I did already tell In-the-moment-man that he could go. I feel bad about just telling him all of a sudden that he can't." Mano stresses over the situation.

"Whatever, we'll be in town for less than 24 hours, Dmitri can just hang out and watch the boat." Sierra says conversely.

"So you're saying that you're ready to go for it, the three of us?" Mano asks excitedly. Sierra grins.

"I was ready six hours ago at sunset! I'd rather take the Russian with no money and just an airline blanket than Khan and all his bullshit anyway. Look at this calm ocean! It's gonna be great," Sierra charms. They both look out towards the faint horizon while sipping their tea.

"Moonset launch!" Sierra chuckles.

The headlamps are all on Mano as he stuffs their only dry bag trying to fit all of their essentials and Dmitri's tiny square of fabric into it. It's not closing properly because the ukulele is just barely poking out.

"Fuck it, it's not gonna get wet, there's no waves for the launch."

They hold hands and pray, asking for Mama Kai to grant them safe passage on this moonlit mission.

"Okay Dmitri, this is how we are gonna do this. You and I will hold the kayak in the surf with Sierra sitting in the front. Then, when I see the window to launch, I'll jump in and Sierra and I will paddle out. Once we make it through the surf break, you swim out and climb into the front seat. Sierra can slip behind you into the princess perch in the middle of the boat and hopefully stay dry. Got it? As soon as we make it past the break, swim out to meet us."

"Yes, Captain. Let's do this." Dmitri states excited.

"Sierra, if you want dry panties on the trip, I suggest you put your panties on your head for the launch," Mano adds.

They ready the boat in the moonlit whitewash. It's the wide-eyed naked Russian, confident Captain Mano shirt-cocking in just a neoprene top, and first-timer Sierra with her panties on her head.

"Okay, I see the break in the sets. Ready? Here we go!"

Mano pushes the boat through the whitewater and jumps in. He calls to Sierra to paddle, and Dmitri just bellies up onto the princess perch right as they take off in the set.

"Dmitri, what the hell are you doing?" Mano yells as Dmitri scrambles aboard.

Miraculously, they make it through the shore break upright as a threesome.

With Dmitri in the princess perch, they continue to paddle out to sea to be safer from any rouge wave. The tippy Russian wiggles around in the tiny princess perch in the middle of the boat.

"How did this happen? Dmitri, you were supposed to swim out and climb onto the front. Alright, you guys are going to have to pull some mad yoga moves to switch places. So Dmitri, if you can get into cat, then Sierra can go...wait!"

The kayak wobbles, then flips. They all get tossed into the black ocean.

"Dmitri!" Sierra squeals. They right the kayak and claw back in, like soaking wet cats. This time they settle in their appropriate assigned positions. Dmitri tries to steady himself in the front and Sierra sits back to back with him in the princess perch, facing Mano in the backseat. Dmitri is still leaning then overcompensating like a drunk in the dark in his seat.

"Okay, smooth and easy Dmitri. One-two, one-two, here-we-go, let's-go-to town." Mano tries to coach the Russian into a steady rhythm.

"One-two, one-two. Easy, Dmitri, easy. Whoa! Dmitri!"

Again, they flip, and again they right the boat and clamber back in.

"Damn it, Dmitri! I sure hope our sleeping bags and everything else are not soaking in that poorly sealed dry bag after you flipped us. Twice!" Mano tries to recompose himself.

"Dmitri, I don't think you can make this mission." Sierra tells him sternly.

"Yeah Dmitri, I think you're just too tippy. I don't know if we can make it to town with you in the boat." Mano adds.

"But Capt..."

"Dmitri, you cannot make this mission," Mano continues coldly.

They paddle back towards the shore break and instruct the Russian to abandon ship.

"Just yell at us when you get back to the beach so we know you're okay," Sierra exhales. He swims in no problem and the duo continues on their way, now without even a trace of moon. The half moon had set, and clouds block out Jupiter, Venus and any other saving grace of a star. Now all the two can see is blackness all around with the slightest silhouette of the cliff-lined coast, and the phosphorescent skyway they're riding on. They can hardly believe it! Each paddle stroke that dips into the black ocean reveals neon green streamers. They leave behind a phosphorescent wake in the water.

They can barely see the outline of the cliffs to guide their course, but they are wet and giddy and empowered by the phosphorescent skyway. They stop for a second to try to soak in their ominous surroundings just bobbing up and down in the calm black ocean. They start paddling again and with their rhythmic streamlined pace they soon near the end of the cliffs. Captain Mano pipes up with enthusiasm.

"I see the spot where we can land, already." He has made the route enough times now that he knows where the reef with the keyhole to the lagoon will be. Even in the dark night he can still make out the shapes and outlines of the cliffs above the landing beach. Of course, they can't see the reef, or the keyhole to slip the boat through it. It's eerie. He can see and hear where water and land meet, but it's impossible to tell how far away it is.

"Just pay close attention to me, Sierra. I'll bring us in. I'm not exactly sure about the spot, but there are almost no waves crashing on the reef, so we'll be fine."

"Pitch black crash-landing, great!" Sierra says with a shiver.

Mano aims for what he thinks is the spot, the keyhole, and they paddle toward the shore, or more so towards the gray silhouette which is most certainly land. He can't really see the breakers or the rocks. Obviously, they are breaking close in, right on the reef with the swell down, but they can't really see anything. Then suddenly, Mano feels a wave forming underneath them.

"Back! Back-paddle, back-paddle, back up," He instructs, hurriedly.

The wave slips by them and sets them back down the right on the reef. They're there already! They jump out and quickly drag the kayak off the reef towards the silhouette of the shore.

"We made it!" Mano exclaims as they clamber onto the sand.

"That was crazy!" Sierra shouts.

"Crazy awesome," Mano laughs.

Chapter 27   When it Rains, it Pours

Mano decides to call Khan's cell phone to see if he made the hike out. He doesn't necessarily want to, but he decides it is the right thing to do. The phone rings and Khan answers.

"Khan, so I guess you made it out, how are you guys?" Mano asks. The rain pounding on the metal roof he's under makes it hard to hear himself speak.

"We got a situation here, Captain." Khan says, hardly acknowledging Mano on the other end.

"Yeah, I know. It's pouring down rain out here and your daughter's stuck with Amy in the valley?"

"Yeah, we got a situation," Khan repeats.

"Ok, it's pouring rain and a bunch of bridges are flooded out. How can I help you?" Mano responds in frustration.

"Where are you?"

"We're on the east side of the island. Sierra and I got a hotel room in town."

"We're stuck on the North Shore, and the bridges are out. We're flooded in," Khan continues.

"Well, if you can get over here…" Mano starts, but Khan cuts him off.

"Captain, you need to make yourself available to me." Mano can hear him flare up over the phone even in the thundering rain.

"We're stuck over here too, Khan. Don't worry, when the rain stops they'll open up the roads. If you get to this side of the island you can stay in our room. Sierra and I got a room here for 2 nights."

"Captain, I was supposed to be on that boat, you need to make yourself available to me now! You've disrespected my tribe, my family, and this storm is putting my daughter back on the inside in danger." Click. He hangs up.

"It's not so easy to help someone who doesn't want to be helped," Mano says, turning to Sierra.

He could sense Khan was pissed the second he answered the phone. He kind of knew he would be pissed regardless. He knew when he left the beach with Sierra last night, He knew even more when it started to rain. He knew even more so when they closed the roads, and that Khan would be stuck on the north side of the island. Khan's pissed and its pouring rain, neither are his problem. Still Khan's not one anybody wants to deal with when angry. Just his tone over the phone sent chills down Mano's spine.

"It's probably better that he's stuck on the North Shore, I don't want to deal with that bad energy," Mano tells Sierra

"Khan's just pissed that he actually had to hike the trail," Sierra states smartly.

"No shit. I'm glad he had to hike it in the rain." Mano responds bitterly.

For three days and three nights buckets of rain pour down. The wind howls and brings in torrents of rain. It rains so hard and so consistently that even the moments when it feels like it's letting up are still a steady drizzle. The streets fill up and low spots become impassable swamps. The sun disappears completely. Everything is wet, grey and cold. Cabin fever in the stale cheap hotel room sets in to the point that Sierra and Mano feel like they just have to make it back to the inside, rain or not. They call but never get a hold of Khan. They might as well just coo him back on the inside. Both Mano and Sierra are over going out of their way to help him.

"He's nearly forty years old, he can take care of himself out here. He'll figure out a boat drop and get back in somehow," Sierra declares.

So, with another $400 of supplies staged on the boat drop with The Pro, Sierra and Mano set out to make the trip back in through the withering storm. Sierra is to hike in with her sister, Katie, who just arrived for her Spring Break, and Mano plans to paddle in alone on the kayak. The foul weather lingers. Thick clouds, wind, swell, and persistent rain taint what should be a joyous return. Still, Sierra and Mano feel it's better to get out of Babylon and back home to Neverland sooner than later.

When Mano gets back to his boat, he notices the bump in the swell immediately. The direction of the waves has changed too. It's a northeast swell as opposed to the typical northwest direction. The ocean looks turbulent and foreboding.

With the swell coming from the northeast, the waves are facing up big directly on the reef. A launch from the keyhole in the reef will be impossible. The launch site a mile back on the protected beach looks sketchy too. Double overhead waves pound straight into the usually calm bay. With strong trade winds and a northeast swell direction, what would a landing on Neverland beach be like? He imagines the waves breaking big and far offshore and having to swim to shore in suffocating whitewash. With the trades blowing as hard as they are, the boat might not even make it to shore upon crash-landing. If he doesn't get in close enough before bailing, the wind might just blow the boat west, and it could miss the beach completely. He cringes at the thought of this. He can't even look at the ocean anymore. The huge crashing surf makes his stomach churn. *Tomorrow*, he tells himself. *Tomorrow will be better.*

He waits the extra day to see if the fierce swell and wind back down, but they don't. For the first time since his very first kayak trip in, he's too scared to launch the boat. He phones The Pro, to ask him for ocean advice.

"What's a northeast swell gonna look like for landing on Neverland beach?" Mano asks.

"With this big storm, the beach has likely changed completely. The ocean has been volatile and unpredictable, lately. I wouldn't get in the water if I were you." Mano swallows at The Pro's grim outlook.

The morning surf report confirms what the seasoned boat captain believed. With no break in the swell in sight, he decides not to wait any longer, and just hike the muddy eleven miles.

He would have to leave his boat with most of the supplies stashed somewhere. He'd have to hike back out for the *SS Salvation*, eventually. Not being a patient person, he just wants to sprint back to Neverland, storm or not, boat or no boat. On the inside he'd have a dry tent, food, and friends. Out here he'd be without shelter or company. Sierra and her sister who left the day before are probably at 8-mile camp already, he thinks to himself.

"Well, I decided I won't try to kayak, so now I can hike in with you." Mano tells a tourist girl Jessie he met. She's been wanting to make it to the beach for months, but she was too scared and not ready to hike the trail on her own. Maybe he's meant to hike, to help this girl make it to the inside.

In an afternoon drizzle, they set off. He's dreading the miles of steep mud, but the trail is beautiful despite its sloppy state. They don't make it far the first day. The first stream crossing two miles in is raging high with runoff from the storms. He could cross, barely, but not safely with a pack, or with her. So they decide to wait it out for a night and cross the next day.

The next morning, he notices the swell has backed down a touch, and he almost abandons the hike to go back for the kayak, but it seems selfish to abandon his new companion, Jessie. They cross the stream in the sunshine safely that morning. It hadn't rained most of the night and the stream is less than half the volume of the evening before. Still, the trail is so muddy that he opts to walk half of it barefoot. Mano quickly remembers what a difficult chore the trail can be, but he enjoys it nearly as much as he did his first time in. Waterfalls gush from the cliffs and they notice at least a dozen that Mano had never seen before. Jessie is thankful and relieved to have Mano guide her and help carry some of her gear. They stop at the 8-mile lookout where the Valley can first be seen. They stare down at the churning ocean from 8-mile perch, not ready to put their packs back on.

"See those big waves breaking way off out there? I bet you're glad we didn't try to take the kayak! It looks pretty intense. Those are some huge sets! It would take all of my strength and some good luck to swim in the *SS Salvation* if it overturned too early in the whitewash."

Just as he says that, he hears the hum of an outboard motor cut the wind. A boat! What's a boat doing out here on a day like today? Surely there's a small craft advisory up. The boat rounds the corner and comes into view.

"I can't believe it! It's The Pro! A boat drop!" *Since when has there ever been a boat drop at four in the afternoon in double overhead surf?* Mano thinks to himself. Then he hears the jubilant yell of a passenger on board.

"Wahoooo!"

"Who's on the boat?" Jessie asks.

"That's someone you'll have to meet. Probably the most loved and feared guy in Neverland."

"Who's that?"

"Khan." Mano tells her.

"Wow, I can't wait to meet him," Jessie snickers.

"Just be wary about joining his *tribe*." Mano jokes back to her. His heart falls to his stomach knowing that their reunion will be anything but jubilant. According to Khan, Mano had disrespected his tribe. Would Khan and his tribe, turn against him?

Still, Mano should be happy to see Khan and know that the supplies he put on the boat would be there even before he arrived. But such a boat drop in the afternoon in this surf and wind is reckless and dangerous.

But this is Khan, and he is just that. Wild and reckless. He must have paid The Pro extra for such a risky mission.

Though already tired, Mano and Jessie strap their packs back on for the final stretch. The duo trots along, pushing through the damp overgrowth. They descend down the last steep, muddy hill into the valley and Mano's heart fills with joy. He's home. Neverland is no longer an escape; instead, it's home.

Chapter 28   Treading lightly in the Face of Chaos

"You've got to go over to the Sanctuary and get that bag!" Sierra explodes, as soon as Mano arrives. Mano tries to digest the situation before getting too riled up.

"So Khan commandeered one of our boat drop bags and took it to his camp at the Sanctuary? How did this happen? Why would he take our food?" Mano asks.

Sierra's animated cries can hardly rouse Mano. The light is fading and he's tired from all day on the muddy trail. He just moved his camp out of a mud puddle and now all he wants to do is sit by a fire and drink chai. But he has to deal with some sort of beach drama. Khan drama!

"Okay, tell me again what happened with the boat drop," he moans.

They put some water on for tea and Sierra retells the story.

"So Katie and I got here early afternoon and we start fixing up our camp. I'm hanging stuff up to dry and just trying to help her get dry and situated when I hear the boat. So naturally I stop everything and go down there to get our bags. Did you see the waves on the beach, by the way? They're huge!"

"Yeah, the ocean is crazy right now. I left the kayak and hiked half the trail barefoot. Anyway, so it was just Khan on the boat?" Mano tries to keep her focused.

"So the bags come in and I'm the only one in the whitewater helping with the bags. Then Khan and one of his minions, I think it was Spacedog, jump off the boat and have a rough swim in. Spacedog pretty much washes in wearing a life jacket. Khan is super testosterone pumped from the swim and marches along the beach wildly. By this time a couple more of Khan's interns arrive on the beach and start helping with the bags. Then Khan, in his adrenaline-infused fury, tells his minions, *'take all the bags with Captain Mano's name on them.'* Katie and I are trying to carry the bags up and Khan just comes and takes the biggest bag out of our hands and his crew carries it away. I was like, *'Hey what are you doing? That's our food,'* and he just glares at me like a madman with his nostrils flailing.

"I thought he was going to hit her," Katie cries out.

"So I just pull Katie away, and get out of there," Sierra continues.

"So we get two of the bags, but Khan commandeers the biggest one, the one with the wine and all the cheese and all the chocolate in it. They just take it with them up to the Sanctuary. They're probably tapping the boob of wine right now!"

"Seriously, he almost hit her!" Katie wails.

"Okay, calm down, we'll get the bag back. I'm sure Khan's tribe hasn't pillaged it yet! Sierra, why do you think Khan was so pissed that he took the bag?"

"I don't know, I'm sure he was super revved up from swimming in and I guess he was pissed about the kayak trip, and that he didn't get a hold of you in town. But what the hell? That's no reason to take the bag and threaten us."

"I can't believe he almost hit her!" Katie sobs.

"Take it easy Katie. We're all fine, nobody's hurt." Mano says.

"I don't think he would have hit me, Katie!" Sierra snaps.

"I wouldn't be so sure. It sounds like Khan's become crazy and irrational. He could totally lose it," Mano counters.

Katie's getting sucked into beach drama already and she's only been in Neverland for just a few hours.

"So you think he's still upset that he got left behind on the kayak and didn't get his way?" Sierra asks.

"I think that's exactly his deal. He's a child that throws a huge tantrum when he doesn't get his way, just like Leia, his daughter. He should simmer down eventually, but it's still bullshit." Mano's fists tighten as he speaks.

"Yeah, you should go over to the Sanctuary now and get our bag back." Sierra tells him.

"That's asking for trouble! I'm not going over there alone in the dark right now. That's just stupid. We should let this simmer down a bit. Besides, we've got plenty of food! You know what? I don't even want to get worked up about this anymore, it's putting me in a bad mood and I just got back!"

They terminate the discussion and share stories about the hike in. Mano tells them about how he and Jessie got denied at the first river crossing, and Sierra explains how she and Katie had to spend a rainy night camped at a makeshift shelter halfway along the trail. This time they all truly earned their way into Neverland. Most importantly, they had all made it back and were safe. What an entrance though, especially for first-timers, Jessie and Katie, who were thrown into storms and drama on their first night at this normally worry-free beach. Mano hates to admit it, but even his fantasy paradise has its drama.

But why does it have to roll down onto him? People like Keith, Kaholo, and Andrew never had to deal with this kind of crap. They just did their own thing, their actions never stirred the pot. It's when you do things for people, helping even, one inevitably sets themselves up for criticism and gossip. Playing an active role in the community requires one to have to defend oneself both verbally and physically. *Why is this?* Mano voices to himself, irritated. Mr. X's motto, FOPS 'Fuck Other People's Shit' certainly works. Good, or bad, if you aren't involved, you don't have to deal with any repercussions. Other people's shit, fuck it!

But if no one cared enough to get involved with other people's doings, community would be dead. Gardens would wilt away, boat drop bags would get lost, and big organized music jams would never happen. Magic could cease to exist, entirely. If no one cared to help out the tourists, they'd be uninspired and would bring down the energy of the valley. There'd certainly be twice as many helicopter rescues and more would drown if qualified people didn't step up to help when needed. Would then there be even more drama?

Of course, Mano is a man of feeling and action. He can't help but be involved. Reasonable or not, his actions induced much of this turmoil. Knowing that Khan forcefully commandeered their boat drop makes Mano especially uneasy. What's worse is that he knows the matter has to rest solely on his shoulders. No one else, not even his so-called *friends* would want to get involved with Khan. Mano knows it will take a lot more than politely asking for his bag back to make peace with him too. As irrational and unbelievable as it is, it doesn't surprise him. Khan, the guy he thought to be his best friend on the island, overnight, even without a confrontation, had become his worst enemy. Mano knows it. Khan turned from a good to a bad avocado without warning.

Mano lets the humble truth sink in. The guy Mano had come out on the boat with, shared food and rum and stories and songs and secrets with, now hated him with a passion. The guy who had given him a surfboard and told him he was *'like a brother he never had,'* now wanted nothing but pain for him. He swallows hard at this, and wonders if sleep will come. The rain comes first, and the pitter-patter on his tent eventually settles him and coaxes him to sleep.

At dawn it's raining harder. His tea jar outside the tent is nearly full. Three inches of rain had fallen overnight; the storm had returned. Every piece of earth around is fully saturated and water is filling up and running off all around his camp. Fortunately, all of his essentials are dry because Sierra had set up more tarps yesterday. They combined their cooking areas to have more dry space together as well as a good-sized pile of dry-ish firewood. Mano wonders about the tourists. How are they faring without tarps and dry cooking space? He wonders about Khan and his army at the Sanctuary on the other side of the raging valley stream. He laughs, imagining their situation. A bunch of cold, wet dudes probably fussing at each other and getting dripped on from the Sanctuary's notoriously ill-fated tarp setup. Sierra and Mano join a couple more wet tourists from the beach at Surf Camp for breakfast under tarps.

It's still raining by midmorning, and the normally dry, steep ravine at Surf Camp has grown into a gushing chocolate milk creek. This is a good indication that everyone will be stuck where they are. The main valley stream will be un-crossable and surely no one will be hiking the trail. He's not going to confront Khan about the bag today.

Embracing the water and the wetness is key to enduring a big storm like this. Mano runs down the beach, naked in the rain and jumps into the ocean. He takes in the beauty and power of the dozen new waterfalls melting over the cliffs. He thinks about the basil plants and salad greens soaking up the moisture. Sierra has a harder time embracing the mud-pit their home has become.

"I hate Neverland when it's raining. I hate having to sit under tarps and constantly having to dry out my shit. I just want it to be sunny again!"

"It will be sunny soon enough, just think of how good the rain is for Thomas's new garden and the basil in Cliff's garden on the beach. Think of how nice it is not to hear any helicopters or have to carry water." Mano encourages.

"I don't care. I just want it to be sunny— it's been raining forever!"

Grizzley comes over and spices up the dismal scene a bit with his *Grizzisims.*

"This is a bear of a storm. Grizzley enough even to make Thriver-Girl Sierra complain! Well, I make storms like this look like the Atacama desert! I make guys like Khan look like Saint Peter." Grizz laughs to himself. "What do you think of that one, Captain Mano?"

"How about, I'm so cool I make hot chai feel like a snowstorm."

"Good one, Mano!" even Katie manages a smile. The crew smokes weed and tells stories, and the morning show progresses seamlessly into the evening show.

"It's not too out of the ordinary for winter storms to last a full two weeks," Grizz teases.

"It's already been a week with little more than a glimmer of sun for a day or two," Sierra says.

"Well, I don't think this one will be as big as it was when you guys were in town. We really got drenched on that one! People were getting nervous, holding up in the cave and just watching the rain hammer down on the beach."

"You got something like fourteen inches of rain in three days, I heard." Mano adds. The crew falls silent in contemplation.

"So what's the biggest storm you've ever been through here on the Inside?" Mano asks Grizz.

"Well, there was one nine years ago. Something like forty straight days of rain. It was biblical!"

"Forty days! That seems impossible," Mano says, wide-eyed.

"I'm telling you, it was scriptural! Forty days without sun. People thought the world was gonna end or something."

That thought gets Sierra, Mano, Katie and the few tourists hanging about even more unsettled. They all spit back their own crazy apocalyptic theories trying to hype up people even more. What an afternoon, huddled up under tarps drinking whiskey chai as a group of suddenly self-proclaimed storm visionaries.

By late afternoon Mano can see the clouds clearing on the horizon to the west and he predicts that the storm will likely clear by morning. He begins to worry about Khan.

Mano feels truly afraid of Khan now. Had he completely turned on him? Whatever motive or reason Khan had for taking the bag and threatening him and Sierra doesn't matter now. He's pissed off, and Mano felt he could act without concern for consequences. Mano could be nice and judicious and fair towards him, but that strategy won't make sense in Khan-world. Mano realizes he can't afford to come across as meek. However, Khan would take any act of intimidation as an invitation to fight. And a fair fight with him would be out of the question. Although Khan is only slightly bigger than him, he could be vicious and would not hesitate to use whatever he could get his hands on. He could release a fury that may not stop until it's too late... Mano can hardly even imagine. Mano fears not so much his fist but his bite and head-butt. His skull is gorilla-like, harder than a mature coconut, for sure. The only other person that would even consider standing up to him, or even dealing with him is Rick, the well over six-foot winemaker living way up-valley. But up there he and Lisa could stay out of any beach drama, and that's what they wanted. Mano consciously decides that fighting Khan would not be worth it, but still he has to confront him.

The rain lets up and he summons the courage to do just that — confront Khan, and ask for his bag back at the Sanctuary. Maybe the weather difficulties would soften the anger Khan holds toward him. The suspense of the whole ordeal is stressful. Mano just wants to put it to rest, to get the bag and somehow make amends with Khan. He walks through the drizzle to see if the stream is crossable.

'Oh man,' he groans to himself the moment he sees the valley stream. It's still a raging torrent. The muddy brown water gushes toward the ocean ferociously. *Well that settles that, no crossing tonight,* he thinks. He turns around and walks back to camp as light fades peacefully in the drizzle.

That night Mano tries to rationalize his fear of Khan by trying to understand him. Khan must have felt slighted as a child, he decides. He had been picked on too much by older siblings and not picked to be on the winning team. Consequently, Khan became the bully that had to be in control. He had to have his team of helpers, his minions, that *he* reigned over. They put up his tarps and tent and cooked the food he provided. He shared almost everything, but he also wanted control of everything. He even thought he should control Mano's kayak! The way he instantly adopted Dmitri as his right-hand man came as no surprise to Mano or others on the beach. Khan knew he could boss around the Russian. Khan loved having *'friends'* he could control — be his tribe.

Mano and Sierra believe the whole tribe thing to be ridiculous, but it makes sense for Khan and it certainly worked for him. Mano had never wanted to be part of his tribe, but he still would hang around as a friend. Now the division is clear. He's out of the tribe, which makes him an enemy by default. Mano heard of irrational explosions and Khan losing it on people for no reason, but he had never witnessed it himself. Now he is regretting that he didn't distance himself more from Khan early on. He ponders what he should or should not have done, but this just makes him tired. His mind plays out what would become of a fight between him and Khan. He swallows and wishes for sleep.

The next morning the sun is still hidden but his tea glass rain gauge reads just a sip. He makes tea and oatmeal for himself and Jessie, who's now camping with him.

His fears have settled overnight. He'll go and try to get the bag and talk to Khan today. He remembers the last time he even saw Khan was almost two weeks ago when he and Dmitri were on the beach in the moonlight. He could see into Khan's fear-driven nature then. He remembers the stress on the whole evening. He remembers how he secretly felt ecstatic knowing that Khan would wake up and see the kayak gone and be forced to hike the trail. Was this some sort of karmic revenge for leaving a tripping hippie to hike the trail out like everybody else?

The situation doesn't seem fair, karmic or otherwise! Regardless, he has to confront Khan and get that bag. He wants this thing over and done with. Surely, the stream is crossable now. Walking down toward the valley stream from his perch spot above the beach camps, he sees Khan and Dmitri walking toward him from the Heiau. He hesitates, but continues toward them. *Well, this is convenient,* Mano thinks. *Now I don't even have to cross the river.* Mano continues down the hill, trying to consider his approach. He notices Khan and Dmitri's gait. Their gaze is down and they walk briskly with their fingers curled under their palms. He doesn't rehearse anything. He decides just to let the words come out naturally.

"How's it going, warriors?" Mano asks sarcastically as they slide by on the trail without even looking up at him. He can feel their energy. Even lighthearted Dmitri is cold.

"What's up? You're not even gonna look up and say hello?" Mano continues, a little more strongly.

"I can't even talk to you right now, Captain," Khan spits through clenched teeth.

Annoyed, Mano searches for the right words to get through to him.

"I just want to get our bag back and find out why you are so upset with me."

"I said I can't talk to you now!" Khan whirls around and glares, nostrils flaring. Mano persists, irritated. He's getting nowhere.

"Look, I understand that you are upset, but taking our food and threatening Sierra, that's ridiculous. You should apologize for that."

"You have no respect for me and my family," Khan huffs.

"What are talking about? What have I done to disrespect you?"

"In town I said you need to make yourself available to me. You were supposed to help me buy plane tickets off the island with the money you owed me."

"Yeah, I called you twice and you hung up on me," Mano huffs.

"You jeopardized the safety of my tribe, my family."

"What are you talking about? That's ridiculous. I was never part of *your tribe!*"

"This valley is a powerfully spiritual place, not a place for your fantasy games and sexual perversion!"

"Perversion? What's is your deal? This valley's not a place for you to boss people around and enslave them into your tribe with food and ganja! You have no respect for this valley, and no respect for women!"

Khan escalates into full tantrum mode. He clenches his fists, pulls his arms down and inhales in audible grunts and screeches like a child gearing up to explode into a violent fit.

"I will hurt you. I will kill you, Captain!" he growls.

Mano had never seen anything like it; Khan is building up pressure like a steam engine, preparing to blow his top. Mano's heart races and fear makes him start to clench his own fists, ready to strike. But he doesn't want to fight Khan. It's not worth it to him. He feels slighted, but still isn't worth a hard blow to the face for either of them just because Khan is overhyped about Mano not helping him in town, or even the stupid food bag. Of course, Mano can hardly analyze it now. Anything he'd say would only provoke the now boiling Khan.

"Mano, run, just run. Leave now!" Dmitri breaks the silence suddenly. They both notice the saliva foam building on the edge of Khan's mouth like a rabid dog. Mano shuffles a step back, his gaze still focused on Khan, who just stands steaming, foaming at the mouth with muscles tensed.

"Yes, Mano, you must leave now. Run, just run!"

Dmitri senses that Khan is about to lose it, but he certainly isn't providing any more mediation to the situation. Mano is sure he'd do little to stop Khan.

"You better leave now or I'll crush you," Khan fumes.

"Yes, sir," Mano spits sarcastically while turning to step back again.

"Don't patronize me, Captain!" He breaks from his standing position but Dmitri is kind of in the way. Mano steps back, glares, and stomps away toward the valley trail.

He just wanted to sock Khan! Give Khan the violence that he wanted. He grinds his teeth thinking about it. He wants to make him feel physical pain for the injustice and mental strife he caused him, and let him know that he would not be controlled. Khan is still controlling him with his threats and taking his stuff, and Mano hates it. He hates himself for not standing up to Khan and putting him in his place. If he were just a bit bigger and more confident maybe he would have went for him when he threatened. He tries to breathe and at least applaud himself for avoiding violence and protecting himself by walking away.

Besides, reacting to the point of violence is what a violent person wants, he tells himself. An aggressive manipulator is not satisfied with a truce, or a reconciliation. Their goal is to push the other person to fear so much that they have no choice but to be violent or to give in to their demands. Mano certainly doesn't want to give in to Khan. It would only let his power grow. Besides, he, himself, is a stubborn person who wouldn't back down. But to give into violence would let Khan win, too. One thing seemed certain: he made the right decision to walk away there on the trail. A bloody defeat would have been certain for Mano with Khan's bodyguard Dmitri there. Dmitri likely would not have attacked Mano, but he certainly wouldn't let his beloved Khan lose if Mano were to gain the advantage in a fight.

So he didn't get the bag, and Khan apparently wants to fight him for ridiculous reasons, and it's starting to rain. Now he's forced to live on edge, in fear, and it disgusts him.

Mano doesn't go back to his camp. Instead, he spends the whole day wandering up-valley observing the gushing side streams from recent rains. He stops at Rick and Lisa's camp and explains to them what happened. They have compassion for Mano's the situation because they had endured Khan's crazy outbreaks on his California farm. They truly sympathize with Mano and try to console him, offering him their food and wine. Still, there is no good solution in sight. Together, they could stand up to Khan, but excommunicating such a character would be a monumental task. Khan would not walk out peacefully like Len-dog. It would take an organized and aggressive team to remove him from the valley.

Oh, how he hates waiting on edge! He drinks wine and smokes weed with Rick and Lisa, and manages to wait out the day. At dusk, he retreats back down to his camp by the beach.

Sierra has good news at camp. Well, sort of good news. Khan had brought her the bag. He apologized to her, but he is still pissed at Mano, and was now raving on about the two hundred dollars Mano owed him for a boat drop well before the storm. The bag is intact. Well except for one thing: *the boob*, the 5-liter bag of red wine, had mysteriously *popped* on the boat drop.

"Well that's pretty fishy," Mano says. The Russian couldn't even pop an inflated boob by jumping on it during a party, yet this boob somehow pops inside of the bag on the boat drop. That seems unlikely. That, and the Sriracha sauce is missing. Sierra claims that a bunch of food smelled like wine, but Mano doesn't notice anything like that.

Khan may be crazy, but he's not stupid. He knows that Mano would never pay him the money he owed him if he didn't return the bag. At least they got the bag. They got the cheese and the chocolate and the whiskey and other essentials. Mano isn't the least bit confident Khan has settled down, but returning the bag and apologizing to Sierra was a step in the right direction.

This time the evening clouds clear just enough to allow a red sun to shine through on the horizon at sunset. Tomorrow the valley will break free from the storm for sure, he decides. He lets out a sigh of relief at that.

Mano doesn't talk to Khan the next day, and he barely sees him in passing the day after. He decides not to dwell on it and just do his own thing; swim and enjoy the sun again. But the weird energy surrounding what had been dubbed the '*Khan drama*,' has sunken in and covered the valley. Normal evening jams and group pizza parties are put on hold. Khan's warriors, his food-sponsored minions, start dropping out of his tribe on the bluffs. Even young Spacedog once completely loyal to Khan decides to set up his own camp. He tells people that he is over all the pointless projects Khan had them slaving on.

"I didn't come here to work for some tribe, I came here to play music and to be free and inspired," Spacedog gripes.

Inspiration is a tricky thing. It doesn't spread linearly. For inspiration needs inspiration to keep going and to grow. Inspired people inspire others. Then magic can be possible. Now it feels like all inspiration reserves are drained from the lack of sun, lack of community, and the stale energy from the '*Khan drama*' that settled over the valley like a fog.

Even this new girl Mano hiked in, Jessie, is kind of a downer. She needed to be inspired. She seemed uninterested in making things fun and exciting, plus she has no initiative. She waited for him to do everything.

"Just boil the water, put the tea in, and pour it into the cups. It's that simple. If you just sit there and let the fire die down, then you will never boil the water." He'd get frustrated coaching her how to help.

She just doesn't really care, and that's hard for Mano to grasp. He didn't mind sharing his tent and taking care of a woman who he wasn't getting sex from, but he wanted her to care for him too. He feels empty realizing he's just being used for food, company, and dry space. Still it would be silly to just kick her out. There were no other new girls around, and in a sense just having someone there through all the drama was better than being alone.

He thinks about his friend Sierra, too. Does she really care about him, or did she just want his protection and the food he helped provide? He thinks about how demanding she was when she wanted him to cross the river and get their bag back, yet how little she really did to help him deal with Khan outside of that. She often just did her own thing regardless. She doesn't care about him. He needed a real friend, yet feels he can't put his faith in anyone.

Caring for Sierra, Jessie, Khan, and Dmitri got him into this whole mess. Khan was jealous that Mano, his brother, wouldn't dedicate himself to him. Now Mano feels bitter about caring at all.

____

198

"Fuck other people's shit!" Mano announces, recalling Mr. X's maxim again.

The next day he foregoes the two-hour tea routine with Jessie, skips yoga, and runs the trail out to get his kayak. The storm had cleared and he decides that all he cares about now is his kayak stashed back in Babylon.

He runs the trail until 6-mile stream. There he decides to take the rest of the trail more slowly. *The trail is like a meditation,* he tells himself. Even with his tiny daypack and being in great shape, the trail is long and difficult, still. But the journey is peaceful, not bothersome.

The beach at trailhead is nearly deserted. He'll just get the kayak and paddle back into the sunset, he decides. He goes to uncover the boat in the bushes but it's not there. The *SS Salvation* is gone! It's been stolen. It's not tucked back in the bushes, not on the beach or anywhere to be seen. A horrible feeling sinks in. He's stuck in Babylon with nothing but a daypack. He's forced to just keep walking to town. He asks a handful of lifeguards about its whereabouts, but they have no leads to give him. The *SS salvation* appears to be lost forever! He's heartbroken.

In town, he just feels more downtrodden. He's alone and out of place. It seems like every time he's in town, he just wants to be back in Neverland. Now he's stuck. He burns some money on a good meal and just waits at some picnic tables for the light to fade, still not knowing where he'll stay.

"Well, well, Captain Mano!" a voice comes out of the darkness. He recognizes it instantly.

He turns around and finds himself face to face with Lennie, who is looking as clean and chipper as can be.

"Da-Len, you made it! You're alive! We all thought you got smoked by the valley. The last I heard, you had lost it and were all cut up with staph, huckin' yourself off of waterfalls in the way back. Everyone thought you were toast, pau-hana!"

"Jumping off of waterfalls! Na, I was thriving back there, just living solo way up in the valley. Look at me now! I lost like 30 pounds, I'm full power. I'm fine."

"Wow, I can't believe it's really you. The last time I saw you was months ago when you were getting screwy in Sierra's yoga class on the Heiau. I'm sorry, man. How are you doing, really?"

"You know, Mano, things have been good— really good, actually. I'm living on the streets, just raging around. But I've been meeting girls and staying healthy, having a pretty good time, too. Things are good."

"Sweet, it was good to run into you Lennie, you look good. I just hiked back out to get my kayak now that the big storm and swells are over, but I get out and find it's freakin' stolen. The valley's been crazy. Khan pretty much lost it and went off on me, even said he was going to kill me. It's been kind of ridiculous this last week. The last two weeks, really."

"Well shit, Captain, I want to hear all about it. Let's go burn one down by the bay."

Chapter 29   Spirit Says Go

Mano doesn't let the *SS Stolen* or Lennie's antics slow him down. He spends a day searching for the kayak, but he eventually gives up and buys another used one to replace her. A local summertime outfitter had a couple of beat up boats they were willing to get rid of, so he picks up an old sun-faded leaker for another couple hundred bucks. It's a *Zest 2*, just like his other boat, however it's missing a hatch cover and it has a three-inch blistering crack in the tail. He's able to fashion a bungee and a piece of plastic trash bag around the hatch, and a guy from the shop helps him patch the crack in the tail with surf epoxy. He prays that it will at least make a few trips before it requires some sort of plastic welding.

He needs a boat out there for fishing, for medical evacs, and for quick re-supply missions. Besides, a pirate Captain without a ship is no Captain at all! He has the paddles from the old boat and a full dry bag of stuff he meant to bring in still stashed at the launch site. A local lady with a truck drives him and the new boat to the end of the road to launch. Close to the trailhead he runs into Kawika hitchhiking back to the trail. His eyes light up when he sees Mano with the boat in the back of the truck.

"I was just asking *Spirit* for any way to get back to Neverland besides hiking the trail. I'm so tired. I said, Spirit, I don't want to go, I don't want to hike, but Spirit said to just get on the road and start making your way to the trailhead. And here you are coming with the kayak."

"Well, I guess it's your lucky day, Kawika. We're fast-tracking on the crest of an ocean wave back to the inside."

Mano is intrigued by Kawika's ability to make easy decisions based on his intuition. He would call his own intuition, '*Spirit,*' and accepts and respects its decision-making ability as some all-knowing guiding light. It gets kinda annoying listening to Kawika say that *Spirit* says this or that, but Mano is weary of letting his own conscience be in full control, so the thought of *Spirit* guiding him intrigues him. *Or maybe Kawika really is possessed and receiving subliminal messages from some great spirit?* Mano wonders.

It's a quick paddle in with a tail wind for two of them, in the big, red *Zest 2*. They are both excited when they see the beach as they pull into the set break. It's a smooth landing, surfing the boat right onto the sand. Mano cracks open a cold beer and he shares it with Kawika in celebration. He helps Mano unload the boat and drag it onto the rocks until he sees Khan. But the sight of Khan's crazy eyes has him bolting for the bushes like a stray cat. Kawika scurries away, leaving Mano by himself to deal with Khan.

Instantly, the beer tastes sour in his mouth. Khan scrambles down the rocks with the fury of a possessed man.

"You've been gone three days. You're supposed to be helping me get off this island and now you're buying beer and another kayak!" Khan roars.

Without even giving him a chance to respond, Khan picks up some beers and starts throwing them against the rocks. They explode like fireworks.

"What the hell is your problem? What the fuck are you doing?" Mano shouts.

"You're off in town buying beers when you should be here helping me and my daughter get off this island. Where's my money?"

"What are you talking about? First off, the kayak was stolen so I had to buy this one. That's why it took so long. And it's not my responsibility to get you and your daughter off the island — that's ridiculous. I'd be more motivated to get you your money quicker if you weren't such a..."

Khan busts a can on the rocks and it sprays up wildly. Mano almost reaches to grab his arm, but he doesn't dare. He just lets him continue his beer slamming fury. Mano marches up the beach and leaves Khan to destroy the better part of a twelve-pack in his temper tantrum. He can't watch. He has to just walk away. He wants to just roll on the sand and brawl with him right then and there, but he can't. He just can't bring himself to risk his own life and limb over some ridiculous stunt from Khan. He lets him have his destructive tantrum. Bystanders peer through the trees and watch as Khan punches the sand and wails and dances about as the inflamed psychopath he has become.

Mano knows that if he does fight Khan and he wins, or doesn't get hurt that badly, he would still be living in fear. If he hurt or humiliated him, Khan might hunt him down and attack him in his sleep. He certainly seems that crazed and unpredictable. In the five days since he confronted Dmitri and him on the trail, Mano thought the delicate situation would simmer down, but it certainly hadn't.

Eventually, Khan runs out of steam and leaves. Mano returns to reclaim the few unexploded beers and drag the kayak up into the bushes, out of helicopter view. Then Khan comes back in a fury, wielding a machete heading for the kayak.

"Buying a kayak when you should be getting me my money! I'm gonna destroy this boat! I'll hack this thing in half!"

"If you hack my kayak, you won't see a cent of the two-hundred I owe you!" Mano yells back. Khan hesitates, retracting the blade, then he comes straight towards Mano.

"I'm gonna kill you, Captain! You better hike out and get me my money right now!"

Mano shuffles back to keep a buffer of twenty to thirty feet between himself and the outstretched blade. The few innocent bystanders simply stare in awe.

"What the hell are you doing? No fighting! Put down that damn machete!" Andrew intervenes finally.

Khan lowers the blade, setting it down and marching down the trail in a huff. Jessie stealthily grabs the machete and hides it in the tall grass. Mano stares, hands trembling. He's so stressed he can hardly think of what to do. Just weeks ago Khan was hugging him, telling him he was like a brother to him. Now he wanted to kill him. And over what? A storm or a kayak trip. Or Mano not having money to give him right away.

"Andrew, what the hell should I do? Did you see that? Khan was about to freakin' hack me with that machete."

"Do you have the money right now? Maybe if you just gave him the money, Khan would chill out. This whole thing might be over."

"I was so focused on finding the lost kayak and getting a replacement, that I didn't even think to take out money when I was in town. Plus, I thought this whole drama was practically over before I left. I have a hundred bucks here now I can give him, but I don't know, even if I did have all the money I don't know if I should give it to him now. In a way, the only thing ensuring that he doesn't destroy me, my camp, or my boat is the stupid money I owe him. But I reckon he's gone so crazy he might just hack up the boat and me anyway."

"You know Khan, he doesn't want to kill anybody. He just…just, he burns hot. Khan burns hot."

"I don't care! That's no way to treat people, coming at them wielding a weapon like that! The beach is as a place of love and sanctuary. Khan of all people should know that. This kind of shit can't happen here in Neverland! It's bullshit!"

"Well, really, the valley is a place of peace and solitude. The beach is where drama happens. But calm down, I'm sure you guys will work something out."

"Work something out? I'm not trying to work something out. I'm trying to keep from getting killed! I need you guys to help stand up to Khan with me and not scurry away like Kawika did as soon as he saw him."

"I'm not getting involved in all this." Andrew shrugs.

"This is what I mean! Nobody here cares when it really counts! Do I have any real friends to back me up and stand up to Khan? This isn't the kind of situation that's just going to be solved with peace and love!" Mano paces back and forth, stressed and disgusted.

"I wish Honu were here. He's a real friend who would stand by me!"

"I'd help you, but I'm not going to fight Khan with you. He's tough and certainly crazy. I don't want to risk getting a broken jaw or getting killed any more than you do," Andrew voices.

"Yeah, I know. Nobody wants to mess with Khan. That's why it has to come down onto my neck." Mano huffs then leaves. He marches up to his camp. Jessie's already back lounging in the hammock seemingly unfazed. He asks for her advice, but she's no more help than Andrew. She doesn't want to get involved.

"I just want this drama to be over with. I'm sick of hearing about Khan this and Khan that," she moans.

Mano kicks over pots and pans and stomps in the mud. "Well as soon as Khan leaves, it will all be over, right?"

Mano sweats through the night, overanalyzing the situation and trying to think of what to do. He has no control over anything. It seems as though he can only react to what Khan throws at him. This bothers him as much as anything. He doesn't want to hike or paddle out the next day just to get him his money. He just got back, and it would only let Khan win. It would just reinforce his violent intimidation tactics. What might happen if he did just fight him? The outcomes he plays out in his head don't look glorifying for either person. They may both be crippled before anyone could stop them. He quivers at the thought of a brutal fight—maybe even a fight to the death. He has to avoid confrontation at any cost, but he wants to end this cat and mouse game of threats, and escape with some pride, still. More than anything, he just wants peace in the valley again. Everyone is sick of the drama that their ongoing dispute has caused.

The next morning he lets Jessie make breakfast. He watches her from the hammock as she toils over some slow cooking pancakes on a weak bed of coals. He casually observes her without directing or managing the operation and it is fine. Still, she acts like it was such a chore when she finishes. He just lies in the hammock waiting for the sun with no motivation for yoga. He has no inspiration to go down to try to talk to Khan or hike out to town as he insisted. He just rests.

His ears perk up and he hears hurried footsteps approaching. He just stays in the hammock until Khan is standing over him.

"You just don't get it, do you? I will cause you serious pain. I told you to come to my camp immediately after sunup so I could give you instructions to hike out to get my money, but instead you're just lying here in this hammock!" Khan fumes.

"We're making breakfast." Mano tells him plainly.

"I told you to meet me at my camp first thing to hike out, or I'd beat you down to nothing. Now I should kick your ass just to show that I'm a man of my word."

"And I'm a man of my word, too. I'll get you the money, but I'm not going to hike out and right back in just to get your money. That's ridiculous! I just got here! You'll get your money soon enough. It's not like you can spend it in here anyway."

"That's not the point. You should go out and get me that money now."

"All you growers out in NorCal make people wait months for money you owe them. This time you're just going to have to wait a few more days. You'll get your money when I leave." Mano says with a smirk.

"This isn't about California. This is about you and me and how your life is in serious danger," Khan snarls, menacingly.

Mano continues from the hammock. "What is your deal? You just wanna threaten people when you don't get your way. You come up to my camp and disrupt our breakfast with your freakin' bullshit!"

"Watch your mouth, Captain. You're asking for pain talking like that. You can't escape me. You can try to run up-valley and hide, but I'll hunt you down." Mano watches Khan fume up and this time it just pisses him off.

"You just really want to provoke me to fight, don't you? I'll tell you what, you want to fight so badly, I'll fight a fair fight with you. I'll go a five-minute round with you right down on the beach, no biting, no head butts."

"I'll tell you right now that's not happening. I fight to kill. I don't care if I use rocks or anything! I'm gonna crush your skull!" Khan's rage builds and Mano senses that he is getting close to his boiling point. Mano adjusts slightly to spin out of the hammock if Khan encroaches any further. Just when he thinks he might spring at him he hears another set of footsteps. They both look back in a moment of reprieve. It's Kawika.

"*Spirit* just told me to come up here and talk to you guys." They are both taken aback by his calm tone. But Khan quickly resumes his threats.

"You need to hike out right now, Captain, if you want any chance of keeping that pretty face of yours!" Visions flash through Mano's head of a brutal biting, head-butting spree that Khan would surely unleash.

"Khan, can you just come here for a second, can I just talk to you alone for a second?" Kawika manages to coax the fuming Khan aside. Mano's relieved to have a second to adjust and collect his thoughts. The whole time Jessie just remains silent, still next to the fire. Two minutes later they return, Kawika leading.

"Captain, I'd like to propose a solution. How about the two of you paddle the kayak out together and you can go to town and get Khan the money you owe him. Then he can catch his plane and get out of here."

Mano sits dumbfounded for a minute, letting Kawika's proposal sink in. Khan would leave the valley on his kayak and Khan's daughter Leia would hike out with Dmitri. Immediately, Mano thinks of the injustice of Khan getting his way and a free ride out, as well as his money, but he allows this thought to pass. If he paddled Khan out, Khan would be forced to cooperate, take his money and leave. He'd save his own face and possibly the face of the community. Truthfully, Kawika conceived the most viable non-violent option. Paddle Khan out. He decides not to try to tack on any pre-requisite apologies for Khan's ridiculous actions and just agrees to Kawika's proposal.

"All right, we leave first thing in the morning in the red boat. You get your money and you leave Neverland." Mano proposes. They both agree. *Thank God for Kawika, no need for a fight to the death anymore.* Now all he has to do is make another fifteen-mile round-trip ocean mission and they'll all be rid of this psychotic surfer.

With fate decided, Mano and Khan get to actually enjoy the rest the day without the thought of a fight looming over them. Khan is even pleased enough with the solution to officially invite Mano to his going away party and music recording session up at Kaholo's. Mano decides to make an appearance there just to show he's not afraid of Khan, but he certainly isn't going to sing or record anything.

He and Jessie stop at Kaholo's briefly, just to see what kind of gathering has formed. It's hardly a party. Neither Mano nor Andrew or anyone else is inspired to play any music at all. People sit back and snicker as hypercritical Khan snaps at people for talking or at Kaholo for playing his flute too loudly during the recording. It's a terrible recording session, completely devoid of magic and communal spirit. Nobody dances, nobody wants to sing Khan's songs with him, and most people just watch the sunset then leave.

"So much for Khan's going away party. I'm more excited about the 'Khan's gone' party tomorrow when you get back, Mano," Andrew says, nudging him.

Mano sleeps through the night for the first time in a week. The next morning Khan is up and ready to depart first thing. Mano launches the boat and they paddle east together. They paddle collected and smoothly in the pale morning light in silence. Their rhythm is sleek and tranquil — beautiful even. Mano almost enjoys paddling with him. In the beginning of the journey the thought crosses his mind to push Khan out of the boat, whack him on the head with the paddle, and leave him in the middle of the ocean, but revenge is never sweet, his conscience tells him. Over the two-hour journey, his pent-up anger toward Khan dissipates with each methodical paddle stroke. It feels like their voyage is a healing process for both of them. Together, in sync, they land perfectly at the protected bay, riding the whitewater onto the sand. Then they catch a quick ride into town. Mano's unforgiving heart considers stiffing Khan once they get into town. Instead of going to the cash machine, he could just hitch a ride right back to the boat and hope Khan didn't catch up.

He decides his own vengeful thoughts have troubled him enough already and have caused him enough strife. The $200 he owes Khan isn't worth losing sleep over. He wants stress-free closure, especially knowing that somehow one day he'd probably run into Khan again. And like Mr. X. advised him, he'd want to be able to just look him in the eye and say, *'how's it.'* So he gets him the two hundred, and Khan buys him breakfast. They exchange a heartless handshake to try to close out any animosity, but the final exchange is cold. There's little forgiveness or mending of hearts for either of them. Mano has no respect for the man who threatened his life, but to wish him ill fortune seems bad juju, so he sends positive energy forward.

Khan's gone. *Now it's time to bring the good energy back.* Mano tells himself as he lets the trade winds blow him and his boat back home to Neverland.

Chapter 30   Bee-ing There for the Land

Spring advances on. Sun and rain make the hillsides bloom. Bees buzz and birds sing, but the energy lull Khan leaves looming over the valley lingers. Residents look for new topics to drown out the gossip and chatter surrounding Khan's departure.

"Bees, Bees, Bees. We need more bees!" Cliff proclaims. "A healthy bee population is essential to pollination, the health of the gardens, and the whole valley ecosystem."

"Yes, of course, everyone agrees that more bees is mo better, but how are we going to get more bees?" Thomas asks.

"You know, there is, or was— a beehive up community garden stream past Seven Trees orange grove." Andrew adds.

"Right! And Keilani was the valley beekeeper taking care of it up there, but that's long past, she doesn't want to do it anymore." Thomas interjects.

"Yeah, she hasn't given a shit about those hives in years." Andrew says.

"Hey, I don't see you hiking way up there and sticking your head in a beehive, either, Andrew." Kaholo harps.

The crew snickers, then just looks at each other disappointedly. The bee situation seems dismal. If one of the valley's tenure residents couldn't keep up with beekeeping, then who could?

All eyes turn to a two-day turned two-week tourist dubbed Beekeeper Matt. His constant talk of the importance of bees and his work beekeeping on the outside probably brought the issue to light in the first place. However, with the obvious opportunity to volunteer, nerdy science guy, Beekeeper Matt, just stares non-committal.

"We just need to bring in more bees—honeybees for the garden." Sierra blurts out breaking up the awkward moment.

"Yeah, we'll just get a bag full of buzzing bees and put them on the boat drop!" Mano laughs. He daydreams of how ridiculous yet still how probable it would be to chuck a trash bag full of live bees into the surf. Then release them into the valley as a dizzy disoriented ornery bunch.

"No, that's not what we need. The bees just need a new hive, then they can propagate and store more pollen and make more honey." Sierra says. Beekeeper Matt and others seem to agree.

"So, we boat drop in a hive?" Mano suggests. People agree, so Mano initiates a formal proposal.

"Sierra and Beekeeper Matt, do you guys want to spearhead this project, get a new hive set up in the valley to help propagate the bees and thus help our gardens?" The two just kinda stare at eachother.

"Well, are you guys beekeepers or not?" Mano asks. Sierra again breaks the awkward silence.

"Well, maybe on your next trip to town, you could get the hive and put it on the boat drop."

Mano smacks his hands across his thighs and stands up, shouting at the heavens.

"This is why community doesn't work! People like Keilani, Thomas, Cliff and I try to do things for the valley and for all of us, but no one else will pick up and carry a community project. You all talk big about 'bringing the bees,' but it's always up to someone else to make happen. It's a burn out man, to try to do something for the Valley! That's why most of the old timers just keep their own gardens and keep to themselves. One person can't carry this place! It's too much. It's a fuckin' burnout."

Mano marches off up valley to forage for fruit alone. The beehive thing *is* a great idea, just like the avocado box. But if no one jumps up and makes it happen, then it's as good as dead. Dead as the seeds planted in the un-watered bluff-top gardens. Communal spirit is dead...The bees, himself, and everyone else here is on their own, stuck in the valley of wandering souls.

Chapter 31   Spirit Says Stay

The negative energy haze lifts and the *Khan's gone* party happens a few days after Mano's homecoming. The crew toasts to celebrate the return of peace to the beach. Everyone gets his or her chance to verbally bash Khan as the whiskey bottle is passed around the fire.

"Biggest egomaniac I've ever met!" Grizzley roars.

"He couldn't even take care of his own kid, and he left trash everywhere," Q chastises.

"He couldn't even make his own oatmeal," Spacedog denounces.

"He had no respect for the land," Cliff declares.

"And he had no respect for women," Sierra adds.

The circle of grievances is brief, but it allows people to say what they had been holding inside. However, fueling anger with anger is no way to return peace to the land. It's important to remember anyone by their good qualities, and truth be told, Khan did have several good qualities. He was generous, and at times very compassionate. He was a charismatic leader and a creator of community. Whether it be for his cultist tribe or otherwise, he still brought a sense of community to the beach. He was high energy and high intensity, and he'd been known to inspire more than just a few people. Khan was a great musician and he brought people together with his music. Mano decides Khan's music will be one positive thing he'll remember about him.

Still, the stale energy from Khan's wake left many in a funk. It leaves Mano burnt out and unmotivated. Even Kaholo feels the energy drain from way up valley.

"We've gotta keep doing, and keep being creative in order to rise out of this lull. We've gotta mix things up and keep it lively for the tourists, too. They are key in this whole rising of inspiration thing. If they're feeling good and inspired, life here will flourish and more good people, with more good energy will come," Kaholo says encouragingly.

"Yeah, this isn't the first time Neverland has had to rise out of a lull. We'll come out of it," Paul adds.

"You know what we can do? We can just exaggerate our strongest, strangest, and best personality traits. Then we'll begin to spice things up for the tourists and ourselves and the vibe will surely improve. That, and more naked girls. That always seems to help." Kaholo continues.

"You mean we should just act wilder to draw more attention from the tourists?" Paul asks, thumbing his beard.

"Well, yeah, but not for attention, for *energy*. We've got to keep upping the fresh energy and I think one way to do that is to accentuate the good energy and different-ness we all have. For example, Paul, you could be even more animalistic, Andrew could be more sexual and outlandish, Gaia could act even more mysterious, and Mano could be more outrageous and silly." Kaholo smiles.

"And you could be more stony," Mano suggests.

"I know, I know. I'm the Cheshire Cat. I can always be more stony!"

"And Grizzley can be more…Grizzly!" They all laugh because it certainly made sense. All they needed to do to revive the energy and raise the vibe was to act more like characters through blatant outlandish positivity. That would bring more hot, naked chicks too. Tourists would be stimulated and the buzz of good vibes in the valley would carry out the coconut wireless and inspire more awesome people to come.

Mano accentuates his character and plays even more of a silly ham, but there is no one new to inspire and he still can't reach his pre-Khan drama level of positivity. Just overplaying his inherent character doesn't restore his energy. He tries to sit down and play a song, but the music doesn't have any heart behind it. He's sick of his own songs and his own thoughts. They're still the same thoughts and dilemmas he had when he first arrived months ago.

He feels numb. He feels his mind drifting away from Neverland and it almost makes him want to just leave. After spring break he'll be burnt out and ready to leave, he decides. The ocean draws him back and gives him peace, still he knows that only a good woman and a strong community could keep him here.

Perhaps he just needs a break from the beach to recharge his energy. A kayak mission to the west side? But is *leaving* is just running away from his own issues? He's tired of all the kayak missions, anyway. He should just be patient and content and wait for new life to arise.

Sure enough, in two or three days, spring breakers arrive and bring fresh positive energy with them. There are lots of new girls and guys and they all want to party. They gather on the beach for a bonfire and Mano brings out a boob of wine to share. Neverland springs out of her lull!

The spring break influx ends quickly as the majority of the tourists stay only a couple of days, as usual. But the energy they leave in the valley is positive and that's what carries forward. Rick and Lisa decide to organize a gathering up in the valley to keep the good vibes flowing. Theirs is an exclusive gathering of just the winter season outlaws for the tapping of their one-year-old banana wine stash up at their campsite. Seventeen residents plus one token tourist make it to the party held in the heart of the valley at their camp beneath a giant mango tree. They share pasta and garlic bread, and get buzzed from the strong homemade wine. The five-gallon banana batch is even smoother than the others these expert winemakers had made. Q and Keith hold down acoustic jams for hours. Everyone eventually passes out with Sierra and Keith being the last ones to bed, singing Beatles songs into the wee hours of the morning.

It's April now. Nights have gotten warmer and days are getting hotter and longer; Winter is certainly behind them. Mano doesn't have to go back to the mainland, but it makes sense for him to go, he decides. He has things to do out there— a future to build, friends and family, plus he needs to make money. But does he really need all that? Does he really belong out there or here in Neverland? He remembers what Andrew said to him just the yesterday—that he couldn't imagine Mano any happier than when he saw him running down the beach naked.

Everything is so involved and complicated out there in the real world. Whereas here, on the inside, things are simple and sensible. It's just sun and rain, ocean and valley, earth and sky, sex and pizza.

Chapter 32 Spirit Guides the *SS Stay-Afloat*

"I don't know about riding the *SS Sinker* all the way to the west side of the island. That boat is sketch," Sierra declares with a laugh.

"Now, now, Sierra. Don't jinx the mission by calling it that— it's *the SS Stay-Afloat*. It will get us there. It's been proven as a four-hour boat already, it will make the 2-hour trip, no problem! Besides, with Grizz coming as well, we'll have the fleet. We can just pirate his boat if ours sinks!"

"I don't know how I get talked into all these missions," she sighs.

"Come on, you know it will be a sweet adventure. And, shells— Everyone finds the best shells over at Shell Beach!"

"Kawika, what does *Spirit* say about this mission to Shell Beach?" Sierra tosses back her ponytail with a smile.

"I did ask *Spirit*. We should get a good launch window tomorrow morning. *Spirit* says to trust in Captain Mano to lead the mission," Kawika says, with a brazen grin. They go to bed to rest for another big day.

"Prepare the fleet for launch." Mano summons the three other sailors before the first morning tourist helicopter. The swell is down and so is the wind. Grizz crams everything inside the hatch of his two-man kayak, including a big pot of already cooked Grizzley beans. Sierra and Mano stuff their essentials into their one big drybag, this time fitting the ukulele in with a proper seal. Mano will launch the *Stay-Afloat* and Sierra will swim out to join him. Then Kawika will launch Grizz's boat, and Grizz will swim out through the waves, and they'll be off.

Mano hits a good launch window between sets and makes it out on his first try. Kawika isn't quite so lucky. Mano and Sierra watch from outside the break like spectators at a boxing match as Kawika gets clobbered by multiple sets of waves. The boat flips and he rights it in the whitewash. He clambers back on only to get flipped again by the next oncoming set.

"It's bean soup by now inside that kayak," Mano jokes to Sierra as the two watch Grizz's boat get pushed upside down to the sand.

Kawika rests, resets then tries again, but he's back on the beach after several failed attempts to launch in the whitewater. Sierra is trying to motion for him to give up and just swim out to their boat. Both she and Mano can tell he's too tired. But *Spirit* finally gives him a good long window and he makes it out, just barely. They all cheer— even Grizz is dancing on the beach.

Old man Grizz backstrokes through the surf break to join them and they're off! The foursome cruise with the current along the seldom-explored waters to the west of Neverland beach. Small waves are still breaking on the outer reef on the point, but Captain Grizzley decides to paddle close in along the cliffs anyway. Grizz leads them right into one of the larger sea caves. The water is surging up and down several feet with the swell and Sierra immediately expresses her concern.

"We don't have to go in there just because they are," she voices nervously.

"Just keep paddling. We're fine." They follow the other kayak through a surging sea tunnel to a room that opens up to the sky! After a fifty-foot long narrow channel with just ten feet of clearance overhead, the passage opens to a circular room with sixty-foot walls that open to the sky above.

"So cool!" Mano exclaims.

"Sketchy, so sketchy," Sierra grips her paddle tight as the boat surges up and down in the tight room. There's a rock in the middle of the room that's just barely exposed at the bottom of each surge of the swell.

"Around the horn!" Captain Mano shouts as they paddle around the rock without looking back. One upward heave throws the boat wildly off-balance, but the duo stays aboard. The up and down surging feeling in the open sky cave is unlike anything he's experienced on the water. It's like riding on the folds of a carpet that's pushed together and pulled apart, billowing up and down.

After another sketchy up and down maneuver, Sierra decides they shouldn't push their luck. "Let's paddle hard and get out of here!" she insists, and Mano conforms.

They paddle out through the tunnel and away from the cliffs to continue west. They pass the undercut rocky point that marks the drier side of the island, and just another mile or so further is Shell Beach.

"Prepare for landing!" Captain Mano asserts. Unlike Neverland Beach, Shell Beach has a reef protecting it and its shells from the pounding northwest swell. The waves are breaking overhead on the outer reef, but there's a narrow channel cutting through the reef that goes right into the beach. Waves only break in the deep channel with the biggest swells. Both teams skirt cautiously through the channel without issue and land on the beach without capsizing. Even the pot of beans inside Grizz's kayak is somehow intact.

When they step foot on the beach they walk over millions and millions of shell chips. Piles of shells are pushed up on the beach. There are no other footprints anywhere. They might be the first humans on this remote beach in over a month. The dozens of sea turtles sunning on the sand seem to agree. Some scoot back into the water as the team pulls the kayaks up on the shore, but others are undeterred by the human intruders

The place feels eerie and desolate, but it provides the kayakers with an additional sense of solitude. It's their *own deserted tropical beach*. They team up to do the normal camp prep duties. Sierra and Mano make a half-mile bushwhack to fetch good water at the only stream, and Grizz and Kawika gather driftwood for a fire. Then it's shell picking along the water's edge.

Mano has little patience for searching out un-chipped puka shells. Instead, he swims along the narrow channel in between the beach and the reef staring at sea turtles. He dreams of being an underwater creature as he swims with them in and out of the pockets and channels in the reef. Soon it's time for sunset and the crew reunites back at their camp.

The sunset from Shell Beach, just a bit farther west of Neverland, even further removed from any society, provides a new perspective. In this even more intimate setting, it's almost like Kaholo's idea for accentuating strong character traits is amplified. Their individual quirks are magnified even more at remote Shell Beach. Kawika's even more engrossed in his own world of intuition, *Spirit,* and Mother Nature. Sierra is more independent and on her own than usual, and Mano falls even more into contemplating love. Grizz is in Grizz-world, even more than ever and the three become more than a bit annoyed with him.

They come together for dinner at sunset, but strangeness settles on them. It's almost like Mano misses Neverland and it's wayward community already. Maybe it's just a bit too much Kawika and Grizz per capita. Sierra and Mano realize that they are both the kind of people better taken in small doses. But that can be said of just about any Neverlander.

The next morning, it's more of the same— solo shell and soul searching in the sun. Over a late breakfast, Grizz and Kawika butt heads. Now Kawika is urging for a sunset launch back to Neverland. After all, *Spirit* says so!

Kawika didn't bring any of his own food, and the extra that Mano and Sierra had for him was running out. They'd all be eating from Grizz's stash by dinner. How did this happen? No big deal, really, but soon debates spark up on whether to spend another night at Shell Beach or to cruise back. The idea of a sunset launch excites Mano and the thought of another evening of Grizz and Kawika together makes Sierra grumble, but really there's no need to rush. It would be better to leave in the morning and spend two nights at the remote Beach. Sierra agrees, but Kawika somehow uses his *Spirit* talk to captivate them both.

"The window to launch the *SS Stay-Afloat* is today at sunset." Kawika commands, as though he's received some divine message.

"You guys should just stay and launch in the morning. We've still got plenty of beans," Grizz tells them.

"Sunset on the kayak, and a night landing in Neverland would be pretty badass," Mano counters.

"Alright, Captain!" Kawika nods his head encouraging.

"Night landing in Neverland. That makes me nervous." Sierra shakes her head.

"I think you guys are silly to launch now. The swell will come down even more tomorrow. And in the morning I might even be ready to go. But you guys do whatever you want. I'm here in the now-wooh. I'll just go whenever I want. That's why I have my own boat! Maybe I'll even stay three more days— oh wouldn't that be Grizzly! I can be even grizzlier out here, Ahh-woooh!"

It's undeniable— Grizzley is somehow getting grizzlier out on Shell Beach. Kawika is getting harder to handle too. And the two together…Sierra and Mano look at the ocean and at each other. They had enough Grizz and Grizzley beans.

Kawika and Mano drag the *SS Stay-Afloat* to the water's edge. Mano gets excited thinking of the intensity of the three of them out at sea on the *Stay-Afloat* as the light fades, as well as a dramatic surprise night landing in Neverland.

"Another night mission, here we go," Sierra sighs.

"Kawika, since us leaving at sunset is your idea, how about you swim out to the kayak after Sierra and I launch?"

"No way, I can't make that swim out through the channel."

"What are you talking about? Be a man and let Sierra and I launch the boat, and you swim out."

"Captain, *Spirit* says…"

"Jesus Christ, Kawika! I'd swim through the channel but I can't trust you to launch the boat. Now just swim! It's almost sunset."

"That's not what *Spirit* says," he moans.

Sierra and Mano roll their eyes. Kawika is not about to deviate from *Spirit*. Sierra opts to backstroke out through the long channel for the team. It takes a while and the waves are close to breaking on her, but they never do. The trio watches Grizz, the lone pirate on the beach, wave them goodbye. They begin to paddle east toward the darkness. All light fades as they pass the undercut point, and an eerie feeling settles over them. Although the darkness sets in slowly, it feels like all of a sudden the trio is paddling through a pitch-black expansive nothingness of ocean. But smooth as ever they cruise, sinking ever so slowly from the small hole in the tail filling with seawater.

"Okay, you guys keep up a good pace. I'm a little nervous being that we have a triple load on the Sinker in the dark here," Sierra voices.

"Don't say that, it's the *Stay-Afloat!*" Mano reprimands. Kawika feathers his paddle, rocking the boat.

"My hands are hurting, I can't really paddle anymore," he whines.

"Just paddle, and don't rock this boat. This is serious— we are in the middle of the pitch black ocean!" Sierra commands. Kawika just keeps up his casual paddling and complaining, paying no mind to her. She becomes more nervous and upset as the swell rolls beneath the boat and the slower pace makes the *Stay-Afloat* scarily unstable in the perch.

"My hands are hurting. Can't we just take a break for a bit?" Kawika just lets his paddle drag in the water.

"God dammit, Kawika! Just shut up and paddle." Sierra snaps.

"I see headlamps on the beach, we are going to make it. I see Neverland!" Mano tries to calm his crew with thoughts of the finish line.

"One-two, one-two, keep it together crew. Lets-get-to-the-beach."

Waiting just outside the breakers for landing is surreal. The trio feels the roll of the swell under the boat get steeper as they approach, and they can hear the thunder of the breaking waves ahead. Mano tries to time the lull on feeling.

"Ok prepare for crash landing." They zoom ahead at Mano's command.

Mano stays aboard and surfs the boat through the whitewater. He hops off in the sandbar without even getting his chest wet. Sierra and Kawika wash in shortly after.

"Night landing intensity!" Sierra exclaims pumped.

"Thank you *Spirit* Thank you *Stay-Afloat*. Thank you Mama Kai!" Mano declares.

"Whoohooie!" they all cheer.

Chapter 33   Granola Bar Rescue

Mano looks out to where sea and sky meet, sipping his morning tea. He reflects back on the past three months he's spent in Neverland. What a season of adventure.

"Man, I'm gonna miss this place," he says to Sierra, still focusing on the horizon. Sierra's organizing her stuff, preparing for her final hike out of the year.

"Do you think you are gonna miss Neverland when you get settled out there?" Mano motions to beyond the horizon.

"Oh for sure. This has been the most incredible experience of my life. I love it out here, too." she sighs.

"Yeah, I kind of don't want to go back, but I guess I'm ready."

"Yeah, I'm ready," Sierra mumbles while poking her blow stick at the smoldering coals of their breakfast fire. They look at each other trying to read the other's thoughts. The drone of a motorboat cuts through their unspoken gratitude and Mano stands up.

"Hey, I hear a boat coming." It's The Pro heading for the beach, she says eagerly.

"Well, looks like we got a boat drop. I should get down there," Mano says. He runs down to the beach to help with the usual bag collecting routine and welcome committee of a morning boat drop. The swell is up a bit, but the morning surf is smooth and glassy.

Strangely, it's just Q and his three bags on The Pro's boat. They all wash in just fine. He manages to swim in during a well-timed lull between sets, although he's panting a good bit when he reaches the shore and certainly happy to see Captain Silly there waiting for him on the beach. It's still early and a bit chilly so Mano doesn't even jump in for a morning swim. Instead, he chats with Q and Mr. X for a bit while they watch The Pro slip back to the east. But as soon as the boat is gone, three more boats suddenly appear heading toward the beach. *Is this another boat drop?* The three boats are loaded with people, a dozen or more. *What the heck are these guys doing? It's certainly not a commercial tour,* Mano thinks to himself. It's not an easy day to be dropping in people, by any means. Q had a hard enough swim in and The Pro got him in extra close with the perfect window for sure. Maybe he's meant to be down here to help these other people. *Na, they'll take one look at the steep break and motor back to Babylon* Mano decides, as he watches one big wave face up and close out completely across the beach.

But that's not the case at all. The boat Captains are weaving in and out waiting for a lull in the waves for a window to hustle the people overboard.

Who are these people? Mano stares out at the boats, but they are too far away to make out faces.

He sees one of the boats zip in close. It's the lull— someone's going to go for it!

One girl jumps off the bow and starts swimming aggressively through the break. Mano scampers down the beach toward her, but hesitates. She's swimming hard— she'll make it to shore just fine. When he sees the young blonde come through the channel, he's transfixed for a moment.

"Melanie?" he calls out.

It's her. She comes trudging up the sand, a bit tired but smiling and just as cute as ever.

"Hey, Mano!" She hardly gives him more than a glance over, then turns back to the boats in the ocean. She's shouting and waving her arms.

"Go back, don't do it. Don't try to swim!" she yells, trying to wave the boats back out to sea. Of course, the bikini model with perfect timing did make it look kind of easy.

"My mom's out there. I don't want her to try to swim in," she says, turning back to Mano.

"What's going on? Who are all these people on the boats?" Mano questions.

"We're trying to come here for a ceremony and meditation on the Heiau." She shouts, hastily.

"So, are all those people gonna swim in?" Mano asks.

"Well, I don't know. When we left we heard the surf report was only one to three feet."

"It was pretty flat first thing this morning, but it's been coming up, big time. Besides, this is the north shore, in Neverland there can always be a swell."

"Well, this wasn't my idea!" Melanie replies with teenager sass.

Just then they watch a seven-foot closeout wave crash down in the impact zone. It closes out so steeply that the spray from the initial impact spits back up through the barrel of the wave.

"Did you see that back-breaker?" Mano points. Right after the set, another boat pulls in close and two people jump off— a guy and a girl.

"That's my sister!" Melanie screeches, watching the two swim in. They take a couple of foam pile punches in the impact zone, while Mano and Melanie wade waist deep into the channel, but they timed the lull perfectly and need no help getting across the channel rip and to shore. Still, they come in breathing hard, not in real swimming shape. Now there are three of them waving off the nine or so less able swimmers on the three boats.

"Don't do it. Don't swim in," they all signal with arms crossed.

Of course, the sisters and Mano know the dilemma. Everyone on the boats sees the beautiful beach and it looks so close. Their friends made it, so they could too? No one wants to be the one left behind, too scared to swim into paradise.

Melanie, her sister and the other man continue to try to wave the others away. "Go back!" they shout. But they don't want to since they're so close. There's some waiting and wave watching from the bobbing boats, then all three Captains zoom in close during a nice lull.

"They're gonna go for it," Mano spits, as seven of the nine remaining tourists plop overboard into the surf. Just one man and a small child stay behind. Mano doesn't know who to swim toward to help as he sees most of them just flailing lackadaisically in the sea, hardly swimming at all. He instinctively swims out towards the farthest person out, an overweight middle-aged woman. She doesn't understand that the time to make it through the impact zone is now, before the next big set comes in. From the water he yells at her, Patricia, and other stragglers to swim.

"Swim, swim! Swim toward me! Really swim!" Mano's voice is urgent.

A teaser wave rolls past them, sending a bit of a wakeup call, but the one woman on the outside still isn't making headway. Then he sees the first set wave building.

"Swim in and dive under the wave when it comes," he yells as he paddles out toward the woman.

"Okay, dive down, hold your breath." Mano shouts to her face as the crashing wave approaches. They go down and come up gasping in the foam-pile.

She's reaching and slapping the water with her arms. She's already panicky and disoriented.

"You gotta go down again, hold your breath." This time he pulls her down with him. They come up again gasping in the whitewash. There's a little break in the waves, an opportunity for them to make some headway.

"Don't panic, hold on to my leg and try to swim with me." Mano decides to try the same method as he did with Q a month ago. He paddles her with his arms for a few seconds, gains a few feet, and then it's time to dive under the whitewater once more. He pulls her drooping body down and back up again. She holds on and Mano is able to paddle her out of the impact zone. In the smaller whitewater two others join him to help. He looks around for anyone else and notices another bigger girl drifting with the current towards the far end of the beach not making much headway.

"Pull this woman to shore. I'm gonna help this other girl," Mano instructs.

Mano swims along the channel and then back out to aid the girl who is just flopping in a life jacket still stuck in the whitewash of the last big set. He paddles her in to where she can stand in the sand bar then coaxes her across the channel. He watches as the other woman he helped is literally dragged up onto the sand by two guys. What a scene— he can't believe it. Finally, he stops to catch his breath and he looks back out to sea.

"Oh crap, here come the bags!"

These boat Captains aren't The Pro, and sure enough one of the bags doesn't catch the surf. Mano goes back out and retrieves it before it drifts past the beach, and he swim's it in. Then it's done.

Melanie thanks him, Patricia thanks him, and the older woman he saved thanks him, too. But they don't seem to realize the gravity of the situation they faced out there. Three people could have drowned. Huminal Paul happened to be on the beach and he had pulled a skinny flailing Frenchmen out of the break to the sandbar as well. But besides being scared and thankful they don't really even seem to feel all that lucky considering the circumstances. What if he or Paul hadn't had been there to help? What if the set had come in even bigger when the group swam in? Somehow Patricia senses Mano's irritation over the whole situation thus comes over to thank him again.

"Oh, here are a couple of granola bars for your help. I know you don't get enough of these out here," Patricia says with a smile.

"Wow, one whole granola bar for each person I pulled out of the surf break. That's awful kind of you." Mano can't help but let the sarcasm slip out. He brushes it off and goes over and sits with Q on the other end of the beach, who is still sorting through his boat drop bags.

"How about a slug of whiskey? That was quite a scene out there!" He pulls out a full bottle and hands it to Mano.

Mano takes a pull and passes it back. Mr. X approaches them.

"Some boat drop, Mano! I watched the whole thing from right here through my binoculars. Man, you were great; you really saved the day again. A dozen people jumping off of boats in wintertime surf. Ha! And half of 'em couldn't even swim worth a shit! I'll tell you, I wouldn't have gone after their asses. No way, not in that surf. And what the hell does that lady think she's doing organizing some sort of spiritual retreat out here? You know Mama Kai don't like that! Of course, she's gonna make them pay on the swim in!"

"Yeah, quite the morning X, and now all of those people are gonna have to hike out of here. There's no way they'll be swimming back out to a boat."

"Yeah, you got that right. Surf's supposed to keep coming up, too. Swell for the next two, three days for sure. And rain. Rain tonight and tomorrow."

"Really? It's April, I thought winter swells should be dying down by now. I was gonna try to paddle out tomorrow, I'm supposed to get back to the mainland."

"Ha! This is the North Shore! Winter ain't over yet! That's the word on the radio, anyhow. If you wanna kayak all the time you gotta come here in the summer Mano, plus babes everywhere too!" X chuckles.

"Speaking of babes, have you seen Sierra? She was just packing up to leave when this whole fiasco started." Mano asks.

"Yeah, she came by already and gave me a hug with her pack on. Hiked out before this whole thing happened nearly an hour ago." X explains. Mano shakes his head, dumbstruck.

"She's gone? She didn't even come down to the beach to say goodbye to me." Mano's taken aback. His friend and teammate that he had helped and supported and brought here couldn't even wait for him to finish pulling people out of the water to say goodbye? She'll be back on the mainland in two days. They might not see each other for months, and she just leaves? Just took her things and split down the trail?

"Hey, Mano, don't take it personally. She's a young girl on a mission. She don't give a shit about goodbyes or what not. She was always into her own game plan." Mr. X tells him, still watching Patricia's group sort bags on the beach through his binoculars.

Mano's bewildered. But he convinces himself that he's not surprised. *Young girl* he repeats to himself, staring into the ocean in reflection. Sierra bolting without a word *was* almost predictable. X is right, she's on a mission. Her mission. She doesn't care otherwise. He knew this already. But he secretly hoped she would grow to appreciate and care about him during her stay there on the beach. Maybe she did care, but she didn't know how to show it. That seems better, he sighs.

Neverland doesn't change people, though, he realizes. He thinks about his own faults, and how the magic land hadn't changed them, either. He ponders his impatience, his stubbornness, and his promiscuity. He hated himself for belittling others only to make himself feel better, but he still did it. He wants urgently to be loved and appreciated and taken care of by the best woman, and to be on top of the social hierarchy of the beach. He is selfish and greedy. Can he or the world ever change?

Still, helping sponsor a friend for a whole season only to be ditched on their last day together leaves him feeling uncared for. Saving people's lives for granola bars makes him feel underappreciated. What is he doing out here? Maybe he *would* be better off in Babylon. *Only one more day*, he thinks to himself. *Just one more day on the inside, then I'll sail outta here.*

Mano trudges back up to his camp, still upset. He hopes to at least find a sweet goodbye note from Sierra, but all he notices are the same dirty dishes from breakfast. *Let it go*, Mano breathes. He grabs his ukulele and a granola bar for one last stroll up valley.

Chapter 34   Mano's Manifestation

Mano hikes up the Hippie Highway trail with feelings of nostalgia. The valley holds so many mysteries still! *Will he ever learn all that she has to teach?* He ponders in melancholy. He stops by Q's spot up near Three Mangos and gets a little revived. He's having his boat drop celebration, which includes whiskey and breakfast burritos. A dozen tourists and outlaws are gathered for the midday boat drop feast. Q got everything going, but then got too drunk and gave up on cooking, so he asks Mano to take over. Instead of grumbling, he cooks willingly, excited about bacon and eggs. He appreciates Q for his generosity in sharing much of what he just brought in. Mano recruits another willing helper and they complete the midday meal.

Afterwards, he joins the group for a swim in outlaw pools farther up the valley. He remembers when he and Melanie jumped up naked from behind the little rock wall to not be 'noticed' by her sister and friends. He remembers finding the calm underwater cave behind the waterfall with Rainbow while tripping the year before. He even remembers his very first swim there many years ago. Now he's privileged to swim there once again. He continues up-valley on his own, stopping to play his ukulele for the birds. He's alone but he feels comfort in his connection with Mother Earth. He can sense the first raindrop being released from the clouds above before it even hits the ground. It's nearly dark and raining a good bit by the time he passes Q's camp on his way down. The fire still smokes but the camp is deserted, so he continues down to the buff-top Sanctuary to seek company.

There are a few people gathered around a nice big fire under the tarps. There's no music playing or much conversation. People just stare into the fire. There's a pot of boiling water off to the side of the fire.

"Is somebody gonna make something with that water? It's boiling." Mano points out.

"We don't have anything to cook," one girl whines.

"Well there's a whole garden just over there with tomatoes and greens and a valley full of taro, and breadfruit, and pumpkins." Mano tells her.

They just stare at the fire unmotivated. *Without breath*, Mano mouths to himself.

"Well, I'm gonna make something!" Mano gets up in disgust, goes over to the Sanctuary garden and picks two big handfuls of the sweet-potato greens that Thomas and Summer had so diligently cultivated months ago. He finds a bowl and rinses it in the rain drip from the tarp. Mano looks over the jars and bottles of cooking spices left over in Khan's wake. He grabs a bit of oil and some cinnamon. He breaks up the leaves in the bowl, pours the oil over them and douses them with cinnamon. He sets the bowl on the grill and stirs the mix. To his surprise it's actually palatable. Random girl then asks to try his five-minute dish.

"Wow, that's pretty good. You should make some of that for everyone."

"The garden is right over there." Mano gets up, quickly finishes his bowl, and walks away.

Drainbows can't even pick greens from a garden, he huffs to himself as he splashes through the puddles on the trail back to his camp.

"Sierra's gone, Honu's gone, Dmitri's gone, all of my good friends, almost all of the doers are gone from the Beach." At the Sanctuary only *Drainbows* remain. Rick and Lisa and Andrew left just yesterday, too. He might as well peace out of Neverland tomorrow morning. He stomps along, frustrated. However, his pace steadies and his mind cools as he crosses the valley stream. A rising moon illuminates the forest slightly through the mist of clouds. He turns off his headlamp and proceeds more slowly, looking at the tree branches above shimmering in the moonlight. He decides to make one last stop on the Heiau to clear his bitter heart before bed.

He kneels and kisses the wet grass in the drizzle. He presses his forehead into the ground. He feels the earth. Feelings of wholeness, and remorse, and love rush through him. He feels all the love and beauty and sorrow and pain of the earth herself sweep over him. He feels sorry for doubting the goodness of this place and the people. Mano thanks Mother Earth for the goodness she has brought into his life and he apologizes for the times he chastised and disrespected this holy land. He weeps into her bosom there on the Heiau in the misty night.

Please help me Mama Kai, help me to love. Help me to grace this sacred land in beautiful, divine love. He feels her love pulse to the rhythm of the churning sea. He unfolds, rising up onto his knees, opening his heart to the sea and sky beyond.

My heart is open to you. I am open to share and receive divine love, he says aloud.

Please send me a partner, a loving woman whose love can equal my own. He exhales and follows it with a deep inhalation rolling up his spine.

Let me find a woman who loves this land and wants to be here with the land as I do. Please send me someone to share this beautiful fantasy with. Closing his eyes, breathing out into space, he dreams his fantasy. He smiles to himself and then bends back down, submitting to Mother Earth with grace. He can feel the wholeness of the earth on the wet grass as his prayer sinks in. He tries to release all his inner fears and just breathe with her pulse for a deep minute. Then a rush of cold wind comes and he feels himself in the spotlight. He uncurls and spins to see *Mahina*, the moon, beaming down on him through a break in the clouds.

Mahina, I love you. Mama Kai, I love you. Mother Earth, I love you!

Mano stands up and spins and dances in the misty spotlight.

I must go, but I will be back. I will be back with love! Let this be my manifestation. I love you Mama Kai, help guide me in Babylon! Let my heart be open to receive. He dances back to his tent with *Mahina* dancing with him in and out of the clouds. He feels each blade of grass under his feet, feeling each droplet of water. He feels alive.

Chapter 35   Out like Outlaws

It's more than a morning drizzle when he wakes up still full of youthful energy from last night's spiritual manifestation dance on the Heiau. He unzips his tent and looks out to see puddles just outside. He's not ready to leave the beach now! He curls back up and listens to the rain. During a lull in the storm he rises and prances down to the beach. The wind has already picked up and there's still a sizable swell. No chance to get his kayak out today. Should he hike the trail with what he can carry on his back and leave the kayak stashed? The latest surf report briefing from Mr. X has Mano thinking that this could be his only option. The swell isn't supposed to diminish by tomorrow.

Leave the boat and hike the trail? His thoughts run impatiently with the swirling rain. He'll leave tomorrow so he doesn't have to hike out in the drizzle, he decides. He sloshes through the mud down at the beach to see Patricia's group packing up, preparing to hike the trail. Their 2-day spiritual vacation to Neverland started with a dramatic swim in, was followed by a rainy evening and night, and would finish with a muddy hike out in the rain. Mr. X was right; Mama Kai wasn't going to make it easy on them.

"It's been raining on and off all night and the storm isn't supposed to clear till tomorrow. Maybe you guys should stay an extra day, the trail right now is gonna be a mess. If it rains more, some of the stream crossings could be dangerous," Mano cautions. He's greeted with placid looks from Patricia's pathetic crew.

"Well, it's Sunday, Easter Sunday, and some of us really have to get back. We were supposed to take a boat out, you know," Patricia responds.

"Yesterday's swim and this storm have a bunch of us feeling uncomfortable. We're kind of on edge and we just want to get going."

Mano examines the dozen or so miserable looking *touri*.

"Some of you don't even have good shoes. You all need walking sticks because it's so slippery. It's gonna be tough, and it may take two days, so be prepared to camp out. I'm waiting until tomorrow to hike, myself." Mano declares.

"Well, with that said, we should probably get going," Patricia says, stuttering.

"Well, at least let me see if I can get you guys a few bamboo walking sticks," Mano insists.

Q comes by to help and the two of them gather and cut bamboo sticks from what they can find lying around the abandoned camps along the beach.

"Stick together and be safe out there." Q tells them, as a smile crinkles his big eyes.

Mano can already imagine them huddled together in a downpour at six-mile camp this evening after a muddy slog all day in the rain. Some group. Some trip!

Mano leaves the muddy beach camp for the ocean. He swims and dances down to the waterfall at the end of the beach in the rain. He hikes back up to his camp on the perch, thinking he'll crawl back into his sleeping bag to warm up. Someone's up there— a visitor— he can sense it before he even climbs the hill.

"Len-dog! What are you doing back in Neverland?"

"Captain Mano, you knew I'd be coming back, I'm an outlaw just like you! Not even Khan can keep me out of Neverland."

"Yeah, I guess you're right. But are you still gonna keep up your reputation as Screwy Lennie freakin' people out at the Sanctuary?"

"You know I'll still be spinning heads wherever I go. But you saw me back on the outside. I'm doing alright. I hiked the trail in less than six hours, trippin' too! I've lost another 10 pounds, I'm doing yoga, I'm legit!"

"So did you bring in any good treats? I'd die for some chocolate or weed right now?"

"Nope, smoked all my weed already, munched shrooms on the trail, ate most of my food, but I think I got a little hash left I'll share with ya."

"Alright Len-dog. Tell you what, you smoke me out, and I'll let you have this whole prime camp. I'm hiking out tomorrow."

"Shoots! Tarps and tent and everything? Too sweet!"

"Well, I'm taking the tent, but you can have everything else. I've even got about 10 packs of ramen, some soy sauce, oil, and maybe a couple cans of tuna."

"Sa-weet Da-Len is stoked out in Neverland again!"

"Yep, and this is probably the driest spot this side of the stream during a storm, too. Sierra really got these tarps dialed."

"Hey, I saw your amiga Sierra hiking out. She gave me a big hug, had tears in her eyes. I could tell that she really loves the Beach. She's gonna miss it here for sure."

"Yeah, I'm gonna miss it here, too. I'm gonna miss it a lot, but I'll be back. After all, I'm an outlaw like you!"

"You gonna bring another hottie like Sierra out here from the mainland next winter?" Len asks, while rolling a hash spliff.

"We'll see, hopefully next time there will be a nice lady for me!" Mano pauses in silence.

"Well alright. Let's smoke this one to a nice lady for Captain Mano." Lennie says handing Mano the lighter and spliff.

They get high and stroll over to the Heiau for sunset. The sun finally wins. It melts away the clouds and pushes back the storm for sunset.

Mano plays a couple of his silly songs on his ukulele then lets Len take over on a hand drum. Gaia is there by herself cloaked in a beautiful white gown from India. She stares placidly toward the setting sun apart from the rest of the small group gathered there. Mano can't help but want to try and break the ice with her. He looks out to the ocean trying to think of words to say, remembering how she waited in the bushes during the big raid and they escaped Titus and The Rock together. Unsure of what to say, he walks over to her and gazes into her eyes. She looks at him and smiles, but just as he's about to mutter something simple like, 'Nice seeing you around this winter, I hope to get to know you better next year,' she lets out a powerful *aum* right as the bottom of the sun meets the horizon. She continues auming, resonating with her Tibetan singing bowl for several minutes until the sun is completely past the horizon. Mano backs away slowly without a word. No chance to enter her world today, he laughs to himself. But it's fitting. He enjoys her toning with the setting sun and almost joins in. He admires her for what he recognizes to be complete contentment in solitude. He wonders if he'll ever reach such a state of inner peace, himself.

The next morning is calm and clear and he feels it's time to leave. The waves are still too big to launch the kayak. With the *SS Stay-Afloat* and a few other items already stashed, he's ready to hit the trail with just his ukulele and a full backpack. He meets a group of tourists he agreed to hike out with down by the river mouth and after a few more goodbyes they all set off on the trail back to civilization.

For the first mile he keeps looking back as if he's forgetting something. He's just starting to look ahead, dreaming of cold beer and a variety of pleasure foods, when the group rolls into eight-mile camp. To their surprise, standing there on the helipad is the big Russian woman Mano pulled from the surf just two days ago as well as the skinny Frenchman Paul dragged out of the water. They're standing on the helipad trying to flag down every passing tour helicopter.

"What are you guys doing? Where's the rest of your group?" Mano asks abruptly.

"We couldn't go on any further yesterday. This trail is too slippery, too dangerous. We are trying to get a helicopter to pick us up."

"Well it's not raining anymore, why don't you just walk out? Take your time, and you'll get there by sunset." Mano encourages them.

"We can help carry some of your stuff if you are having a hard time balancing on the trail with your packs," a tourist from Mano's group offers to the meek Frenchman.

"No, we will wait here for a helicopter. This trail, it's too steep, too dangerous, we cannot," the big woman insists.

Just then, the whole group turns to see a big bearded man huffing up the trail from the other direction, heading toward Neverland. He's sporting a ginormous backpack on his back with a small, but still heavy looking backpack strapped to his front. He's double-posting it with two walking sticks, sweating profusely.

"Looking good man, just a couple miles to go, mostly downhill," Mano elates seeing the man's spirit of excitement.

"I know, I can't wait to get back to the valley." The man stops for a moment to catch his breath. "What's going on here?"

"These two are too weenie to hike the trail, they're trying to flag down a helicopter for a ride out and we're trying to talk them out of it." Mano answers.

Disgusted, the big man drops his front backpack, bats his eyelids and wipes the sweat off his brow.

"Helicopter! You can't be calling for a helicopter unless you are seriously injured, in dire need!"

"Well, we nearly drowned in the ocean two days ago and I had a heart attack! This man here saved me, and now we just can't go on, we need a helicopter," the woman wails.

"Heart attack! Let me take your pulse. I'm a nurse," the man insists.

"We'll it was a *spiritual* heart attack...I almost died." The bearded man rolls his eyes and spikes one of his trekking poles into the ground.

"I don't care, you've gotta hike the trail like everyone else, no calling for a freakin' helicopter, that's bullshit!" He grabs his extra backpack and his poles and keeps sweating down the trail toward paradise.

"Man, that guy must have been carrying seventy pounds. What a workhorse, a real trail-dog!" one tourist proclaims. They all watch him trudge off in awe.

"That guy's right, the helicopters aren't supposed to pick people up or land at all unless someone is seriously injured," Mano concurs.

"But I had a spiritual heart attack," the lady moans.

"Shut up already and start walking. We all hiked the trail, so can you," another tourist chastises while the rest of the group snickers.

"No, we are not going down that dangerous trail. We wait here." The Frenchman nods in agreement.

"I'm sick of talking to these people. Let's just keep going." Mano starts down the trail and soon the group follows.

The group proceeds at a fast pace. Faster than Mano wants to travel, but he keeps up with them. They turn toward six-mile valley after the long climb up from seven-mile at a steady trot. Just on the other side of the valley stream, they hear the buzz of a low flying helicopter. Then they can feel the wind from the blades. It's landing. It's the Rangers!

"It's landing right ahead of us, what do we do?" The lead hiker asks. No one in their party has a permit. They start to walk back the other way down the trail, but pause, realizing that a confrontation is inevitable. Two big Rangers in full camo gear with pistols on their hips approach the string of backpackers. They examine the group sternly before speaking.

"Have you guys seen a couple of injured backpackers? A man and a woman?"

"Yeah, they're back at the eight-mile heliport," the leader manages to utter in response.

"Okay, and all you guys are okay," one Ranger huffs in a deep Hawaiian voice.

"Yeah, we're just on our way out."

"You guys got your camping permits?" The group just looks dumbly at each other in silence.

"Those guys at eight-mile have been trying to get a helicopter, they need help," someone breaks in.

"Well, you guys better just keep hiking out now." The men turn and leave in their helicopter nearly as quickly as they landed.

"We're so lucky," Mano sighs.

"Did you see that? They landed that thing on a patch of grass the size of a picnic table!"

"Yeah! That was something. Those guys were in full riot gear, intense!"

"That Russian lady doesn't know what's coming. She thinks she's getting a rescue, and instead it's gonna be the Rangers!"

"Yeah, and we're safe and outta here! No tickets for us!"

"We're out like outlaws!"

~ Part III ~

Chapter 36   Return with Love, Fear, and Tears

It's the other side of the world. Across an ocean to a land where dreams become reality and thoughts become truths. A tropical island where logic is sidestepped and love and magic prevail.

"Neverland here we come!" Mano grips her hand tightly with nervous excitement as the airplane descends through the clouds and the island comes into view.

"When you get here, look for the van at the beach park down by the bay. It'll have a long-board on top and a bunch of short-boards inside. I'll probably be out surfing when you arrive!"

"Alright, Honu. We'll see you soon, brotha!" He hangs up the phone and the two of them bus over to the north shore of the island.

They open up the van and shove their bodies and backpacks in amongst the tangle of towels, t-shirts, sandals, and surf leashes. They rattle and shake back to the main road.

"Sweet ride. Smells pretty dank in here, too!" Mano jokes.

"You know we be staying irie in the van with the Mendo-man," Honu chuckles.

"Jah know this!" Zoe giggles, taken aback by her first glimpse at this hippie-island-life through Honu's shared surf-wagon.

The three cruise around the island to the one bulk-foods grocery store.

"So we should probably get about three or four-hundred dollars worth of food if we want to stay on the inside for 3 or 4 weeks without needing to come back out for re-supply." Mano explains to his girlfriend Zoe, confidently.

"So how do we decide what to get? I mean, there's so many things I want." she questions.

"We gotta get stuff that will keep well in a tropical environment without refrigeration, and things with good durable packaging. Think simple, and think big!"

Zoe watches wide-eyed as Mano casually tosses a two-liter bottle of olive oil and a ten-pound bag of rice into their cart. They continue down the said list of essentials. Sugar, flour, onions, potatoes, raisins, oats, cans of sardines, tomato paste, big blocks of cheese, and jars of peanut butter. All these blue-collar staples have fresh, organic-minded Zoe feeling a little leery.

"We're really gonna make good food for a month in the wilderness with all this basic stuff?"

"All this, and lots of love." Mano says, pulling her close for a full body kiss there in the aisle.

"There'll be fresh fruit and veggies out there, too, and we'll plant a garden— just you wait!"

They move down the aisle and stop to stare at a ten-pound bag of Krusteazs® instant pancake mix. Mano approaches Zoe, delicately.

"I know this isn't something you would typically eat, but this here, Krusteaz®, is key to sustained existence out there. I mean you can add just about anything to pancakes and it works. Just ask Honu or anyone who's been in Neverland!"

"I don't know. Let's look at the ingredients here." She picks up the package wearily.

"Don't do it, man!" a voice lurches from behind as a hand grabs at Mano's shoulder.

"Andrew, how are you! What are you doing here?"

"Just came out of the Valley, and man, let me tell you— Rangers all up in there! All the camps are destroyed. They're like on some crazy man-hunt still. The trail was closed for weeks! It's open now, but they're flying in with new guys every week. Neverland's done—it's over. Go find yourself a new Neverland cause this fantasy is crushed!"

"Whoa there! What are you talking about? Neverland's not finished. They'll find that wanted guy and things will settle down. It's just a Ranger Raid, right?"

"I don't know, man. Things might be different now. They got more funding from the government to chase us outta there too! I'd hold off on the Krusteaz, or any sort of big boat drop for now. And as far as I'm concerned, our community in Neverland is pau!"

"This can't be for real. This Ranger scare will blow over just like any North Shore storm that seems to last forever."

"I dunno man. I'm just gonna cruise in the van with Honu and see where things go. I'd do the same if I were you guys."

Saddened, they put back the Krusteaz® and Mano scales back their shopping cart, removing a few more items.

"Yeah, the Rangers even seized a couple of boat drop bags a few weeks ago. Whatever you bring out there, be prepared to lose it!" Andrew cautions, dismally.

"Don't worry. I'm sure this will blow over. We'll just take a few extra precautions and we'll avoid the Rangers. They'll find their wanted dude and things will calm down." Mano states, reassuringly.

He kisses Zoe on the forehead and smiles. "Don't worry."

They buy a hundred pounds of food and supplies and sort things into double-bagged trash bags in the parking lot. They all load back into Honu's van and drive to the North Shore to meet The Pro.

"No worries mate, if I see Rangers on the beach, I won't drop the bags." The Pro assures them, confidently. Him and Mano devise a system of simple hand signals to confirm a safe drop. The method seems fool-proof, and Mano breathes easy as they bump along toward the trailhead. With the boat drop in order, now all he would have to do is take care of Zoe and get her safely down the trail. That, he knew he could do. He looks into her eyes and is captivated by her natural beauty. He lets himself bathe in her wavy chestnut hair, sun kissed cheeks and freckled nose. Mahalo Mama Kai for sending me this gorgeous woman to love and cherish in her most holy land. Mano closes his eyes in a prayer of thanks. The dream is now!

After another day of prep and metering countless stories from other Neverland outlaws in town, the duo decides to go for it. They trade Andrew's scare story for other more recent accounts of the beach being peaceful and safe. They put their faith in the coconut wireless to warn them of any Rangers that may be in the valley. Surely, they'd be notified by hikers on the trail of any Ranger danger. Honu bumps and grinds the van to the trailhead to drop them off. Mano grips Zoe's hand and she squeezes his back compellingly. Her touch is not excited elation; it's fear. He looks at her eyes and his euphoric heart sinks. Just sitting in the van on the way to the trailhead he knows that she's trembling inside. The spirits had sent him a young woman, who shared undeniably the most love he had ever experienced, but who also held her fears so deep rooted and close to her heart, it made her easily triggered, unruly, and anxious. He swallows hard and prays for grace. He kisses her cheek and turns to look her in the eye.

"Honey, what are you scared about?" Mano asks, endearingly.

"I'm nervous about the trail, Rangers, and other girls on the beach."

"Don't worry. I'm sure you'll be the prettiest girl on the beach. Besides, you'll be *with me*."

"I'm worried about the Rangers and other girls on the beach — naked girls that you're attracted to, I just know it." she chatters.

"Remember, you're *my girl*, my princess."

"Just know that if you do anything stupid, like look at another girl, I'll freak out, ok?" Mano grits his teeth hearing Zoe snap out of fear.

"Just try to remember I'm here with you. Other girls don't matter, even if I do glance at them."

"You just can't do that. It hurts me too much." She cries. Mano pulls her head into his chest. The scene is all too familiar and frustrating for him, but all he can think to do is pull her close and reassure her.

Still, he doesn't understand it. His girlfriend Zoe couldn't be described as anything less than stunning. Her big, bold smile accented her warm brown eyes, cute dimples and round face. Her wavy layered hair flowed long down her back. She had an amazingly soft feminine body with perfect perky tits, smooth tanned skin, and a honey sweet smell that just drew him in...But it didn't matter if he adored her; she was young and insecure in herself. She couldn't let herself believe how beautiful she really was. Despite their hot and cold relationship, he's still convinced she is the divine manifestation of the love he prayed for on the Heiau nearly a year ago. He was her manifestation, too. Neither is even close to perfect, but they had love — beautiful love. The kind that could surely grow and blossom like a flower in Neverland. And the valley would help them heal, too. The valley could, and would strengthen their love.

"Just wait till we get to Neverland, you're gonna love it out there, and the people out there are gonna love you too." Mano assures her.

The van lurches to a stop at the trailhead and Honu jumps out to open the sliding door from the outside.

"Ok, I expect to see you in the valley on the inside in two weeks! Don't get caught up in places bought up. Neverland is where it's at, you know!" Mano pesters his friend.

"I'll get in there, you just hold that one boat drop bag for me. Neverland will always be there. I'll get there when I'm ready. You two lovebirds enjoy, and don't forget to stay silly, Mano-banano!"

"Oh, we will!" Mano shouts, as he slams the van door and Honu peels off.

Mano sighs as he waits impatiently for Zoe to rearrange a few things in her backpack and ready herself. He's excited to hit the trail. However his excitement makes him less than accommodating to Zoe's usual lengthy preparation processes.

He glances around as to not pressure her anymore. His eyes catch and hold on a hot shapely bikini body rinsing off in the showers across the parking lot. Zoe looks up and catches him in the act. She's instantly triggered and lets herself become angry to the point of shutting down.

"Why don't you just go ask her to hike with you cause I'm not going with you anymore!"

Before he can say anything, she rushes off to the bushes sobbing. He grits his teeth, and snaps out of frustration.

"Goddammit, why can't we just have a good start to this beautiful trip?" Mano shouts into the air. — He knows it's not the *other girl,* he knows its her anxiety about the journey to a whole new world they are about to enter, but he certainly acted insensitive to her fears.

He keeps his distance, sensing there's nothing he can do. He's being punished. Fine! He goes over to the trailhead and tries to ignore her by asking backpackers coming back to Babylon about the trail conditions and any potential Rangers ahead.

"The trail's great, hardly muddy at all," one young man replies. Two girls eager for the finish line approach him next and offer their walking sticks.

"It was just too slippery and too scary. We had to turn back at seven-mile." they respond conversely, handing him the one bamboo pole and one store-bought trekking pole.

"Oh thanks. My *girlfriend* and I could really use these. Walking sticks are essential for this trail." He's sure to annunciate *girlfriend* but he fears just talking to them is 'forbidden'. Still worth it at this point to get the walking sticks. He waits another minute then tries to approach the closed-down Zoe.

"Hey, I got us some good walking sticks, now let's try to make this magical journey *to-ge-ther*."

"I'm not going with you. I hate you." She grabs the trekking pole from him and marches ahead on her own up the trail. He starts after her, but hesitates, knowing that he'll never catch her in her anger-fueled power-hike. Why should he, anyway? *Let her go*, he tells himself. Eventually, the trail steepens and his slow, steady slog catches up to her. He tries a simple *I'm sorry*, to gain her back.

"I don't care. I hate you!" She turns on him with evil eyes and slams her pole on the ground in disgust. He picks it up and starts to fume up himself.

"I shouldn't even let you have this! You don't care. You just want to ruin this beautiful journey to paradise by being angry." He throws the pole up the mountainside in a violent burst. Zoe storms ahead, still in a fit.

The start of their beautiful journey of love is tainted with fear, ferocity, and anger. He's frustrated. His past programming has him thinking that all he is for her is simply *not good enough*! To make matters worse, he threw his frustrations right back at her, shouting harsh words and throwing away her pole violently. How could she make him so frustrated he could lose his temper? They'll both sweat their frustrations out along the trail, he decides. Things will blow over, as usual. He tries to let it go, but it pains him so to not have her happily by his side. He takes on her emotions, it's his own weakness and he knows it. She knows it too and she uses it, he decides, negatively. He tries not to let a sadness that broods from it weigh him down as he lumbers slowly up the trail.

The climb helps him breathe and sweat through his struggles. This *feeling her pain* will pass, he decides. Still, thoughts of their relationship linger as he trudges along deflated with a sunken heart. *Would he ever be pure enough to settle her fears? Could she feel secure with him?*

The trail winds up, up, high above the ocean before switch backing down to the first stream crossing. He sees her there and crosses the creek a bit behind her. On the other side of the stream he sets his pack down and wanders along the small rocky beach at the mouth of the creek.

He doesn't know how to reach out to her, but something needs to happen, after all it will be getting dark soon. She's already continued on the trail, but before he decide to chase after her she turns around and finds him.

"The trail splits and I don't know which way to go," Zoe states, disappointedly.

"Why can't you just let me love you, and be happy?" Mano asks, looking saddened.

"Just tell me if it's left or right up there." she motions ahead.

"It's *right*, the trail follows the coast, and the other way goes up to a waterfall up this valley. But why don't you just sit down. If you go running off on your own, it will get dark and mosquitos will consume you…I have the tent in my pack remember!" he states, perturbed. She doesn't respond, so Mano continues.

"I love you. This should be a great trip, just love and enjoy, ok?"

"You don't love me. If you loved me you wouldn't do those things!"

"If I didn't love you, I wouldn't be taking you here to this very special place of love as my princess."

Zoe almost manages to smile under her tear-stricken face.

"Can't you just see that I'm scared?" she sobs, submissively.

Mano approaches her with newfound gentleness.

"Here, let me hold you." She lets him in and cries in his arms as he rubs her back.

"I love you still. Remember I love you no matter what. Do you believe that?" His words are soft but deep.

Be patient, be compassionate, choose love, he says to himself in silence. They hold each other and regain strength and empathy through their loving embrace. The stillness of dusk falls upon them.

"Let's go and make a camp— it's getting dark," Mano suggests.

The two work together to set up their tent and prepare dinner. They hold each other next to the glow of a small fire in the dark, damp, guava forest. In the tent their naked bodies hold tight throughout the night. Birds sing as they make love again at dawn. For those precious moments, all fears and past wounds are forgotten. Imperfections are forgiven. Love is pure.

The next morning is bright and beautiful on the trail. They detour up to the waterfall after breakfast and plunge into the cool deep pool. This refreshes the energy, and Mano tells Zoe about the different plants and trees they pass and she listens excitedly. They stop at all the lookouts for photos, taking breaks often for they're both now in backpacking shape.

For Zoe, everything is beautiful, amazing, and new. For Mano, the trail is a familiar meditation. They plunge into the pools at six-mile and again at eight-mile camps. Mano suggests they stop there and save the last few miles to the beach till morning. They're tired, and even though they could make it to the valley well before nightfall, they enjoy a relaxing sunset from the pristine camp perched on the cliff. Mano can tell that Zoe is still nervous, letting her mind catch on fears of *other girls* in Neverland. But it seems like they left the *trail of tears* back at two-mile stream. They sleep deeply side by side.

The next morning there's no news of Rangers in the valley from people hiking out, thus Mano and Zoe descend cheerfully toward the beach. They pick out a tent site and plunge into the Pacific.

"Mama Kai, I love you!" Mano exclaims, as he dances across the sand. The ocean makes him feel powerful and alive. He's back again. Returned with love.

"Mahalo nui loa!" he exclaims, hugging his naked girlfriend in the whitewash.

Chapter 37   Manifest Destiny

She's so beautiful, she's so loving, I'm so loving. Mano practices words of affirmation for himself and his partner. Then he thanks the great spirits of the land and the ancients for sending him such a beautiful, loving goddess to be with him in this most precious land. Mano whispers positive prayers to the stars before bed. Zoe is a beautiful flower on the inside and out. He just needs to be patient and wait for her to blossom into the true goddess that she is. She's still hiding her true nature and holding onto her fears. But her fears are beautiful in themselves, he decides. Even her flaws are beautiful. He didn't totally understand it, or like it, but he knew it to be true.

He ponders his own *inner beauty* for a moment. Was there beauty in his bluntness, lustfulness, and insensitive honesty? There must be some, but he certainly didn't see his shortcomings as beautiful. Mano couldn't hide his true self, nor did he like to admit to his defects, most of which shone right out in the open. Zoe on the other hand knew well what plagued her and she wanted to hide it, entombing her childhood wounds deep inside until a trigger would overwhelm her and awaken her fears. *Humans must be the source of their own love, but just as well, they are the creators of their own demise*, Manos thinks to himself.

Mano wants her to just be Zoe and love herself, but she seems to uphold whatever face she needs to please or infuriate him. She gives herself to him, telling him that he's all she needs. However, instead of feeling needed and fulfilled because this is all he really wants, he feels trapped under her love. And feeling trapped, he holds onto lust.

With a deep sigh he lies down in the grass on the Heiau perch and tosses twigs up into the wind. He misses her already. He breathes with the gentle rumble of the ocean swell against the rocks. They got in an argument this morning and he forced himself away to let them both cool down. Why did it pain him so much to be away from her with things unresolved? Why couldn't he accept her being upset and not wanting him? It made him feel so helpless and not good enough. He tries to surrender his thoughts to the wind and just listen to the birds.

A male and female cardinal swoop down and land in front of him. He watches their behavior and interactions intently. Birds seem just as uncertain with themselves, he decides. The male hops back and forth while the female cocks her head watching him. She doesn't come to him, but instead hops along the short grass of the Heaiu further away from the suitor.

Then she's hiding behind a rock, teasing the male and chirping away, cheerfully. Intrigued, the male flies over and above her, and looks down at her from a perch on a boulder. She takes a seed from the grass in her beak and flies off a few feet, just as another male frolics in more curious than the first. She's impressed and gives two short hops in the direction of the new suitor. But she changes her mind and flies back to the first giving him a slight squeak. Then she takes off into the sky like nothing ever happened. The two male cardinals just look at each other confused before they fly off together.

"Going gay isn't the answer boys!" Mano chuckles to himself, quite pleased with his cardinal encounter.

Still not ready to approach Zoe, Mano decides to solo up to community gardens and welcome himself back to the valley. *Just do something for yourself, don't worry about Zoe*, he encourages his being. Maybe he'll run into Paul and bring back some fresh greens. By that time, she'll be cooled down enough to receive him with love again. He scurries up the valley trail, sucking on baby mangos the whole way up. He finds the secret turnoff trail and enters the sanctuary of the garden that marks the center of the valley with care. He skirts around a grove of mossy-trunked mature orange trees and down to the cleared, sun-bathed main terrace of the garden. He soaks in the panorama of edibles and flowers planted along the stream diversion that feeds the loi terraces of edibles. Water trickles pleasantly from loi to loi along careful cut trenches to feed the sun-kissed broadleaf plants all around. With tall trees on all sides blocking the view out, the garden holds a mysterious, secretive aura. Mano's glance catches on the naked man just below the big mango tree walking toward him.

"Well for once it's not the Rangers or the pigs— it's you! Hello there, Captain Mano. Back for another winter season?" Paul greets him with a big sweaty hug.

"So did you crash-land back in with Khan and more hot interns?" Paul smiles, staring face to face with him all too endearingly.

"No interns, no Khan, thank God, but I did bring with me a girlfriend from the mainland."

"What's that? Lovesick Mano finally found his princess." A sweet voice flows from the terrace below.

"Sky! You're here too? So great to hear your voice. I heard you guys were back from California and madly in love."

"Absolutely! Mano-banano, we've just got married and we're having a baby!" Paul exclaims, as he scoops up naked Sky.

"Yeah I'm pregnant! Isn't it incredible and exciting! We're here for a couple more weeks then we will go out and have the baby in Babylon."

"And we hope to bring it back with us to raise here in the garden by the end of the summer." Paul adds, enthusiastically gesturing to the grandeur of community garden.

"You mean him or her, our baby's not an *it*," Sky interjects, calming Paul's excitement.

"Yeah sure. I'm pretty convinced he's a boy anyway." Paul chuckles, kissing and rubbing Sky's belly merrily.

"So it's really happening— you guys are gonna have the Neverland kid! This is for real!"

"The start of the lineage!" Paul exclaims.

Mano's heart sinks a little looking at them, they're so filled with love he's almost jealous.

"Yeah, I got my *stayer girl* and we're living the dream— a family in the valley." Paul continues, proudly.

"So tell us about this new goddess of yours? Why is she not here with you now?" Sky insists.

"Well uh… She's still getting used to life out here. We just got here and she's transitioning…" He fumbles his words but manages to continue.

"She's totally amazing and loving and caring. It's just, she gets super jealous and fearful especially when other girls are around. I still don't quite understand it. We've been together almost 6 months now."

"Oh yeah, other wahine walkin-on-the-beach make a sister go crazy, huh." Paul humors, mocking Pidgin-talk.

"Yeah, she's kind of crazy jealous but I know it's also just because she loves me so much…Things got kind of bad this morning when this other girl showed up and camped right next to us."

"What do ya think, honey? I just can't picture Captain Mano with a jealous girlfriend, can you?" Paul asks Sky.

"Maybe he needs a jealous girlfriend to help keep him in line!" Sky scoffs.

"Honey! This is Captain Silly here. He's supposed to be a bit out of line…" Paul affronts.

"I can behave myself…well I certainly can be true to her. It's just sometimes I get distracted and she can read right into me, thoughts and everything. Plus, she watches me like a hawk, you know!" Mano sighs.

"Mano with a jealous girlfriend in the valley. I can't wait to meet her!" Paul declares, joking.

"But Paul, she's a really nice girl, and I really think she's Neverland material. I mean, she loves it here already. She loves the valley, the energy, the simple life. She's the kind to stay.

"I most definitely will affirm one thing. To find a girl who really wants to stay isn't easy. It sure took me long enough, but I got my goddess. Our intentions came true. I knocked her up, and we're staying right here." Paul plants his bare foot proudly.

"Stop it! Don't you call me *knocked-up!*" Sky answers her hubby with a sharp pinch to his arm.

"You see the wahine, she gets excited…"

"Our family of 3 will be back for good after we have the baby and save a little money." Sky states with a smile.

"Well I should harvest some edible hibiscus leaves and a few other things for dinner and get back down to the beach. Wahine waiting, you know." Mano jokes.

"You waiting on a boat drop *Cap-i-tan* or you got a kayak for re-supply?"

"Yeah, I'm afraid the kayak is no more. The report on the *SS Stay-Afloat* is that last spring Kawika used *Spirit* to guide him to it. He found it where it was stashed by massage camp, and then used it with only moderate success for a couple weeks before he left it on the beach and the Rangers helicoptered it outta here. Yeah, Kawika's on my shit list, but I haven't seen him yet."

"Right behind Khan, I'm sure." Paul chuckles.

"Khan's gone forever for all I care," Mano denounces.

"Oh no, he'll be back, just like lolo Lennie, 'em loonies always be comin' back." Paul spouts.

"Yeah, I know, but I'm not worried. I'll just look him in the eye and say *howz it?*"

"Just like a wild boar, you just look 'em right in da eye." Paul confirms, with a father-like look.

"Anyway, I got the wahine, and aside from her being a little lolo herself, life is good. We're expecting a boat drop any day now." Mano concludes.

Paul offers Mano some fresh dill and a ripe breadfruit to take back down to the beach. Mano takes his time looping around going down the hippie highway to reconnect with Zoe. He scurries merrily down the trail to the beach with the warm afternoon sun staring him in the face. He turns off the trail maka side to their shady camp just off the first helipad.

"Where were you this whole time?" Zoe probes upon his return.

"I thought you didn't want to see me so I went up the valley and hung out with my friends Paul and Sky for a bit."

"Well, I had plenty of fun here on the beach without you." She sniffs.

"So are you happy to see me now?" Mano questions.

"Yes, I'm happy to see you. I feel much better now. I just got upset and scared."

"I'm sorry I triggered you hun-buns, you know I love you, right?"

They embrace and enjoy the rest of the evening. The birds coronade the sunset as always, and on the fire a warm tea brews. Settling in, Mano feels at home, and the two feel whole in each other's arms.

"Do you think we'll get our boat drop tomorrow? Zoe asks, as their fire smolders.

"Na, the waves are still too big— but soon. Maybe in the next couple of days."

"Are you upset that you don't have your kayak?"

"No, I've got you, and we've got a boat drop coming. Besides, the swell is too big for kayaking this time of year anyway."

"Are you happy to be here with me?"

"I feel like I'm meant to be here with you, my love. This is the best thing that's ever happened to me."

The two sleep soundly, snuggling close. The next morning, they sow seeds for a garden during a daylong rainstorm. Mano builds up a rock-lined garden just outside their tent and they plant arugula, basil, kale and lettuce in the soaked earth. They sprinkle a few lettuce seeds up valley as well. In the rain, they work together to weed and clear around some big basil plants in the beach garden, too. While doing so, they uncover some arugula and kale that's being crowded out by weeds and thick vines.

Zoe loves the land already and enjoys gardening and exploring, despite the all-day rain. Mano encourages the warm feeling he has that love will prevail for him and Zoe in Neverland.

The next morning, the sun returns and dries up the muggy beach. The Pro comes with their boat drop in the morning under fair weather and a break in the swell just as predicted. Mano and Zoe rejoice in their now plethora of food and supplies. The sun even encourages the cute neighbor girl to move along back down the trail to Babylon. Without her to make Zoe uneasy, she lets go and the next few days pass effortlessly.

In fact, they pass marvelously! The two swim naked together in the ocean. They make love on the beach, by the river, and swim and make love again. In this tropical paradise, there's ample opportunity to get the physical contact they both crave. They lie next to each other in love — In the hammock, in the sunny grass of the helipad, and under the shade of the java plum trees.

The rest of the Beach seems to have the good vibe harnessed, too. Recent raids had scared away most of the tourists and left a hearty crew at the beach campsites. The most notorious outlaws like Grizzley, Mr. X, and Ella are hardly deterred by the Ranger scare.

"I got three tickets in a month. I guess I'm supposed to be worried or something!" Grizz laughs.

"The vibe has changed. I'm digging the new Neverland. With the Piscean age ending we should begin seeing even more great change. Change for the better!" A man in dark sunglasses who calls himself the Star-man makes the widely accepted declaration. So positive and profound is Star-man's foretelling, it's almost the catalyst of another party night on the beach.

"Yeah, it's like a time of flip-flop — Mr. X moving off the beach, Keilani with Captain Bligh, and Kaholo out of the valley… Things are getting weirder — that's for sure!" Q laughs at his own words.

"And Captain Bligh with Keilani, that's the best never-saw-it-coming flip-flop example ever." Mano bursts back.

Mano walks along the trail to fill up water still hung up on Star-man's astrological talk, as well as thoughts of the up-valley mystic, Keilani, taming the reckless toothless pirate, Captain Bligh.

A new Age, The age of Aquarius, What does that even mean? What's going to change? A lot of crazy hippies thought the world would end on December 21, 2012, but of course it didn't. This Star-man fellow sure spoke profoundly of *big changes*, though. For some reason the new prophetic character stirs Mano's psyche. It wasn't necessarily what he said, but more how he let go of the words— like they were a message, a truth, that was not at all his own. The way he just stood and stared out past the horizon from behind his dark glasses made him even more of an enigma.

"So you gotta tell me a little about your manifestation of love come true. I wanna hear about meeting Zoe and bringing her here." Mr. X asks Mano surprisingly, when they catch each other alone on the way to the waterfall to fill jugs. X never took any interest in Mano or anyone else for that matter. Now he's asking him about his manifestation for love, as if he knew about it?

Mano is hesitant to engage at first, but he soon becomes enthralled with his own story. He tells X how they met on the mainland, fell in love instantly and moved in together. He continues on with a brief version of their history together up until their arrival in Neverland.

"So what I really want to know is, did you get everything you asked for? After all, you did have some points built up after saving those people's butts in the surf last winter." Mr. X spurts, without hesitation.

"The amazing thing is, yes! I got absolutely everything I wished for when I prayed and wished for true love on the Heiau. But everything I failed to mention, straight blew up in my face!"

"Yep, yep, you gotta be careful what you wish for. You know, Mama Kai likes to throw curveballs. I told you that already. When manifesting something, you've got to be very, very specific!"

"Well, I was pretty specific in some ways. I thought about the type of girl I wanted. I even thought about little quirky desires and traits, both physical and personality. I emphasized that I wanted the most loving woman ever, and I got just that. I wanted a beautiful passionate woman, and I got just that…"

"Yeah, she's pretty much a jungle 10 as far as physical beauty. You got that right. I've seen all the pretty ones pass through, you know." Mr. X smirks.

"But X, it's crazy. She doesn't believe it! No matter how much I tell her, she'll never fully believe it. I show her, too, with my actions as best I can..."

"So, that's the part you left out, huh. Got a gorgeous loving woman who sees herself as an awful person inside." Mr. X scratches his beard in deep thought.

"I know, I didn't say anything about desiring a woman who was secure in herself and not jealous, and that certainly blew right back in my face. Zoe is so jealous and fearful to the point it makes her crazy. She's already run out on me or threatened to leave me a half-dozen times over misplaced words or glances. Plus, she can hammer on the hate just as profusely as love it seems. The passion swings both ways.

"Young girls, they take a ton of work sometimes." Mr. X releases staring off into space.

"I don't know X, somehow it seems much more than just jealousy or young girl insecurities. Her fears are rooted deep from her childhood."

"Mano, everyone has their inner child to deal with." X adds, calmly.

"And her inner child is a kicking, screaming bitch!" Mano flares up, defensively.

"She gets so angry and hateful over the slightest trigger and it makes me so frustrated that it almost makes me violent. She just gets so crazy...Crazy mean out of fear. It's her fear that she can't control, and that sets me off reacting out of my true self."

"Well most people, and even animals go crazy out of fear. Still, that's tough. Especially if it makes you lose your temper. And you just can't do that. You can't let things escalate to violence. You know that."

"Yeah, it rips me up inside when I lose it like that. I mean I've never hit her or anything and surely I never would, but it seems she tries to push me to that extreme, just like Khan almost did. She tries to draw it out of me."

"*Khan crazy*. I can hardly believe that!" X raises an eyebrow.

"Crazy-passionate out of love and fear— it's hard to explain." Mano looks out to the beyond, pensively.

"Well, Mano, you've been out here and you know this place is hard for any young girl or young man even. You really gotta come to grips with yourself out here. It may take a while for her to find herself and settle in. Settle down and love her inner child, love yours, and if the love is as strong as you say it is, then maybe it's worth swimming in rough waters for a bit."

Mano contemplates the metaphor. It reminds him of his conversation with Hitman about *water women*. He may not be apt to grow gills, but how long could he swim for?

"Another thing, X. If I truly believe that Zoe is a manifestation from Mama Kai, does that mean if I screw it up with her I could be cursed in love forever?"

"Don't read into things so much, Mano. You can manifest and re-manifest. It will all come around. We all get what we deserve, you know. Just be patient and live in the flow."

Chapter 38   Dolphin Speak

"I've just re-learned how to walk, but you should see me dance!"

The potbellied man laughs as he hobbles about the beach campfire. People are drumming and chanting as a huge blaze lights up the sand on a calm night. Honu is back and he initiated a bonfire gathering on the beach. A few more new characters have arrived as well. Mano sits down with Zoe on the rocks behind the glow. Hesitant to join in the hubbub, he casually watches this new character comport around the circle. Zoe keys in on him as well.

"Oh, Thank goodness for my partner here for bringing me out here to this amazing place. I'd never made it out here... Alone no way! Goodness if it weren't for…"

"Honu," someone spouts up.

"Oh yes, that's what you call him." The strange man's perfectly doofy smile shines under his push-broom mustache.

"I came to this island…" he begins, with the bravado of a circus ringmaster captivating the crowd.

"I came here with the whales all the way from Alaska down the trail. Took me three days to hike in. And if it weren't for my bravest helper Honu over here being patient with me and guiding me along, I'd never have made it. But thank *Spirit*, and thank my turtle-steady friend here. I made it. Made it just to be here with you good people right now!"

The man spins around and leans over a tourist girl gesturing to her and the whole crowd at once. This old guy is not shy at all. Mano recognizes immediately

"I'm a healer from all over the world, but I come from Alaska!" The man announces over emphasizing the word *Alaska* like it's a signature dish at a fancy restaurant.

He sits down clumsily, yet somewhat majestically, in front of the shy, little, young thing. He draws his eyes into hers and clasps both his hands around hers as if proposing.

"I'm a healer, but I've come here cause I was told this is where the healers come to heal. I've been guided by medicine men and shamans in Alaska and I've healed people all over the world." He reaches out and spins one hand to the group, still clasping the fingers of the young maiden with his other.

Mano nudges Zoe to get her to pay more attention.

"See how excited and silly looking he gets when he says *Alaska*." Mano whispers. He too is strangely captivated.

"Do you know about the Dolphins?" the man asks, peering over his thick-rimmed glasses to look through the girl capturing the whole group with his gaze.

"Dolphins can feel each other underwater from miles away. They are the smartest creatures of the sea with their sonar. Damn, they're smarter than us even! Well, definitely smarter than me, anyway!" he chuckles to himself, as if he were the only one listening.

"And I've felt them! Through spiritual connection, and in the water, too. Because I AM a Dolphin!" he spouts wildly, and then takes a moment to admire individually each face that shines up in the light. The group focuses on the strange charismatic mustached *healer*, with mixed attentiveness.

They all watch as he sends true energy of grace into the girl's hand he holds all while giving his lengthy life-story, trail-story introduction.

"I got a steal plate in my head, and I almost died several times, and I just relearned how to walk from the dad-gum screws in my ankle, but I got here, and I'm a healer, and I'm here to heal myself and the divine goddess, mother earth."

"What is your name, *healer man?*" The girl suddenly speaks up with bright blue eyes and a French accent.

"You can call me Dolphin!" He smiles and removes his spectacles to let them dangle happily on his chest from their cords.

Mano looks at Honu. They all share the same smile, and Honu just falls into drumming and chanting louder.

"And now you gotta see me dance!" Dolphin declares, hobbling to his feet and strutting around the fire. He walks about shirtless, waving his skinny arms above his head, spreading his push-broom smile around the circle.

"Now, the monkey dance." He shimmies and waves his pumpkin belly in front of the tourists with delight.

"I've been at a world healer conference where I did massage for some of the best healers in the world...Why? Because I can feel what others are feeling, cause I am a dolphin! You know, dolphin sonar is so complex they can sense each other's emotions through the water."

The group is captivated and some start to dream about the dolphin-world as the chanting and sound of the waves crashing and Dolphin-man's fireside folklore spit out with the crisp rhythmic beating of the drum.

Honu is back and the vibe is on the rise. Mano squeezes Zoe's hand tight in his and daydreams about the weeks to come with the excitement of a rising moon.

Eventually, Dolphin tires out enough to exit the stage. Honu switches from drums to guitar, and his own heart song is felt by the group.

Not just faces, but souls shine in the firelight. Perhaps Dolphin does in fact help feelings transmit between those in the group.

The fire wanes and Mano leads Zoe back to their camp under the moon's glow. They kiss and hold each other at the entrance to their tent.

"So, were there any girls at the fire that you were attracted to?" Zoe asks suddenly, breaking up their intimate moment.

"Of course not, and besides should that even matter?" Mano replies in disbelief. *They had a great night, why should she feel the need to spoil it now?* He thinks to himself.

"It's just that I saw you looking across the fire when you were playing music and there were other girls there. I just want to know if there was anyone that you were attracted to so I know whether or not to be scared?" Zoe looks at him with pleading eyes. Mano sighs, taken aback. They enter the tent and prepare for sleep.

Zoe senses Mano's frustration and tries to calm him.

"I just felt something. That's all. I'm really sensitive to sexual energy, you know."

"I think a lot of times you *want* to feel something. You want to make yourself scared. You want to play into your own fears and that's retarded. It self-detrimental." Mano releases, rudely.

"You're just not sensitive at all!" Zoe snaps, and shuts down. She turns away and burrows on the edge of their double sleeping bag.

After she's fallen asleep, he cuddles back towards her and buries himself in her warmth. It's that closeness, that loving touch that makes him feel whole, but at dawn she's still cold, stricken with fear.

"I had a horrible dream that you were with another woman." Zoe tells him.

"Well come here, let me love you." he responds, sincerely.

"I can't, not right now."

"Fine, I'm gonna start a fire and make oatmeal... for myself!" Mano huffs defensively.

He tries to just let it go and boil water for breakfast. *Boil water for just himself!* He can hardly stand the harshness of his own words he hears echoing in his head. He might as well make her oats...

"Well good morning, Captain Mano!"

The man's voice is full of morning cheer.

"Hey there, Dolphin. How are you rising today?"

"Well, my back hurts, my ankle hurts, but I just swam in the ocean and my soul feels wonderful. How are you?"

"I'm feeling ok, just making breakfast, you know." Mano mumbles.

"So, where's your goddess, Ellie, Kelly, oh I'm just so bad with names."

"Zo-ee," Mano annunciates.

"She's in the tent still, not feeling real well. I was just gonna bring her some oatmeal."

"I don't want any oatmeal, I'm fine." Zoe's voice calls out sharp from the tent.

"Well, that's too bad, darling. I'll send some good *Alaska* energy to ya, help you feel better!" Dolphin responds for Mano, enthusiastically.

"Say... I see you got a bunch of oats. I could really use some oats and nuts. You need protein out here you know... mind if I have a bowl?"

"Uh sure... here you go." Mano hands him a bowl of prepared oats, hesitantly.

It's sort of an awkward situation, Zoe sulking in the tent while the two men eat oats just footsteps away. Dolphin blabbers on about himself, his life as a misplaced, misunderstood, injured, wandering healer continues. Mano just wants him to go away but shunning his newly arrived camp neighbor seems inappropriate. A woman comes by to say hello, making things more awkward.

"I heard from some people last night at the bonfire that you were a healer of sorts. I was wondering if you could work any magic on my ankle? I rolled it badly on the trail and it hurts to walk on it, and I'm supposed to hike out tomorrow with my group."

"Ankles! I know all about busted ankles. I got screws in my ankle years ago and I'm still relearning how to walk. Why don't you sit down right here, you lovely goddess."

Dolphin is already starting to sound like a broken record, but he shows a big toothy smile and the blue-eyed hiker sits down on an upturned bucket in front of him. She shyly offers him her slightly swollen ankle. He gives her ankle a gentle massage all around stimulating blood flow.

"There, feel better now?" Dolphin smiles broadly. His eyes light up from behind his glasses.

"Now, we're not done yet. If you really want to get this ankle ready for that trail tomorrow, then we're gonna have to send it as much love and good energy as we can. So it can heal! Do you know about toning?"

"Toning?" The woman counters reluctantly.

"Yes, toning. Healing and energy work powered by vibrational tones. One person's own voice can only heal so much, but two people toning can raise the vibration by a factor of 10, and 3 people toning all together— that's a hundred times as effective." She looks at Dolphin perplexed, yet eager.

"Now just practice with me. Make a tone with your own voice and hold it, all while at the same time focusing love and healing toward your ankle."

The woman lets out a full breath tone and Dolphin matches hers, raising the vibration.

"Ok great. Now we need you, Mano, over here, too. Let's all tone with her together, sending love and healing energy to her, together. So Mano, we'll try to match her tone and then raise it up just slightly, giving her a higher vibration."

They all breathe in and tone together. The unified sound is amazing. It's almost like their voices are vibrating off one another, lifting up the tone and creating a beautiful resonance.

"Thanks, that was great," the woman releases, after they all stop and breathe.

"Yeah, that felt great for me too." Mano declares. Then he swallows his words. What's Zoe gonna think. Here he is *healing* another woman in their camp and enjoying it. She can hear it all from the tent too. This time fear sweeps over him and makes him uneasy. He's nervous after Dolphin and the woman leave.

He cautiously asks Zoe if she wants a cup of tea from outside the tent.

"I don't even want to talk to you," Zoe yells at him and turns back into the sleeping bag.

"Okay, I guess I'll just leave you alone." Mano replies sorely.

"Inviting another girl to our camp, what were you thinking? You know how that's gonna make me feel! You're so insensitive."

"You know what! You can just sulk to yourself over nothing! I'm going up valley for the day on my own!" Mano zips up the tent, grabs his small backpack and storms off.

Alone in the valley he reacquaints himself with the peaceful serenity all around. Beneath the quiet canopy of the jungle, away from the thundering sound of the surf at the beach, he reenters a daydream. He lets his bare feet feel the forest floor and sounds and smells lead him up the valley to Cliff's hidden veggie garden. There, through a window cut in the canopy for the garden he shares the sun's rays with the papayas and hibiscus and edible greens. He feels inclined to just *be there* with the plants. Meditatively, he waters the garden with the gravity-fed hose from the stream.

He munches on different greens and observes the progress of the valley's currently most developed veggie garden. Even early in the season there's already plenty of edible hibiscus and Okinawa spinach and some early arugula. He recognizes kale, tomatoes, basil, papayas, carrots, eggplant, peppers, and several types of salad greens started. He finds room to plant a few more seeds as well. Afterward, he continues up valley to gather a dozen oranges from his favorite hidden tree. Despite adequate distraction from Mother Nature, he can't help but think of Zoe. How could she be so jealous? She allowed herself to be so easily triggered. What could he do to dispel her fears? He feels like he is a loving, caring, loyal partner to her, but she somehow doesn't. Should he try to care less to encourage her to win him over like Paul might suggest? Somehow, that just doesn't feel right. — He couldn't do that and still really be himself. He needed guidance, and she needed help from someone other than him...Maybe they needed Dolphin.

He's back at the beach close to sunset and finds Zoe playing hand drums with Honu, Dolphin, and a few other dudes at the old Buddha Sanctuary spot. He's almost angry when he notices her having such a good time without him. She's topless, surrounded by other guys playing music, while he was up valley gathering fruit feeling bad about himself for not settling her fears. *And the attention from the opposite sex she gets is somehow ok*, he thinks to himself egocentrically, but puts it aside.

He catches himself feeling insecure seeing her enjoying his friends. *Friends.* Wait, we all need friends. He decides he's happy to see her smiling with his friends. He walks up and she gives him a slight smile. It's not the smile that says, *oh you're back, I care about you,* but instead it gleans *here I am having fun without you.*

"Who wants an orange?" He offers to the crew, releasing the bundle of dripping oranges in his sarong. The group excites and welcomes him in.

Everyone goes out to the perch to eat oranges and watch the sun slip behind a haze of low-lying clouds just above the horizon. It's almost sunset.

"How was your day?" Mano asks Zoe, casually.

"Oh, it's been a great day. We've been making great food and drumming." Her response is quick with a turn of her head. She still doesn't want to talk to him.

"Say, Captain Mano. Zoe is a real goddess, you should see her drum. She's a natural, she's just started and she's already better than me."

"I don't know about that, Dolphin, but I do like drumming." Zoe responds, with a smirk.

"Well, come on! Let's play together." Dolphin spouts encouragingly.

Dolphin sits across from her and they beat the Djembe to a unified rhythm. He sets the base beat and she follows with ease. He smiles, staring goofily into her enchanting eyes. She woops and smiles, letting her perky naked tits jiggle for all to see. She clearly loves all the male attention she's getting. Mano can hardly watch as she rubs it in.

But her drumming is great, and maybe this drum is just the outlet she needs. *Let it be,* he tells himself, trying to stop reading into the situation. They all play through the sunset. Zoe's eager to share food and make dinner with her new friends, so she and Mano go back to their beach camp to gather a few items for dinner and the evening show.

"Why didn't you save some of those oranges for us? You just gave them all away." she pesters him back at camp.

"Why should you care? You didn't hike all the way up valley to get them. You were just flaunting your titties all day long for a bunch of dudes, and you harass me for a five minute conversation with some tourist!" Mano flares up.

"Everyone runs around naked here, why should you care?"

"I don't, it's just, just… you didn't even get up to hug me or want to sit with me for sunset."

"Cause I was still upset with you from this morning."

"Well, can we forgive each other now, you know, go on and have a good rest of the night?"

She says nothing—instead she just holds angry eyes.

"So you are just choosing to be upset and be mean? That's ridiculous!" Mano announces.

"Well, I am still upset. That's how I feel. Look, I don't want to argue with you anymore. Let's just go back and play music."

Mano winces. There's nothing more to say, it seems. The whole interaction leaves him with a lead heart and a feeling of emptiness.

Sweet flute music by the glow of the fire brings him back. She sits next to him and eases up a bit, allowing Mano to hold her hand and rub her back. Loving on her makes him feel so much better. When she lets him in, he feels whole again.

"Who is that playing the flute? Your music is so soothing, so healing!" Zoe asks to the dark open air once the music pauses. The face with the flute leans over from across the fire and radiates its glow. The soft tones continue. When another ensemble finishes, the man humbly bows and introduces himself.

"My name is Dolphin. I've been a long time resident of this sacred valley. I've gone around the world, and now I'm back, and I'm delighted!" The thin little man proclaims with great pizzazz.

"Whoa there. Dolphin? We already have a guy named Dolphin— right over here." Mano points to Dolphin right next to Zoe, holding a drum between his knees.

"Yeah, we can't have two Dolphins? Who's the real Dolphin here?" Honu lurches out.

"Well, I can assure you, I am Dolphin. That's the name I acquired at the Sanctuary years ago, and I embody the playful spirit of the dolphin, always." The little man adds a bright, playful fluttering of his flute to complete his statement.

"Yeah, this Dolphin was back at the Sanctuary in the days of Mayor Don even. He's pretty much a dolphin-guy already." Grizz chimes in, verifying the newly arrived Dolphin's tenure in the valley.

"But, I've always been Dolphin. It's the spirit animal that was bestowed upon me by powerful medicine men in Alaska!" Dolphin testifies, removing his glasses pleading before the group.

"Well, we can't have two Dolphins, that's all there is to it." Mano insists.

Flute Dolphin pushes his nose in the air, flippers his hands daintily at his sides and releases an impeccable dolphin-like chirp. All eyes draw to him, then everyone skips back to the older potbellied man who just smiles, sheepishly. Grizz chimes in to judge.

"Yeah, this guy over here is pretty much Dolphin-ed out already, Alaska guy here, I dunno, he's kinda more like a walrus or something!"

Mano and the rest of the crowd lose it on this one. The push-broom mustache and big front teeth mimic walrus for sure.

"But, I've always been called Dolphin. I don't see why we can't just have two Dolphins?" The older man continues to plead, clumsily.

"Walrus!" Someone coughs.

"Well, what is your real name, *Alaska* man?" Mano announces.

"Well, my real name is…Carey. Yeah Carey is the name my mother gave me, bless her heart."

"Well then you can be Carey, Carey-Dolphin, or Walrus. What will it be?" Mano concludes.

"I don't like Walrus. I'm not a walrus! I'm a dolphin," Carey whines. The *Real Dolphin* flaps his flippers and squeaks. Carey cocks his head and thumbs across his thick mustache.

"So I guess I'll be Carey-Dolphin," he states, begrudgingly.

And so, it is decided. The two Dolphins seem to accept it and music plays together in celebration. Drums and flute, guitar and ukulele, together and separate as the fire lights up the circle.

Mano tries drumming with Zoe on the same drum for the first time. Their natural rhythms come together quite well and they follow each other's beat. The role of the lead drummer transfers between them seamlessly throughout their cohesive rhythm, but they have a hard time keeping balance between them. It's almost like the drum cannot handle their unified power at once, one must be dominant and the other must follow. Once again Mano is reminded of the shear fierceness of his partner's energy. Zoe senses the same.

That night in the tent Mano wants to talk about the issues that came up throughout the day and work to improve on their relationship, but Zoe just wants him to love her, so he accepts the love he craves and he keeps his mouth shut. They make love passionately and hold each other through the cool, windy night.

The next morning, their tent neighbor Carey-Dolphin smells their coffee and invites himself over. Mano almost rolls his eyes as he approaches, empty cup in hand.

"Sugar! Man, I could really use some sugar. You guys got sugar don't ya? And coffee, I smell some good coffee over here."

"Alright Carey-D. You want a cup of coffee? It's just about ready." Mano answers, plainly. Mano is a bit uneasy seeing how yesterday's morning with Carey led to a day of distress. But Zoe's up with him, and her mood is good.

"Man, I swam in the ocean already this morning. I feel great. This place, you know, it's *so* healing! Now, I just need some sugar and I'm set."

"We don't have any extra sugar, Carey." Zoe responds coldly.

"Say, after breakfast maybe I could do some healing work on you." Carey offers back to Zoe.

"Yeah, well of course with your boyfriend's permission. I'd love to help you." He sends his warm walrus-like smile to both of them.

"Sure, Carey-D. I think that could be a great idea. I could even help too." Mano answers, agreeing.

"What do you say, Miss Zoe? You know I've worked with medicine men and healers from all over the world. I'd love to work on you." Zoe's hesitant, but she agrees to let Dolphin-man feel into her heavily guarded inner-self.

"Ok, just breathe with me, nice and slow, let yourself be open." Dolphin tells her, calmly. They sit across from each other with eyes closed. They start to breathe deeply together. Carey moves his hand along her back, up to her shoulder and neck. He presses gently with his thumb on her third eye and then moves to her heart chakra, feeling, toning, and healing. He feels her past. He listens. Listens to the deepest wounds of her inner child. He listens and sends love.

"Ok Mano, I want you to tone with me sending healing energy over her root chakra. Just put your hand here, just over her lower abdomen and tone with Zoe's tone. Remember to match her tone and raise it up just a little bit. We're lifting her up from her root chakra."

"Oooooooh…" She starts her tone and the two men join in, matching, then raising the vibration. They continue through several breath cycles for several minutes, then Carey calmly removes Mano's hand and his own. Carey thumbs her third eye briefly and instructs her to open her eyes.

"That was so soothing. Thank you." Zoe exhales, wide-eyed. Carey takes her hand, gracefully.

"Thank you for allowing me to feel you, and tone with you. You are a supreme goddess. I am honored. Thank you. Thank you. Thank you." he bobs his head, gleefully.

"I never knew about toning. I love it. It feels so good, so healing." Zoe voices. Mano can see her filled with new light. Some of her pent-up fear has been released. Her eyes shine soft and true.

"Can I share something with you that I felt. Share it with you and your loving man here?" Carey leans in glowing with his own light.

Zoe is cautious yet curious. She stares back into Carey's eyes ready to absorb. He takes her hand and cups his weathered palms around hers.

"You are a woman's woman. Do you know what I mean by that?" He pauses and smiles into her, feeling her non-verbal response.

"You carry all the wounds of Mother Earth and generations of women's strife inside. Thousands of years of patriarchal male-dominant society have created deep wounds in the womb of Mother Earth." Zoe looks on steadily as Carey continues.

"And you, being a woman's woman, you carry the pain of that wound from Mother Earth deep inside. It's an incredible burden, but one that can be released."

A tear slips down Zoe's face as she smiles slightly. Mano cannot quite grasp what Carey Dolphin is saying, but being inherently sensitive he can feel the deep pain of this wound inside his partner. Dolphin places his hand on the small of her back. Crouching beside her, he sends loving warmth.

"I understand and can relate to your inner child, too. I too have a deeply rooted fear of abandonment." Dolphin's words make Zoe's face tighten, but with added pressure from his hand she releases.

"This man here, Mano. He loves you." The three wrap arms around each other with their heads touching.

"Let's all tone together for the healing of Mother Earth." The three resonate together in a beautiful unified hug. Mano turns to Zoe with a look of upmost care. "I love you." He inhales surrendering into her arms.

"I love you forever," she sobs, squeezing him back, tightly. The two return to the tent and just hold each other in love. They're tantalizing need for each other's love is magic in itself. With fears released, love flows and it feels great.

Mano is overly curious and wants to ask Carey Dolphin about Zoe. How can *he* facilitate her healing? He runs by his camp when she's not around to notice.

"Dolphin, I want to know more about what you felt in Zoe. I want to know so I can help her. Tell me more about what you felt." Mano pleads, eagerly.

"Zoe is a woman's woman and she holds tight the wounds of Mother Earth. We have to be patient while they heal. We can't heal her, but we can love her, and listen. And we can tell her she is great. That's all."

"Well, I already love her and I try to be attentive. What do you really mean?" Mano feels Carey's answer is a regurgitation of what he already heard.

"Women don't want to be helped. They want to be heard! And us men sometimes just can't hear them. We can, but not all the time so really women need to be heard by other women. In the old days they used to have sewing circles, and that was a place women could go to be heard. We need to create something like that here. For all the women!"

"That's an incredible idea, just what I needed to hear. We should try to put together some kind of moon camp for them or something."

"Remember, Mano! Listen, observe, and let her be heard. Don't try to do or fix everything!" Mano freezes, catching himself. Then Carey sighs, seeming perplexed by his own advice.

"Well, I don't know, really. My advice hasn't got me far. I lost every good woman I had to my own foolishness. Nobody stays with me. I've got serious abandonment issues, for Christ sake!" Dolphin sulks in his thoughts.

"There's got to be love out there for all of us, and real love, you know, comes from within." Mano answers, trying to brighten the mood.

"I know, I know. But I've got abandonment issues, and you know what happens to people with abandonment issues?" Carey doesn't wait for a response.

"People with abandonment issues recreate abandonment for themselves over and over again!"

Mano swallows, and mouths to himself, *Zoe.*

Chapter 39   Nothing's out of reach

The arugula is the first to sprout in *Zoe's Dishwater Garden*. That's the name Mano bestows on the tiny salad greens garden the two planted just outside their tent. The little garden is less than half the size of their tent, tucked between the tent door and the thick lantana bushes that separate their camp from the beach trail. The kale sprouts next, but is slow to grow. Still only 3 weeks after sowing the seeds, there are arugula leaves worth thinning. Outside of their tiny garden, other plants are flourishing in the tropical sunshine too. Some of the mature basil and oregano plants in Cliff's beach garden are three feet tall and tomatoes are starting to pop up along the beach trail. Oranges and liliquoi fruit have been easy enough to come by too.

"Abundance, Abundance, Abundance!" Rainbow shouts merrily, showing off a sarong full of watercress and mint she gathered up valley along the stream.

"And look at these pumpkins Uncle Dan gave me. I'm gonna make a pumpkin quinoa stew and a special hot cacao drink for all the goddesses." She says glowing with excitement. Rainbow had returned to the beach and like Carey-Dolphin, she was really into toning and healing the divine feminine. She and Zoe become sisters in toning and cacao fudge making. Zoe looks up to her as a woman of self-confidence and admires her for seeming to not need a man for anything. *She is the Queen of the Fairies; she's so down to earth, yet so wildly cosmic.* Mano jokes to himself.

Their love for the land and sea helps bring Mano and Zoe together once again. Zoe loves the ocean like a true mermaid. But not being from the coast, the steep breaking waves and shore rips intimidate her. She hasn't really swum in the ocean there yet, but with the swell currently way down, Mano convinces her to give it a try. Mano coaxes her into a swim-float in along the channel inside the break. They swim and frolic in the relatively tame channel. Mano explains to her that they can just drift down the *lazy river* to the west end of the beach and walk back rather than be concerned about the strong shore rip. *Just go with the flow*, he encourages. She agrees and they let the current rip them along the coast. Then, all of a sudden, the channel deepens, and she can no longer reach the sand beneath with her feet. She starts to get scared.

"Don't worry, the shore is just right over there," Mano assures, swimming right next to her. Then it's big surges of whitewater rolling in from the break. She's more than nervous now, diving under the powerful whitewash. They're almost down to Captain Bligh's camp at the other end of the beach. They are just 10 yards from the shore but the deep channel is surging back against the breaking waves, not pushing them toward the beach like Mano envisioned.

"Ok, lets swim in," Mano calls to her, seeing her face struck with fright. But she's already too scared to swim. Zoe just dives under as the next wave rushes over and they are pushed further along the deep channel in the current.

"Just reach for me right here! Swim a little toward me— we're almost there." Mano shouts, anxiously. Zoe's face deteriorates more. She can't even mutter *'I can't swim'* or *'help me.'* Mano's eyes catch on Captain Bligh running down the beach to help.

"Just grab a hold of my ankle and I'll paddle you in." Mano instructs. He paddles a few hard overhand strokes and they're out of the channel and standing waist deep on the sand before Captain Bligh even gets to the water. It's an easy rescue, but Mano's still relieved to see Captain Bligh ready to swim out to them with a buoy. He remembers the two recues from last year. The *'grab the-ankle routine'* was the same for Q.

What's it like to be paralyzed with fear? He ponders. He half expects her to chastise him for the scary swim, but her thoughts quickly fall toward her other fears. She scans the beach for potential *threats*. She's so preoccupied looking for *other naked girls* that she doesn't even notice a huge monk seal sleeping on the sand right in front of them!

With both Zoe and Q, the safe zone was just a couple of hard paddle strokes away. But both were immobilized with their fears, their rational brains could not make their bodies do a simple task that they knew how to do. Why is this? Once fear takes over, you lose control over yourself both mentally and physically. You're acting sub-consciously; you are only *reacting* out of fear.

Mano makes this distinction and he looks to apply the concept to Zoe's ingrained fears and distrust for men. It gives him new understanding to her difficult reactive state. Zoe's fears are real, but just like the swim in the channel, the other side is within reach. Letting love rule instead of fear seems like just a few strokes outside of her comfort zone.

In the surging waves, some people just need a swim coach to tell them they are ok and they'll swim out of the rip on their own as long as you are by their side. But others in the same situation need a full-on rescue. What makes some lose their ability to swim entirely and fall in to panic when they can't touch bottom? They are not drowning, but they let themselves drown in their fears. Mano's biggest fear was being without love. *Would he make it through with just a swim coach, or would he need a rescue?*

Mano lets the afternoon winds and choppy surf stir up hope for him. As evening settles in, the trade winds lay down, the sea calms and so does he. He reminds himself to abandon his grasp on his fears. Staring out at the ocean, he lets himself feel as peaceful as the waves and sky. He gently hums one of Kaiko's catchy songs.

'*Be who you wanna be, nothing's out of reach, lying naked at the beach…*'

"Hola Cap-i-tan! Is that a Naked J song you are humming?"

Honu's voice perks him up out of his trance instantly.

"You know it, surf-baba! I got Kaiko's '*Where the river meets the sea*' stuck in my head!"

"Yeah, that's a good one, cuz! Hey, I heard from irie pirate Bligh you had to help the wahine swim through the channel today."

"It was just swim practice." Mano responds to Honu with a smirk.

"Yeah, Neverland beach will make a strong swimmer outta her!" They both laugh as Mano puts a hand on Honu's shoulder.

"How bout we roll a J, in the spirit of Naked J. I got some Cali herb." Mano offers.

"Yeah, I'll smoke one to Aloha, unconditional love." Honu chuckles, enthusiastically.

"Embrace the Aloha!" Mano shouts into the breeze. The two men share a bonding moment with the sacred medicine and watch a Mars-red sun sink peacefully beneath a thin veil of clouds and disappear into the ocean.

It's all smiles and chanting and drumming at Honu camp after sunset. Zoe is in a good mood and Mano allows himself to ease up a bit at the mostly male gathering. There are two sets of cast irons cooking pizzas on a big bed of coals. Looks like everyone will get more than a tiny slice tonight. Grizz is offering his usual over-the-top cooking advice and the crew is starting to get silly, dancing and rapping about. More joints are being passed and Mano starts rapping about cave-man valley cats getting jiggy in the way back.

"Getting grizzly up there in the va-alley, making caveman love, ever-y day. Up there making caveman love." he sings out.

"Caveman lov-ing woo ooh!"

"Hey Captain Silly, I think you're on to something there, just keep singing away and lemme get my Uke." Honu encourages.

"How about this…Caveman loving, wooh ohh, F-sharp minor to B-minor." Honu plays the riff and Mano keeps rapping. Together, *Caveman Lovin,* an instant Neverland classic is born.

"Ok, we just gotta refine it a little bit more. You know, make it pretty, but keep it silly." Honu encourages. They ramble and rap well into the night. The next morning, they all come together again for the morning show. More great music shared in the open air with pancakes and Nutella®.

"Abundance, Abundance, Abundance!" Zoe declares, mimicking the *Queen of the Fairies.*

"She really loves Nutella," Mano jokes.

Before the pancake party kicks into full swing, a messenger comes to deliver news from the coconut wireless. A scrawny man stands up tall and delivers the telegram in a stately, yet stuttering proclamation.

"I'm delivering this message to the beach, news sent via coconut wireless, by Q on the outside. Outlaws in town report that Khan has landed on the island and is on his way to Neverland."

The crowd hums, excitedly.

"Well, just as good. I'd rather deal with his ass in here than out there." Honu is the first to speak up. Mano is hesitant to say anything.

"Who's Ka-on?" Zoe mouths, copying the messenger.

"Oh, you'll know Khan. You'll surely meet him! He's probably the most loved and feared character of the whole beach. I'm certain, you've heard some of the stories from last year. He threatened to kill your boyfriend Mano-banano, and others too." Honu announces for all to hear.

"Honu, you know that you're the most loved character!" Mano jokes back.

"So, what do we do when he gets here?" Zoe chatters nervously.

Honu and Mano, the two with the roughest past history with Khan look at each other and share a mutual understanding.

"We blast him with Aloha! So much Aloha that he won't know what to do!" Mano declares.

"And if he starts to go all crazy attack mode on anyone we'll bash him over the head with Mano's busted guitar, not my good one!" Honu adds, with only a touch of humor.

Blasting him with Aloha certainly seemed like the most reasonable approach. Mano already felt a lot more confident about dealing with Khan now that he had real friends like Honu on the beach and Paul in the valley. He wouldn't take any shit from him in any case — he had already decided that long ago. But Khan didn't have any real reason to be upset with either of them. They knew him well enough to know that he'd likely be in good spirits upon arrival and it would take at least a week or more in the valley for him to deteriorate to his infamous volatile state.

They jam on through the morning show while Rainbow and Zoe flip pancakes. Mano and Honu refine *Caveman Lovin'* into a lyrical masterpiece, if such a thing could be said for any song with *Caveman* in the title. No sooner than three pancakes later, they hear the drone of a motorboat.

"Listen, shush. Do you hear that?" Mano lurches.

"Dual outboard, yeah that's him. It's The Pro." Honu infers.

"Bet-cha it's Khan too. I can sense it. I can feel his energy!" Spacedog, one of Khan's former minions, announces.

"Well, we'll be ready to blast him full of Aloha and Nutella pancakes as soon as he lands!" Honu chuckles.

The crew jams on. Space-dog volunteers to go to the beach to investigate the possible *Khan drop*. Soon enough, Khan, Spacedog, and some new girl approach the river mouth camp from the Heiau trail. As soon as they cross the stream, the whole crew starts in song. *'Neverland I love you so, thanks for calling me to live like a rain-bow...'* The five or six people playing and singing are unified and smiling as they approach. Khan just kind of smiles back and stares placidly toward the open air. They all exchange nonchalant welcome greetings after the song is finished.

Khan breaks out a brand new ukulele to play a song. Old feelings of past conflicts make Mano and Honu leery about joining in. They are cautious in befriending him. Khan lights up a joint as sort of a peace offering. He offers Mano a small bud and Honu a pack of sunflower seeds. They both take his nominal gifts with hesitation. Mano recalls the lyrics of one of Khan's old songs, *For-give-ness, for they know not what they do.* Khan's smooth voice echoes in Mano's head but he can't stomach the meaning. This is the man who threatened to kill him and made life in paradise edgy for weeks not even a year ago. Khan had no respect for him— why should he forgive him? Mano's rational mind battles with his desire for wanting to make peace. He can sense Honu is experiencing the same dilemma.

Khan is welcomed, but only half-heartedly for the rest of the morning show. Zoe is quick to get some drumming instruction from him. Khan is an incredible Djembe drummer and Zoe has natural rhythm and is a great listener, which makes her a great drummer. Mano can hardly stand to see Khan with her, but he refrains from opening his mouth and instead Honu and him hike up valley to gather some liliquoi, and just take a break from the scene. Walking up the Hippie Highway, Mano can't help but let his mind catch on the similarities between Khan and his girlfriend.

They are both very passionate and caring, yet they tended to act irrationally out of fear. Would Zoe, like Khan, ultimately resort to violence when all control is lost? Childlike tantrums are common when both don't get their way. Both are generous and nice to everyone, yet they are threatening toward those closest to them because they act out of fear of losing the ones they love. Even the way their hands struck the skin of the drum was strikingly similar.

Mano can't help but wonder if Khan's energy had anything to do with receiving Zoe in his manifestation for love on the Heiau a year ago. For most of his life, he'd parted ways or run from people who tried to intimidate or manipulate him. People would walk over him till they pushed him to his breaking point and induced conflict. He hated this and didn't like to admit to being a subject for manipulation or intimidation, but it was true.

Would he be forced into fight or flight with his lover? Of course, with her, he couldn't fight her physically. There had to be another way of dealing with this kind of person that could produce positive results. How could he stand up for himself with Zoe but not fight her, or run from her? How could he hold his ground, yet help her? He must be compassionate yet as solid as a rock in himself for what he stood for. This idea seems reasonable, but where do compassion, understanding, and forgiveness fit into the equation? With Zoe, as with Khan the year before, he'd rather bend excessively to keep the peace. Still, was this always the best resolution?

There seemed to be an easy answer for Khan. Just keep your distance— don't be his close friend. And this is what happened. Not just with Mano and Honu, but others too. Spacedog and Q and everyone who already knew Khan kept their distance. No one really befriended him despite his efforts to be friendly, share, and be caring. A friendship with him just wasn't worth the risk, most seemed to decide. This was a sad truth to see played out, for deep on the inside Khan is a beautiful soul with a lot of love to give. With no *tribe*, Khan left the beach and the valley he loved after less than a couple weeks, disheartened.

One beautiful day of sun and wind, Honu invites the resident crew of a dozen or so to trip mushrooms together. Mano is hesitant, still remembering the depth of his two trips last winter, but everyone else seems to embrace the idea, so he joins in. At midday, the ceremony begins. They all sit knee-to-knee in a circle on the Heiau. The sacred medicine, as well as offerings of oranges and chocolate, is placed in the center of the circle. The group prays together. They all tone each other up and pick a couple stems and caps from the bag. Mano opts for just a small dose and Zoe takes a medium one.

Soon its giggle fits and dancing on the Heiau in the sun. Honu and Dolphin serenade the group sweetly with flute and ukulele while Carey-D and Zoe hammer on the drum and chant tribally on the lower Heiau. Mano lays back and soaks in energy from the earth. Then he gets up to fly a kite in the breeze with Uncle Dan. The kite has an incredible fifty-foot tail and it dances back and forth with him in the wind. He calls it his pet dragon and he passes it along to his friends. Zoe goes off with the *Queen of the Fairies* laughing and dancing merrily all along the beach. They roll and splash in the water like beached mermaids. Everyone comes back together in song at sunset.

Mano's low dose has him coming down a little before the rest. Spacedog is drumming off beat to his song disrupting his and a few others' rhythm. Carey-D is talking annoyingly and irritating him too. Mano just can't play through any longer; he stops suddenly and scowls at Spacedog.

272

"Hey Spacedog, why don't you let Carey-Dolphin play the drum to this one, it may keep him from running his mouth so much!"

"Love my family, love my family, love my family," Rainbow starts to sing out in her fairy-like voice which Mano finds rather annoying, too. Others around join in. Mano figures he just gave up his turn, and thus just starts to sing with them.

"Love my family, Love my family," he tries to match their mismatched pitch. Then his heart sinks when he realizes that the message is directed at him. They all stare into him and for a moment he sweats feeling his soul being judged at the pearly gates. *Be nice, don't put down others*, he tells himself. He tries to redeem himself by hugging Spacedog and sending a look of compassion toward Rainbow, Carey, and Zoe. But still he feels shame in his own being. His personality flaws came right to the surface under the influence of the psilocybin. The group feels his and other's true selves just as strong as ever too. They all seem to realize that he realizes, and forgiveness is exchanged without words. They keep up the chant together.

"Love my family, love my family, love my family." Carey-D breaks down and starts weeping out of shame for always wanting to be the center of attention, or maybe just out of love. Love he feels for being accepted with flaws by his newfound island family. They all circle in around him and tone love into him just like he taught many of them to do. They keep toning louder and louder, higher and higher. The resonance vibrates through their hearts down into the Heiau beneath them to the womb of mother earth. Cosmic worldly healing radiates with each pulsing heartbeat, the unified toning, and each rhythmic wave thundering against the shore.

Chapter 40   Embrace the Aloha

Days fly by with the spring trade winds and twist and flow together with the morning show. Honu's camp becomes so popular as a breakfast hangout it's nicknamed the *Pancake Heiau*. The smells of blossoming weeds and flowers and the back and forth calling of songbirds to their mates keep Mano deliberating over love and balance in his relationship with Zoe. He's unsure how to further his relationship with his lover while still being his own bright vibrant silly self. He shakes his head. He's thinking about it too much, he decides. He distracts himself and decides he just wants to think about bananas. Ripe, yellow, sweet, little Apple Bananas or big bold Cuban Reds with the outsides crisped dark in coconut oil. How good would banana-Nutella pancakes be?

He hikes up valley when the morning show turns afternoon. He plunges into the cool clear waters of outlaw pools gulping up the divine tasting water right out of the stream. He smiles to himself, thinking of how Ella once told him that drinking the water straight from the valley stream alters your DNA. He passes the rope swing at Thomas's garden and follows a side canyon fittingly named Banana Creek to where several racks of bananas were awaiting maturity in a banana grove above a ten-foot high cascade way up the narrow canyon. Unfortunately, the bananas that he and Honu had been watching still aren't ready. The local outlaw consensus is that the flower of the rack has to be all the way open or fallen off and there should be at least one yellowish banana. The rack is close, but it's not in bug danger at all and there's not even a hint of yellow. Alas, he should wait another week! Mano does find two ripe pumpkins and he brings those down along with some edible hibiscus, dill, and other greens from community garden.

Coming back down the Hippie Highway, Mano stops by the old Sanctuary on the bluffs and finds Rainbow toiling over some damp twigs trying to get a fire started. Mano's a bit surprised. With all her patience, she's not able to get a steady flame. The earth was still moist from an early morning sprinkle and there are rarely caches of dry wood up at the Sanctuary. She kindly asks Mano for help and he offers, gladly. With the two of them working together, they turn wet twigs into coals and boiling water. He stays for a tea and plays a few songs on Honu's guitar he left in her care.

"I can't believe Honu left after just a couple weeks on the inside. I'm really gonna miss having him here to hold down the good vibes." Mano sighs, submissively.

"Yeah, he had so much Aloha. He inspired me to learn music, too. I'm gonna play this guitar, you just wait! I've already started writing a song." Rainbow's words are pure joy.

"Wow, what's the title of your first song?" Mano's asks, encouragingly.

"I think I'll call it, Forever-ever land." She smiles.

"Like Neverland, but forever. I love it!" Mano verbalizes. They smile at each other and for a moment, they share the same curious fairy-tale gaze they had for each other during the outlaw pool acid trip two spring seasons ago.

"Ok, one more song and I gotta get back down to the beach to deliver these pumpkins to my Zoe," Mano smirks. Again, their twinkling eyes catch on each other for a long second. He hikes back down to the beach and leaves her to enjoy the solitude of the now deserted bluff camps.

"Where have you been, and where's the bananas you said you were trying to get?" Zoe scans him voodoo-like looking for a trigger.

"The bananas need four or five more days, but I brought you back some pumpkins. Maybe we can make pumpkin pie? I miss you." Mano reaches to hug and kiss her as a means to avoid further interrogation. She pulls away.

"Where else have you been? You've been gone most of the day." She's already building up anxiety as he formulates his answer. Mano opts for pure honesty knowing he's got nothing to hide. He couldn't hide anything anyway.

"I stopped by the Sanctuary on my way down the Hippie Highway and Rainbow was there, and she asked me if I could help her build a fire, so I did. Nothing more, I assure you."

"You were hanging out alone with another girl— my friend!" Zoe starts to fume up.

"Hey, she's my friend too, and she needed help. Why would I not help her?" Mano states bluntly, feeling perturbed.

"Cause you're supposed to be here helping me! Was she naked?" Her triggered brain hunts for negative thought fuel.

"What's the point— she's always naked and so are you! Look, I was only up there for maybe an hour and all we did was light a fire, make tea and I played a few songs."

"You're such an idiot. You're off playing music for a naked girl— how do you think that's gonna make me feel? You know you're not supposed to be hanging out with other girls and you go and play music for a naked girl."

Zoe's starting to get crazy eyes letting the anger build up inside.

"Hey, you know I'm not even attracted to Rainbow— not at all!" He's drawn in getting defensive and irritated himself.

"How could you? You don't care about me! I'm down here gathering firewood because there's supposed to be a storm coming and you're up on the bluffs playing music for naked girls!" she cries, stomping around camp.

"How could you!" she wails.

"Look I'm sorry, I just didn't think it was a big deal."

She gets right in Mano's face, stares with crazy eyes and screams.

"You're horrible. I hate you!" The build-up to boiling point is a flashback of Mano's near violent confrontation with Khan last spring. His eyelids flutter and he takes a breath. He puts his hands on Zoe's shoulders, preventing her advance.

"Don't touch me!" she screeches, then spins away from him and storms off.

"You're fucking horrible. I hate you!" she spits back at him in rage.

"That's it, I'm outta here. I'm not putting up with your jealous craziness!"

"I'm not putting up with you, either. I hate you!" she continues to scream.

He marches off frustrated and upset, leaving her sulking in hate and rage. He couldn't have said or done anything worse! The rest of the day is ruined again. Ruined for nothing. Just replaying what happened stirs him so much it makes him clinch his fists and want to scream. He goes off to the beach and runs and kicks the sand and yells.

"This is not working! Why must I be pushed to the edge? I want to give up. This is not love!" He cries out and pounds his fists and digs into the sand, furiously. He tries to calm down and sit and breathe rhythmically, but he's so frustrated. If only he just went straight back after community garden, then he'd be holding and loving her right now. Instead, he's forced to suffer! *He could just be done with her.* Break up with her and be done. It's not the first time the thought crossed his mind, but now it settled in his stomach into a real option. The feeling made him uneasy. This just isn't working! Her blow-ups are too dramatic, almost making him violent. His heart feels tortured and he has no idea how to resolve the sensation inside.

The whole situation makes him edgy, making him more prone to lash out and lose his temper. It seemed like only a matter of time till he would. He feared the fury of his own fists just like he did with Khan. Retaliating with violence or threats would only make things worse; it would be an end-all for sure. *He couldn't, he wouldn't hit her no matter how angry she made him.* He made a pact with himself then and there. Eventually, he'd just have to abandon her. Paddle her out like Khan? Uhh! It just sounded so cold and horrible. This was the woman he loved — not Khan, some drug crazed, hot-tempered haole.

Nothing made sense. *Love her through it?* He tries to calm himself with the words from Honu but the phrase feels rundown, stale, and drained of love at this point. He bites his tongue and decides to try and go back to her with love.

Zoe's cold but calmer when he returns after dark. She doesn't even acknowledge him. Wanting to make peace more than anything, Mano tries apologizing to her.

"I'm sorry I triggered you and made you so upset earlier."

She's silent, offering nothing in return. He grits his teeth, trying to suppress his true feelings.

"I made some pumpkin and bean soup for us." she states humbly. He sits down and serves himself a bowl of soup from the pot on the coals.

"This is really good, thanks." He bargains with a compliment, trying to shoot a smile her way. She does her best not to even let her eyes catch on him as she shuffles around their camp organizing.

"I have to clean this place up before this storm comes and soaks everything." Zoe says with her head down. The wind had already picked up and was blowing in a sprinkling mist.

"I heard the weather report from X. It's just supposed to be a light rain tonight and clearing tomorrow. I hope it rains more, though. The gardens need it." Mano follows.

"If I don't organize the stuff, things will get wet and ruined." She continues.

"As long as everything is under the tarp and the food is in the buckets it will be fine, but if you want, I'll help you organize it the way you want to, then we can relax."

She continues to ignore him. He stands up and approaches her.

"Here, let me give you a hug. I love you."

"I just don't feel loved," she pouts, as she receives him.

"If it's not raining tomorrow, I'm going to go up-valley on my own to do that solo vision quest thing you suggested." Zoe states, boldly.

"Well that's a fine idea. I think that would be a great way for you to find your Aloha." Mano responds hesitantly.

In the tent he tries to roll toward her and snuggle her but she just turns away.

"Do you still hate me?" he sighs, feeling empty inside.

"I can't decide. I'll talk to you in the morning," she mutters against her pillow. He decides he doesn't really want to hold her anyway. Eventually, a restless sleep finds them both.

By late morning, the rain had stopped and the sun is out. Zoe's up packing her backpack, readying herself for her solo mission. She's still edgy and hardly speaks to Mano.

"Don't you want any breakfast before you go?" he asks, already knowing the answer.

"No, I want to get going and be on my own!"

"So I'll see you on the Heiau at sunset the day after tomorrow?" he shouts, watching her splash away along the muddy beach trail with her boots on. No response. *She'll come back when she feels like it, and if not, he'll live on in peace without her!* he thinks to himself.

"I hope you find your *Aloha* out there!" Mano shouts into the wind, watching her wavy sun-kissed hair bounce over the top of her backpack as she storms off. Maybe he'll find some solace of his own too. Maybe he can learn to not be so dependent on her love, he wonders.

"Come hang out with us here at our camp," Honu offers him, after returning from his quick turn-around town mission that afternoon. Mano spends the next two days with music, toning and self-reflection alone and at 'healing camp' with Carey-D and Honu. They reassure him that he is a good man after all. He complains about his tight back and Carey gives him a nice massage. He begins to feel loved even without her. Something he never thought possible since their inseparable connection seven months ago.

"Most of your tenseness and pain is on your left side. That's your receiving side. The left side of your body is where we receive good energy from the world," Carey explains to him with a sigh. Mano's thoughts still drift to Zoe wandering up in the valley.

"Relax! Don't even think about Zoe for a while. I'm sure she's fine and will come back full of Aloha." Carey reassures him, feeling his thoughts.

"Dolphin, have you ever been crazy in love with a woman?" Mano asks.

"Ahh, maybe never as crazy as you, but I've certainly been in love. And those *Alaska* women will drive you crazy. But ya see, I drove 'em all away— made them abandon me." He chuckles and then stares off into space as if looking for a long lost something.

"So what are the women like in Alaska, anyway?" Mano asks, curiously. Carey responds with a warm-hearted toothy smile.

"The women in Alaska become the men they want to marry!"

Up in the valley, Zoe wanders and explores in peaceful solitude. She feels comfortable, capable, and at home in her jungle environment. Still, she's never camped alone and the idea makes her a bit nervous. *I'll be all alone in the forest when the daylight fades to darkness*, she thinks to herself. The idea intrigues her, but leaves her unsettled. She decides to distract herself. She diverts from the main valley trail and continues along haplessly following side-trails, singing to herself. '*Embrace the Aloha here and now*,' she hums sweetly, trying to forget about her and Mano for a while.

She detests herself for being so triggered and reactive with him, but she feels that the love she holds in her heart doesn't match the love he or anyone has. She doesn't understand this or why she feels this way, but she accepts the feeling and lets herself hum it away and return it to the earth like the fallen java plum leaves that crunch under her feet as she hikes deeper into the forest canopy. She wonders about being alone and pure on her own in the valley with her own love for weeks and weeks. She would have a secret camp, her own magical fairy garden with wonderful fruit trees and a little perch with a swing that had a window through the jungle to view to the ocean. She could be an up-valley goddess mystique? *That could be fitting*, she supposes.

She sets her heavy pack down and watches water trickle over the rocks of a small side stream. Taking her boots off, she lets her feet cool in the little brook, settling back into her daydream of her own perfect camp sanctuary. Maybe she'd pick a spot next to a trickling stream with a perfect little gravel bottom pool. There would be passion fruit vines and red ginger flowers all around. She envisions the setup while twinkling her toes in the water. *Ouch!* She slaps across her forehead and smears the blood of several mosquitos. Maybe a goddess camp on a windy ridge-top would better suit her. She'd get strong arms and legs from hauling water up to her garden spot on the breezy ridge, she decides. She looks up toward the canopy, scanning for a breezy, bug-free ridge nearby. With a glimpse at the sun's position, she realizes it's late afternoon already. *I don't even have a camp set up, I need to find a spot and build a fire before dark.* She turns around realizing that she's diverted from the main trail and she's unsure of how to retrace her steps. *I'll follow the water down to the main stream and I'll surely run into the trail.* She's relieved that she can revert to logic, but she almost wishes that Mano was there to help her find and set up a good campsite.

Ambling along through the java plum and mango trees, she descends. She's singing to herself another made up song when she notices what appears to be a faint side trail. *A-L-O-H-A* is spelled out in small rocks on the ground, marking the turn-off. She smiles on the inside at the coincidence of the moment. Looking ahead, she can see and even smell smoke from a nearby campfire, but she hears no one. *How did I end up here?* She wonders. Overcome with curiosity, she follows the trail into the camp, creeping quietly. Zoe notices a big tan-skinned man with long, curly hair with strands of grey tending the fire. His back is turned and he doesn't notice her.

"Aloha," she sings out softly.

"Aloha!" the man exclaims, spinning around and noticing the beautiful estranged goddess standing in his camp.

She's suddenly nervous and stammers. "I saw your sign and I just thought I'd see who was here."

"Well, that's great, cause I was just wishing that someone would stop by for dinner." The man stares at her excitedly with a gold-rimmed front tooth and big amber eyes.

"Well, I was looking for a place to camp in the valley..." She delays finishing her sentence as she looks around at the man's very disorganized, dirty camp. The man responds, reading the situation.

"There's a good spot to put a tent just over this little hill, but if you don't wanna be around me and be off on your own I understand." There's an awkward pause, but the stranger breaks the silence.

"Do you have a tent?" he asks, still trying to place this girl who just wandered in.

"Yes, I have my own tent." She looks around again, accepting that where she is, is ok. They sit and have tea together after she sets up her tent just out of sight. Even though she wanted to be self-sufficient and alone in the valley, somehow she's happy she found this man she nicknames *Grandpa Aloha*. Her arrival is a manifestation to him for a dinner guest and he's eager to hear her story and help her. The old man's eyes glow in the firelight as he tells his own sob story of love.

"You got to have compassion for love to work," Grandpa Aloha reminds her.

"It's taken me so long to learn compassion, oh man, and I'm still learning. But this valley here will teach you everything you need to know…if you just let her. It's important to have compassion for what you don't understand in your partner and love for yourself, too." The old man can sense that Zoe struggles to love herself. He realizes she doesn't even believe how beautiful she is. He sighs at the sheer beauty of it.

The fire smolders and Zoe gets up off her little rock seat. Suddenly, the dark forest consumes her.

"It's so much darker here than down on the beach," she stutters, as she fumbles for her head torch.

"I think I should go to bed now," she tells the man, sheepishly.

"Ok, Alright, just one more hug for Grandpa Aloha." She hugs him and he holds on for too long, but he can't help but try to soak up the love from this youthful goddess.

In the tent alone she writes down the words to the song she was singing to herself on the trail, *Embrace the Aloha*. She hums the tune over and over in her head until she drifts asleep.

She wakes up at first light in a sweat and realizes that Mano's not there by her side. She recognizes that they'd slept next to each other for hundreds of nights straight and she feels almost not herself without him. She realizes how attached to him she'd become. What does this really mean to be attached? For a yearning moment she wonders how he feels, how he's doing— is he missing her? Of course, he would be. *Be your own strong woman*, she tells herself. But what does that really mean? She chuckles and lets herself be unbothered. She almost revels in the unknown.

After breakfast with Grandpa Aloha, she extends aloha and cleans up and organizes his whole camp. The old man can hardly decide what he is more grateful for, having his camp cleaned and organized, or just getting to watch this beautiful young maiden walk around and pick up things in the morning sun. He feels truly blessed.

She leaves her pack at camp Aloha and continues her solo exploration up valley hoping to find some hidden gardens and other wonders. She swims naked in a beautiful deep pool she discovers. She wanders and wonders looking for community gardens but never finds them. She does find and eat tons of mangos, though. She comes across an orange tree full of ripe oranges way high up. The longest bamboo pole nearby won't reach. She thinks to climb the tree, but she can't pull herself up. Besides, there's giant thorns on nearly every branch! *How does he do it?* She ponders for a moment. Then she reaches down to slap a mosquito on her leg and realizes that she's being bitten all over.

"Ahh!" Zoe yelps as she slaps at the cloud of mosquitos all around her head and runs all the way back down the trail to Grandpa Aloha's. Again, they share dinner and stories and smiles across the fire. The second night in the tent she misses Mano even more. Her mind catches on her fears and she wonders if another woman is tempting him this very night. Has he overlooked her already? Insecurity rushes over her and her heart races. Stop it! She voices to herself, she'll see him at sunset tomorrow. Wherever he is and whatever he's doing is beyond her control. Her core settles and accepts peace in this.

Again, she sings herself to sleep and she wakes at dawn yearning for his loving touch. She goes back to the pools she found and swims and writes in her journal. She toils through reflections of her youth and how she got to this point. Why was she so hurtful and fearful toward the ones who loved and cared about her the most? She hated it and didn't understand it. Just thinking about it made her angry. She kicks her feet in the water as if to kick her thoughts out of her head.

"Don't abandon your inner child. Instead, love her." a soft voice sings, as if it were coming from the stream itself. Zoe looks around and sees no one. Then she notices Ella gathering fresh mint from another pool just upstream.

"Sorry to startle you. I was just reflecting a message I received from the spirits of the valley for myself or anyone. This is a special spot, the Hawaiian ancestors told me so, and I just had to speak what they spoke to me. Just to be, you see."

Zoe is perplexed and still having difficulty grasping how many of Neverland's residents spoke in *riddles* and *messages*. She looks at Ella and their brown eyes meet for a moment.

"It's good to see another woman on her own up here." Zoe smiles.

"Yeah, I was kinda thinking the same thing." Ella responds, endearingly in her Aussie accent.

"Say, have you done any work with your inner child," *little Zoe?*"

Zoe looks down at her toes in the stream.

"Loving and healing our inner children is one of the best things we can do for ourselves. Not just for our spiritual growth, but for our whole body, and for mother earth, too."

Ella continues while hugging her knees to her naked breasts from her mossy perch at a pool just above Zoe.

"The valley is a wonderful place of healing energy. Here, we can easily connect with the crystalline grid of mother earth."

Ella sighs, looking at Zoe who is still focused on her feet in the water.

"You know we have to love our inner children, but we can't let them drive our school bus. Recognizing this and not allowing our inner children to be in control of our lives frees us to be our higher selves."

"Would you like to tone with me— tone for healing?" Zoe asks, looking up to the older woman.

"How about we sit and meditate and connect with the feminine energy of mother earth." Ella suggests, alternatively.

"I feel like this spot could be ideal for connecting with the ancients of the valley, too." Ella walks over and places a soft hand on Zoe's shoulder.

"You know you can manifest whatever you truly desire here in the valley."

They begin the meditation with what Ella calls a grounding exercise where they focus in on rooting down into the earth.

"Imagine that you are a big, old tree with roots that go deep, deep, deep into mother earth. Let your inner child sit in your abdomen," Ella voices, deliberately.

They sit with the ancients and their inner children in mediation on a ledge above the pool. Zoe has a hard time staying still with flies and mosquitos buzzing about, but just the presence of Ella helps put her at ease. She focuses some love to her child inside and it feels good— truly liberating, actually. They both come out of their meditative states simultaneously when a shaman bird drops in to whistle and sing right in front of them. The two open their eyes and stare at each other and smile. It's a moment of intimacy Zoe's never quite experienced before.

———

284

"Well it was nice to share this moment, and this meditation with you. I must head back down valley. My partner, Mr. X awaits me." Ella disappears just as quietly and mysteriously as she arrived.

Zoe stays alone nearly an hour after Ella leaves at the spot she names *Little Zoe's Bathtub*. The cool water feels so refreshing on her skin, her face, and her soul. Ultimately, she rallies herself to make the trek back down to meet Mano for sunset. She sings with each step down the trail sending love to little Zoe inside.

Mano is on the Heiau two hours before sunset playing music. He hopes and wonders over Zoe's return in the cool afternoon light. He muses on his thoughts of his own solo journey and journals a few poetic verses of a love poem for Zoe.

Zoe is sure to keep him on edge, arriving almost in twilight, but when they meet, it's glorious. Hugs and kisses and I love you to the moon! He tells her about *healing camp* and she tells him how she found her *Aloha*, and sent love to her inner child up-valley. They hold each other so tight that they can feel their rapid heartbeats as one. The last golden rays of sun christen a long, drawn out kiss and they feel filled with love again. They go back to the beach and cook pizzas together. They hold each other and make love in the tent. Her skin and taste enchant him. To her his touch feels cosmically right. They soak in all the love and touch they both missed.

The next morning, they host the morning show with Carey-D cooking up maple syrup pancakes. Washing clothes turns into more amazing lovemaking down at the river mouth. With no one around they dance naked with sarongs blowing in the wind on the Heiau. Could they feel more *loved*? Is it a dance of free beings, or a dance of wounded souls addicted to each other's love? Regardless they embrace the Aloha for the moment is now.

Chapter 41   Earth Quakin' Soul Shakin'

Strange wave, rogue wave, or no wave at all? Mixed opinions or possible fake news rolls in from the trail via the coconut wireless. It's another classic spring evening where the steady trade winds calmed at sunset and the ocean is transformed into a shimmering slick of tranquility in the fading light. No reason to be anything but chill, right? But talk of a *rogue wave* has amped up the energy on the beach. Everyone can feel it. With more than a tinge of curiosity, Mano and Zoe approach a lively group of tourists at some sort of celebratory bonfire on the beach. He recognizes a few outlaws around the twilight blaze, and they join the group feeling welcomed. Uncle Dan hollers at him upon arrival.

"Hey Mano, did you see this tsunami wave everyone's talking about?"

"What? There hasn't been a tsunami here! Unless you're talking about the Japan one from two winters ago!"

"No, there was a tsunami to-day." one tourist persists.

"If there was a tsunami, there'd be a helicopter warning. Remember two winters ago, '*Tsu-nami move-to-higher-ground!*'" Mano mimics the voice blasted from the helicopter loudspeaker comically.

"No, this is for real. The seismic wave hit the north shore at 10 am. I waited to hike the trail till it passed." one young backpacker continues.

"Wait… so you actually saw the wave come in?"

"A bunch of people watched and waited for it. It was a six-foot wave, and it landed at 10:10 in the morning. Surely someone here saw it too?"

The few locals and four or five other tourists around the fire just kind of look at each other dumbfounded. 'Tsunami? What Tsunami?' their faces seem to say.

"So…what did it look like when you saw it?" Zoe queries the young wanderer in.

"Well, it wasn't like a big crashing wave. Instead, all of a sudden, the tide drew out twenty feet or so, and the ocean just came rushing back in to the fill the space. It came up pretty big and fast, maybe ten to fifteen feet up the shore. And then it did the same thing like three more times, but lesser each time. Well maybe the second time the tide came out almost just as much, but the last few times were smaller for sure."

"Whoa, so you just got to stand there and watch it? You weren't like being ushered to higher ground or anything?" Grizz interjects.

"Yeah, I dunno. They weren't really evacuating the coast like I thought they might be. But it was supposed to only be a six-foot wave and, from what I saw, it wasn't that dramatic."

"They didn't send any helicopters in here to warn us. For other tsunami's they've been all about sending helicopters." Grizz, spouts feeling underappreciated as usual. Mano, Zoe, and everyone else seem to agree that there were no helicopter warnings in Neverland. A few even comment saying it seemed to be a slow day for helicopter tours in general.

"So none of you beach guys even saw this Tsunami, or tidal wave or anything?" Grizz persists. He doesn't give space for a response.

"I dunno, I kinda think this Babyloney tourist guy is full of shit. He smoked all his Pakalolo and is making up stories of seismic waves trying to scare us into giving him all of our weed. Ha! But I'm a bear, I just hang onto my weed even if the Rangers try to peel me from my camp!" Grizz cackles, picking the backpacker apart.

"There is a chance that there just wasn't anyone on the beach to see the wave right when it hit. It's kinda unlikely, but not that unlikely." Mano counters back.

"Hey man, I believe you." Uncle Dan declares boldly, looking at the youngster square in the face. The group turns to the valley elder, perplexed. Dan would almost always rather toil in his tobacco pouch than engage in any debate. He continues with all eyes focused upon him.

"I didn't see any kind of strange wave myself, but I could feel something this morning, like a weird shift in the earth itself. I've been out here alone a long time and I'm real sensitive to new energies. Something's happening for sure."

"Did they say there's gonna be more tsunamis?" Mano questions.

"They didn't say anything about another tsunami, but I think earthquakes are kinda unpredictable, and that's what causes them, you know. The government's been kinda weird lately, too. They closed down a bunch of offices, said they're gonna do another shutdown, like they don't have money to operate or something, I dunno."

"They don't have money to warn us, but they do have money to helicopter in here and write us tickets! Yeah, I know how it is." Grizz comments sarcastically.

"Well, we haven't seen the Rangers since that big multi-day raid after new years." Uncle Dan adds inquisitively. Mano and other outlaws engage there seldom needed 3-D brains and compute. Two months plus without a raid or even a maintenance visit— That *is* unusual.

"Well, I don't think all this tsunami talk should keep us from partying!" Spacedog breaks an awkward silence.

"But here we are, right here on the beach in the dark of night. We'd never see one coming," Zoe moans.

"Ya-mon, one big wave could come and wipe us out right now!" Uncle Dan chuckles.

"What are we supposed to do, live in fear of what we don't even know exists? That's the craziest thing I've ever heard of! Why don't we all run up valley and never come down to the ocean again?" Mano exclaims, looking toward Zoe and sending her an all-too-blunt dual message.

"Alright! Enough with the doomsday talk. Let's jam." Honu shouts, as he lifts a big log onto the already blazing bonfire. A rush of embers flies up and sends everyone rolling back into the sand wincing. Drums play louder and louder drowning out the waves and any lingering conversation. Chants and yelps ring out with the pops and cracks of the wet wood. Soon the fire and the vibe relax again. Mano holds Zoe, wrapping his body around hers beside the comforting glow. Almost everyone trickles off to go to sleep. Just Carey-D, Honu, Mano, and Zoe remain. They watch the peaceful glow of the fire wane together under the starry night.

"This is what life is really all about," Mano proclaims, holding Zoe in the glow. The shimmer of firelight catches on the faces of the other two men and Mano smiles to himself, feeling the beautiful beings beside him. He sighs in thanks for Zoe and wishes love for these two men. He can't help but feel it in their souls, their wonder and hope that they too will be loved and held so sweetly.

Just then a rush of water comes in! They all hear it just in time and jump up, instinctively grabbing the drums as the ankle deep whitewash floods over the beach fire. It fizzles out instantly and they all laugh together in the darkness. Not a tsunami, just a rogue wave washing high up on the beach. Off to bed they go.

It's the first week of March, he figures out with thoughtful interpolation of dates in his journal. He reconfirms the exact date with a tourist and realizes it's just two more days till Zoe's 24th birthday. Excited to throw a party, he spreads the news all across the beach. Everybody seems to be into a big sunset show on the beach helipad. Mano gathers a bunch of oranges and Honu hunts mid valley for bonfire logs. All sorts of other people plan and prepare exquisite dishes for the birthday potluck party. Grizzley even plans to break out some body paint he was saving for a special occasion.

"You and X coming down to the beach for Zoe's birthday?" Mano stops Ella on her way down from the Heiau.

"You know Mr. X's birthday is the same day! He may not be too keen on sharing the show, but we'll try to at least stop by and say hello."

"Whoa! No way, Zoe really has the same birthday as Mr. X!" Mano can hardly digest. *'The king of not going out,'* the most stubborn outlaw of the whole valley shares a birthday with his lover!

As predicted, instead of being excited to share his birthday, Mr. X is perturbed. He shows a little Pisces jealousy — the hottest goddess on the beach was stealing his birthday thunder!

The birthday potluck turns into quite a show. Outlaws and tourists arrive on the helipad an hour before sunset. Exquisite camp-kitchen dishes are carried out to be blessed and toned by Zoe and Rainbow, both of whom are tastefully covered in body paint and glitter. Dueling fires compete with dancing goddesses and a spectacular sunset for attention. Flute Dolphin is so full of joy, he dances around filming everyone on his *heart cam,* looking out at them through a heart shape he forms with his hands. Over thirty people are gathered by the time the food is served. There's not two, but three Dutch oven birthday cakes. Even more incredibly, there's ice— *Neverland diamonds* and a few ice-cold beers! A couple of backpackers with a boat captain connection had a bag of ice and beer thrown off one of the tour boats and they brought the exquisite booty to the party. Mano serves up rum and liliquoi drinks on ice! Some tourists even leave the birthday girl gifts of chocolate and hand-made treasures.

Even Mr. X is laughing and smiling from his chair at the edge of helipad. Grizz is hollering, Captain Bligh is singing. Everyone is singing, blasting off like there's no tomorrow. It's cosmically good times!

Just when the music and the mayhem seem to be reaching climax, two tourists waltz in with a trumpet and saxophone and the dance party turns into a marching Mardi Gras parade.

"This is the best birthday I've ever had, and more than I could have ever wished for. I love you so much my Mano!" She kisses him wildly, and he scoops her up carrying her with the marching procession.

They are living their best lives in the moment, dancing freely under a rising moon. When their feet finally tire from dancing, the two lovers hold each other by the glow of the fire and just let saxophone and flute serenade them. Orion is high in the sky before anyone trickles off to bed. The birthday girl escorts her man back to their tent and they make love to the music of the party nearby. The vibes are still too high from the helipad and they decide to return for one more set of music and dancing. Many partygoers pass out right there by the fire, and coffee is served from the still hot coals at dawn.

Mano and Zoe reconvene with Dolphin back on the helipad for breakfast. They drink coffee together still waiting for the sun to rise over the back wall and warm the beach.

"What a great party last night. What a wonderful night of joy and celebration." Mano praises.

"Some of the best music, and sheer wild awesomeness of the whole year. Mahalo to the birthday girl and to everyone!" Dolphin bows elegantly in thanksgiving.

"I know, everyone came together with such vibrancy and heart, it was truly magic." Mano reflects. Zoe stares out toward the horizon dreamily.

"Look at the surf, it looks calmer than I've ever seen it," she proclaims, still in her own dreamy world.

"Yeah, there's hardly a swell at all. I bet you could swim past the break and hear the whales no problem today." Mano offers.

"You know what? Maybe today is my day to swim out there." Zoe chatters back to Dolphin and Mano with eager eyes.

"We'll wait till the sun comes out and touches the beach, then I'll go out there with both of you guys." Dolphin adds. They patiently await the arrival of the sun, staying warm holding their coffee mugs.

"Look, it's dolphins!" Dolphin giggles with delight as all focus in on a pod of dolphins passing right in front of the Heiau heading toward the beach.

"There must be fifty of them out there!" Mano excites watching the dark-colored, smooth creatures casually glide along the surface.

"This is totally your day, birthday girl. We gotta try to swim out there with them." Dolphin exclaims clapping his hands together daintily.

"This is a dream. I'll grab the surfboard so we have something to float on out there!" Mano bursts with excitement.

The three hold hands in the always-intimidating whitewater preparing to dive under the break to meet the dolphins on the other side. The pod of dolphins is still playing 150 yards offshore.

"You can do this, Zoe. Just dive under three or four little waves and you're there." Mano reassures her.

They all take a deep breath and dive through the break to meet in the calm crystal blue on the outside of the waves.

"I can hear the whales! I can hear them singing!" Zoe splashes with excitement.

"Now let's go swim out further to meet the dolphins!" Dolphin encourages. The two swim together and Mano paddles alongside on the surfboard. It takes a good while to get to them as the dolphins are now further offshore, but the playful pod seems to wait for the trio, patiently. They have one snorkeling mask between them and they take turns diving under and observing the dolphins. The pod floats curiously, effortlessly amongst their human observers. Some of the spinner dolphins circle around them as if welcoming them in.

"They are kind of resting right now, just floating and swimming about slowly. They are even more exciting when they are playful." Dolphin comments, being the only one who has ever swam with spinner dolphins before.

"What do you think they are feeling from us?" Mano asks Zoe with childlike excitement.

"I wish I could talk to them—hear the secrets of their ocean world," Zoe giggles.

"What would you ask them if you could?" Mano probes.

"We *can* communicate with them." Dolphin interjects confidently.

"Ok let's all dive underwater at the same time and just try to send as much love to them as we can, all at once, and thank them for swimming with us." Zoe suggests. The two men agree.

"Ok. One, two, three."

They dive under together and send them a message of love and gratitude, hoping their friends can feel their message of love with their sixth sense or sonar. Zoe is designated observer for she is the one with the mask. And the dolphins respond! At first they just float and absorb, but then they are clearly signaling each other. They start to group together and gather slowly below them, deep down, almost at the bottom, fifty or sixty feet below the surface. The trio stares at them below, still sending love. The pod starts to circle slowly counterclockwise beneath them. More and more of them join and they circle the trio like an underwater merry-go-round. They drift slowly, receiving the love in their sleepy, almost dazed states. Then something happens and they snap to swimming instead of drifting. The merry-go-round picks up speed and they spiral up around their human observers as if following the coils of a spring up to the surface. As soon as they all break the surface, they spread back out into groups of four or five and slow down again. Then they slowly swim away together to the north, their silhouettes fading with the tops of the waves.

"That was incredible!" they all exclaim, hugging each other on ocean surface.

"I could feel their love, too!" Zoe exclaims.

"That was Magic!" Mano bursts with glee.

"Mahalo Mama Kai! Mahalo for Magic!"

Chapter 42   Biblical Storm

"It isn't supposed to rain like this, right? I've never seen rain like this!" Zoe exclaims in a panic looking outside their tent at the pelting rain.

"Only once or twice a season does it come down with this kind of intensity," Mano shudders.

"So you're saying rain this crazy intense is normal? Look out there, it's gushing down!" They both pop their heads out of the tent vestibule to observe the storm.

"I can't believe it! This is like a hurricane of rain! No way is this a normal spring storm!" Zoe shouts, as sheets of rain slam their tent and tarp.

"Well, I wouldn't call it normal, but last year in March there was a hell of a storm. For two weeks it rained and at times as hard as this."

"We should go out and dig more trenches. It's really filling up out there!" Zoe's tone changes from excited to frantic.

"No sense trying to dig now. Wait for a lull, it will come." Mano tries to calm her down. He doesn't want to admit it, but he's a bit nervous too. The water is gushing down harder than he can remember in the worst of last spring's torrents. They crawl back into the tent and give thanks that their tarp and tent are holding up and water is more or less draining away. Their kitchen is already a mud pit, but that was inevitable. At least they are dry inside their tent. They relish in steamy *hurricane love* and run out into the rain to shower afterwards. Mano tries to trench a bit more around the tent but it hardly makes a difference. Muddy water just fills in from all sides.

"First the tsunamis, now this!" Mano exclaims, frustrated.

"Don't get frustrated, we have each other and a dry tent still." Zoe reminds him.

"I love you, birthday girl." Mano kisses her as they roll in the cramped shelter together.

"Well, I'm glad you weren't born just two days later or your birthday would have been rained out!"

"Oh thanks for making my 24th so special, my Mano."

The rain eventually slows to a drizzle by mid-day, but it doesn't look to be clearing anytime soon. The whole beach and valley are a thick gray cloud.

"Well, this is just what we need for the gardens— water for the basil and tomatoes on the beach." Mano says trying to brighten the mood.

They summon the energy to go out in the rain and gather more firewood rather than try to mess any further with the muddy trenches. Everything outside of the ten-foot by ten-foot square where their tent is pitched under the center of their tarp has become a muddy swamp.

The two get wet collecting wet wood. They make a good-sized pile under another tarp they set up. Mano decides to make a quick run up to the Sanctuary on the bluffs to see how Honu and everyone else are faring in the storm.

He gets to the valley stream and of course it's flooding. It must still be raining quite hard up valley, he decides. He reminisces on the time last March when Khan had seized the boat drop bag and held it hostage at the Sanctuary on the other side of the un-crossable stream. Even with all of Zoe's ups and down's, there was nothing like that drama, he reassures himself.

After seeing the gushing stream, Mano decides to turn back to camp. Surely everything is fine on the bluffs anyway. Honu has probably got the tarps dialed in and everyone is jamming tunes and drinking coffee high and dry. He and Zoe have a simple dinner of rice and tuna and just stay in their still dry tent reading books and trading massages as the rain pitter-patters outside. The next morning, it's barely sprinkling but the valley is still socked in with clouds. The flooding creek has subsided and is now safely crossable. Of course, every tourist on the beach seizes the opportunity to hike out in the mud and mist. They're so silly! Why not wait a day or two to hike when the trail is dry and the weather is beautiful!

Mano and Zoe are ready to do a re-supply run, but they'd wait three, or even four days for optimal weather conditions. Stressing out on a slow, slippery trail in the drizzle isn't worth getting back to Babylon for just because they were out of beans, cooking oil, and chocolate. The two run down the now deserted beach naked in the rain together and enjoy the storm for what it is. On the other side of the river, some of the less prepared hippies are struggling to stay dry, but Honu and the Dolphins are holding down the Sanctuary with 24-hour hot coals and dry space. The team had collected a massive amount of wood, too.

All of the two-day tourists who left this morning kicked down their remaining food so the community kitchen was back open. Most of the veggies, rice, and beans are thrown together in a giant pot on the grill. Love Soup as Carey-D calls it, is served hot to whoever shows up with a cup.

Mano and Zoe stop by for a few songs, but they opt for *love pizza* at their camp instead.

"Well, that's the last of the tomato paste, the last of the yeast, and the end of the last onion," Mano proclaims as he seals up the one bucket of food that they have left. I guess that's gonna be our last pizza until re-supply.

"Maybe this storm will clear by tomorrow and we'll hike the next day. What-cha think Zoe?" Mano offers his usual optimistic air.

"Yeah that sounds good. But the funny thing is, I'm not even that excited to go back, I don't want to hike the trail in the mud and I don't really have any major desire to go to town." She wraps her arms around him and kisses him sweetly.

"Oh sweetie, that's just the answer I wanted to hear. But trust me, you'll love a trip to treat-land. We'll get ice cream, and smoothies, and cold beer, and we'll eat steaks and have rum drinks on ice. Then we'll blast right back to the inside with the biggest baddest boat drop ever! Bacon and eggs and avocados and a dozen different kinds of chocolate!"

"Treatland!" She cheers playfully.

"That's right, *treatland*. Let's get pumped!"

"Ooo, ooo! Can I bring back special goddess treats for Rainbow and all my fairy friends."

"Absolutely! Whatever you wish, my princesa!"

They start to play the dangerous game of thinking of the most exquisite treats they could indulge upon that are only possible in the outside world.

"How about an ice cream sundae with strawberries and whipped cream." Mano spouts.

"With hot fudge, too." Zoe adds.

"Ok, maybe we shouldn't get too caught up in all this. It's still raining, you know." Mano bends over her and nuzzles her stomach, making her giggle.

"Ma-Ze-Ze" he teases, kissing her all over.

The next morning, there's only a fresh half-inch of rain in Mano's coffee cup, but there's no sun in sight. They decide to make it a rum and coffee day up at the Sanctuary. They share the rest of their rum, which is just enough to give everyone a slight midday buzz.

"Hey, we wanna hear your song— the aloha one Mano told me about." Honu nudges Zoe with excitement.

"You told Honu about the song I wrote? I told you to keep it a secret, silly!"

"Oh, come on sister, music is to be shared." Rainbow spits back before Zoe has a chance to get upset.

"Well, I don't really know how to play it. I just wrote the words and I've only just sang it to myself up in the valley." she fumbles.

"It's a beautiful song and I'm sure we could figure out some music to go with it." Mano encourages. Honu and Mano experiment on the ukulele to try to find cords to match Zoe's singing. On their first try with Mano playing and Zoe singing the song comes together impeccably well and the lyrics to *'Embrace the Aloha'* stick in everyone's head. Zoe's voice is soft and sweet and flows naturally like a midnight rain. Soon, she's inspired enough to try to play it and sing it herself on the uke. By the time the evening show rolls around she's ready for a second performance on her own. She sings even better resonating with the tone of the ukulele against her body. Everyone claps and cheers in amazement— Zoe's first song of her own.

"I love it, I love it, I love it!" Rainbow jumps up and shouts and hugs her fairy sister and they dance around with glee. Carey Dolphin gets up and kneels before her.

"You are the supreme goddess of mother earth," he says, humbly kissing her ankles. The song has direct meaning and application to Zoe herself too. This is possibly why she was so timid in sharing it. Her biggest struggle is to embrace the love she has and the love from others around her. Embrace loving her inner child and others unconditionally.

Mano and Honu share a heartfelt discussion on how some of the best songs written have a message that's often one of the hardest things for the songwriter themselves to do and this itself is quite beautiful. Magical even.

Can we teach ourselves to live the songs we sing? This is the golden question of the day.

Rain, rain, and more rain. Right when everyone thought the storm was over, it comes back in a fury. Waves of intense rain come in thirty-minute spurts every few hours it seems, with the same steady, dismal drizzle in between.

"We haven't seen the sun for three days." Mano gripes.

"Yeah, I'm over it already. This on and off rain and drizzle is ridiculous. It needs to just rain and be done with it." Grizz whines.

By day four of the storm everyone is thoroughly fed up with the rain and the semi-aquatic environment they are all now living in. Mano and Zoe's tent is damp and now harbors a funky mildew smell. The mud towel they use to wipe their bare feet before going inside is now more mud than towel. Lighting a fire has become a 15-minute chore and cooking in their mud-pit kitchen is anything but pleasant. Everyone else on the bluffs seems to agree. Not seeing the sun in four days has people getting moody and edgy. Even such positive vibe creatures as Honu and flute Dolphin can't help but gripe.

"I've moved my tent three times and I still get water pooling up in the bottom. It seems like everywhere I put it, water just comes up from the ground and soaks in." Honu groans.

"I just can't stay warm at all in this storm." Dolphin complains.

"This watered-down *love soup* just keeps getting worse and worse." Spacedog laments.

"Almost all seem to agree that as soon as the rain lets up, they'll hike out, re-supply, and refresh in town." The five holding down the Sanctuary are pretty much out of their own food and relying solely on fruit, coffee, and Carey's never ending, but never good tasting soup pot. The morning of day five of the storm it's pouring hard again. No chance of hiking the trail today— it's too dangerous. Six-mile and two-mile streams are surely flooded out. It looked to be another day held up under tarps for the Sanctuary crew. Hunger gripes start promptly after the meager amount of tourist-kicked-down oats is consumed. Now all that's left is the soup, which no one can stomach for breakfast.

"Alright, enough complaining! We're gonna just have to go out in the rain and into the valley and find food." Honu announces. Space dog and Dolphin just kind of stare at each other as if to say: *Really, in the rain?*

"This has to happen guys. We're gonna have to work and get wet to sustain ourselves and keep up the good vibes during this storm. Come on! Are we drainbows or are we self-sufficient outlaws?" Honu rallies.

Nobody wants to be deemed a drainbow, so they decide together that they'll all bust out in the rain and bring back sustenance. They divide into teams for different foraging tasks.

Rainbow and Spacedog trap and kill a goat. Instead of setting up snares and waiting patiently for a few days they tried a quicker approach. The beach goat herd was spotted in their usual safe haven in the pocket valley above the waterfall. Spacedog scrambled up above the waterfall despite the slick conditions and spooked the herd along the slippery edge. One frantic goat couldn't hold it's footing on the wet rock and with Spacedog's ambitious advance, it tumbled over the cliff right down to the beach camps where Rainbow grabbed the injured goat and slit its throat just like she did to the captive one two years before. It was a brash and brutal exercise, but it worked.

Dolphin and Zoe manage to forage nearly three pounds of tiny cherry tomatoes and heaps of basil and some arugula, filling almost a quarter of a five-gallon bucket. Honu and Mano go way up valley and bring back three big taro, eight oranges, a ripe papaya, and a green one. Grizzley goes up valley to raid one of his few remaining stashes and brings down a bucket of food containing some much-needed cooking oil, pinto beans, and a full 10 pound bag of Krusteaz® pancake mix. Carey-D, who of course was *still learning how to walk*, gets assigned to keeping up the fire at the Sanctuary and organizing the remaining food and spices. Incredibly by dinnertime all 8 of the Sanctuary team together had brought back enough food for a meal for 30.

The butchered goat, taro, basil, and beans turn the soup into a real meal that tasted better than the first round of love soup, but still wasn't good. The tomatoes, basil, green papaya, and arugula are made into an amazing salad complete with liliquoi dressing rounding out the meal. As a bonus, Rainbow offers up the last of her cacao powder and they make a hot chocolate for all to try. Just tasting the chocolate makes Mano want more though.

Only four residents miss out on the rainy day forage and feast. Mr. X and Ella didn't participate as they rarely came to Sanctuary anyway. They were still comfortable and supplied at their riverside camp. Keilani was said to be still hiding out at her up valley camp waiting out the storm. Gaia was either tucked in her camp in the way back or out of the valley altogether, no one really knew for sure. Oddly enough, all the other up valley residents were out of the valley for the storm anyway.

Krazy Red was on Maui, Kaholo was in California, and Cliff, Captain Bligh, Uncle Dan, Paul, and Sky were on-island on the outside somewhere. Many had left the morning after Zoe's big birthday bash before the storm even started. Of course, not a single tourist remained and no one was hiking in or out of the certainly closed trail. Those that were there just had to wait it out, hunker down and be patient. After nearly a week, people were starting to wonder how many days it had been since anyone had seen a boat, a helicopter, a tourist hiker, or the sun. An eerie feeling of being cut off from the rest of the world grew in the stomachs of each of the 11 or so outlaws that remained.

The next day the rain subsides enough to where some consider hitting the trail. Obviously, Carey couldn't go. Rainbow and Zoe were too sketched to consider the still swollen stream crossings and slippery exposed ledges, and Dolphin and Mano decided they still had the patience to wait for a better day. But Honu and Spacedog are eager to push through the mud and get to town to set up a boat drop for the crew. They volunteer themselves eagerly and set out in the drizzle just after coffee. However, it's not even midday before they're back.

"What happened? Rainbow asks. Obviously, you didn't make it very far."

"You guys won't believe it, a whole 200 yard section of the trail is just gone! A huge landslide pushed everything right down into the ocean just past eight-mile camp." Spacedog gestures with exploding arms.

"He's right, there's just a swath of mud where the trail used to be, like the whole mountainside just gave way, and slid into the Pacific. There's no crossing that thing, it's a death trap, you'll slip right down into the ocean and get crushed against the cliffs by the swell." Honu continues grimly.

"So you're saying we're trapped here?" Rainbow squeaks in fear.

"Well for now yeah, we're stuck. Once everything totally dries out, I'm sure it would be possible to carve out a few steps and scramble across the landslide, but who knows. Maybe they'll be more landslides on the other side."

A wave of confusion and terror rushes over everyone. All of a sudden the situation is much graver than anyone had imagined.

"And it's still raining. This is horrible!" Rainbow shrieks.

"Calm down everyone, it's not like anyone was really gonna get out of here today anyway. Just like the tsunami, it's not like we've never seen a mudslide across the trail before. After the storm clears they'll send a trail crew in on a helicopter to eight-mile, they'll fix the trail and life will go on." Dolphin speaks coolly yet sternly trying to reassure the fear-stricken bunch.

"I don't know." Zoe hesitates. "I kind of have this weird feeling that *they* don't care about *us* anyone."

"What do you mean, *they don't care*." Mano interjects.

"What if Babylon doesn't fix the trail? Remember they didn't even send helicopters to warn us about that last tsunami." Zoe says.

"Fake tsunami!" Spacedog corrects.

"Well, when's the last time anyone saw a helicopter, or a boat, or the cruise ship for that matter?" The crowd grumbles in disagreement.

"Wait a minute, what about the cruise ship?" Mano jumps up.

"I remember seeing the cruise ship the day after Zoe's birthday, the evening before the storm. Ok, and today has been the 7th day of the storm, right? That means the cruise ship should be coming today for sure. That's how we'll know that Babylon is still operating, we just got to wait for the *Maid of the Mist* at sunset."

"Are you sure it's been seven days already?" Grizz scratches his head. Others seem just as uncertain. It takes a 20-minute discussion on accounting for time to get everyone in agreement. Today is the 7th day, and the said cruise ship is due.

"I got an idea. Why don't we take the instruments in trash bags and all go down to the cave on the beach and hang out and drum for the arrival of the ship. It will get us out of this Sanctuary mud pit!" Honu rallies.

Everyone latches on to Honu's idea and they all go down to the beach cave to watch and wait for their ship to come in.

"Oh, *Maid of the Mist* where are you now!" Mano chants looking out toward the ocean of gray. With the misty rain they can't see the horizon, but normally the ship comes in close— so close you can see the camera flashes from those on board. There's no way they could miss it in the mist. They'd see its lights, as it turned around when darkness set in. The drumming corresponds with the suspense of the setting sun and the arrival of the great boat beacon of Babylon. But neither the sun or the ship show and they all walk back to the Sanctuary at dusk dismally.

"So no cruise ship, no other boats. Does this signify the end of the world or something!" Spacedog shouts excitedly as they hike along the beach trail in procession.

"Maybe it's the end of Babylon, but not our world." Honu adds boldly.

"Maybe that damn boat saw the whole island socked in and they decided to turn around early so the crew could have evening cocktails at the port." Mano tries to snuff out any more doomsday talk.

"It's the end of the world, grab your woman now!" Carey-D yelps wildly. Mano reaches his arm tighter around Zoe's waist. All eyes catch on Rainbow. Flute Dolphin slips his hand into hers but she shakes him off with a smirk.

The group still seems to accept Mano's theory the most. The beach was clouded in and the boat just turned around early.

Mano thought about Ella and how she used to tease in years past about, 'When the boats stop coming...' Everyone would look at her like she was nuts, but maybe that 'when' is now. Mano and Zoe opt out of another wet trek up to the Sanctuary, deciding to stay down at their camp and save love soup for Rainbow and the boys on the bluffs.

They dine on rice and sardines while casually discussing end of the world couples matchups and the goodness of sardines. At this point sardines have become a treat, and a valuable source of protein. They both eye the last can like hungry cats. In just one week, how different their world had become.

"So Rainbow will eventually re-accept men and she'll go for Dolphin, for sure." Mano starts off.

"Yeah, he's certainly the charmer of the bunch with his flute playing and all." Zoe agrees.

"So that just leaves Keilani for Carey, Spacedog, and Honu to fight over. What do you think?"

"Honu." Zoe says without hesitation.

"Yeah, sure that sounds good to me. I guess Carey, Grizz, and Spacedoggy will have to manifest a mermaid!" Mano ponders this for a second.

"But say, if Babylon is really going down for sure there'd be all sorts of outlaws and hippies crazy enough to do whatever it took to get back to the inside. Shoot, Gaia would hike to 8-mile, jump in, and swim the rest of the way to the beach if she had to." Honu offers.

"What if Gaia is still here tucked back in the valley. It's not like anyone checked every camp. She might be chanting her way through the storm, subsiding on nuts and granola." Mano offers.

"Alright, enough doomsday talk, Captain silly. I'm just thankful that I'm here with you." Zoe dismisses Mano's wandering mind.

"Me too," he exhales nuzzling her playfully. They sit next to their tiny fire together and try to take comfort in each other, but still a feeling of loneliness sweeps over them. They think about their families on the outside, thousands of miles away. They look into each other's eyes saddened, scared, and confused. After dinner they crawl into the tent without a word. The feeling of each other's hearts pressing up against their bodies soothes them in such a way neither can understand. But alas, in this land of mystery and magic that's perfectly ok.

"I have a little something for us!" Zoe snickers reaching into her little cosmetic bag.

"Oh my goddess is it chocolate? Please, let it be chocolate!"

"It is! I've been saving a tiny little morsel for us, and I think we should enjoy it now."

"Ahh Ma Ze-Ze, I just knew you had some chocolate squirreled away somewhere." They savor the flavor of the quarter bar of dark chocolate and over accentuate sounds of enjoyment to really soak it in. Mano thanks his cacao goddess. Zoe lies back down on her back and sighs.

"Mano, something's bothering me. It's a bit of a secret, but for some reason I feel like I should tell you." Zoe hesitates almost starting to tear up. Mano's mind hurries as if preparing for something big, now realizing the chocolate was given to soften the blow.

"Oh, what is it my sweet pea? You know you can tell me anything. I won't judge you. I love you no matter what, remember."

"It's just, it's just, I'm not sure if it's true, but I have this horrible deep feeling that this whole never-ending storm really could be forever. I feel like us being stuck out here is all my fault!"

"Oh, come on! This storm, this horrible weather has nothing to do with you. How could it possibly be your fault that the trail is washed out and we're trapped here in this wet mess." Mano ensures. Zoe's face remains pale, motionless.

"Wait, what is it? I'm sorry, I really should just listen." Mano sees that the look on her face is serious… It's real.

"Remember when I went up valley on my own to find my Aloha?"

"Yes, and you found Grandpa Aloha and you wrote that wonderful song."

"Well I also ran into Ella up valley and we had a special moment together." She pauses as if trying to collect her thoughts. Mano looks on enchanted.

"Well, before we began a meditation with the ancients, Ella put her hand on my shoulder and told me at this spot I could manifest whatever I desired. And during the meditation I just put my wish out there." she sighs. Now Mano's face is as pale as a ghost.

"What did you wish for?" He breaks the silence.

"I wished to be here in Neverland with your love forever." She starts to cry and Mano stares for a second mouthing her words. Mano takes her and holds her sobbing face against his chest.

"I just said it over and over in my head, hoping that it would be true." she sobs.

"Well, it is true Zoe, I'm gonna be with you. I'll be here and you'll have my love forever."

"But I don't know. It's just that now I have this feeling that it will mean that we'll be trapped here forever with this storm and landslides and tsunamis."

Mano's heart suddenly sinks to his stomach. He remembers his own manifestation and how it twisted itself to truth. He hesitates but tries to give a confident reply.

"Oh baby I... that's a wonderful wish, but no storm lasts forever, and we won't be trapped here for eternity, that's nonsense. Remember Uncle Dan and Grizz's tale of the 40 days of rain? This has only been a week. At the very worst we'll have another week of wet weather. They'll send a maintenance crew to fix the trail— spring break has to happen eventually right?"

"I guess I'm just scared, that's all. This place is just so powerful and the feelings I get seem so real that it's hard not to believe them."

"I know exactly how you feel, this place is real. It's more real than anything out there in Babylon. And the magic that happens here is cosmic. It's impossible to explain. And manifestations do come true— that's how I got you."

"Am I everything you wished for?" Zoe sniffles.

"Absolutely honey, everything." He raises his eyebrows, wrinkling his forehead. She doesn't know what more to say so she just holds him and squeezes him tighter than ever.

The next morning the birds are chirping louder than the rain.

"The sun is gonna come out this morning, I can feel it!" Mano tells Zoe after he runs out to the beach and sees clouds clearing, lifting out of the valley. For a moment he can even see the back wall. This is cause enough for celebration, Mano decides. He reaches into their bucket and grabs a plastic baggy with a few fistfuls of steel cut oats in it.

"What do ya say ZeZe, let's go up to Sanctuary and share these with the team?"

"Hey now that's the last of our oats." she retorts.

"Well I know, but we still got some rice and lentils and dates and dried mushrooms and one can of sardines. Those guys up there have been eating love soup and pancakes for days, what do you say, let's live dangerously and share these with the Sanctuary crew."

"Mano-banano, you just get a little feeling of sun in you and you just wanna give, give, give!"

"Ma-bay-bay, just a few oats for the Ohana."

"Ok fine, just save enough in another bag for us to each have one small bowl sometime. Here, I'll got you a bag, cause I know you don't know where they are!"

They go up to the downtrodden soup-eaters camp and Mano presents the small bag of oats.

"Alright, now that's what I'm talking about!" Spacey pipes up.

They all look on as Mano stirs the oats into the boiling water.

"You know what, this is already gonna be good, but I want this to be really good. I'm gonna toss in some raisins from my secret midnight snack stash." Spacedog spouts to everyone's amazement, getting up to fetch his precious raisins. They look on still as poised mimes for steel cut oats take a long time to cook.

"Ok, they are finally ready." Mano announces. Grizz gets up and heads right to the pot with his bowl.

"Hold on there, Grizzley bear! Ladies first!"

Mano lets Rainbow and Zoe serve themselves, then he serves a healthy portion in his bowl and hands it to Honu.

"I know you're too damn humble, and you're the skinniest, so there." He takes a cup and serves himself a slightly smaller portion. Grizz is getting antsy now that the bottom of the pot is clearly visible. Carey is fidgety and gets up too. *Don't do it, Carey,* Mano says to himself watching the inevitable unfold. Just as Grizz is about to serve himself, Carey reaches ahead of him and dips his spoon into the pot.

"What, you think you're just gonna cut in front of me like that?" Grizz threatens, slamming the pot down looking Carey right in the eye.

"I just wanted to make sure I'd get some too, Mr. Bear." Carey stares back at him goofily. Then Grizz goes off on him.

"You know what? I don't like you Dolphin-dude. You come into this valley with next to nada thinking everybody should serve you just cause you're some healer-guy, and all you do is creep on girls and eat other people's food. I'll help you write your ticket straight out of this community kitchen!"

"You can't be telling me I'm all that, that's baloney," Carey backpedals.

"Creeper by day, healer in every way," Rainbow slides one in to everyone's surprise.

Come on Carey, just apologize to the Grizz, or half the community is gonna turn against you. You'll get ousted. Mano thinks to himself.

"Dolphin-dude is a phony and that's no Baloney, what do you guys think?" Grizz is rhyming on him, gathering steam.

Mano's mind races. *Damn it! Carey's bringing abandonment on himself, and that's his biggest fear. I can't let this happen! I've got to step in and save him.* He steps in front of the two men and stands in front of the pot of oats.

"I'll tell you what I think. I think both of you greedy old men should sit down and let Spacedog have a bowl. He's been waiting here patiently and he's the one who put in the raisins from his own private stash. Probably all the food he has left! I say let the *man* with the best sounding apology clean the bowl after he's through!"

That pretty much settles the crowd and apologies are passed. Rainbow even apologizes for her somewhat misplaced comment to misunderstood Dolphin-dude. All this over what should have been cheerful oats. Mano can hardly imagine what the situation could be like during a *real* food shortage.

The crew on the bluffs finished the love-soup-goat stew last night, but the taste of oats and the bickering it brought didn't seem to satisfy. Honu decides they must be smart about the little supplies that they have left and he closes the food bucket on breakfast.

"We'll start cooking beans and fried taro this evening, but now we have to conserve." Honu announces.

"What else can we eat right now?" Rainbow whines.

"Eat a mango, there's plenty of Mangos." Spacedog provides the short answer.

Rainbow bites into a mango and attests to its sweet juicy flavor.

"Wow, that is really good. I guess I could just live off of these for a while."

One thing that seemed would never run out was mangos. They could just have mango everything until the storm cleared, it seemed. Honu seizes the opportunity and proposes the mango initiative. Everyone at the Sanctuary would be required to go out in the rain and gather and peel at least 10 mangos a day. All community meals would be supplemented with mangos.

By midday the drizzling stops but the sun never shows, and by sunset it's raining again. This seems like a low blow, for everyone was truly excited with the break in the clouds this morning.

That evening, hunger and loneliness bring Keilani down to the Sanctuary to join them. She sets up a camp and agrees to help out in exchange for food and company.

"Of course you can hang with us, we'd love to have you," Honu speaks for the group. All can appreciate a fresh face, and another soft voice around the circle.

"The only rule is you got to bring mangos," Spacedog jokes, edging to get a word in with possibly the last remaining available goddess of the valley.

"Ah, mangos! All I've eaten for the last two days have been oats and mangos. You guys are on the mango diet here too!"

"Well it's pinto beans and taro with tomatoes and mangos for supper, so I guess we'd have to say yes."

"And fried mangos for dessert, and goddesses get to eat first, of course." Carey-D reiterates with a smile.

Keilani continues. "Have you guys talked to X? Got a radio report on what's going on out there? Weather and all that. Also, I was gonna check on Gaia, but I was so cold I just headed straight down to Sanctuary. Anyone seen her?"

"Yep, tried that. Radio's busted, all we can hear is static— no weather report, no nada. And no Gaia, nobody's seen her since the birthday party." Spacedog answers, nonchalantly.

"Well, I wonder if Kaholo has a working radio up in one of his stashes, and I'm pretty sure Gaia is still up valley. I saw her a few days ago and I'm sure she wouldn't hike out in this muddy mess."

"Wait, there's still stashes up there? At Kaholo's camp, like food and stuff?" Carey-D perks up.

"Yeah, we might have to go up there tomorrow and you know... borrow a few things. It's kinda looking desperate down here. *Mango-beans* in all." Keilani's voice is calm, like she's not even worried.

"I betch-ya he's got cheese!" Spacedog lurches gleefully.

"Spacedoggy if you want, I'll take you up there tomorrow and we'll see what we can find. And then we'll fetch Gaia too." Keilani smiles. The other lost boys look at her like abandoned puppies. *So she goes for Spacedog?* Mano finds himself staring into her curiously.

Zoe pinches him, huffing, realizing that she's no longer the center of attention.

"Maybe it's time we head back down to camp." Zoe shuffles him along the muddy trail back to the beach. He's tired and doesn't put up a fight. Still, his mind catches back on Zoe's reactive behavior as they amble through the night. *Why does she always feel the need to control him? Why does she still let herself get so scared? Why did he still let it get to him? Maybe he should just surrender. After all, he's destined to be stuck here with her love anyway!* He chuckles to himself at the silliness of it all.

"I really just hope we see the sun tomorrow," Mano sighs, falling asleep with his head on Zoe's breast.

Dawn brings another morning of clearing clouds and growing confidence. The rain stops for the whole morning show even. The water level in the valley stream drops significantly, approaching normal flows.

The crew approves a *'go ahead'* for operation stash raid. They ask for Mama Kai's blessing and forgiveness and agree to limit the stash raid to just one bucket focusing on cheese and a radio up at Kaholo's.

Keilani and Spacedog return with Gaia and a stash bucket at sunset.

"Gaia, you're still here!" Rainbow giggles with delight.

"And you brought with you peanut butter!" Dolphin flippers his hands excitedly!

"Ok, just one scoop each for everyone right now," Honu forces rationing authoritatively.

"Hey everyone, I can see the sun!" Zoe dances into camp. They all rush out to the bluffs to see. Despite the evening drizzle, they all observe a rose-colored sun, beam through the clouds and dive into the ocean. The peanut butter jar is passed around and they all tone together in hopes of seeing more sun tomorrow.

"Glorious! A peanut-butter sunset show, what more can we wish for?" Zoe announces to the heavens.

"Uh, how about a full day of sun, blazing hot, and a bunch of hotties on a giant boat drop with ice cream." Spacedog scoffs, stealing her thunder.

"Alright, that's enough Spacediggity, we got to celebrate the small victories here. Maybe we'll get blasted with solar energy tomorrow. Now let's make a pizza!" Mano excites.

Spacedog and Keilani scored big stash raiding up at Kaholo's. They brought back a five-pound bag of whole-wheat flour, yeast, four pounds of cheese, peanut butter, sugar, and maple syrup. They searched all around trying to find coffee, but only found a small tin box with some old tea bags in it. They found Kaholo's radio, but it wouldn't turn on. The battery appears to be dead and the darn thing takes one of those funky rectangular 9-volt batteries that nobody has. Most are hardly phased by the radio disappointment because they are eating pizza! They make three great cheese pizzas with a mango sauce base (of course) and even a dessert pizza with sugar-glazed mango. All to Dolphin's joyous flute-playing and the pitter patter of the rain on the tarp. Alas, the evening pizza and jam sessions have returned. The good food brings back positive energy and it feels like Neverland again!

Overnight, the storm intensifies. Torrents of rain come down all night in sporadic waves with bursts of wind. Mano tosses and turns and wakes Zoe beside him. She calms him from his nightmare and coaxes him back to sleep. He's swimming in the dark black ocean lost at sea in his dream. Wind from the storm shakes their tent and tree branches fall to the ground nearby. They grasp each other in the tent as the rain, wind, surf, and falling limbs crash loudly outside. At dawn it's all over and the birds sing out loud again.

Mano is still restless and just wants to hold his lover, not wanting to go outside. When they finally do go out into the mud to pee, the wreckage that surrounds them is unsettling. There are not so much broken branches but whole logs washed up onto the helipad and all along the beach trail.

"What's all this debris from?" Zoe asks, looking curiously at pieces of weathered plastic and inundated driftwood just 20 meters from their tent.

"This came from the sea." Mano states frankly.

"You're telling me that a big set wave washed all the way up to the helipad, all the way to the beach trail and into the trees!"

"Zoe, this wasn't high surf. This was a tsunami wave! Multiple tsunami waves!" Mano points to the three lines of debris at different levels strewn along the coastline.

"Tsunamis. That's what all those crashing sounds were last night, not just branches falling from the trees."

"This is crazy! Another five feet higher and the waves would have engulfed our whole camp. We'd be washed away." Zoe yelps and starts to lose her composure.

"I can't handle this anymore, Mano. I just want to go home! Back to the mainland, back to the desert where there aren't any crazy storms or tsunamis."

"I think we should move our whole camp up to the bluffs this morning." Mano's voice is calm, focused.

"Ahh, I thought we were going to have sun today. Now we have to move everything in this god-awful drizzle. Now everything is gonna get even more soaked!" Zoe whines.

"Well, if a bigger tsunami comes then we'll really be soaked, if not washed away."

"Don't even say that! That's a horrible thing to say!" Zoe wails.

They start to gather up their stuff grimly without even talking. They transport most of the gear in big trash bags and buckets and ford it across the once again swollen stream to set it up near the bluff-top Sanctuary. Just getting everything packed and ready to move is a muddy chore that takes all morning and puts them both in a miserable, foul mood.

"I told you to let me carry the bags across!" Mano harks at Zoe after she slips in the stream and nearly loses a whole trash bag full of essentials to the current.

"I'm sorry, I thought I could do it." she cries.

"Well, you should have listened to me! Now our sleeping bag is half wet, and guess what, all of your clothes in the bottom of the bag are soaked."

"Why do you have to be so mean!" Zoe sits down and cries in the rain. Mano curses himself and gets even more frustrated.

"Fuckin' storm, fuckin valley, let Zoe take back her manifestation and just get us the fuck outta here!" He turns to Zoe, still crying hopelessly in the rain.

"Just keep crying, I'll go set up camp super-soaker." Mano marches off carrying the dripping bag up the hill. He could hardly contain his frustration still. *We'll be spooning in a soaking wet sleeping bag, thanks a lot Zoe!* He harps to himself. *Ugh! He was so mean! Now he won't get to share her love at all, instead he'll be forced into the wettest corner of the tent. Now things would be miserable for sure, and who knows for how long! Would this storm ever end?*

He's forced to set up the whole camp by himself. It takes the entire rest of the day. Now he wanted her help, but of course she wouldn't even consider it. She checked out and was just hanging out at the Sanctuary making pizza and receiving love from other men. And the thought of this just makes him feel more horrible, more inadequate. He tries to just grit his teeth and focus on the task at hand. He wants to go home. He feels like he's losing it, and nobody's there to comfort him. He's an asshole in her eyes and he knows it. The only thing keeping him going through all this chaos is Zoe's love and now she hates him…Again.

Focus, breathe, gratitude, he tells himself. He hunts and finds a spot for the tent and tarp that drains well. Besides the half soaked sleeping bag and nearly all of Zoe's clothes, the tent, the sleeping mats, and all of the other little things like head torches and books and journals are dry. Zoe's clothes were half wet before anyway, he jokes, trying to charm some goodness back into himself. He's shivering profusely from being soaked himself, and from the lack of love for himself he holds inside.

Walking back to the Sanctuary shivering and pale holding a pile of drenched clothes under his arm, he feels like a beaten man. When he sees his lover half naked and dry by the fire soaking up a massage from Carey's loving hands he feels anger. He proceeds to string up her clothes on a line around the fire under the tarp.

She glances at him with that same sly smile that gleans *look can't you see that I'm loved and taken care of without you*. The coldness seizes him and he hunches over the fire. Carey finishes the massage. To Mano's surprise he gets up and goes over to him. Carey stands him up and gives him a big hug. He rubs his hands up and down Mano's arms and back trying to warm him up.

"Thanks Ca-rey-D." Mano stutters, slowly coming back to life.

"Now I'd like to give you a massage." Carey Dolphin offers politely.

Carey holds and massages Mano by the fire and sends him the love that he needs to help him regain his composure. Carey turns to Zoe who's still closed off to her man.

"Now Zoe, Mano's not perfect, but he does love you. You have to forgive him and love him back anyway." Carey tries to open her closed body and heart with a soft hand on her shoulder. She softens, but still holds her hate.

"Let's all hold hands and tone together. Let's tone for love and light—for glorious sunlight." Carey initiates and they all follow, smooth and graceful. After about a minute, they start to hear birds chirping! The drizzling stops. They keep toning louder and louder till they all seem to run out of breath at the same time. The rain has stopped and the birds just keep singing.

"Hey everybody, I just got this funny feeling that we are all inside of a rainbow," Rainbow declares.

"Well, let's go out to the bluffs to see." Honu prompts. They all run out to the edge of the bluffs and stare straight up at a glorious rainbow beaming from the sea to the back wall. To the east remains the dark grey storm but to the west shines the sun, bright and orange from below the clouds. They stare at it and soak up its warmth.

"I can really feel it, I feel it warming my very soul." Mano cries out with delight. He sneaks behind Zoe and hugs her from behind. She receives him and he kisses her neck watching the clouds fill with orange glow.

"Let the sun save us." he whispers.

The next morning, the only clouds that remain are stuck behind rainbow alley east of the valley. It's a bit of an eerie feeling looking back past 8-mile camp and Babylon beyond and just seeing the darkest, thickest gloom ever, but the sun is shining on the valley and the sky is blue to the west. No new tsunamis seem to have occurred overnight, at least so it appears. But there's no boats or helicopters or signals from the outside world of any sort, either. Rainbow and Zoe make cinnamon-less mango cinnamon rolls and Spacedog makes a tough trade of some sugar for coffee with Mr. X so everyone can have coffee to go with. They all enjoy breakfast in the sun. Glorious beaming tropical sun! Hard-to-heat creatures like Mano and Dolphin finally feel warmth to their cores again. Everyone dries out their soppy gear and many take a much-needed bath.

With everyone juiced from the fresh coffee, outlaws are quick to engage in apocalyptic coffee talk, with many theories revolving around the total lack of usual boat and helicopter traffic.

"So, I can see why they are still not running tour boats, with the storm still likely raging on the outside, but you'd think they'd send a helicopter of some sort. You know, at least to check on the tsunami aftermath. A rogue heli-tour pilot would fly in this weather, too." Mano pitches.

"Well they didn't send a helicopter to warn us about either tsunami." Honu counters.

"Well they had no reason to send a warning or to check on us. The trail is closed. There's no permitted campers back here. We don't exist!" Dolphin practically giggles. Grizz gets up disgruntled.

"Well I'm happy those stupid copters are gone. Mechanical mosquitos is all they are. Buzzing in all low just to pester us and snoop on us all the time. And then they come in and land and sting us with Rangers and tickets! No more helicopters now-wooooh! Yeah, that's my manifestation!"

"I still think the cruise ship not showing is the biggest red flag. Maybe Babylon is not coming around." Mano jesters.

"But if there's no more boats or helicopters coming, that means the whole outside world just abandoned us. We're out here and they don't even care. Here I am abandoned again!" Carey-D moans.

"Carey, I'm absolutely sick of you *asking to be abandoned*. Realize this once and for all! The only one who can abandon YOU is YOU!" Honu retorts.

"Well said, Honu. We care about us. It doesn't matter what the outside world thinks or does." Keilani's calm voice reassures them all.

Chapter 43   Inside or Out

The muddy earth is drying out even more the next morning. By early afternoon, the sun is out strong and the clouds against the back wall are thinning. Everyone is trying to dry out his or her wet world in the sun. With morale up and the hope of more sun tomorrow, Honu and Spacedog plan another trail mission. They'll scope out the landslide past 8-mile and see if they can find a way to climb over or around it, then they can try to make it to town to see what's been going on. If the sun persists, surely the trail will be passable tomorrow.

Even with the glorious arrival of the afternoon sun, Mano and Zoe are on edge again. Zoe starts to build fear around Gaia's presence in Sanctuary camp yesterday.

"I saw how you and her exchanged smiles last night when making those pizzas." Zoe snips. Mano can hardly believe her eagerness to delve back into pain and thus retorts back, irritated.

"So now you need to control who I smile at!"

"Maybe you should stay here with her, and I'll hike out!" Zoe pesters.

"Don't be silly. The trail, if there still is a trail, is a slippery, dangerous mess. Let Spacedog and Honu do a recon first."

The two walk out onto the edge of the bluff and watch the wall of gray that still enshrouds the whole coastline past 8-mile valley.

"See, it's better here in Neverland. You don't want to hike back to the outside world now." Mano tells her softly, trying to ease her fears.

"I don't trust this place or Babylon anymore! And I don't like not knowing what's going on. I want to hike out and call home, maybe just fly home." Zoe sobs, feeling confused. She drifts back toward Sanctuary leaving Mano uneasy and alone. Most everyone had to feel the same way. Confused and fearful of what loomed ahead in the gray clouds of the future. It was easy to be free and in the moment when things were blissful and smooth, but keeping that same attitude when confidence in the future is bleak feels nearly impossible.

Mother nature was crying out with her storms and tsunamis, and in Neverland all felt that energy. Surrendering to the blissful present moment would take more than a ray of sunlight piercing through the squall.

Mano walks back to the Sanctuary hoping to find Zoe. Instead, he stumbles upon Spacedog, Dolphin, and Gaia huddled over the smoldering midday fire. Spacedog and Gaia are carefully twisting finger-length ganja buds by their stems over the coals.

Mano looks at them perplexed. Spacey is quick to offer explanation.

"With all this rain I thought my pacalolo flower would get moldy, so I just went ahead and harvested everything this morning and now I'm speed-drying it by the fire."

"Speed-drying? Don't you wanna just dry it slowly under a tarp or am I talking spacey science?"

"Oh, Mano! This is the super-crypt Spacedog fire cure, guaranteed to give you the headiest, pure vibe high. Free from all that Babylonia bullshit energy of the outside world. "

You must of run outta your super-crypt Cali stash, huh?"

"I tell you what, Mano. You keep the pizza train rolling and we'll all be getting super stoned on Spacedog's pre-apocalyptic pacalolo at sunset."

Gaia falls back off her rock seat by the fire giggling and almost singes her long blonde hair on the coals. They'd already sampled the fire-cured bud.

"Have you guys seen Zoe?" Mano asks, after they all catch their breath.

"Methinks she went searching for mangos up valley." Dolphin giggles back, fairylike.

"And Honu?"

Community Garden with Carey." Spacedog coughs.

"You ready to try the trail again tomorrow, Spacedog?" Mano asks enthusiastically.

"Na, I'm not going. I got weed now, so I kinda lost my motivation. I told Honu already, it's all good."

"Well maybe I'll go with Honu then!" Mano spouts back impatiently.

"I dunno, all this Babylon mission-talk has got me super spun out, I'm over thinking about it. If that sun comes out tomorrow, I'm gonna roll me a fat joint and chill at the beach. I'll watch the waves and I'll even call in the tsunamis for Babylon." Spacedog responds with a mischievous grin.

He keeps rambling on in his semi-decipherable spacy blabber, causing Mano to roll his eyes and trudge up the hippie highway alone. Maybe he'll run into Honu or Zoe. He grabs some limes, tangelos, and mangos up in Tom's garden but turns around before Community Garden and heads back to Sanctuary for sunset. He figures he'll save his energy for the trail. Honu and Zoe are already making a pizza when he gets back. The doomsday debate continues after a peaceful sun dives below the hazy horizon.

"All this sun this afternoon and still no helicopters!" Carey laments.

Conversation soars with curiosity over the state of affairs of Babylon and the trail. Over the course of the day, the vibe had changed. Outlaws were starting to feel edgy, ambitious, and tired of feeling cut off from the outside world. People seemed to want more than anything some sort of resolution with the real world beyond. Someone needed to explore the trail and find out what was going on in Babylon.

With Spacedog out, everyone turned to Mano to partner with Honu on another recon mission. A new plan is made. Tomorrow, if the weather held from dry to no more than a drizzle, Mano and Honu would try to climb above or over the landslide past 8-mile valleyand onward to 2-mile valley where possibly the stream was still flooded. If at all flooded, they would head back that same afternoon and report on the trail conditions to the group and thus wait for the whole North Shore to clear up before trying again. If 2-mile stream were to be encountered low and easily crossable, Honu would cross and cruise to town. Per Zoe's adamant request, Mano would come back the same day regardless and let the crew know of the situation.

The evening show winds down early with prayers and toning for sunny trail conditions for the duo's early morning mission. Mano and Zoe go back to their camp on the bluffs to wind down and rest for Mano's early hike. Mano's anxious and decides to make a small fire to boil some calming lemongrass tree back at their camp. Zoe is anxious too.

"I don't know if you should be trying to cross over that landslide out there. That sounds too dangerous." Zoe voices her concern.

"Honu and I will be safe, and we'll stick to the plan. If the landslide or anything else on the trail looks sketchy, we'll turn back."

He tries to comfort and settle Zoe in order to settle himself and his own fears over the trail ahead. Even with the taste of the warm, soothing tea, his stomach feels tight trying to digest tomorrow's mission. He tries to hold Zoe by the fire, but she won't relax into his touch. He can feel her getting more agitated the harder he tries. All he can think of is how he should get some sleep before tomorrow's journey. He'd give up his best knife for a bottle of Cliff's homemade wine just to settle him and her.

"We'll get up at dawn and if you feel up for it, you can hike the first bit of the trail out of the valley with us." Mano encourages.

"I still don't understand why you have to go, we're not out of food!"

"I'm not even going all the way to town. I'm coming back the same day no matter what, remember?"

"I'm just so scared and I don't have a good feeling about it. The trail, this unpredictable weather, the chaos there could be in Babylon."

"I know you're scared. That's ok, but can't you just love me and be with me in peace tonight?"

"How am I supposed to love you when you are leaving me?" Zoe starts to stomp around their camp, steaming.

"Hey, settle down. Why don't you just lay down with me for a bit?"

"I don't wanna lay down with you. I want you to listen to me!"

"I am listening!" Mano bursts. She gets right in his face in a fury.

"If you leave me I'll go crazy inside. You're so stupid if you still can't figure that out!"

"Calm down, get out of my face!" He roars right back at her.

"Don't you do this to me, Mano. You're making me crazy!"

"You're already crazy. I'm going for a walk so I can get away from your craziness!" He turns his back to her and marches off. She runs after him and grabs his chest digging her fingernails into his shirt.

"Get off of me, Zoe. Now!" he yells, still trying to march away.

"Don't you leave me," she wails, latching on even harder. Frustration overtakes him and he shoves her off of him pushing her hard with both hands. She falls over backwards to the ground taking a piece of the shirt with her.

"I can't believe you just did that!" she wails on the ground in tears. He can hardly believe himself, either. For a moment he's paralyzed, still hearing his heart beat through the hole ripped in his chest. The power of his own hands pushing her seemed not his own. He keeps marching off to get away from it all.

"You just keep running away from your problems!" Zoe wails.

"You're craziness shouldn't have to be my problem!" Mano shouts into the night.

How did it have to come to this! Why couldn't she just let go? Let go of her fears, let go of him! He tries to push the instance away as if it were another scared Zoe reactive moment. And she caused him to react, violently even. *How could he let himself succumb to pushing her, to letting his own fear and frustration overtake him? And he's still frustrated!* He stomps about fuming. *Breathe, let it go, at least you walked away,* he corrals his conscience.

Whatever! He'll get a break from her tomorrow, no sense in even trying to resolve things now. Uhh! But that's exactly what makes her so upset and scared...*Leaving. Calm down and go back and stay and be quiet now, at least!* He summons himself. Instead of rationalizing or pouting about anymore, he goes back to their camp, walks right past her by their fire and crawls into the tent.

"I'm sorry I pushed you. Can we just get some sleep now?" He mutters an apology to her through the nylon barrier that separates them.

"You're horrible. I can't believe you were violent with me. You're horrible, and worst of all you don't even care! You won't even listen to me."

"I do care. I care about you more than anything!" he shouts back. It hurt his heart to hear her say he didn't care.

"Well then listen to me!" she wails.

"No, I'm not listening to you now! Right now I just want to get some sleep. I'll listen to you when I get back tomorrow afternoon." Mano buries his face in his jacket pillow trying not to listen anymore.

"Arrahh!" Zoe steams up outside of the tent. He wants to say something to calm her down, cause now he's a bit calmer himself, but anything he says would be useless, if he's not going to listen to her anymore then he's not gonna talk! He presses his mouth against his jacket.

"You just don't listen, and you wanna leave me!" Zoe wails louder than ever!

"Arrah!"

She boils up again, Mano's body tenses in the tent. He sits up, and starts to crawl to the vestibule. He can hear her panting in rage right next to him.

Whack! Something smashes him hard right in the back of his head through the fabric of the tent. He turns over rapidly, but he's off balance and seeing stars, his head in a daze.

"Ouch! What the fuck was that!" He stutters trying to regain his bearings on all fours.

"Did you just throw a rock at me? Are you trying to kill me?"

He crawls out of the tent holding his throbbing head and he scans across the fire looking for her, but she's gone. Disappeared into the night. He glances around their camp in hazy rainbow-blurred vision. His eyes catch on a big, round, unripe mango at the edge of the vestibule, the object that impaled him.

He picks up the bruised fruit and hucks it over the edge of the bluffs to the ocean in a burst of rage. He wants to go and hunt her down at the Sanctuary and shake her violently, as if to shake a possessed demon from her body, but his eyes pause on the waning fire and the hazy rainbows melt from his vision.

He stares deep into the smoldering flame and sees the little Zoe trapped crying inside. He sees beyond the anger, and the uncontrollable fear. He sheds a tear knowing that all her fear, and aggression is really just love. Love is behind it all, he can see it radiating in their fire somehow. *Let her go…Let go of your need for her love.* He whispers to himself before crawling back into the sleeping bag alone.

He hears the birds singing at dawn, but he rolls over, sluggishly. Honu would come get him for the recon mission, he decides. Zoe probably crawled under the communal tarp at the Sanctuary and stayed warm with a borrowed blanket. Like Spacedog before, last night's incident caused him to lose his motivation for the mission. He lets himself fall back asleep, for just a moment…Two hours later the morning sun steams him out of the sleeping bag. He shuffles out of the tent in a panic. Where were Zoe, Honu and everyone? He goes over to their pile of gear where his backpack and trail shoes were carefully laid out the night before. Right away he notices that her boots and pack are gone.

Mano rushes over to the Sanctuary and encounters the crew chatting around the breakfast fire like normal.

"Where's Honu and Zoe?" Mano pesters as he marches into camp.

318

"You're too late, Mano-banano. They both left on the trail mission before anyone here even got up." Spacedog blabs from his hammock.

"Yeah, they must have hiked out super early. Nobody even saw them leave but they left this little note by the fire." Rainbow states, handing Mano the note written in Zoe's handwriting.

'Left to town, be back in a few days, H + Z.'

No apologetic note to him. No hug goodbye. Nothing. Mano can hardly comprehend the note, but he can believe it. He can see her fears propelling her down the trail right now! Would they really try to hike all the way to town though? Would she be back or was she through with him and done with Neverland, too? Uncertainty almost makes him jump at the chance to chase after them, but he knew better. *Let her go.* He sighs. Maybe this was a sign from the land that their love wasn't meant to be. He rubs the tender spot on the back of his head in wonder. He'd never catch them on the trail anyway. Zoe may or may not come back. Honu would come back eventually and that's when he would find out about Zoe, he decides.

After a half-hour of contemplation without conclusion, Mano jumps in the valley stream to clear his head of the whole thing. And it works! For the first time in his existence he lets himself surrender to the moment, to the out-of-control unknown. He, Spacedog, the Dolphins, Rainbow, Keilani, Grizz, and Gaia all hike down to the beach to soak up the bit of sun, and smoke Spacey's speed-dried pacalolo in celebration of *the moment.*

They sprawl out naked on the warm sand and splash happily in the whitewash along the channel, diving under the waves, playing like children.

"Tsunami! run for your lives!" Mano calls out and they all scramble frantically up the beach.

"Just kidding, just kidding!" Mano giggles, seeing the looks of terror on their faces. The tsunami drill sparks a new game where they all play in the surf till someone yells *tsunami* and then everyone tries to push each other out of the way to race back to the highest patch of dry sand.

Eventually the crew tires and returns to the bluffs for the evening show. Dolphin's soft flute serenades the setting sun and livens the group gathered on the rocky edge. Mano sits separately, staring out at the horizon on a rock perch, feeling empty and alone. The events of the last 24 hours settle uneasily in his stomach. His heart feels like a heavy stone, but his body doesn't know how to feel. In the midst of his moment of deep introspection, he feels a soft hand gently touch his shoulder. He recognizes her rosy aroma. It's Gaia. He turns and his brown eyes meet her cool ocean blues.

"I want you to know how proud I am of you for letting go and embracing the unknown today." she tells him.

Mano feels her words as smooth as her silky white Sanskrit sarong wash over him like the valley stream. He doesn't know how to respond so he just stares into her deep eyes and lets himself become entranced. She reaches for his hand and clasps it in hers, breaking the awkward stare. She pulls his hand to her heart for the slightest touch, then locks eyes with him again.

"You're a good man, Mano. You deserve peace."

He uses her grip to pull himself closer to where their foreheads almost touch. She squeezes his hand tight and pulls his lips to hers for a soft kiss. He holds the cosmic kiss for a second then feels her pull away. She releases her grip, turns and fades into the night. Her golden hair shimmers in the twilight and her long sarong dances around her bare feet as she walks away.

What just happened? His overactive mind analyzes. He tries to cool it down and steady his heart, which pounds with the waves crashing below. He exhales and releases his breath into the humid night and walks back over to the Sanctuary.

With darkness settled in and the evening soup brewing, the Sanctuary doomsday talkers continue their typical debates.

"Yeah, I bet Honu and Zoe are stuck at 6-mile stream crossing, humping in a tent in the rain right now!" Spacedog laughs, looking Snoop-Dogg-like with a cloud of smoke billowing up around his head and a fat spliff in hand.

"It's certainly raining harder there than here. Let's just hope they are safe." Keilani calls out, keeping the group in check.

Already the wind had kicked up and was blowing in flurries of mist and sprinkles of rain. The fierce gusts were wreaking havoc on the Sanctuary's well-worn tarp-covered cooking area. It appeared they were on the cusp of a windy nighttime squall—the kind where the wind swirls moisture around the back valley and bursts across the bluffs in sporadic surges, stretching and billowing the tarps from above and underneath. Mano and the Dolphins scramble to tighten things down in the misty wind. They all huddle around the fire and tone up the love soup, tuning out the flapping of a loose corner of the tarp.

"Man, I wish Honu never left. He'd have the Sanctuary tarp-ology dialed." Spacedog continues.

It certainly was a tricky thing to figure out, and once you had the tarps dripping just right in the big rain, you were peeling them back to dry out the saturated earth when sun returned. And the wind was the hardest to combat. A loose tarp would billow back and forth like an untethered sail. But a tarp too tight would pull and tear. At the Sanctuary the tarps needed just the right amount of give, weight balance, and fortunate direction to the wind to work well in a squall. It wasn't working well and that was unsettling. Thinking of Honu and Zoe stuck somewhere along a slippery trail was unsettling. The sudden bursts of wind were unsettling. The vibe had wavered with the wind from the *free in the moment* sunny afternoon everyone had experienced.

Drums bring spirit and unity back to the group during the windstorm. Tomorrow would be another mission. Excitement sails through the tribe with a chance to have the unknown revealed tomorrow...

A new plan is thrown together. This time Mano and Spacedog would hike to 6-mile valley after breakfast and see if their comrades had made it beyond this valley stream. They would return with their report early afternoon, not risking any stream crossings themselves, as creeks would likely rise if a real rain came down overnight. It wasn't much of a mission, but it seemed like enough to shed some light on the real state of the trail and find out if Honu and Zoe really went for it on their proposed town mission.

Conversation, drumming, and tea continue for another hour, but eventually the drummers, doomsday talkers, and tarp adjusters tire. With the fire smoldering, few feel the motivation to dodge the smoke and wind, so the crew disperses to their camps in a cooperative push after a pot of lemongrass tea is divvied up. Gaia and Mano catch each other along the bluff edge trail.

"Gaia, wait!" Mano calls to pause her as she scurries around the edge, seeming to not notice him at all. With the wind howling and the surf pounding the rocks below, Mano has to practically yell to stop her on the path. She turns abruptly and they stand face to face.

"What do you think about the mission tomorrow? I mean do you think Spacedog and I will find them, do you think that the trail is safe?" Mano's confused and doesn't really know what to say, feel, or do.

"The trail is safe if it feels safe under your feet. Trust your intuition, Mano." Gaia responds, unwavering.

"I want to trust and have faith. Still, I feel everything everywhere is so uncertain. Catastrophic even!" Mano exclaims, panting.

"Take a breath, Mano. Just go on a little hike with Spacedoggy, and see what you see. You don't have to get anywhere or find Honu and Zoe. If the trail feels dangerous, turn around and come back to Neverland. I want to see you here tomorrow for sunset."

She leans towards him with a smile. He reaches around her waist to pull her in close for a hug. Her body tingles with his touch and she turns her head toward his lips and ignites a passionate full body kiss. They embrace and hold the kiss while the wind howls and the surf pounds the sea cliffs below. She pulls away slowly, her body still tingling. Mano is speechless, staring at her love-struck.

"I'll see you at the Sanctuary tomorrow for breakfast, and I'll see you back home in Neverland after your mission." Gaia manages to release before turning back down the trail to her tent. Mano doesn't know what to think. Her taste lingering on his lips almost makes him feel ashamed, with Zoe and the love they shared still fresh in his heart. He thinks of how crazy Zoe would be if she actually knew of his kiss with Gaia. The mere thought of her rage makes his body quiver, but he shakes it free. He lets the taste and the feeling of Gaia linger on his lips and he falls asleep with the image of her blue eyes peering back at him from under her Sanskrit sarong as she faded into the night.

Mano and Spacedog wake at first light to set out on the recon-rescue mission. At the Sanctuary, Rainbow and Gaia force them to scarf down a hearty breakfast of coffee and mango pancakes. The night was sleepless for most as the squall shook everyone's tents and blasted torrents of rain from all angles. Both Dolphins and Keilani claimed they heard a thunderous explosive boom in the middle of the night, but most agree it was just the pounding surf, which kicked up to more than double overhead with the night's squall. The wind had lessened and although grey clouds loomed to the east, the rain had ceased on the bluffs. Mano could tell Spacey was nervous, and they both elect to subdue their anxiety with a morning toke. The group tones them up, praying for the safe return of the now four that had departed the valley.

Honu and Zoe had been gone over 24 hours and that certainly should have been long enough to hike back from 2-mile stream. Did they decide to go all the way to town? Did they make it before whatever thunderous quake shook the island last night? Did they get held up at a stream crossing and were simply waiting out the weather in a tent? Would they come back at all? This fear of the unknown has everyone unsettled, but hope that Mano and Spacedog's mission could provide some new info carries the vibe onward for the tribe.

After the duo departs with their boots and backpacks, the morning show crew moves out from under the dreary tarps at the Sanctuary to the base of the big red clay hill at the entrance of the valley to hang out and await the return of the two— and hopefully four— trail-bound outlaws. Mr. X and Ella even hike to the base of red hill to join. They, along with Gaia, patiently play their singing bowls as the sun brakes through the mist over the back wall. Mano and Spacedog are spotted coming back down red hill no more than four hours after they departed.

"Something happened, X exclaims. There's no way they hiked to 6-mile stream and back that quickly."

The crew anxiously awaits the trail report from the duo descending the switchbacks to the valley.

"What's up now? More landslides?" Rainbow asks when she sees Mano and Spacedog approach, their faces looking grim and pale as if they had stared at death.

"Just some landslides, hah! Oh no, what we're dealing with here is much more incredible!" Spacedog drops his pack and extends his arms wide with presidential prowess.

Everyone focuses on Spacedog as he sits down on his pack meditatively and prepares to tell all with fluttering eyes. He concentrates, then delivers his theory in epic Spacedog fashion.

"Tectonic plates shifting and crazy magnetic forces from the center of the earth. Magma flowing up through seams in the earth's crust! Continental plates are shifting and drifting creating a giant fault." He gestures, fanning his fingers out explosively.

"What are you talking about, Spacedoggy? Just tell us how the trail is out there." Rainbow insists.

"Well, what he's saying is the theory behind all this. What we saw was a giant fissure in the island itself, a huge fault all the way up the mountainside likely caused by some plate shifting or volcanic activity below the surface of the earth. It's likely it's this fault that's earth-quaking and causing the tsunamis too." Mano clarifies, his face as pale as a ghost.

Spacedog takes back over with intensity, explaining how they came upon this massive un-crossable fault where they could not see the beginning, end, or other side through the clouds and mist.

"So basically, what Spacedoggy is saying is that the whole island is splitting in half and we're fucked. We're stuck here on the inside." Mano bursts through the increasing hubbub.

"Or we're saved. We're here on the inside. I guess it depends on how you look at it." Keilani beams, glowing with grace. They all just kind of look at one another not knowing what to think. Finally, Carey cries out in tears.

"If I'm stuck anywhere, I want it to be here with you guys. You are the most beautiful souls, the best family I could ever imagine being stuck with. Thank you, thank you, thank you!"

"We love you, Carey!" Rainbow fires back radiantly. "We love you all! We are all saved!" Rainbow smiles wide and opens her arms to the heavens.

Mano and Gaia look at each other and sort of half-smile. So this is the reaction everyone is having to doomsday? They glance across at each person in the group. X, Ella, and Keilani assume peaceful meditative poses. With their eyes closed, they exhibit an aura of peaceful gratitude. Carey smiles goofily, but exudes an aura of a man whose worries had vanished. Spacedog and Grizz seem unfettered, just living in the now and rolling with it. Rainbow and Dolphin jump up and down with delight, cheering. "Mangos and Magic and fairy fun forever!" It seems like Mano is the only one still pensive. X turns to Mano in disbelief.

"So you're sure the trail is completely a no-go—there really is some massive uncross-able fault all the way up the mountain?"

"Yeah, you don't even want to think to go there, it's as wild as Spacey described. It really is like the island is splitting in two or something" Mano responds, dismally.

"What do you think happened to Honu and Zoe? Do you think they are alright?" Ella asks pleading.

"I certainly hope they made it to the other side before whatever erupted last night, but we saw no sign of them at all."

"Do you really think we'll be trapped here in Neverland forever?" Carey asks Mano endearingly.

"Well, there is another way out of here besides the trail." Grizz erupts.

"What do you mean? The impassable back wall?" Mano catastrophizes.

"No—the Ocean, Captain Hollywood! Salvation via kayak." Grizz proclaims.

"My boat's gone. Kawika stole it, left it on the beach, and the Rangers took it, remember?"

"Yeah, but Grizz's kayak is still here stashed just off the beach, paddles and everything." Spacedog states with a smirk.

"That's right! Grizz's boat is still here. Once the waves settle down, I could paddle his boat to the outside and see what the hell's going on."

"You could come back with more supplies so we'd have what we really need to survive out here." X encourages.

"Or I could get a helicopter to come in and rescue everybody. That is, if the rest of the island hasn't been destroyed or abandoned already. Who really knows what's going on out there? When the surf lays down, I could make the ocean mission and find out." Mano conjures.

"Whoa, Whoa, Whoa, Silly Mano, slow down. You're right, we don't know what's going on out there, and the ocean could be even more unstable than the trail. More tsunamis even, and who said anything about being rescued?" Rainbow sputters.

"I don't know, but we're gonna need more supplies if we're gonna be able to survive and sustain ourselves out here. Oats and rice and stuff we can't grow out here. Coffee and sugar and hundreds of pounds of chocolate. We'll need lighters and guitar strings and triple-A batteries."

"Yeah, but do we really need all that stuff? With the taro, and the goats, and the pigs, and the veggie gardens, and all the fruit in the valley, we should have more than enough to sustain all of us here indefinitely." Keilani ensures.

"Well indefinitely sure seems like a pretty long time. I mean we haven't even been out here two months, and what about our families out there?"

Spacedog sighs deeply. "Our *Ohana* here is the best family I've ever had. I'm sure most of the rest of the crew feels the same."

Mano sinks into deep thought for a second. Suddenly he's confused to the meaning of family. What does *Ohana* mean out here? What does it mean now in this new potentially *changed* world. What was his family on the outside doing right now? His mind holds on to the thought of connecting with the outside world. Just letting people know they were alive would comfort him. Then he begins to ponder whether he would be happier here or out there in the long run anyway. He tries to define what happiness is for him and struggles to decide what he thinks he really needs to be fulfilled. *Love.* Love is what both his heart and his mind finally settle on. Then there was the great mystery that stirred him. What had really happened to Honu and Zoe and the outside world anyway? He was just so damn curious. But why? Why couldn't he just accept the mystery as a beautiful reality and live in the now? Run naked and carefree and eat mangos and be content. Dolphin senses Mano's inner dilemma and proposes an idea.

"Hey, let's stop thinking about all this and go for a quick plunge in the ocean. You know what I just realized Mano-banano? That favorite cruise ship of yours is due back tomorrow. What do ya say we give the Babylonians one more day to show themselves before we conjure up any possible kayak mission to the outside."

"Ok, that sounds like a good deal, let's all go swim and live in the now, enjoy this bit of afternoon sun."

Again, they all go down to the beach in procession and play happily in the whitewash along the channel. They don't venture out to the waves for the surf is still pretty big with plenty of wind swell. But diving and playing in the shallow water's edge lets them feel free in the moment like children.

Flute, ukulele, and drums serenade the setting sun yet again. A peaceful night rain swoops in and cools the land. They all sleep in peacefully for there's no sound of slashing helicopters to disturb their morning dreams.

Sure enough, the next evening the cruise ship doesn't show. And few can decide whether to feel worried or relieved about it. A whole slew of doomsday theories and conspiracies develop regarding the outside world and curiosity stirs amongst the crew. But does it really matter what's going on out there? What if the whole island is abandoned? What if it's not? What if there is another tsunami coming right now? They can't fear the unknown, but it would be better to *know* to be prepared, right? After much back and forth, this is the only solid thing that's agreed upon. *Live without fear, yet try to be prepared.*

The next morning, with the wind and the surf settled down, Sanctuary talk resumes regarding a possible kayak mission to the outside world.

"Think of it like Columbus, re-discovering a new world!" Carey exclaims, trying to pump up the idea of a voyage. Carey-D, Spacedog, Mr. X, and Mano think an ocean route could yield safe passage beyond the giant fault. Rainbow, Keilani, Gaia, and Dolphin are leery and question not only the trip's safety, but also its purpose.

"The purpose of a kayak mission is connecting, seeing what's going on, and resupplying. It makes sense to know what's out there." Mano claims.

"What you don't know won't kill you!" Rainbow yelps back.

"Nonsense, I've seen Captain Mano paddle to town and back in a headwind in one day multiple times. He could easily paddle out, get supplies, and see what the hell's up with Babylon." Spacedog counters.

"Yeah, Captain Mano could go out and bring back pounds of tobacco and coffee and other stuff we really need to survive out here."

"Carey you're not gonna die without cigarettes and coffee." Gaia chastises.

"Do you think there's any more coffee or chocolate or tobacco left in Babylon if the island's abandoned?" Carey moans.

"If it were really the apocalypse or some crazy volcanic eruption there would be fire in the sky and flocks of birds going haywire like they were evacuating the island. There'd be some sort of greater sign from out there." Grizz declares, motioning out to the calming nighttime seas.

"We don't know. We are not in control, but we should investigate what's going on. That's part of what this mission is all about—to explore and see what's out there, and if there is anyone left there in Babylon to let them know we are alive, too! Christ, our mothers are probably worried sick about us already, hearing about tsunamis and giant faults on the news and all." Mano retorts. The mention of the *mom* word suddenly creates quite the hubbub.

"Mano, if you go out there, you gotta call my mom for me," Carey pleads.

"Mine too!" "Me too!" everyone pipes up, even Spacedoggy. Suddenly the mood had swung, everyone was thinking about their families on the outside.

"Well, what if this is really it? There'll be no more chocolate or moms or anyone left on the outside. I mean there's no more boats or helicopters—does that mean there's no more moms?" Keilani proposes curiously.

"But we still need food and supplies, and if this island really is splitting apart maybe, Mano should make a run for stuff before it's too late, or before the Babylonians eat all the chocolate in all the stores!" Grizz's brain holds onto bear mode.

"I don't know, this all sounds foolish to me, why don't we wait till we are completely out of everything to make this kind of decision." Rainbow pipes back.

"Well, cause of what Grizz said, and the mom thing!" Carey squelches.

"Well, I think it should just be up to Mano to decide, no one else is qualified to paddle out there anyway." Rainbow tries to settle the crew.

"I can't really decide and I wanted to get you guy's thoughts, so maybe we could put it up to a vote or something." Mano professes, feeling at odds with his whole being. His mind can't escape wanting to know what happened to Zoe and Honu. *Life, Death, Love.* His heart beats loudly feeling fate on his shoulders.

Spacedog surges, "Let's do a vote!"

"Who here thinks this kayak mission is a worthy idea and encourages Mano to attempt to reconnect with the outside world?" Carey, Grizz, Spacedog, and Mr. X put up their hands to vote for the mission.

"Spacedog, how could you!" Rainbow wails.

"What? I know he'll be able to do it just fine, and he'll bring back all sorts of goodies and stuff we need. And I got a mom too, you know!"

Rainbow takes over. "So, who thinks Mano should stay here and we just eat everything we got and try to live off the land and sustain ourselves on our own till things calm down."

Ella raises her hand as well as Keilani, Dolphin, and Rainbow. They all opt for the mango challenge route. Gaia refused to take a side and just left the Sanctuary upset as soon as the wayward discussion began. The vote is 4 to 4, leaving the decision up to Mano anyway.

"I loved Honu and Zoe! If you perish out at sea I'll be even more devastated — don't leave us now!" Rainbow wails, tugging at Mano's arm.

"Don't worry, I'll be back in two days tops safe as can be, I promise."

"You don't know that. Who knows what's out there? Even if you make it past possible earthquakes and tsunamis, there could be chaos on the other side. What if there's a war or they don't let you come back for some reason? What if all the food is all gone, anyway? You know that if you didn't come back we'd all be devastated. Can't you see that?" Rainbow declares.

"Rainbow, just like Zoe, you can't let yourself fear the unknown!" Mano announces. Rainbow storms off in tears.

"You know, Mano, you don't have to be the hero all the time. We'll do just fine, whatever happens." Keilani utters, then drifts away outside the circle.

"If I don't go then we'll all be just be eating taro and mangos and all our moms will think we're dead! I don't wanna eat mangos and taro forever!"

"Well, go then, and we'll all pray for your safe return." Dolphin sighs.

"I just wanna go tomorrow, get it over with, and get back here where I belong."

"Patience, Mano. Patience." Dolphin encourages.

"What good does having patience do in a situation like this? Waiting is just gonna keep me and everyone else on edge and wondering."

Mano runs to the edge of the bluffs to check the surf and see if he'd be able to get the kayak out of the break. It's much smaller than the day before when they all played in the whitewash. With the wind down there was plenty of time between sets, too. Just what he thought. He makes up his mind in a frantic push, he'll go in the morning.

Mano goes back to the Sanctuary and tells the crew that he's mentally and physically ready to make the mission to the outside tomorrow morning.

"Are you sure?" Dolphin tries to edge him.

"*I just wan to make dis mission.*" He accentuates mimicking the Russian Dmitri.

"I'll take Grizzley's kayak and leave just after sunrise and try to come back the following day." He concludes.

"Alright, you have our full support, of course." Dolphin warms.

"Everyone except Rainbow and Gaia." Mano moans.

Mr. X discusses with him the most essential items to get for their long-term sustainability. Realizing the outside world may now be a whole new shopping scene, Mano makes no promises. He hopes to encounter such important items as a big bag of brown rice, honey, sugar, coffee, oats, cheese, chocolate, seeds for planting, cooking oil, peanut butter, batteries, lighters, and guitar and ukulele strings. Even if he can get large quantities of just a few of these items safely back to Neverland it would be a worthwhile trip. Going would also settle his inner dilemma of needing to know the fate of his best friend and lover. He gets everyone's, even Mr. X's mom's phone number, and agrees to call the lot of them, if possible.

"Now give me all of your Babylonian money. This may be the last time you get to use it!" Mano announces, and they all happily hand over their cash and plastic.

He then goes down to the beach with Spacedog to uncover and prepare the kayak for tomorrow's launch.

"You know, I think it's pretty master stoker of you to go out there and try to do all this for the *Ohana*. We really can't thank you enough for stepping up to this challenge." Spacedog praises him admirably as they carry the kayak to the helipad.

"Spacedoggy, this will be a piece of cake. It's just a supply run, right? Done it dozens of times. You can thank me when I come back with a chocolate bar and a fat block of cheese for ya!"

Back on the bluffs, the sunset show is edgy. Gaia is standoffish and hardly says a word to anyone. Mano is anxious, too. This makes everything edgy and unpleasant. All he could think about already was getting to town and back here, so the unknown would be known and his and other's fears would settle. The whole evening show feels fast and out of sync. The music being played is at too fast a rhythm. The sunset serenade sounds like a chase scene in his head. They should be relaxing, after all. They're all stuck here forever right? He can't keep his thoughts from Zoe and Honu. He needed to know what happened with them before he could let his heart move forward with Gaia. He hated to admit it, but he was so confused inside that being alone on the ocean for a day seemed easier than another day of mixed feelings with Gaia and hanging out at Sanctuary. He feels as unsettled in the moment as mother earth herself. With thoughts of Rainbow, Gaia, Honu, and Zoe clogging his head and the fate of the Ohana resting on his shoulders, he was in no state to make *mission decisions*, but his ego continued to rally his heavy heart. It told him the decision had been made. Now he just had to live in the moment with it.

He tries to comfort and settle Gaia in order to settle himself. He cozies up to her by the fire, but she won't relax into his touch. She gets more annoyed the harder he tries, it seems. *'Hear the voice inside, allow your heart to guide you.'* He repeats a mantra bestowed on him to encourage himself to act from his heart. He manages to clasp and hold Gaia's hand, and together they stare into the glowing embers. Dolphin-like, he can feel her warmth and deep love radiating through him. She sends a message of calmness and peace like she first exuded when their eyes caught each other on the Heiau trail years before. His heart takes over boldly and he whispers in her ear.

"I love you." They are both caught off-guard by the abrupt declaration. Mano feels sheepish; his heart spoke without his brain's permission.

She squeezes his hand in hers and sends him a fire lit smile.

"I think we should all retire early tonight so Captain Mano can rest for his big kayak mission tomorrow." Gaia suggests to the group.

"We'll all get up at dawn to tone you up, and see you off." Rainbow encourages. Everyone agrees.

Mano and Gaia stand up unceremoniously and start to gather their things. The rest of the crew continues to stare at the glowing coals in introspection. This time, Gaia whispers into his ear. "Meet me at my camp in ten minutes."

He hugs her and wishes her goodnight, letting her depart the group alone. Mano squats down to sip his tea next to the glowing embers. His heart races with excitement, but his body feels heavy and confused.

"So… Captain silly and Gaia, the up valley mystique. Maybe this is the birth of a new world, you sure you want to paddle out tomorrow?" Dolphin declares, fluttering his eyelashes and whistling his flute fairy-like.

"Captain Mano's twitter-pated again! I think he should go to town and chase after Zoe — and let the rest of us misfits have a chance!" Spacedog announces. Mumbling and snickering proceeds amongst the crew.

"Enough!" Mano spits into the fire. He gets up and walks away.

He follows the well-worn footpath to the edge of the bluffs, his bare feet carefully avoiding protruding boulders and soft muddy patches. He walks slowly on feeling. At his camp, near the edge, he tosses his tea mug beside his tent and stares off at the hazy black merger of sky and sea far beyond. His heart turns with the churning sea below. His heart, his love, his mission, and the whole world held in a hazy limbo. He knew his heart wanted to surrender to the moment, surrender to love, but he didn't know how. He felt too disheveled and ungrounded to fully throw himself into love with Gaia. He laughs at how once again, how crazy out of control everything is. It should be freeing, but in the moment to him it felt like entrapment. He takes a cooling breath and approaches Gaia's tent hesitantly.

"It's nice and dry in here," Gaia sings, holding back a slight giggle. She could feel him approach. He unzips the damp outer rainfly and crawls inside the small blanket lined tent. He feels his bright headlamp is invasive so he quickly switches it off, but the pitch black inside is equally as awkward.

"I still wanna be able to see you silly! Let's try this. " Gaia jokes as she reaches for her headlamp and turns it to the dim red light setting and beams it up from the corner of the tent, allowing them to look at each other through red ambient glow.

Her blonde hair is down with curled ends covering her bare nipples. Her lower body is buried in the folds of her sleeping bag.

Mano reaches for her hand and runs his thumb gently over her delicate fingers. He feels her and fumbles for what to say.

"You look beautiful in this red light with your hair down."

"You don't have to woo me, Mano! I can tell you are well confused, but let's simply share in this moment." They both laugh. He reaches to pull her hair back and purposely, playfully slips his fingers over her nipple. He reaches around her back to draw her whole body toward him. They feel their warm breath on each other's lips with eyes locked, for several seconds before mutually succumbing to a kiss. He lifts her onto him and they kiss and caress while her legs wrap around him. Their bodies press against each other with primal instinct, but gentleness guides the movement under the red light glow. Gaia giggles and coos as Mano teases her nipples with his mouth. He winces with primal pleasure as her fingernails dig into his back. They fully surrender to the moment and nothing else matters.

Each inhalation draws in truth, and every exhale releases life. They fall asleep with their bodies intertwined. With her head on his bare chest they snuggle peacefully well past dawn.

She wakes and crawls over him like a curious kitten. Dangling her breasts and hair over his tan body.

"I don't think I'm ready to kayak to town anymore." Mano whispers before rolling on top of her again. Her soft skin and sweet smell are so enchanting he can hardly contain himself. Neither do, and they don't depart from the tent until the sun has crested the back wall.

They stroll by the Sanctuary to see what's up, trying to act like nothing happened. No one bats an eye, but Mano can sense the crew can smell the lust in the air. Again, Mano wavers over the kayak mission that he planned to launch hours ago.

"Are you gonna give up on the mission and stay here?" Rainbow asks right away. Mano responds hesitantly.

"I'm not sure, I don't think I could leave now with this full sun likely to bring in the trade winds. I think I'm too late."

"Spacedog and Carey went down to the kayak on the beach to look for you. They didn't see you at your camp, so they just went down there already." Dolphin sputters back.

No sooner than Dolphin's mention of them, the two thrust back into Sanctuary camp.

"Oh, there's Captain No-show, too twitter-pated to paddle out, I presume." Spacedog says, marching in with an aura of boyish exuberance, but stares into Mano's eyes with an unwavering stone cold gaze. He thrusts a black ball cap into Mano's stomach.

"Got a present for ya, yar!" Spacedog spits pirate-like.

Mano grabs the hat and stares at the white lettering on the face of the hat above the brim. He reads the lettering out loud.

"I heart HI."

"*I love Hawaii*—this is Honu's hat. He surely hiked out wearing this. Is Honu here?" Mano's heart pounds with excitement.

"Maybe he's here in spirit," Carey chimes in.

"Yeah, we found it washed up on the beach." Spacedog mumbles humbly.

Mano's tries to speak but his voice falls to his stomach like a lead brick. The whole crew stares at each other in awe.

"Maybe it blew off his head on the hike out and landed in the ocean." Rainbow pleads, excitedly.

Mano's stomach turns as he tunes into the artifact of Zoe and Honu.

"Maybe he threw it into the ocean at Space Rock knowing the current would take it here to let us all know that Zoe and him made it out after that crazy earthquake that night." Gaia offers, tugging at Mano's hand.

Mano latches onto the positive implication to steer the crew's mood to anything but utter doom. His gut tightens around the feeling that it should have been him out there with Honu on the trail instead of Zoe. He fumbles the brim of the ball cap between his fingers. His hands begin to shake. He can hold Honu's essence no longer. With hands still shaky, he walks over to Rainbow and offers the hat to her.

"I think Honu would have wanted you to have this."

She thanks him, taking the ball cap, then shuffles away in tears.

Mano looks to his heart for what to say. He tries to calm his shaky hands and harness his inner strength.

"I feel I should make the kayak mission this evening for the Ohana in honor of Zoe and Honu."

"But what about the trade winds, and that mysterious huge fault you and Spacedog saw?" Gaia pleads grabbing hold of Mano's shirt.

"I won't leave until the wind has calmed down near sunset. And I'll turn around if anything looks at all unreasonable." Mano tries to reassure her and the rest of the crew. He closes his eyes and tries to re-align with his heart.

"I need to do this for myself as much as for resolution with Honu and Zoe." Mano states boldly.

334

"That's it! You're so selfish!" Gaia erupts and marches off toward the hippie highway. Mano starts after her but Carey and Dolphin grab his arms to stop him.

"Relax, Mano! Let her go, let her have space to process."

He eases up and tries to digest what he just said. It didn't come out right! His words almost never came out right in the heat of the moment when it mattered the most! He stomps his feet and pulls his own hair.

"She never even gave me a chance to explain my feelings or anything!" he shouts aloud.

The three do their best to settle him down, but in the end, Mano leaves up the Hippie Highway to Ginger Pools in near midday sun. He tells them he needs to clear his head by jumping in some fresh water before this evening's 'whatever mission.'

He passes Three Mangos and descends to Ginger Pools quietly, hoping to spot Gaia there. He's almost relieved to find the pools deserted, as he still doesn't know what he'd say to her. He strips his clothes and slips into the deepest lower pool in delicate surrender. He lets the cold water numb his overactive brain and tries to dismiss all thought.

He dries off naked in the sun on a rock with the luscious desire that Gaia will show up and seduce him. He senses she's far up valley at one of her secret spots, though. His manifesting powers can't draw her in so he trots back down the Hippie Highway refreshed.

Back at the Sanctuary, the re-assembled crew anxiously awaits some news. The Dolphins, Spacedog, Grizz, Keilani, Mr. X, and Ella are gathered around. Nobody's seen Rainbow or Gaia but the consensus is they are up in the way back valley, Community Garden or beyond. The crew had been stuck on doomsday thoughts the whole sunny helicopter-less afternoon and they looked to Mano for answers. He restates his decision in another formal announcement.

"I will make the mission to the outside this afternoon one hour before sunset if the trades drop down, which I'm pretty sure they will."

"Be extra safe out there and don't risk anything." Dolphin inserts hurriedly.

"Yes, of course. I'll do the best I can. I'm not going to risk anything, that's for certain; any weirdness and I'll just turn around. I'll be gone for two nights at the most."

"Mano, don't tempt fate with this tumultuous earth right now. You can always come right back to the inside if anything is dangerous or sketchy, on the water or out there even." Keilani adds.

Mano tries to quiet his own concerns on the pending mission as the weight of the uncertainty around Gaia, Zoe, Honu, and the whole Ohana sits heavy in his stomach. Dolphin rallies some enthusiasm by serenading the crew with his flute. Even Mr. X plays the drum and sings. He and the rest of the crew choke down a bowl of love soup. To ensure he has energy for the mission, he forces himself to down another bowl. They all pray and tone and sing together once more.

It's quite the scene, but he's excited too. He chuckles to himself, thinking he is like one of *Khan's warriors* and this is his mission for the beloved *tribe*. He almost wishes Khan were here to pump him up with good *mana* for the expedition.

The golden hour to head down to the beach can't come quicker. They all walk down to the beach in a grand drumming, toning procession. Somehow, he dismisses his distress over Gaia and rallies himself to the uncontrolled present moment. He lets himself be charmed along by the procession and filled with good valley juju for his mysterious voyage to the beyond.

The wind died down just as he predicted. It would be a calm evening launch. He takes a deep breath, staring out toward the ocean of mystery. He kneels on the sand looking out to Mama Kai and prays. *Mama Kai, please humbly and gracefully accept me into your waters. Please carry me safely on this journey to the outside and back home to my beloved Neverland. Let me rest in the arms of my love once again.*

He turns and faces his tribe, his Ohana.

"You guys just keep jamming until I get back." He hugs each one of them and they offer their blessing. He looks out to the horizon and asks for a blessing from Honu, Zoe, and Gaia as well.

He waves goodbye to the seven on shore and turns to meet the ocean without a word. He drags the kayak into the whitewash and waits patiently. As calm as can be, he breathes with the churning of the swell. The swell falls flat and the waves let him in. He slices through the break and turns on the outside to wave another farewell to his family on shore. They all dance and cheer from the beach. He looks toward the gray clouds to the east and paddles forward. He doesn't look back. He's on a mission.

Just two and a half hours — less even — and I'll be there, he says to himself, confidently. He paddles past the bluffs and he can see and hear a couple of them hollering and toning for him. He glances over — it's Rainbow and Gaia — he can't make out their faces but Gaia's long blond hair is unmistakable. He waves his paddle high and shouts *'I love you.'* Could his voice carry over the waves crashing against the rocks? He hopes she can see beyond his words to the love he holds in his core. He had to give their love a chance to grow, he had to return to her. Then the two females disappear into the folds of the rolling bluffs and he sits alone in his kayak, wondering. He looks ahead at the still gray clouds enshrouding Babylon six nautical miles east and he almost thinks to just turn around right there. But a spirit, almost a tailwind, propels him forward.

But wait! Is that the souls of Honu and Zoe trying to push me to meet them in the afterlife? He shakes the morbid thought away, and tries to focus on his route. *Do it for yourself first, do it for the Ohana, do it for love in the moment.* He smiles. His mission may be for himself as much as anyone else but it's not selfish. He decides to paddle a little farther off shore and out to sea. The threat of tsunami's lingered in his head, and the thought of them coaxes him farther from the rocky coast. He paddles off shore almost a half-mile.

Then he realizes that being farther away from the cliffs will make the take-out beach harder to recognize at night and darkness would arrive in just over an hour. Ah, but tonight there is Moon! Mahina, thank you. The half moon should rise up above the cliffs anytime now. His paddle blade strikes the water rhythmic and powerful; he's cruising steady, approaching the cloud-covered 7-mile valley. *He was made for this mission,* he tells himself boldly.

He looks back toward Neverland and the setting sun for the first time since he waved to Gaia and Rainbow on the bluffs. The sun is just twenty minutes from touching the horizon. He sighs, wishing he could pause it for the rest of the mission. *You'll have the moon,* he tells himself again, *don't worry.* He looks to the right at the mysterious low hanging clouds up against 7 and 8-mile valleys now alongside him. *I wonder if I can see this crazy fault just past 8-mile I witnessed with Spacedog?* He surveys the cliffside with a keen eye, but the land is masked in clouds. His heart plunges after a more careful look. *Those aren't clouds, that's steam!* Steam billowing up from the lava-hot crack in the earth's crust — the fault. His stomach tightens as he notices the steam rising as far as he can see, engulfing the highest peaks.

His mind races and he thinks to paddle the boat farther from the coast, away from the steam, which rose up from a hole in the earth. The mere consideration of a magma seeping gouge across the island sends a quiver up his spine. He thinks of Honu and Zoe. Did this steaming fault consume them? The thought makes him nervous and cold. The eerie feeling of their souls billowing up above the island like the clouds of steam engulfs him like a cold wind and he paddles frantically to gain warmth and another quarter mile away from the coast. He adjusts his bearing easterly toward town but his mind toils with the thought of turning back. There really is something crazy going on from inside the earth itself. He's so cold to the core from the thought that his whole body is covered with goose bumps.

Mano decides to try to regain his composure by turning to watch the sunset and taking a drink of water. He relaxes watching the bottom edge of the orange sphere kiss the placid ocean. He breathes and lets out an *Aum* of prayer as it descends. He imagines the Ohana watching the sunset from the bluffs and praying with him, too. He thinks about Zoe, Honu, and Gaia. What where they doing and feeling right now? He rolls the shaft of the kayak paddle across his thighs barely fluttering the blade of the paddle in the water. He looks at the misty coast, at the setting sun, and at the endless ocean all around. He feels alone and out of place on Grizz's kayak in the fading light. He looks at the shimmering silhouette of his body, boat, and the paddle against the water. He realizes even his shadow would leave him soon. Why couldn't he just embrace the mystery, let go of Honu and Zoe, and the unknown and accept the loving arms of Gaia and his home in Neverland as it was? His mind starts doubting his physical self, the mission to Babylon, everything. Suddenly, he feels foolish, abandoned, and lost in an ocean of mystery and grief.

He'll just go back. He could rest in Gaia's warmth tonight! Maybe Zoe and Honu made it to the outside before the massive fault struck and would return via boat. Maybe they were engulfed by the steaming seam in Mother Earth and would never be seen again. He had no way of knowing, no control at all. Did Zoe still love him? Was Gaia his soul mate? Or was she just a fluke of romantic chance? His heart sinks into his stomach full of unsettled emotions and he feels seasick. He tries to shake negative thought from his mind. *No! No, everyone will return!* They could all live in harmony together in Neverland somehow. But he's scared of what could be true. Does he even want to know his friends' or the island's fate? He can't bring himself to turn toward the darkness and away from the afterglow. Instead of continuing on his mission to Babylon to reveal the unknown, he paddles back toward the comforting light. Toward the simple life, Gaia and his wayward island Ohana. He's not disappointed; he's gracious, he's whole. There's nothing to prove.

I'm over halfway home, he chuckles to himself passing back in front of 7-mile valley again. He stares at the foreboding, billowing steam clouds that enshroud 7 and 8-mile valleys, but keeps his focus toward the comforting sunset afterglow and Neverland beach in the shadows beyond. A chill surrounds him as he stares again toward the steaming cliffs alongside him. He really can *feel* the spirits of Honu and Zoe along the misty palis. He honors their beings, wherever they may be.

Boom! A sudden, thundering explosion echoes all around. It's so powerful he's nearly bucked from the kayak. What just happened? He instinctively looks around trying to find where it came from. Then his mind makes the connection. *Earthquake-Tsunami!* His heart races and he turns the boat toward the open ocean and starts paddling out to sea like a madman. He can feel the massive wave building even before he can see it.

I have to paddle to the outside before it breaks, is all his mind can fathom. He feels the wave pulling him in toward it as the wall of water builds rushing up the face. He paddles with all his strength, but the wall of water just seems to grow and grow. Not looking back, he surges ahead on pure adrenaline.

This is it! He gasps in horror, realizing that this giant wave could be his fate. He can see it cresting, he's near the top, he's not gonna make it! The kayak sweeps up the face of the wave, he's about to go over the falls on this giant terminal wave!

At the last moment he dives off the kayak through the face of the wave, crawling for the outside. Instinct and adrenaline propel him. He holds his breath and feels the pull try to take him down, but she releases. He surfaces in tumultuous backwash confused, gasping. Instinct is still all he knows, so he continues to swim, swim as hard as he can for the outside, trying to get away from the surge that took the kayak. Turbulent water swirls around him, and he feels that some sort of whirlpool is sucking him under. He panics and treads water frantically. He prays for calm and finally it comes. The black water steadies around him. His heart pounds as he rotates full circle and all he can see is the rolling sea of black all around. He decides to close his eyes and let his body just float for a moment. He's alive. He comes up to the surface, treading water, attempting to look around again, still thinking that at any moment he could be sucked under or washed away by another wave. Eventually his breathing steadies, but his heart sinks. He's alone in the dark black ocean.

Mano settles into floating. He looks up at the sky for some sort of hope or orientation. He sees just speckles of stars twinkling out from behind clouds and mist. The earth still exists? He wonders in awe for a moment. How is he still alive? Somehow his heart finds some peace there in the steady black water. He's alive, floating in the great Pacific. Then he trembles and swallows. He's lost.

Alone and adrift in the dark, cold, black, endless ocean. He tries to put together what just happened. Did he really just dive through the crest of an 80, maybe even 200-foot tsunami wave? He releases his breath and lets his body sink underwater momentarily. He feels temporarily secure in the serene, unexplainable calmness that's underwater.

Tuning in underwater he hears the whales singing loudly, their bellowing appears more scattered and frantic than the slow soothing calls he remembers. This can't be real. "This is all a dream," he laughs! Swimming through a tsunami wave in the middle of the ocean! Okay. I'm ready to wake up now. *Wake up!* He calls out. *I'm ready to be warm and safe lying next to my lover again!* He rolls over in the water attempting to stir himself awake. The stillness of the sea takes over and he feels the endless ocean all around. He wiggles again in the water. Still, the watery abyss holds him. No, this isn't right. This can't be! He's still treading water. He can hardly see the outline of land in the misty haze.

Where's my boat? I can't survive swimming out here! He cries out to the night. A cold fear rushes over him. Will he ever make it to land again? Will he see Neverland or Gaia or anyone else ever again? Or will he rest in peace with the spirits of Honu and Zoe? Will he soon know their fate? Are they alive? Will he even know after his own death? Or will his soul just vanish to the bottom of a dark abyss? Oh, why did he do this! Why did he ever leave—his foolish pride, his selfishness would cost him his life. He'd soon be drowning. He sinks back underwater in despair, sinking down underneath to the calmer world of the whales below the surface.

He thinks of Gaia and the others waiting for him, praying at sunset. He thinks of Zoe, and her manifestation to be with him in love forever. *To be with her in love forever.* He repeats her words. Would he or she ever return to the sunlight? Or would they return as wandering souls lost in the valley? His stomach sinks. The thought of her fate and Gaia mourning him is more than he can bear. He surges to the surface and kicks on his back, staring up at the misty moon shining out from behind the clouds.

I must try to swim—swim home to Neverland, just maybe I can make it. I'd give anything to be safe and back on land again. He pleads to the great spirit of the Pacific.

"Mama Kai, please let me make it home, home to live and love once again," Mano cries to the night.

He orients himself, gazing toward the faded silhouette of the cliffs—an eternal distance ahead. If I'm looking at the island, Neverland Beach will be somewhere to my right, he conjures while treading water. But how far? He was certainly about halfway along when the Tsunami came. But now he's an additional mile or even more offshore. He had paddled out so far it seemed, to meet the giant wave. So far, so cold, so dark. How could he ever make it? *All I can do is be patient and just start swimming slowly that way* he sighs. He certainly could make it, he charms himself. He's tired and delusional and cold, still unsure of the exact direction back to the beach.

He must try though. Swim home! Back to the beach and back into Gaia's loving arms. He rallies himself beginning a slow overhand crawl stroke westward. Not even ten minutes pass and he looks up and senses he's veering of course, swimming more out to sea. He's tired and it's so black that he can hardly discern direction. Escaping the tsunami spent all his energy and adrenaline already. Mano can't convince himself whether he's making real progress, or merely treading water. He just wants to lie limp in the water, go to sleep even. His body quivers from the cold. He shutters at the thought of a never-ending aquatic sleep that looms once he would become too tired to swim. He swims anyway in a dreamy state of humble acceptance of his fate. He hums along with the whale's song, feeling sort of in a trance as though the ocean is moving with him.

The creatures singing in the mysterious dark sea beneath give him hope, too. *They're cheering for me,* he chuckles inside. His pace slows and he reaches what feels to him a sort of equilibrium with the ocean all around. He's maintaining, not getting more tired, it seems. But his eyes sting from the saltwater. He's hungry and thirsty and cold. His one-millimeter surf top does little to hold in his internal heat. He feels incredibly slow but he's still swimming smooth and forward, it seems. The intricate whale's song is all he can focus on to keep from falling asleep. He relaxes even more and surrenders to Mama Kai.

Surrender! How beautiful it is! Oh, to be loved and held by her! *I traded my love for this loving ocean to love me. How could it be? But it is. It's ok.* He surrenders to her and her liquid tranquility. An hour or so into his never-ending swim, he decides to take a break and just let himself float for a bit, bobbing up for breaths casually.

"Do you love me Mama Kai?" He manages to spit toward the heavens when he spins on his back to float with his mouth to the moon. He decides talking aloud is too much energy. Instead, he just broadcasts his heart feelings through the water. *Save me, oh save me Great Spirit! Don't let my love drown here in these dark waters.* Breath fills his body and he feels the courage to keep swimming.

Once again, he opens his stinging eyes at the surface to re-plot his course for Neverland. He looks around panicky searching for the silhouette of the cliffs to reorient himself, but his vision is a blur—so much that he cannot see land at all. He spins around and all he can see is fuzzy mist through his burning eyes. He's nearly blind. He turned around so much trying to look for land, that now he has no idea of his direction at all anymore. He swallows and sinks, feeling despair overtake him. He'll never touch land again. His love will be lost in this endless ocean. No more Gaia, Honu or Zoe. No more world. Should he just open his mouth underwater and let the black sea fill his lungs and find his eternal sleep—end this nightmare now?

Listen to the whales, let them bring you comfort he tells himself. His brain doesn't let his body give in and just swallow the sea. If I swim toward the whales, they will lead me back to the beach—back home. He gets a touch excited and attempts to hone in on their direction through auditory inference. Oh, but wait! The whales aren't going to the beach now. It's late spring, they are supposed to be swimming back to Alaska. Following their song will lead him farther out to sea, he considers. He realizes that he has no idea at all where he is, and how far from land he must still be. His heart sinks and again despair sweeps over him. Floating in a tired limbo, he listens to their tune. He feels them.

I can still hear. I can swim toward them and spend my final breaths immersed in their song he encourages himself. He likes this idea, or at least he likes the distraction of it. Mano swims toward the whale's song, slowly, no longer using overhand strokes. He treads water and develops float strokes to edge closer to their echoing. Eventually his mind admits it—he's exhausted. Maybe it's time to go to sleep now. He fills his lungs with air and lets himself bob limp just holding his breath. Sleep. Sleep is good. Sleep is warmth. A feeling of warmth and comfort relaxes him.

The whales cry louder and wake him. He was sleeping? How? He's delirious. He treads water frantically to ensure his head remains above the surface. *Swimming and swimming* – is this his fate? Is he already dead? Swimming in an endless sea, never even knowing if he is dead or alive. Is this his afterlife? Would he even reach heaven? Or is he destined to remain in this watery limbo? Cold fear rushes over him. He's cold and just wants to sleep again. Sleep off this horrible nightmare and wake in the arms of his lover. I can do this. I can sleep through the nightmare and wake up on the other side. Be on land again. He takes another deep breath and bobs in a warming fetal position.

He's warm, so warm he wants to take off all his clothes.

"I'm hot, this fire is blazing!" Mano bursts.

"Well, why don't you take off your clothes and dance farther away from the bonfire!" Zoe laughs, pulling his shirt off and tossing it to the sand. Honu is drumming and chanting.

"Mangos and mayhem. Captain Mano has returned." Honu chants to the beating of the drum. Gaia's there, too, and she dances over and shoves a juicy mango into Mano's mouth. Mano bites it and lets the juice run down to his bare chest.

"Waaahoo!" he shouts tribally and takes another big bite. Gaia tickles him and he pulls her down on top of him for mango kisses, rolling in the sand. Zoe lies down with them and the two girls take turns caressing him, kissing and licking his mango-covered body.

"I love you, my mango Mano!" Zoe releases, between torrents of kisses and laughter.

"I love you more, mango-licious." Gaia giggles, sweeping her long golden locks over him. Then suddenly, it's whales screaming and the whole bonfire crew stops dumbstruck, and looks toward the ocean. A giant wave crashes over the beach and sweeps them all out to sea.

"Ereeek! Waoooo!" the whales screech, as everyone is pulled out to the ocean in the whitewash. They all get pushed back over the falls of another huge wave rushing in. He's separated from his lovers and he screeches louder than the whales as he sees Gaia's body float limp in the water. He fights an incredible current to reach her. Then somehow the ocean calms and he is able to swim to her. He reaches for her, grabbing her golden hair to pull her head around to see her face. Her cool blue eyes are open but her stare is lifeless. "Noooo!" Mano screams underwater, turning away.

"Ehhhheeew!" the whales scream. He scrambles and claws his way to the surface to the air on the other side of the water. He looks around searching for something, anything, but his vision is fuzzy and his eyes sting. He can't see anything. He's still in the middle of the ocean. There's no Gaia, no Zoe, no Mango taste in his mouth.

"Ehhhheeew!" a whale calls out to him, louder than ever. Again, those whales woke him from his dream! In his delirious, blind and tired state, he can't help but wonder why this ocean won't just let him die. The whales call to him again. They sure are loud. So close. Wait! They are getting closer. He's not swimming to them. They are coming to him. Suddenly, he remembers his underwater cry for help. He repeats his call to them by telepathic heart transmission. *Save me, oh save me, my whale friends. I believe in you!* he manages to transmit with clear conscience. They sing in response. He hears them. He feels them. They are so close! He convinces himself he can smell them even. He smells mangos, too. Is he dreaming again?

He startles and wakes, remembering he must swim to the surface to take another survival breath. His arms flutter at his sides, but there's no water. His feet kick against a warm, wet mush. He flutters his arms again. Air? He takes a breath. He breathes in hot moist air. He's not in the ocean at all. Through his blurred vision he sees pure darkness — not even a hint of fuzzy moonlit mist as before.

And the cold? The overwhelming cold he battled in the ocean is gone. Everything smells fishy, too. Too fishy for an ocean. He's so confused. He feels around his warm, mushy surroundings as blind as a bat. Another dream? Purgatory? *Where are the whales?* He wonders, trying to remember their most recent echo. He feels a thundering breath, certainly not his own. It can't be. But it is. He's inside the mouth of a humpback whale.

He claws at the mushy living flesh that is the whales mouth, still trying to convince himself he's dreaming. *Is he being eaten? No, he's being transported* he realizes.

"Oh, take me home to Neverland, sacred sea beast" he pleads out loud, collapsing onto the warm mush. Just the very though of actually being inside of a whale, being rescued by a whale, is more than his weary mind can handle. He falls into a dreamy delirium once again.

He feels her lips on his. Tasting the sweetness of her love melts him, deeper into the dream. *All I want to do is love you forever* he sends and receives. He holds her tight and feels her warmth, nuzzling in. Then a fierce wind comes and jostles them. He doesn't understand, he should be able to just hold onto her, but she is being pulled from his arms by the wind. He tries to keep his grasp, but his hands are weak. His whole body feels weak. *Let go. It's okay, just let go* his heart tries to say. He gives in, and releases. He's spit out into a crashing wave.

Cold water rushes over him and he's awake again. He's swimming again, flailing miserably in the turbulent water. He's weak and disoriented and blind. He holds his breath and tries to relax — just float in the water like he did before. His mind somehow catches up with his new surroundings. He's no longer inside the whale, or way out at sea — he's in the surf break. The beach, could it be just there?

He feels his limp body being pulled by an approaching wave. He tries to dive down and toward it, but it catches him. The wave picks him up and slams him into the sand. He feels the sand scrape against his face. *Sand!* He realizes, coughing at the surface. He tries to reach for it, but the ocean just pulls him away again. Another wave comes and sends a surge of water down his open mouth. He feels helpless in the water. He tries swimming to the sand. He spits and gasps at the surface, but he can't get there. He can feel the top surface of the water but he can't reach his head to it. He has to breathe so he breathes in water. He sinks to the sandy bottom and is pushed forward again.

Again, he feels the sandy beach and he claws for it, but the sea carries him back. Dreams take over once again. He lets go of her and everything and it feels good. *Surrender* — the thought fills him. His whole body relaxes, surrendering to the ocean — surrendering to love. His mouth opens and water rushes in once more. Then a surge of whitewater comes and carries him to the shore. A wave pushes him up onto the sand, and here he lies.

The Beginning

The sun rose and warmed the earth. The weeks of spring rain helped the gardens to flourish. The land was cultivated and seeds were gathered and new plants were made to sprout. They would eventually develop and explore and procreate. But they were in no hurry. The natural cycles that guided their very existence led the evolution of all things and history began. Stories were told by spoken word and passed down. Lives were lived and legends were made. The story of love lives on.

Copyright © Michael Gary Devloo 2020

If this story of love and magic touched you, please write a review or comment, send an email, and tell a friend.

Mahalo,

Michael Gary Devloo

Look for Music from this story on Spotify and YouTube in Spring 2021

ABOUT THE AUTHOR:

Michael **G**ary **D**evloo shares a life of adventure with his son Kale in Pagosa Springs, Colorado. Michael's travels have taken him across five continents to many remote and pristine natural areas. Michael cherishes the simple outdoor lifestyle, living in harmony with nature, and enjoys creating his own fun. You'll find him singing around the campfire, or exploring the mountains with his family. When he's not writing stories or music, he's connecting with nature on a mountain bike, kayak, surfboard, or snowboard. Michael is also an English-Spanish Interpreter, Professional Engineer, and off-grid homebuilder.

mikedevloo@gmail.com   Facebook and Instagram: @michaeldevloo

Other Books by Michael:

Casa Construction, Exterior © 2008
The Legend of the Weminuche Ware-pig © 2019

Made in the USA
Las Vegas, NV
12 January 2021